George Alfred Henty

Orange and Green

A tale of the Boyne and Limerick

George Alfred Henty

Orange and Green
A tale of the Boyne and Limerick

ISBN/EAN: 9783337027155

Printed in Europe, USA, Canada, Australia, Japan

Cover: Foto ©Andreas Hilbeck / pixelio.de

More available books at **www.hansebooks.com**

CAPTAIN DAVENANT AND HIS OFFICERS DRINK TO KING JAMES.

ORANGE AND GREEN:

A TALE OF THE BOYNE AND LIMERICK.

BY

G. A. HENTY,

Author of "The Young Carthaginian;" "With Clive in India;" "In Freedom's Cause;"
"The Lion of the North;" "With Wolfe in Canada;" "Facing Death;" &c.

*WITH EIGHT FULL-PAGE ILLUSTRATIONS
BY GORDON BROWNE.*

LONDON:
BLACKIE & SON, 49 & 50 OLD BAILEY, E.C.
GLASGOW, EDINBURGH, AND DUBLIN.
1888.

PREFACE.

My dear Lads,

The subject of Ireland is one which has for some years been a very prominent one, and is likely, I fear, for some time yet to occupy a large share of public attention. For many years the laws in Ireland and the rights of Irishmen have been identical with those which we enjoy in England. The discontent manifested in the troubles of recent years has had its root in an older sense of grievance, for which there was, unhappily, only too abundant reason. The great proportion of the soil of Ireland was taken from the original owners and handed over to Cromwell's followers, and for years the land that still remained in the hands of Irishmen was subject to the covetousness of a party of greedy intriguers, who had sufficient influence to sway the proceedings of government. The result was the rising of Ireland, nominally in defence of the rights of King James, but really an effort of despair on the part of those who deemed their religion, their property, and even their lives threatened by the absolute ascendency of the Protestant party in the government of the country. I have drawn my information from a variety of sources; but as I wished you to see the matter from the Irish point of view I have drawn most largely from the history of those events by Mr. O'Driscol, published sixty years ago. There is, however, but little difference of opinion between Irish and English authors as to the general course of the war, or as to the atrocious conduct of William's army of foreign mercenaries towards the people of Ireland.

Yours sincerely,

G. A. HENTY.

CONTENTS.

CHAP.   Page

I. A Shipwreck, ... 9

II. For James or William, ... 33

III. The King in Ireland, ... 51

IV. The Siege of Derry, ... 68

V. The Relief of Derry, ... 90

VI. Dundalk, ... 114

VII. The Coming Battle, ... 131

VIII. Boyne Water, ... 150

IX. Pleasant Quarters, ... 174

X. A Cavalry Raid, ... 196

XI. The First Siege of Limerick, ... 218

XII. Winter Quarters, ... 238

XIII. A Dangerous Mission, ... 255

XIV. Athlone, ... 283

XV. A Fortunate Recognition, ... 313

XVI. Peace, ... 341

ILLUSTRATIONS.

Page

CAPTAIN DAVENANT AND HIS OFFICERS DRINK TO KING
JAMES, ... *Frontispiece.* 65

"JOHN EAGERLY DEVOURED THE BOOKS WHICH WALTER LENT
HIM," 21

JOHN RELIEVED BY WALTER IN THE ROYALIST CAMP, . . . 84

"CAN YOU GIVE ME SHELTER?" ASKED WALTER, ... 131

KING WILLIAM RECONNOITRES THE IRISH POSITION, . . . 147

THE HESSIAN TROOPERS DRIVEN FORTH, ... 193

WALTER ESCAPES FROM THE ENGLISH SOLDIERS, ... 269

"KILCOWAN IS ON FIRE, SIR!" 321

ORANGE AND GREEN.

A TALE OF THE BOYNE AND LIMERICK.

CHAPTER I.

A SHIPWRECK.

A FEW miles to the south of Bray Head, on the crest of a hill falling sharply down to the sea, stood Castle Davenant, a conspicuous landmark to mariners skirting the coast on their way from Cork or Waterford to Dublin Bay. Castle Davenant it was called, although it had long since ceased to be defensible; but when it was built by Sir Godfrey Davenant, who came over with Strongbow, it was a place of strength. Strongbow's followers did well for themselves. They had reckoned on hard fighting, but the Irish were too much divided among themselves to oppose any serious resistance to the invaders. Strongbow had married the daughter of Dermid, Prince of Leinster, and at the death of that prince succeeded him, and the greater portion of Leinster was soon divided among the knights and men-at-arms who had followed his standard. Godfrey Davenant, who was a favourite of the earl, had no reason to be dissatisfied with his share, which consisted of a domain including many square miles of fertile land stretching back from the sea-coast.

Here for many generations his descendants lived, for the most part taking an active share in the wars and disturbances which, with scarcely an interval of rest, agitated the country. The castle had continued to deserve its name until forty years before the time this story commences, when Cromwell's gunners had battered a breach in it and left it a heap of smoking ruins. Walter Davenant had died, fighting to the last, in his own hall. At that time the greater part of his estate was bestowed upon officers and soldiers in Cromwell's army, among whom no less than four million acres of Irish land were divided.

Had it not been that Walter Davenant's widow was an Englishwoman and a relation of General Ireton, the whole of the estate would have gone; but his influence was sufficient to secure for her the possession of the ruins of her home and a few hundred acres surrounding it. Fortunately the dowry which Mrs. Davenant had brought her husband was untouched, and a new house was reared within the ruins of the castle, the new work being dovetailed with the old.

The family now consisted of Mrs. Davenant, a lady sixty-eight years old; her son Fergus, who was when Cromwell devastated the land a child of five years; his wife Katherine, daughter of Lawrence M'Carthy, a large land-owner near Cork; and their two sons, Walter, a lad of sixteen, and Godfrey, twelve years old.

Two miles west of the castle stood a square-built stone house, surrounded by solidly-constructed barns and outbuildings. This was the abode of old Zephaniah Whitefoot, the man upon whom had been bestowed the broad lands of Walter Davenant. Zephaniah had fought stoutly as lieutenant in one of Cromwell's regiments of horse, and had always considered himself an ill-treated man, because although he had obtained all the most fertile portion of the Davenant estate, the old family were permitted to retain the castle and a few hundred acres by the sea.

He was one of those who contended that the Amalekites should be utterly destroyed by the sword, and he considered that the retention of the corner of their domains by the Davenants was a direct flying in the face of the providence who had given them into the hands of the faithful. Not that had he obtained possession of the ruined castle Zephaniah Whitefoot would have repaired it or set up his abode there. The followers of Cromwell had no eyes for the beautiful. They were too much in earnest to care aught for the amenities of life, and despised as almost sinful anything approximating to beauty either in dress, person, or surroundings. The houses that they reared in this land of which they had taken possession were bare to the point of ugliness, and their interior was as cold and hard as was the exterior. Everything was for use, nothing for ornament. Scarce a flower was to be seen in their gardens, and laughter was a sign of levity to be sternly repressed.

Their isolation in the midst of a hostile population caused them no concern whatever. They cared for no society or companionship save that of their own households, which they ruled with a rod of iron, and an occasional gathering for religious purposes with the other settlers of their own faith. They regarded the Irish as Papists doomed to everlasting perdition, and indeed consigned to that fate all outside their own narrow sect. Such a people could no more mix with the surrounding population than oil with water. As a rule they tilled as much ground in the immediate vicinity of their houses as they and their families could manage, and the rest of the land which had fallen into their possession they let either for a money payment, or more often for a portion of the crops raised upon it, to such natives as were willing to hold it on these terms.

The next generation had fallen away somewhat from their fathers' standards. It is not in human nature to stand such a strain as their families had been subjected to. There is an innate yearning for joy and happiness, and even the sternest discipline cannot keep man for ever in the gloomy bonds of fanaticism. In most cases the immediate descendants of Cromwell's soldiers would gladly have made some sort of compromise, would have surrendered much of their outlying land to obtain secure and peaceful possession of the rest, and would have emerged from the life of gloomy seclusion in which they found themselves; but no whisper of any such feeling as this would be heard in the household of Zephaniah Whitefoot so long as he lived.

He was an old man now, but as hard, as gloomy, and as unloveable as he had been when in his prime. His wife had died very many years before, of no disease that Zephaniah or the doctor he called in could discover, but in fact of utter weariness at the dull life of repression and gloom which crushed her down. Of a naturally meek and docile disposition, she had submitted without murmuring to her husband's commands, and had, during her whole married life, never shocked him so much as she did the day before her death, when for the first time she exhibited the possession of an opinion of her own by saying earnestly:

"You may say what you like, Zephaniah, but I do think we were meant to have some happiness and pleasure on earth. If we were intended to go through life without laughing why should we be able to laugh? Oh, how I should like to hear one hearty natural laugh again before I die, such as I used to hear when I was a girl!"

Jabez Whitefoot inherited his mother's docility of disposition, and even when he grew to middle age never dreamt of disputing his father's absolute rule, and remained strictly neutral when his wife, the daughter of an old comrade of his father, settled a few miles away, fought stoutly at times against his tyranny.

"You are less than a man, Jabez," she would say to him indignantly, "to put up at your age with being lectured as if you were a child. Parental obedience is all very well, and I hope I was always obedient to my father; but when it comes to a body not being permitted to have a soul of his own it is going too far. If you had told me that, when I became your wife, I was to become the inmate of a dungeon for the rest of my existence, I wouldn't have had you, not if you had been master of all the broad lands of Leinster."

But though unable to rouse her husband into making an effort for some sort of freedom, Hannah Whitefoot had battled more successfully in behalf of her son John.

"You have had the management of your son, sir, and I will manage mine," she said. "I will see that he does not grow up a reprobate or a Papist, but at least he shall grow up a man, and his life shall not be as hateful as mine is if I can help it."

Many battles had already been fought on this point, but in the end Hannah Whitefoot triumphed. Although her husband never himself opposed his father's authority, he refused absolutely to use his own to compel his wife to submission.

"You know, sir," he said, "you had your own way with my mother and me, and I say nothing for or against it. Hannah has other ideas. No one can say that she is not a good woman, or that she fails in her duty to me. All people do not see life from the same point of view. She is just as conscientious in her way as you are in yours; she reads her Bible and draws her own conclusions from it just as you do; and as she is the mother of the child, and as I know she will do her best for it, I shall not interfere with her way of doing it."

And so Hannah won at last, and although according to modern ideas the boy's training would have been considered strict in the extreme, it differed very widely from that which his father had had before him. Sounds of laughter such as never had been heard within the walls of the house since Zephaniah laid stone upon stone sometimes issued from the room where Hannah and the child were together alone, and Zephaniah was out with Jabez about the farm; and Hannah herself benefited as much as did the child by her rebellion against the authorities. Jabez, too, was conscious that home was brighter and pleasanter than it had been, and when Zephaniah burst into a torrent of indignation when he discovered that the child had absolutely heard some fairy stories from its mother, Jabez said quietly:

"Father, I wish no dispute. I have been an obedient son to you, and will continue so to my life's end; but if you are not satisfied with the doings of my wife, I will depart with her. There are plenty who will be glad to let me a piece of land; and if I only work there as hard as I work here, I shall assuredly be able to support her and my boy. So let this be the last word between us."

This threat put an end to the struggle. Zephaniah had, like most of his class, a keen eye to the main chance, and could ill spare the services of Jabez and his thrifty and hard-working wife, and henceforth, except by pointed references in the lengthy morning and evening prayers to the backsliding in his household, he held his peace.

Between the Castle and Zephaniah Whitefoot there had never been any intercourse. The dowager Mrs. Davenant hated the Cromwellite occupier of her estate, not only as a usurper but as the representative of the man who had slain her husband. She never alluded to his existence, and had always contrived in her rides and walks to avoid any point from which she could obtain so much as a distant view of the square, ugly house which formed a blot on the fair landscape. She still spoke of the estate as if it extended to its original boundaries, and ignored absolutely the very existence of Zephaniah Whitefoot and all that belonged to him. But when her son and Jabez grew to man's estate, at about the same period, they necessarily at times crossed each other's paths; and as in them the prejudices and enmities of their elders were somewhat softened, they would, when they met on the road, exchange a passing nod or a brief " Good morning."

Another generation still, and the boys of the two houses met as friends.   Thanks to his mother's successful rebellion, John Whitefoot grew up a hearty, healthy boy, with a bright eye, a merry laugh, and a frank, open bearing.

" One would think," his grandfather remarked angrily one day, as the boy went out whistling gaily to fetch in a young colt Jabez was about to break, " that John was the son of a malignant, or one of the men of Charles Stuart, rather than of a God-fearing tiller of the soil."

" So long as he fears God, and walks in the right way, he is none the worse for that, father," Jabez said stoutly; " and even you would hardly say that his mother has failed in her teachings in that respect.   I do not know that so long as one has the words of Scripture in his heart, he is any the better for having them always on his lips; in other respects I regret not that the boy should have a spirit and a fire which I know I lack myself.   Who can say what may yet take place here!   The Stuarts are again upon the throne, and, with James's leaning towards Papacy, there is no saying whether some day all the lands which Cromwell divided among his soldiers may not be restored to their original possessors, and in that case our sons may have to make their way in other paths of life than ours; and if it be so, John will assuredly be more likely to make his way than I should have done."

"We would never surrender, save with our lives, what our swords have won. We will hold the inheritance which the Lord has given us," the old man said fiercely.

"Yes, father; and so said those whose lands we have inherited; so said Walter Davenant, of whose lands we are possessed. It will be as God wills it. He has given to us the lands of others, and it may be that he will take them away again. The times have changed, father, and the manners; and I am well pleased to see that John, while I am sure he is as true to the faith as I am myself, will take broader and, perhaps, happier views of life than I have done."

Zephaniah gave a snort of displeasure. He grieved continually at the influence which his daughter-in-law exercised over her son, and which now extended clearly to her husband; but Jabez was now a man of five-and-forty, and had lately shown that, in some respects at least, he intended to have his way, while Zephaniah himself, though still erect and strong, was well-nigh eighty.

"Remember, Jabez," he said, "that it goes hard with those who, having set their hands to the plough, turn aside."

"I shall not turn aside, father," Jabez said quietly. "I have gone too long along a straight furrow to change now; but I am not ill pleased that my son should have a wider scope. I trust and believe that he will drive his furrow as straight as we have done, although it may not be exactly in the same line."

But neither Zephaniah nor old Mrs. Davenant knew that their respective grandsons had made friends, although both the boys' fathers knew and approved of it, although for somewhat different reasons.

"The Whitefoot boy," Mr. Davenant had said to his wife, "is, I fancy from what I have seen of him, of a different type to his father and grandfather. I met him the other day when I was out, and he spoke as naturally and outspokenly as Walter himself. He seems to have got rid of the Puritanical twang altogether. At any rate he will do Walter no harm; and, indeed, I should say that there was a solid good sense about him which will do Master Walter, who is somewhat disposed to be a madcap, much good. Anyhow he is a better companion for the boy than the lads down in the village; and there is no saying, wife, how matters may go in this unhappy country. It may be that we may come to our own again; it may be that we may lose what is left to us. Anyhow, it can do no harm to Walter that he should have as a friend one in the opposite camp."

Somewhat similar was the talk between Hannah and Jabez, although in their case the wife was the speaker.

"John has told me, Jabez, that he has several times met young Davenant, and that the boy is disposed to be friendly with him; and he has asked me to speak with you, to know whether you have any objection to his making a friend of him."

"What do you say, Hannah?" Jabez asked cautiously. "My father, I fear, would not approve of it."

"Your father need know nothing about it, Jabez. He is an old man and a good man; but he clings to the ways of his youth, and deems that things are still as they were when he rode behind Cromwell. I would not deceive him did he ask; but I do not see that the matter need be mentioned in his presence. It seems to me that it will be good for John to be friends with this boy. He is almost without companionship; we have acquaintance, it is true, among the other settlers of our faith, but such companionship as he has there will not open his mind or broaden his views. We are dull people here for a lad. Had we had other children it might have been different.

"I have heard my mother speak of her life as a girl in England, and assuredly it was brighter and more varied than ours; and it seems not to me that the pleasures which they had were sinful, although I have been taught otherwise; but as I read my Bible, I cannot see that innocent pleasures are in any way denied to the Lord's people; and such pleasure as the companionship of the young Davenant can give John will, I think, be altogether for his good."

"But the lad is a Papist, Hannah."

"He is, Jabez; but boys, methinks, do not argue among themselves upon points of doctrine; and I have no fear that John will ever be led from the right path, nor indeed, though it is presumption for a woman to say so, do I feel so sure as our ministers, that ours is the only path to heaven. We believe firmly that it is the best path, but others believe as firmly in their

paths; and I cannot think, Jabez, that all mankind,
save those who are within the fold of our church, can
be condemned by the good Lord to perdition."

"Your words are bold, Hannah, and I know not
what my father and the elders of the church would
say were they to hear them. As to that I will not
argue, but methinks that you are right in saying that
the companionship of the young Davenant will do our
boy no harm, but the lad must have his father's consent. Though I reckon that we could count pounds
where they could count shillings, yet in the opinion of
the world they assuredly stand above us. Moreover,
as it is only in human nature that they should regard
us as those who have despoiled them, John must have
no dealings with their son without their consent; if
that be given I have nought to say against it."

And so John told Walter next time they met, and
learned in reply that Walter had already obtained his
father's consent to going out rambles with him; so
the boys became companions and friends, and each
benefited by it. To John, the bright, careless ease
and gaiety of Walter's talk and manner were at first
strange indeed, after the restraint and gloom of his
home; but in time he caught something of his companion's tone, until, as has been said, his altered manner
and bearing struck and annoyed his grandfather.

On the other hand, the earnestness and solidity of
John's character was of benefit to Walter; and his
simple truthfulness, the straightforwardness of his
principles, and his blunt frankness in saying exactly
what he thought, influenced Walter to quite as large an
extent as he had influenced John.

"JOHN EAGERLY DEVOURED THE BOOKS WHICH WALTER LENT HIM."

So the companionship between the lads had gone on for two years. In fine weather they had met once or twice a week and had taken long rambles together, or, throwing themselves down on the slopes facing the sea, had talked over subjects of mutual interest. Walter's education was far in advance of that of his companion, whose reading, indeed, had been confined to the Scriptures, and the works of divines and controversialists of his own church, and whose acquirements did not extend beyond the most elementary subjects.

To him everything that Walter knew was novel and strange; and he eagerly devoured, after receiving permission from his mother, the books which Walter lent him, principally histories, travels, and the works of Milton and Shakespeare. As to the latter, Hannah had at first some scruples; and it was only after setting herself, with great misgivings as to the lawfulness of the act, to peruse the book that she suffered her son to read it. The volume only contained some ten of Shakespeare's plays; and Hannah, on handing the book to her son, said:

"I do not pretend, John, to understand all that is written there, but I cannot see that there is evil in it. There are assuredly many noble thoughts and much worldly wisdom. Did I think that your life would be passed here, I should say that it were better for you not to read a book which gives a picture of a life so different from what yours would be; but none can say what your lot may be. And although I have heard much about the wickedness of the stage, I can see no line in this book which could do harm to you. I do not see it can do you much good, John, but neither do I see that

it can do you any harm; therefore, if you have set
your mind on it, read it, my boy."

It was a stormy evening in the first week of
November, 1688. The wind was blowing in fierce
gusts, making every door and casement quiver in
Davenant Castle, while between the gusts the sound
of the deep roar of the sea on the rocks far below
could be plainly heard. Mrs. Davenant was sitting in
a high-backed chair on one side of the great fireplace,
in which a pile of logs was blazing. Her son had
just laid down a book which he could no longer see
to read, while her daughter-in-law was industriously
knitting. Walter was wandering restlessly between
the fire and the window, looking out at the flying
clouds, through which the moon occasionally struggled.

"Do sit down, Walter," his mother said at last. "You
certainly are the most restless creature I ever saw."

"Not always, mother; but I cannot help wondering
about that ship we saw down the coast making for the
bay. She was about ten miles out, and seemed to be
keeping her course when I saw her last half an hour
ago; but I can see by the clouds that the wind has
drawn round more to the north, and I doubt much
whether she will be able to gain the bay."

"In that case, Walter," his father said, "if her captain knows his business he will wear round and run
down for Waterford. I agree with you," he continued,
after walking to the window and watching the clouds,
"that a vessel coming from the south will hardly
weather Bray Head with this wind."

He had scarcely spoken when the door opened, and
one of the servants entered.

"Your honour, a boy has just come up from the village; he says that John Considine sent him to tell you that a large ship is driving in to shore, and that he thinks she will strike not far from the village."

"Why, on earth," Mr. Davenant exclaimed, "doesn't he tack and stand out to sea!"

"The boy says her foremast is gone, and they have lost all management of her."

"In that case God help them! there is little chance for them on this rocky coast; however, I will go down at once and see if anything can be done. Katherine, do you see that there are plenty of hot blankets ready in case any of the poor fellows are washed ashore. I shall, of course, send them up here. I suppose, Walter, you will come down with me."

But Walter had already disappeared, having slipped off as soon as he had heard the message.

"Don't let that boy get into mischief, Fergus," old Mrs. Davenant said.

"I am afraid, mother, he is beyond me," her son said with a smile. "No Davenant yet could ever keep out of mischief, and Walter is no exception; however, fortunately for us, we generally get out of scrapes as easily as we get into them."

"Not always, Fergus," she said, shaking her head.

"No, not always, mother; but exceptions, you know, prove the rule."

"Well, Godfrey, do you want to go?" he asked the younger boy, who had risen from the table, and was looking eagerly at him. "Of course you do; but, mind, you must keep close to me. Ah, Father John!" he broke off as an ecclesiastic, muffled up to the throat in

wrappings, entered the room, "are you going down
too?"

"Assuredly I am, Fergus; you don't think a trifle of
wind would keep me from doing my duty?"

In another two minutes the two men and Godfrey
sallied out. They staggered as the wind struck them,
and Godfrey clung to his father's arm. Not a word
was spoken as they made their way down the steep
descent to the village, which consisted of about a dozen
fishermen's huts. Indeed, speaking would have been
useless, for no word would have been heard above the
howling of the storm.

The vessel was visible to them as they made their
way down the hill. She was a complete wreck. The
light of the moon was sufficient for them to see that
she had, as the boy said, lost her foremast. Her sails
were in ribbons, and she was labouring heavily in the
sea, each wave that struck her breaking over her bows
and sweeping along her deck. There was no hope
for her; she could neither tack nor wear, and no
anchor would hold for a moment on that rocky bottom
in such a sea.

On reaching the village they joined a group of fishermen who were standing under the shelter of the end
of a cottage.

"Can nothing be done, Considine?" Mr. Davenant
shouted in the ear of one of the fishermen.

"Not a thing, yer honour; she has just let drop one
of her anchors."

"But they could not hope it would hold there," Mr.
Davenant said.

"Not they, your honour, onless they were mad.

They hoped it would hoult so as to bring her head round; but the cable went as soon as the strain came. I saw her head go sharp up to the wind, and then fall off again; not that it would have made much difference in the end, though it would have given them half an hour longer of life."

"Could we get a boat off with a line if she strikes?"

"Look at the sea, yer honour. Mr. Walter has been asking us; but there's no boat could get through that surf, not if all Ireland dipinded on it."

"Where is Walter?"

"Sure and I can't tell ye, yer honour. He was here a few minutes since; but what's come of him is more nor I can tell ye."

"He went off with Larry Doolan," a boy who was standing next to the fisherman shouted.

"Then as sure as fate they are up to some mischief," Mr. Davenant said. "Walter is bad enough by himself, but with Larry to help him it would take a regiment to look after them."

"They can't be in much mischief to-night, yer honour," the fisherman said. "Look, sir, she's coming in fast. She draws a power of water, and she will strike in a minute or two."

"She seems crowded with men. Can nothing be done to help them?" the priest asked.

"Nothing, your reverence. Praying for them is the only thing that can help the poor sowls now."

"You are sure it's not possible to launch a boat, Considine?"

"Look for yourself, yer honour. There's not a boat

on the coast that could get through them breakers. There she goes."

Even above the noise of the storm a loud cry was heard and the crash of breaking timber, as with the shock the main and mizzen masts, weakened by the loss of the foremast, went over the sides. The next great wave drove the vessel forward two or three fathoms.

"That's her last move," Considine said. "The rocks will be through her bottom now."

"They are off," a boy shouted running up.

"Who are off?" Considine asked.

"The young squire and Larry Doolan."

"Off where?" Mr. Davenant exclaimed.

"Off in the curragh, yer honour. Me and Tim Connolly helped them carry it round the Nose, and they launched her there. There they are. Sure you can see them for yourself."

The party rushed out from the shelter, and there, a quarter of a mile along on the right, a small boat was seen making its way over the waves.

"Be jabers, yer honour, and they have done it," the boatmen said as Mr. Davenant gave a cry of alarm.

"I didn't think of the curragh, and if I had she could not have been launched here. Mr. Walter has hit on the only place where there was a chance. Under the shelter of the Nose it might be done, but nowhere else."

The Nose was a formidable reef of rocks running off from a point and trending to the south. Many a ship had gone ashore on its jagged edge, but with the wind from the north-east it formed somewhat of a shelter, and it was under its lee that Walter and Larry had launched the curragh.

The curragh is still found on the Irish coast. It is a boat whose greatest width is at the stern, so much so that it looks like a boat cut in two. The floor is almost flat, and rises so much to the bow that three or four feet are entirely out of water. They are roughly built, and by no means fast, but they are wonderfully good sea-boats for their size, and can live in seas which would swamp a boat of ordinary build. Walter had, with the assistance of Larry Doolan, built this boat for going out fishing. It was extremely light, being a mere framework covered with tarred canvas. As soon as Walter had reached the village, and found that the fishermen considered that no boat could possibly be put out, he had found and held a consultation with Larry.

"Do you think the curragh could go out, Larry?"

"Not she, yer honour. She would just be broke up like an egg-shell with them breakers."

"But she might float if we got beyond them, Larry."

"She might that," Larry agreed, "seeing how light she is."

"Well, will you go with me, Larry?"

"Sure and I would go anywhere with yer honour, but she could never get out."

"I am thinking, Larry, that if we carry her along beyond the Nose we might find it calmer there."

"Well, we might," Larry agreed. "At any rate we can try."

So calling together two or three other boys they had lifted the light boat and carried it with its oars along

the shore until they got beyond the Nose; but even
here it was a formidable business to launch her, for
although the rocks broke the full force of the seas,
throwing the spray hundreds of feet up in the air, the
waves poured through the intervals, and dashed over
the lower rocks in such masses that formidable waves
rolled in to the shore.

After much consultation the boys agreed that their
best plan was to scramble out on the rocks as far as
possible so as to launch the boat beyond the break of
the surf.

It was a hazardous enterprise, and the whole party
were several times nearly washed into the water as
they struggled out.   At last they reached a spot
beyond which they could go no farther, as a deep passage was here broken in the rock.   But they were now
beyond the line of breakers.   After several vain efforts
to launch the boat, in each of which she narrowly
escaped destruction, they agreed that the only plan was,
after a wave passed, to drop her on to a flat rock, which
then showed above the water, and to jump into her.

The two boys on shore were to hold the head rope
to prevent her being dashed towards the land by the
next wave, while Larry worked with the oars to get
her away from the ridge.   The moment the wave had
passed under them the head rope was to be thrown off.
This plan was carried out.   The two boys had but just
time to jump into the boat and get out their oars when
the next wave lifted the boat high on its crest. The lads
holding the rope were nearly torn from the rock, but
they held on till the strain ceased, then they threw in
the rope, and Walter and Larry bent to their oars.

"Row easy, Larry," Walter said as the next wave passed under them, "and put her head to each wave."

Terrible as was the sea, the curragh floated buoyantly over it, though several times, as she rose to the steep waves, Walter thought that she would be thrown right over. The worst part of their task was over when they got beyond the end of the Nose, for up to that point they were forced to row across the course of the waves, and continually to turn the boat to face the great masses of water which ran between the rocks. But once beyond the end of the reef they turned her head north and rowed straight towards the ship.

"She has struck, Master Walter," Larry said, glancing over his shoulder, "and her masts are gone."

"Lay out, then, Larry, there's no time to lose."

But in spite of their efforts the boat moved but slowly through the water, for the wind caught her high bow with such force that at times it needed all their strength and skill to keep her head straight. At last they were close to the ship, which already showed signs of breaking up. They ranged up alongside of it.

"Fasten a line to a keg and throw it in," Walter shouted.

In a minute a keg was thrown overboard with a line attached. As soon as it drifted a little way from the vessel's side they hauled it into the boat.

"Now, back, Larry; these waves would sink us in a moment if we turn our stern to them."

The wreck lay within a hundred yards of the shore, and the boat backed until close to the line where the waves toppled over in a torrent of foam.

"Now, Larry, keep her steady; we are as near as we dare go."

Then Walter stood up in the boat, took the keg and a foot or two of line in his hand, and waited till the next wave passed under the boat. He swung the keg round his head and hurled it towards the shore. Then he dropped into his seat and gave two or three vigorous strokes, and, when safely beyond the line of breakers, sat quiet and watched the result.

"They have missed it the first time," he said. "Look! they are going to run into the surf for it."

The group on the shore joined hands, and the next time the keg was borne forward in the tumble of foam Considine ran forward and seized it. The back rush took him from his feet, but the others held on, and before the next wave came the line was safely on the beach. A strong cable was soon pulled ashore and firmly fixed. A light line was attached to it, and the sailors at once began to pass along.

"Shall we turn back now, Master Walter?"

"We will keep near the wreck for a few minutes longer, Larry. She can't hold together long, and may be we can pick somebody up."

The vessel was indeed breaking up fast. Her stern was burst in, and the waves, as they poured in at the opening, smashed up the deck. Many of the crew had been washed overboard, and had instantly disappeared. As the boat approached the wreck an officer who had climbed the shrouds shouted out:

"Will your boat hold another?"

"Yes," Walter shouted back, "she will hold two more."

"I will try and swim to you," the officer said.

He threw off the long cloak in which he was wrapped, and unbuckled his sword and let it drop, unbuttoned and took off his military coat, and with some difficulty got rid of his high boots.

"Can you come a bit nearer?" he shouted.

"We daren't," Walter said. "A touch from one of those floating timbers would send us to the bottom."

The officer waved his hand and then sprang head foremost into the sea. So long was he in the water that Walter began to think he must have struck against something and was not coming up again, when suddenly he appeared within twenty yards of the boat. They rowed towards him instantly.

"You must get in over the stern," Walter said.

The officer was perfectly cool, and, placing his hands on the stern, drew himself partly over it, and Walter, grasping his hand, dragged him in. No sooner was he in than Walter again hailed the wreck.

"We can carry one more."

But those who were still on board were huddled up in the bow waiting their turn for the rope.

"There is a big un coming now," Larry exclaimed, "that will finish her."

A wave, towering far above its fellows, was indeed approaching. Higher and higher it rose. There was a wild cry from the wreck as it surged over it. When it had passed the sea was covered with floating timbers, but the vessel was gone.

"We can do nothing now," Walter said. "We daren't go in among that wreckage, and any who got hold of floating planks will drift ashore. Now, Larry, back quietly, and let her drift down round the Nose. We must keep her head to the waves."

Ten minutes and they were abreast of the reef. As soon as they were past it Walter gave the word, and they rowed along under its shelter to the point where they had embarked.

"Now, sir," Walter said, "we will back her up to that rock. When we are close enough you must jump."

This was safely accomplished.

"Now, Larry, row alongside when the next wave comes; we must both scramble out as well as we can."

But by this time help was at hand. The boat had been anxiously watched from the shore, and when, on the disappearance of the wreck, she was seen to be making her way back to the Nose, Mr. Davenant, with Considine and the priest, and the boys who had assisted in getting her afloat, hurried along the shore to meet her, the rest of the fishermen remaining behind to aid any who might be washed up from the wreck. As soon as it was seen that they intended to land at the spot where they had started, Considine and Mr. Davenant made their way along the rock and joined the officer just as he leapt ashore. The boat came alongside on the top of the wave, and as this sank it grazed the rock and capsized, but Walter and Larry grasped the hands stretched out to them, and were hauled on to the rock, while the next wave dashed the curragh in fragments on the beach.

CHAPTER II.

FOR JAMES OR WILLIAM.

"MY dear Walter," his father exclaimed as he embraced his son, as he scrambled on shore, "you have behaved like a hero indeed, but you oughtn't to have done it; and you too, Larry. You both deserve a sound thrashing for the fright you have given us."

"They may have frightened you, sir," the officer said; "but assuredly I owe my life to these brave lads. I have scarcely thanked them yet, for indeed until I felt my foot on the rock I had but small hopes of reaching shore safely in that cock-boat of theirs. After feeling that great ship so helpless against the waves, it seemed impossible that a mere egg-shell could float over them. My name, sir, is Colonel L'Estrange, at your service."

"My name is Davenant, colonel, and I am truly glad that my son has rescued you; but the sooner you are up at my place the better, sir. This is no weather for standing talking in shirt-sleeves."

They now made their way along the rock back to the shore, and then hurried to the village. There they learned that six men had succeeded in getting to shore along the rope before the vessel broke up.

C

Telling Larry he had best have a glass of hot spirits and then turn into bed at once, and that he was to come up to the house the first thing in the morning, Mr. Davenant, with the priest, Colonel L'Estrange, and Walter made his way up to the house, to which the men who had reached the shore had been already taken.

The party were met at the door by Mrs. Davenant, who had been extremely anxious, for Godfrey had been sent home by his father as soon as the wreck went to pieces, and had brought the news of Walter's doings up to that time.

"He is quite safe, Katherine," Mr. Davenant said, "but you mustn't stop either to scold him or praise him at present. Hurry off, Walter, and get between the blankets; I will bring you up some hot spiced wine directly. Katherine, this is Colonel L'Estrange, whom Walter has brought ashore in his boat. You will excuse him at present, for he has been for hours exposed to the storm, and must be half-frozen as well as half-drowned. Now, colonel, if you will come along with me you will find a bed with hot blankets ready, and, I doubt not, a blazing fire. Ah, here is the spiced wine; take a draught of that before you go up stairs. You can have another after you are in bed."

Three more survivors from the wreck were presently brought up. They had been washed ashore on planks, as indeed had many others, but the rest had all been beaten to death against the rocks by the breakers. Walter slept late the next morning, and when he came down stairs found that the others had already finished breakfast. When he had eaten his meal and listened to the gentle scolding which his mother gave him for risking his life, he joined his father, who was, with Colonel L'Estrange, pacing backwards and forwards on the terrace in front of the house. The first fury of the storm was over, but it still blew strongly, and a very heavy sea was running.

"Ah, my young friend," Colonel L'Estrange said, advancing, "I am glad to see you, and to be able to thank you more warmly than I was able to do last night, when the very words seemed frozen on my lips, for having saved my life. It was a gallant deed, and one which your father may well be proud of. It showed not only bravery of the highest kind, but coolness and judgment, which are virtues even more rare. I predict a brilliant future for you, and if in any way my aid may be of use to you, believe me, it will be at your service."

"It was well you were a good swimmer, sir," Walter said, "for we could not have helped you if you had not been able to help yourself, for the sea was covered with pieces of wreck, and as the boat was only covered with canvas the slightest touch from one of the jagged ends would have made a hole in it. I am very much obliged to you for your kind offer of assistance; but at present we have not made up our minds what I am to be; have we, father?"

"No, indeed, Walter. You have told me that you would like, at any rate for a time, to see something of the world before settling down here for life; but it is no easy matter to say what is best for you to do. Ireland offers but little field for anyone's ambition. Since King James came to the throne, and especially since Tyrconnell became governor, things have been a little more favourable for us; and I have hopes yet that justice will be done to the Catholic population of this unhappy country. Is it not monstrous, Colonel L'Estrange, that the very men who had a hand in the rebellion against King Charles the First should still be in possession during the reign of his son of the lands which were taken from my father because he was loyal to his king? And so it is all over Ireland, the descendants of Cromwell's men lord it in the homes of those who were faithful to King Charles."

"It certainly seems so, sir," Col. L'Estrange said; "but I am no politician. I am simply a soldier, and obey orders; but I own that it does seem a cruel injustice that the great portion of the lands of this country should be held by the descendants of Cromwell's soldiers, while the lawful owners, whose only fault was that they were loyal to their king, should still be dispossessed of it."

"But I think better times are coming," Mr. Davenant said. "There can be no doubt of the king's leaning towards our religion. He has been restrained from carrying his good-will towards us into effect by his privy-councillors and by the English party here, whose interest it is to prevent any change being made, and who constantly misrepresent the feelings of this country. From the days when Strongbow first landed this island has been the prey of adventurers, whose only object has been to wrest the land from the native population."

"But you are yourself a descendant of one of the early English settlers, Mr. Davenant."

"That is true enough," Mr. Davenant said smiling, "and no doubt he was as bad as the rest of them; but you see we have held the land for some centuries now, and, like the other descendants of Strongbow's men, have come to look at matters from the Irish point of view rather than the English; however, I hope for better times."

"You haven't heard the news, then, about the Prince of Orange?"

"No; what is the news?" Mr. Davenant asked. "There have been rumours for years that he intended to make a bid for the English throne; but I have heard nothing else."

"There was a report before I left London that he has already sailed from Holland," Colonel L'Estrange replied; "and indeed I have no doubt the rumour is well founded."

"But he will never succeed," Mr. Davenant said eagerly. "He will be put down as easily as Monmouth was."

"I do not know," Colonel L'Estrange said gravely. "The Protestant feeling in England is very strong. Monmouth was vain and empty-headed, and he wrecked his own cause. The Dutchman is a different sort of man altogether, and one thing is certain, if King James can make a mess of matters he is sure to do so. The Stuarts have always been feeble and indecisive, and James is the most feeble and indecisive of them. If William succeeds in effecting a landing, I think his chance of success is a good one."

"He may reign in England," Mr. Davenant broke in passionately, "but he will not reign in Ireland. But forgive me," he broke off. "I forgot for a moment that you are an Englishman and my guest."

"You need not apologize, Mr. Davenant. As I said, I am a soldier and no politician. My ancestors were royalists, and I have no great love for the Dutch stadt-holder, who will be supported in England by the class who rose against King Charles. At the same time it is difficult to feel much enthusiasm for the Stuarts. The first was a pedant; the second threw away his chances over and over again by his duplicity and want of faith; the third was utterly selfish and unprin-cipled; the fourth is a gloomy bigot. Charles was, and James is, a pensioner of France. How can men be ready to sacrifice everything for such a race as this?"

"That is not the way in which we look at it in Ireland," Mr. Davenant said. "The wars here are waged under various pretences; someone is goaded into rebellion, false charges are preferred wholesale, or there is a religious pretext; but we all know what is at the bottom of them all, simply the greed of English adventurers for Irish land; and not content with having dispossessed the ancient owners of three-fourths of the cultivated land of the country, they want the re-mainder, and under the pretence that we, the descen-dants of the early settlers, are in sympathy with our Irish neighbours, they have marked us out for de-struction, and already a great portion of our estates is in the hands of Cromwell's men. So gross have been the abuses that the commission, which the king appointed to inquire into the seizure of our estates, only ventured to sit one day, for the proofs brought for-ward were so overwhelmingly strong that it was seen at once that did the inquiry continue it would be made manifest to all the world that justice could be satisfied by nothing less than a clear sweep of all those men who have seized our estates.

"If Ireland rises in favour of King James it will not be for any love for the Stuarts; but it will be to recover the land which has been illegally wrested from us, and which, if Dutch William and his Whig adherents gain the upper hand, will be taken from us for ever. The religious element will, of course, count for much. Already we have suffered persecution for our religion; and if the Whigs could have their way they would stamp it out utterly with fire and sword. Things have looked better during the last five or six years than they have done since Cromwell first put foot in Ireland. We have begun to hope for justice. Tyrconnell has stood up for us, and with the good-will of James has gained many concessions. We have now what we never had before, an Irish army. The land thieves have been fairly alarmed, for they have seen that the long-delayed justice will be done us at last. Many have sold back their lands to the original owners and have left the country; others are only holding out for better terms. Another ten years of James's reign and things would have righted themselves; but if the Dutchman ascends the throne of England there is no hope for Ireland save in the sword."

"Well, we must hope it will not come to that," Colonel L'Estrange said. "I am ready to fight the battles of England on the Continent, but civil war with all its horrors sickens me; and civil war here is not like our civil war in England. There were no race

animosities there, no memory of cruel wrongs on one
side or the other; men fought for a principle, but
there were no atrocities committed on either side like
those which have devastated Germany. The peasant
ploughed the land, and the trader kept open his shop
unmolested. It is true that towards the end there
were confiscations of the property of those who still
continued the strife, and a few executions of indivi-
duals; but, taking it as a whole, no war has ever caused
so little suffering to the people at large as did the civil
war in England; but assuredly a war in Ireland now,
like those which have gone before, would be marked
by the foulest atrocities, massacres, and destruction on
both sides."

"Yes," Mr. Davenant said, "I must own that for
downright brutal and bloody ferocity the wars in Ireland rival those of the Huns."

Walter had listened in silence to this conversation.
His father now turned to him.

"Have you heard whether Larry has recovered from
his adventure of yesterday as well as you have?"

"No, father, I have not heard anything about it.
I came out here directly I finished my breakfast.
How are the people who were brought up here?"

"They are going on well, Walter, but they were all
so bruised as they were being drawn up through the
surf that it will be some days before any of them can
leave their beds. How many had you on board,
colonel?"

"I did not see the list of passengers, but there were
twelve or fourteen aft, and from what I saw I should
think as many more forward; there were twenty-three

men in the crew. I suppose altogether there were some fifty on board."

"Are you going to make a long stay in Ireland?"

"No; I shall only remain here a week or two. I am the bearer of some letters from the king to Tyrconnell; and that reminds me that I must be making my way on to Dublin."

"I will ride in with you," Mr. Davenant said. "I must tell my friends this news that you bring; it seems to me to be most serious. I will have a horse round for you here in half an hour if that will suit you."

"Perfectly," Colonel L'Estrange replied; "that will just give me time to walk round to the village to see the lad you call Larry, for I could not go without thanking him for the share he had in preserving my life. Perhaps you will go down with me, Walter, and show me his house?"

When they reached the shore they found the whole population of the village engaged in dragging up the spars, planks, and pieces of timber with which the rocks were strewn.

"There is Larry," Walter said; "it is evident that there's nothing the matter with him."

Larry was indeed just coming up dragging a piece of timber behind him, while in his left hand he held a large bundle of fragments of wood of different sizes, which, as well as the timber, he was taking home for firing.

"Larry, come here; the English gentleman wants to speak to you."

The boy dropped his wood and came up.

"My lad," Colonel L'Estrange said, "I am greatly indebted to you for your work of last night. Take this," and he placed a purse of ten guineas in Larry's hand. "And remember that I am still greatly your debtor, and that if at any future time you should be in a position in which my aid may be useful, you have only to let me know and I will stand your friend."

The sum appeared to Larry to be enormous.

"Long life to yer honour, and it's proud I am to have been of service to such a grand gentleman. It's thankful I am for your kindness, and if ever you want a boy to do a job for you it's myself that will be proud to do it. As to yesterday, I just came because the young squire tould me to, and thankful I am that he got back safe to shore, for if we had been drowned I don't know whatever I should have said to the squire."

Two days after the shipwreck Walter and John Whitefoot met at the place which they had agreed on when they last saw each other four days before.

"I heard of your brave deed on the night of the storm, Walter—everyone is talking of it; and even my grandfather, who has seldom a good word for any of you at the Castle, said that it was a noble deed. It was as much as I could do not to say, 'Yes, he is a friend of mine;' for I felt proud of you, I can tell you."

"It is all nonsense, John. I have often been out in a curragh in bad weather, though never in quite such a storm as that; but, once launched, she rode lightly enough, and scarce shipped a spoonful of water."

"I should like to have been there," John said; "but I should have been no use. My people have always been against my going down to the sea, deeming it a pure waste of time, except that they let me go down to swim. I can do that well, you know; but they have always forbidden my going out in boats. Now, you see, it is proved that it is not a waste of time, for you have been able to save many lives. The thought must make you very happy."

"Well, I don't know that it does particularly," Walter said carelessly. "Of course I was glad at the time, but I have not thought much about it one way or the other since. You see the news that has come has driven everything else out of our heads."

"Is it true, then, the report that we heard yesterday, that William of Orange has set out for England?"

"Yes, it is true enough; and I am afraid, by what I hear, that it is likely to cause all sorts of troubles."

"I suppose so," John said gravely; "and of course in this matter my people think differently from yours. You know we agreed that we would never talk on these subjects, but I am afraid the time is coming when there will be nothing else to be talked of."

"I am afraid so too, John. My father thinks that there will be civil war again."

"Of course my grandfather is delighted," John said quietly; "he has been greatly disturbed in his mind for some months owing to the leanings of King James towards the Irish, which seem to point to his having to give up no small portion of the lands."

"We thought so too, John; and although it is your father who would lose and mine who would gain, I don't think that even you can deny that it would be reasonable. Your grandfather got the land from mine

because he fought for Cromwell against the king, and
Cromwell got the best of it. Well, it seems only reasonable that when the king again came to the throne,
those who fought for him should get their own again."

"It does seem so, Walter, I must own; and I am
sure I should not have cared for myself if the land
was given back again to your father to-morrow. Then
I suppose we should go back to England; and as I
know my grandfather has done well and has laid by
a good deal of money, they could take a farm there;
and there would be more chance of their letting me
enter upon some handicraft. I would rather that by a
great deal than farming. All these books you have
lent me, Walter, have shown me what great and noble
deeds there are to be done in the world—I don't mean
in fighting, you know, but in other ways. And they
make the life here, toiling on the farm from sunrise
to sunset with no object save that of laying by every
year more money, seem terribly empty and worthless.

"By the way, my grandfather was yesterday evening rating my father because, instead of always keeping me hard at work, he allowed me once or twice a
week to be away for hours wasting my time—which
means, though he didn't know it, going about with
you. My father said stoutly that he did not think
the time was altogether wasted, for that in the last
two years I had made a notable advance in learning,
and he was satisfied that I had benefited much by
these intervals of recreation. Thereupon my grandfather grumbled that I was too fond of reading, and
that I was filling my mind with all sorts of nonsense,
whereas true wisdom was to be found in one book only.

" My father said that was true of religious wisdom, but that for the advancement of the world it was needed that men should learn other things. Of course my grandfather had three or four texts ready at hand; but my father had him by saying: 'You see, father, all the commands issued to the Jews are not strictly applicable to us—for example, they were ordered not to use horses; and I do not remember that Cromwell felt that he was doing wrong when he raised his ironsides.' That was a poser, and so the matter dropped."

Ten days later, when the boys met, John said:

" This is the last time we shall meet for some time, Walter, for I am going up to Derry to stay with a cousin of my father who is settled there and exercises the trade of a currier. I said some months ago that I should like to learn a trade, but everyone was against it then; they seemed to think that, as I should some day have the land, it was flying in the face of Providence to think of anything else. But I suppose the fact that everything is so unsettled now, and that there is no saying what may come of these events in England, may have made them think differently.

" At any rate my father said to me yesterday: 'We have been talking over what you said about wishing to learn a trade. If all goes on well there is no occasion for you to learn any business save that of farming; but none can say what the Lord may not have in store for us, or what troubles may come upon us. In any case it will do you no harm to see a little of the world outside our farm; and therefore your grandfather and I have settled that you shall go for a few months to my cousin, who, as you know, is a currier in Derry.

He has often written asking you to go and stay
with him, seeing that he has no children of his own.
Learn what you can of his business; and if it should
be that you find it more to your liking than farming,
I should not be one to hold you back from following
the bent of your inclinations.

"'But this is between ourselves. My father's ideas
on these subjects you know, and it would cause much
trouble did he think that you had any idea of not
following in the path in which he and I have trod.
But to me it seems better that each should go on
the path towards which his mind is turned—that is,
when he has made quite sure, after long reflection and
prayer, that it is no idle whim but a settled earnest
desire. If, then, after your visit to your uncle you
feel that you are truly called to follow a life other
than that you would lead here, I shall not oppose you.
The Lord has blessed our labours, the land is fertile,
and I can well provide the moneys that will be needful
to start you either in business with my cousin, or in
such way as may appear best.'

"I thanked him gravely, but indeed Walter I had
difficulty in restraining myself from shouting with
joy, for a life like that of my father and grandfather
here would be very grievous to me. I have no desire
to gain greater wealth than we have, but I long for a
higher life than this."

"I don't know, John," Walter said doubtfully. "Unless, as you say, these troubles make a difference, you
will be a large land-owner some day; and these bit-
ternesses will die out in time, and you will take a
very different position from that which your grand-

father holds. Of course we regard him as a usurper, but you know in the third generation the grandson of a usurper becomes a legitimate monarch. My ancestors usurped the land from the native Irish by the sword, just as your grandfather did from us; but we came in time to be regarded as the natural lords of the soil, and so will you. But to be a currier!—that strikes me as a tremendous come down!"

"I care nothing about coming up or coming down," John said simply; "I long only for an honest mode of life, in which, instead of dwelling solitary, and seeing no one from year to year save at our Sabbath meetings, I may mix with others and take part in a more active and busy life. In itself I do not suppose that the trade of a currier is a very pleasant one; but that matters little if when work is done one has leisure for some sort of communication with others and for improving one's mind. It will be to me something like what going to court in London would be to you, Walter. I am most grieved about my mother; she will miss me sorely.

"She said to me last night, 'I fear somewhat, John, that the course I have taken with you has greatly unfitted you for settling down here as we have done before you; but although I shall miss you sadly, I do not blame myself for what I have done. I think myself, my son, that there are higher lives than that spent in tilling the soil from boyhood to old age. It is true the soil must be tilled. There must be ever hewers of wood and drawers of water; but God has appointed for each his place, and I think, my son, that you have that within you which would render the life with which your father and grandfather have been well-contented an irksome one for you.

"I have no fear that we shall be always separated. Your grandfather is an old man, and when the Lord pleases to take him, your father and I will be free to do as we choose, and can, if we like, dispose of this land and quit this troubled country and settle in England or elsewhere near where you may be. It is true that we shall get little for the land; for, broad as are its acres, who will give much for a doubtful title? But there is ample laid by for our old age, and I see not the sense of labouring incessantly, as does your grandfather, merely to lay up stores which you will never enjoy. Did I see any signs of a decrease in the bitter animosity which parties feel towards each other here I might think differently; but there is no prospect of peace and good-will returning in your time, and therefore no object in your father and I toiling on for the rest of our lives when the return of our labour will be of little worth to you. Such being so, I do not regret that your thoughts turn to the world of which you have read in books. The world is but a secondary consideration to us, 'tis true, but I can see no special goodness in a life of dull monotony."

"I wonder where your mother got hold of her ideas, John; she is so different from most of your people?"

"She is indeed," John agreed. "It was from her mother that she received her teaching. I know she was not happy with her husband, who was as gloomy and fanatical as is my grandfather, and she ever looked back to the happy days of her girlhood in England. I think she did for my mother just what my mother has done for me, only the difference is that she never had sufficient influence with her husband to enable her to carry out her views for her daughter, while my mother—

"Has managed to have her own way." Walter laughed.

"I suppose so, and that in spite of my grandfather. Certainly I owe everything to her, for I am sure if it hadn't been for her my father would never have ventured to oppose the old man, even so far as to let me know you. It makes one sad to think, Walter, that religion should sometimes make those who think most of it tyrants in their families. My grandfather is terribly earnest in his religion. There is no pretence or mistake about it; but, for all that, or rather because of it, he would, if he could, allow no one else to have a will or opinion of his own."

"I don't think it's the religion, John, but the manner of the religion. My mother and grandmother are both as religious as anyone could be; but I don't think I ever heard either of them say a hard word of a soul. Their religion is a pleasure to them and not a task, and I know that some years ago, when we had a priest who was always denouncing the Protestants, they very soon managed to get him changed for another. What a funny thing it is, to be sure, that people should quarrel about their religion! After all, we believe all the same important things; and as to others, what does it matter, provided we all do our best in the way that seems right to us?"

But this was too liberal for John. He had been

brought up in too strait a sect to subscribe to such an opinion as this.

"I do think it makes a difference, Walter," he said slowly.

"I don't," Walter said; "it's just a matter of bringing up. If you had been born in the Castle, and I had been born in your place, you would have thought as I do, and I should have thought as you do; and of course still more if you had been born in a Catholic country like Italy, where you would never have heard of Protestantism, and I had been born in a Protestant country like Holland, where I should never have had a chance of becoming a Catholic. Very few people ever change their religion; they just live and die as they have been born and educated."

"It seems so," John said after a pause; "but the question is too deep for us."

"Quite so," Walter laughed, "and I don't want to argue it. Well, when are you going to start?"

"I am off to-morrow morning. My father has an acquaintance in Dublin who is starting for Derry, and I am to go in his charge."

For another hour the boys chatted together, and then with mutual promises of writing regularly, whenever they had the chance, they said good-by, and the following morning John started with his father to Dublin, and next day journeyed north towards Derry.

CHAPTER III.

THE KING IN IRELAND.

N the 12th of November a vessel arrived in Dublin with the news that William of Orange had landed at Torbay on the 5th. The news created the wildest excitement. The Protestants, who had been deeply depressed by the apparent intention of James to hand back to their original owners the land which had been wrested from them, now took heart and began openly to arm. Upon the other hand, the Catholics felt that if William and the Whigs succeeded to the chief power in England their faith, their remaining property, and their lives were alike menaced, and they, too, prepared to fight to the last for all they held dear.

Walter rode several times with his father into Dublin. The streets presented a strange spectacle. They were crowded with Protestant fugitives from the country districts. These had forsaken all and flocked into Dublin, fearing that the Irish would retaliate for past grievances by a general massacre. The banks of the Liffey were crowded by these fugitives, who with tears and cries besought the captains of the vessels lying there to give them passage to England.

All sorts of rumours of bloodshed, massacre, and destruction circulated through the city. The Protestants in the north were said to have fallen upon the Catholic population and to have put them to the sword, while in the south and west it was said the Catholics had taken the same measures against the Protestants. Both reports were equally false, but they were generally believed, and added to the panic and dismay. In fact, however, both parties were waiting. The Protestants dared not commence hostilities until assured that William was firmly seated on the English throne and ready to come to their assistance; the Catholics were equally desirous to maintain the peace until assured that no hope remained save the sword.

A month after John Whitefoot had left, Walter received a letter from him:—

"Dear Friend Walter,—You will have heard, no doubt, of the troubles that have arisen here. My father sent me here to learn a trade, but at present all men's minds are so agitated that there is no talk save of arms and of fighting. My kinsman is as bad as the others. He spends the day going hither and thither among the townsfolk, and has been made an officer in one of the six companies which have been raised here, and pays no further heed to business. The town is mightily divided: the younger and more zealous spirits are all for fighting, while almost all the older and wealthier citizens are opposed to this.

"This is how the trouble began. The Earl of Tyrconnell sent, as you know, three thousand soldiers to help King James at the first news of the landing of the prince, and to do so he withdrew the regiment which was in garrison in this town. On the 7th of

this month of December the people here heard that
the regiment of the Earl of Antrim was approaching
the town to take the place of those troops. When the
news arrived there was a sort of panic in the town,
and the news was spread that this regiment was intended to massacre the people.

"Why this should be I do not know, and I cannot
but think that the alarm was a false one; however,
the regiment arrived on the river bank, and some of its
officers crossed and entered the city. When they were
in council with some of the leading citizens, a party
of apprentices, with some of the rabble, shut the gates.
For some time there was great debate. The older
citizens were mostly in favour of admitting the earl's
regiment. Why, they asked, should Derry alone defy
the power of Tyrconnell and King James? If King
William made his cause good and came over to Ireland to aid the Protestants, it would be time enough
for the men of Derry to join him and to fight for their
faith; but if they now stood alone they could do no
good to the cause of King William, and would bring
destruction on themselves and their city.

"But these arguments were of no avail. The apprentices and all the young men of the town, and the
fugitives who had come in from the country round,
were all for fighting, and so the gates were kept shut;
and Lord Antrim, seeing that he could do nothing
against such a strong place as Derry, marched away
with his regiment. This seems to me a fair account
of what has happened. What will come of it I know
not; but, being a Protestant, my feelings would in-
cline me to the side of William. Yet it seems to me

that his friends here have acted hastily in thus adventuring themselves against all the forces of King James, and that sore trouble is like to come upon the town. However, it is not for me to judge. I am as warm as any of them in defence of our religion, and shall try to do my best in case of need. I am sorry, dear Walter, that we have to take different sides in this quarrel, but of course we are each of the opinion of our elders, and must not blame each other for what is indeed not of our own choosing.

"This is a fair city, standing on rising ground by a stately river, and with strong walls; and at any other time life would be very pleasant here, although living among so many people seems strange to me after my life on the farm. I hear all sorts of tales about fighting in other parts, and of the slaughter of Protestants by Rapparees, but know not whether they are true. As my cousin, who is an earnest man, is wholly taken up with the present affairs, and all business is at a stand, I have little to do, and spend much of my time by the river side, and have taken to fishing, which I like mightily, and yesterday I caught a fish weighing three pounds, and we had him for dinner. I often wish you were with me. Write me a long letter and tell me all that you are doing.

"Your affectionate friend,

"JOHN WHITEFOOT."

Indeed, throughout all Ireland preparations for war were going on. All over the north the Protestants were banding themselves in arms; and, under the excuse of some outrages committed by a few isolated

parties of peasants known as Rapparees, were everywhere harrying the Catholics, carrying fire and sword
into quiet villages, burning, slaying, and carrying off
their grain and cattle. Throughout the whole of Ulster
Charlemont and Carrickfergus alone remained in the
hands of King James's troops.

England and Scotland had now accepted William
as their king, and James had fled to France. With
the exception of Ulster, Ireland remained staunch to
King James. In the south Lord Inshiquin, and in
Connaught Lord Kingston, had each raised corps
among the Protestant settlers for William, and were
the first to commence hostilities, and the latter, marching north, made an attack on Carrickfergus.

Tyrconnell now issued commissions to several of the
Catholic nobility and gentry to raise troops for the
king's service, and as the people responded to the call
readily some fifty regiments of foot and several troops
of horse were soon raised. But though men were
forthcoming in abundance, there was a great want of
arms and all munitions of war. There were in the
government stores only twenty thousand arms, and
most of these were old weapons that had been returned to store as unserviceable, and only about a
thousand muskets were found to be of any use. There
was no artillery or ammunition, and no money with
which these necessaries could be purchased abroad.
The gentry would have willingly contributed, but all
had been well-nigh ruined by the confiscation of their
property, and could do little towards filling the trea-
sury.

Never did a nation enter upon a war so badly pro-

vided with all necessaries as did Ireland when she
resolved to adhere to the cause of her king and to
resist the power of England and Scotland, aided by
that of Holland and the Protestant States of Germany.

Mr. Davenant had been one of the first to respond
to the invitation of Tyrconnell, and had set about
raising a troop of horse. He had no difficulty in
getting the number of men in Bray and the surrounding villages, and the difficulty in mounting them was
overcome by the patriotism of sundry gentlemen and
citizens of Dublin, who willingly contributed their
spare horses to the king's service.

Their arms were various. Some had swords, some
short pikes, while a few only had pistols; but the
smiths everywhere toiled hard converting scythes and
reaping-hooks into swords and pikes, and before they
were ready to take the field the whole troop were
provided with swords. Walter had eagerly begged
his father to appoint him cornet of the troop, and Mr.
Davenant might have yielded had it not been for his
wife's entreaties. Even old Mrs. Davenant, intensely
loyal as she was to the cause of James, sided with her
daughter-in-law.

"Of course, Fergus, you will do your duty to the
king. It would indeed be a shame for a Davenant to
hold back; but at Walter's age there can be no occasion for him, as yet, to take a commission. I am ready
to give my son as I gave my husband to the king;
and when Walter becomes a man he too must go if
duty demands it; but for the present, assuredly there
is no reason why such a boy should mix himself up
in this unhappy struggle. Besides, if aught befalls you

it is to him that his mother will have to look in the future. There are hundreds and thousands of strong and active men in Ireland, and the necessity has not yet come for boys to take the field."

So Walter, to his intense disappointment, was refused the cornetcy of the troop, but his father, who fully entered into his feelings, finally told him that when the troop took the field he should accompany him.

"You are not to carry arms, Walter, or to mix yourself up in any way with it. You will be a sort of camp-follower, you know; but you will see all that goes on, and will be able to prepare yourself to take your place in the ranks, if the war should unhappily go on for any time."

With this Walter had to be satisfied; and, indeed, although somewhat disappointed at not being at once allowed to join the troop, he felt sure that it would not be very long before his father, once away from the influence of his wife and mother, would allow him to join.

"May I take Larry with me, father? He would look after my horse, and would be useful to you for running messages and all sorts of things. He wants to go very much; you see his uncle and two or three of his cousins have joined the troop, and he would have joined too if you had not thought him too young."

"The worst of you and Larry is, that you are always getting into some scrape together," Mr. Davenant said with a smile.

"But I should not get into scrapes on such a business as this," Walter said indignantly. "This is a serious affair, and of course going with you I should be very particular."

"Yes, as long as I was close by, Walter; however, I don't mind your taking Larry; he would, as you say, be useful, and you will want somebody to look after your horse and act as your servant. We may be separated sometimes, for the troop may be sent on detached service when I could not take you with me."

The permission to take Larry quite reconciled Walter to the downfall of his hopes of going as cornet, and in high spirits he hastened down to the village to tell Larry that his father had consented to his accompanying him.

All through January Mr. Davenant was busy drilling his troop. Throughout all Ireland both parties were preparing for the storm which was soon to burst. Lord Mountjoy, a Protestant nobleman, was sent with his regiment, which consisted for the most part of Protestants, to Derry. He held a meeting with the leading townspeople, who agreed to admit the Protestant soldiers, upon the condition that no more troops were sent. Accordingly, the Protestant troops, under Colonel Lundy, entered the town, and Lord Mountjoy assumed the governorship.

Tyrconnell soon perceived that he had made a mistake in sending Mountjoy to Derry, for instead of overawing the inhabitants, his regiment had in fact become a part of the rebel garrison; he therefore recalled Mountjoy and sent him over to France on the pretence of an embassy to King James, but as soon as he arrived there he was treacherously thrown into prison.

The people of Derry received quantities of powder and arms from Scotland, and on the 20th of February the Prince of Orange was formally proclaimed king in Derry; and this example was followed throughout Ulster. This was, in fact, the beginning of the war. Anxious to save Ireland from the horrors of civil war, Lord Granard and other Protestant noblemen of the council joined Tyrconnell in issuing a proclamation, ordering the Protestant corps to lay down their arms; and as they did not obey, Lieutenant-general Hamilton was despatched to the north with a thousand regular troops and a considerable number of irregulars.

These came up with the insurgents at Dromore, and defeated them with great slaughter. They rallied at Hillsborough, but again were defeated and scattered. Hamilton divided his force, and marching through the north reduced Ulster to submission, with the exception only of the fortified towns of Enniskillen and Derry. In the south General M'Carty was equally successful in clearing Munster of William's adherents, and defeated Lord Inshiquin in every encounter.

On the 14th of March Mr. Davenant, who had ridden into Dublin, returned in the evening with the news that the king had landed at Kinsale two days before, with fifteen hundred Irish troops in the pay of France, and a hundred French officers, intended to aid in drilling the new levies.

"I am glad, indeed, that he has arrived, for had he been met on the seas by the English fleet all our hopes might have been dashed at a blow. Now that he is with us it will rouse the enthusiasm of the people to the utmost. **If he is** wise he will surely be **able to unite** all Ireland under him, save of course the **fanatics of** the north, who, however, can do nothing **against the whole strength** of the country, since Hamilton's little **force alone has** been sufficient to put down all opposition, save where they remain shut up behind the walls **of Derry** and Enniskillen. **It is** not with them that we have **to cope** alone—they would be utterly powerless—it is with the army of England and Scotland we shall have to fight. Unfortunately we have no fleet, and they can land wherever they choose; but now the king is really among us, all who **have** hitherto wavered **will join.** Let England and Scotland choose their **king as they** will, but there is no reason why Ireland should desert its rightful monarch at their bidding."

"When will the king arrive at Dublin, father?"

"He goes **first to Cork, Walter;** Tyrconnell has set out, and will **meet him** there. They say he will be here in about ten days' time. The French ambassador, the Marquis d'Avaux, comes with him, **and** many French nobles."

"Do you think, father, he will at once order that his friends shall receive the land again which **was** taken from them by Cromwell's soldiers?"

"I hope not, my boy. It is his interest and not our own we must think of now; and if Ireland is to resist successfully the English and continental troops of Dutch William, we must be united — we must be Irishmen first, Catholics and Protestants afterwards. I trust that he will issue such proclamations as will allay the alarm of the Protestants and bind us all together.

"King James is not like his father. In no single case since he came to the throne has he broken his royal word once given; therefore all may feel confidence in any promises he may make. I have, of course, no hope that anything he can say will influence the fanatics of Derry and Enniskillen, but we can afford to disregard them. They are entailing misery and suffering upon themselves without the slightest benefit to the cause they advocate. If we beat the English, of course those places must finally surrender; if the English beat us, they will get their Dutch William as king, without any effort on their part. I think myself that it will be very unwise to attempt anything against those two places. The people there can shut themselves up in their walls as long as they like, and by so doing can in no way harm us. If we take their towns it will only add to the bad blood that already exists. Better by far leave them to themselves, until the main battle is fought out."

On the 23rd the news came that the king was to arrive in Dublin the next day, and Mr. Davenant, or, as he was now called, Captain Davenant, went over with all the gentry of the neighbourhood to meet him.

King James was received with enthusiasm. Addresses were presented to him by the several public bodies and by the clergy of the Established Church. His answer to these addresses gave satisfaction to all. He promised favour and protection to the Established Protestant Church; issued an invitation to the Protestants who had fled the kingdom to return to their homes, and assured them of safety and his particular care; and he commanded that, with the exception of the military, no Catholics should carry arms in Dublin. Finally, he summoned a parliament to meet him in Dublin on the 7th of May.

One day a messenger arrived with a despatch for Captain Davenant.

"We are to move into Dublin to-morrow, Walter," he said when he read it. "We are to take the field at once; the king himself is going to march in command of us against Derry. I think his majesty is wrong; and I know that Tyrconnell has argued strongly against his intention. There are three reasons against it. First, as I told you, I think it were better to leave Derry alone until the main issue is settled; secondly, King James has no military experience whatever, and if ought goes wrong with the expedition he will lose prestige; thirdly, although it were well for him to be with the army when it fights a foreign foe, it were better that he should not lead it against men who are, however much they may rebel against him, his own subjects.

"I know Tyrconnell has set forth these objections to him; but unhappily obstinacy is a fault of all the Stuart race, and it generally happens that they are most obstinate when most wrong. However, I trust that when Derry sees so strong a force marching against it, it will open its gates without resistance. A siege can only entail horrible suffering on the town; and that suffering will in the end tell against James's cause, for it will excite the sympathy of the Protestants in England and Scotland and make them all the hotter to conquer Ireland."

The following day the troop was mustered in front

of the castle, and, after a tender farewell to his wife and
mother, Captain Davenant placed himself at their head
and rode off. A quarter of an hour later Walter, with
Larry Doolan on a rough little pony by his side, rode
after the troop. Dublin was reached in the afternoon.
The town presented a festive appearance; the principal
streets were still draped with the flags which had been
hung out at the king's entry five days before. The
streets were thronged with people, for loyalists had come
in from all parts of the country to welcome the king.

Large numbers of men belonging to the newly raised
regiments wandered among the crowd, and with these
were mingled the French uniforms of the Irish troops
who had come over with James. The troop was loudly
cheered by the crowd as it passed through the town
to the spot assigned to it in the camp of the force
gathered near the city. Walter and Larry rode a short
distance behind the troop, and joined it as soon as it
reached the ground allotted to it.

"It was a brave sight, father, was it not, to see the
city decked out and all the people cheering for the
king? Dublin is setting a fine example—isn't it?"

"You must not set much weight upon the cheering of a crowd, Walter. I do not say that the people
of Dublin may not at the present moment be loyal to
the king; but if he were defeated and William were
to march in, you would see that they would cheer him
just as heartily. The mob of London cheered King
James as he passed through it a week before he was
so ill advised as to fly, and they threw up their hats
for joy a fortnight later for William. No, my boy—
there is no dependence on a mob. They worship suc-

cess, and the king who is present is sure to be vastly more dear to them than the king who is absent. And now you had better help Larry picket your horses. Put them by the side of mine. See how the troopers fasten theirs, and do yours the same. When that is done send Larry to get hold of some wood and light a fire; it will be cold when the sun goes down. As for food, we have brought enough with us for to-night; to-morrow, I suppose, we shall get rations."

Captain Davenant now posted a certain number of men to look after the horses, and the rest set off to cut firewood; and in an hour four or five great fires were blazing. Forage was served out for the horses from the stores which had been collected, and also a truss of straw to every three soldiers as bedding. Walter had in the meantime strolled away among the other camps, and was greatly amused at the various shifts and contrivances that the men had made to make themselves comfortable. A few only of the officers had tents; for these, as well as all other necessaries of war, were wanting; and the troops, who had for some little time been in camp there, had raised all sorts of shelter from the weather. Some had constructed little huts of turf thatched with straw or rushes; others had erected little tents, some of sail-cloth obtained from the shipping, others of blankets, coarse linen cloaks, or any other articles on which they could lay hands. All were in high spirits at the prospect of the termination of the monotony of continued drill and of the commencement of active campaigning. Huge fires blazed everywhere, and the country for some distance round had been completely stripped of its wood.

Everywhere was life and bustle. Men were cleaning their arms preparatory to the march of next day; others were cooking at the fires; troopers were grooming their horses; snatches of song and loud laughter rose in the air. After wandering about for an hour Walter rejoined his father. Captain Davenant was sitting with the two officers of his troop, Lieutenant O'Driscoll and Cornet Heron, by a fire, the materials for which the three troopers who acted as their servants had collected. There was no cooking to be done, for sufficient cold provisions had been brought with the troop.

"You are just in time, Walter," his father said; "we are going to fall to at once at our meal. Hand over that cold chicken, Larry; and do you, Tim Donelly, broach that keg of claret. Give me the bread, Fergus—that's right. Now, gentlemen, here's a hunch each; plates are a luxury which we must do without in the field. Now let us fall to."

Walter seated himself on a truss of straw beside his father, and thought he had never enjoyed a meal so much in his life as the bread and cold chicken, eaten as they were in the open air in front of the crackling fire. Each was provided with a horn, and these were filled from the keg."

"Here's to the king, gentlemen; success to his arms!"

All stood up to drink the toast, and then continued their meal. Three chickens vanished rapidly, and the troopers kept their horns filled with claret.

"If we always do as well as that," Captain Davenant said as they finished the meal, "we shall have no reason to grumble. But I fear that's too much to expect.

(377)   E

Bring me my pipe and tobacco, Larry; you will find them in the holsters of my saddle. Fergus, do you undo these trusses and lay the straw out even—that will do. Now, lads, you will find plenty more provisions in the wallet. Do you go and get your own suppers, then give an eye to the horses. We shall not want anything more."

For two or three hours the three officers and Walter sat chatting by the fire, occasionally piling on fresh logs. Gradually the din of voices in the camp died away and the bright fires burned down.

"I think we had better turn in," Captain Davenant said at last. "We must be astir an hour before daylight, for we march as soon as it's light."

Rolling themselves in their long cloaks, they lay down upon the straw. It was some time before Walter got to sleep. The novelty of the situation and the strangeness of lying with the night air blowing in his face made him unusually wakeful. Occasionally, too, a laugh from some party who were sitting late round their fire attracted his attention, and the sound of the snorting and pawing of the horses also kept him awake; but at last he, too, went off to sleep. In spite of his warm cloak he felt stiff and chilled when the sound of the trumpets and drums roused the camp.

"Well, Walter, how do you like sleeping in the open?" his father said as he rose to his feet and shook himself.

"I don't mind the sleeping, father, but the waking is not so pleasant; however, I shall soon get accustomed to it, I suppose. But I always did hate getting up in the dark even when we were going out fishing."

"You won't always get as comfortable a bed as this, Walter; so don't expect it. The time will come ere long when you will look back upon this as absolute luxury. We are not likely to get straw another night, I can tell you. Now, Fergus, bring that wallet here. We must breakfast before we get in the saddle."

Walter came to the conclusion that breakfast eaten in the dark was a very inferior meal to dinner before a great fire; however, he kept his thoughts to himself, and, as soon as he had finished, went to aid Larry in saddling the horses.

"I suppose I can ride with you to-day, father?" he said as he mounted.

"Yes; there will not be any military display by the way. Many of the soldiers have got nothing in the way of uniform at present. So you can ride with me. But if any general officer comes along, you must draw off a little and drop behind with Larry, who will follow in the rear of the troop."

As soon as daylight appeared the bugles gave the signal, and the force, preceded by its cavalry, started on its march towards the north.

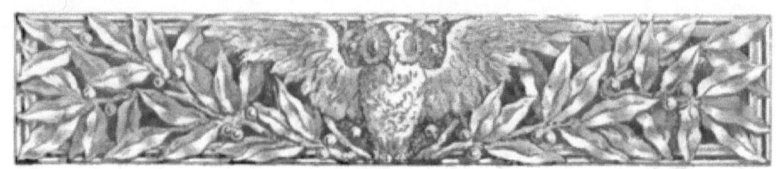

CHAPTER IV.

THE SIEGE OF DERRY.

THERE was an air of excitement in the streets of Derry. Knots of people were gathered talking excitedly, women stood at the doors of all the houses, while men moved aimlessly and restlessly about between the groups, listened for a time to a speaker, and then moved on again. The work of strengthening the defences, which had gone on incessantly for the last three months, had ceased, while numbers of persons were gathered on the walls looking anxiously towards the south. A general air of gloom and despondency hung over the place; the storm which Derry had braved was gathering around it at last. King James and his troops were advancing against it.

Opinion was strongly divided in the city; almost without exception the older citizens deprecated resistance. The walls, indeed, were strong and the position formidable. The king had no artillery worth speaking of, and the walls, manned by brave men, might well for a definite time resist assault; but the stores of food could not long support the large population now gathered in the town, and there seemed no possibility whatever of assistance from England before the horrors of famine would be upon them. To what purpose, then, oppose resistance, which must, even if successful, cause frightful sufferings to the inhabitants, and which, if unsuccessful, would hand over the city to the vengeance of James.

The garrison had been strengthened by two regiments and a vast quantity of supplies. But including everything there were but provisions for ten days, and as many weeks might elapse before assistance could come. The younger and more ardent spirits were for resistance to the last. "Better," they said, "die of hunger than surrender the Protestant stronghold to the Papists." Every hour brought crowds of fugitives, the inhabitants of all the villages deserting their homes at the approach of the royal forces, and flying, with what goods they could carry, to Derry.

Archdeacon Hamilton had arrived with a message from the king, offering that if the city would, within four days, surrender, there should be an amnesty to all for past offences, and that the property of all the inhabitants should be respected. This proposition was now being considered by the governor and his council, together with all the principal officers of the English regiments.

John Whitefoot had been out all day, and had just returned to his cousin's house, which was crowded with fugitives, as the tanner had friends and connections in all the villages, and had opened his doors to all who sought shelter, until every room was filled.

It was a pitiful sight to see women with their babies in their arms and their children gathered round them sitting forlornly, almost indifferent to the momentous consultation which was going on, and thinking only of their deserted homes and wondering what had befallen them. The men had for the most part been out in the streets gathering news. The tanner's wife, assisted by two or three of the women, was busy at the great fire on the hearth, over which hung some huge pots in which broth and porridge were being prepared. One by one the men dropped in. No news had yet been heard as to the decision of the council. It was dark when the tanner himself entered. His face was stern and pale.

"It is settled," he said shortly; "the council have broken up. I have just spoken to one of the members. They and the officers are unanimously in favour of accepting the terms of James."

Exclamations of anger broke from some of the men.

"I cannot say aught against it," the tanner said, "though my heart feels well nigh broken. Had we only men here I should say let us fight to the last, but look at all these women and children; think what thousands and thousands of them are in the town. Truly I cannot blame the council that they have decided not to bring this terrible suffering upon the city."

"The Lord will provide for his own," a minister who had come in with his flock, said. "Friend, I had looked for better things from you. I thought that you were steadfast in the cause of the Lord, and now that the time of trouble comes you fall away at once. Remember how Sennacherib and his host died before Jerusalem. Cannot the Lord protect Londonderry likewise?"

"The age of miracles is past," the tanner said. "Did

we not see in Germany how Magdeburg and other Protestant cities were destroyed with their inhabitants by the Papists? No, Brother Williams, the wicked are suffered to work their will here when they are stronger than the godly, and we must look for no miracles. I am ready to fight, and, had the council decided otherwise, would have done my share to the last, but my heart sickens as I look round on the women, the weak, and ailing. Did James demand that we should renounce our religion, I would say let us all die by sword or famine rather than consent; but he has offered toleration to all, that none shall suffer for what has been done, and that the property as well as the lives of all shall be respected. Truly it seems to me that resistance would be not bravery but a sort of madness. There are promises of aid from England; but how long may we have to wait for them, and there are but ten days' provisions in the town. If these English officers of King William think that resistance is hopeless, why should I, who know nought of war, set myself against them?"

"Because they have not faith," the minister said, "and you should have faith; because they think only of carnal weapons, and you should trust to the Lord. Remember Leyden, how help came when all seemed lost."

"I do," the tanner replied, "and I remember how the women and children suffered and died, how they dropped in the streets and perished with famine in their houses; I remember this, and I shrink from saying let us resist to the end. I should rejoice if they had decided that Derry should be deserted, that the women and children should be sent away to shelter in the mountains of Donegal, and that every man should march out and do combat with the army of James. We are numerous and far better armed than the Papists, and victory might be ours; but were it otherwise, were every man fated to fall on the field, I would still say let us march forward. It is not death that I fear, but seeing these weak and helpless ones suffer. I should not envy the feelings of the men who decided on resistance, when the time came that the women and children were dying of hunger around them. There is a time to fight, and a time to sheath the sword and to wait until a chance of drawing it successfully again arrives, and methinks that, having such good terms offered, the present is the time for waiting."

The preacher waved his hand impatiently, and, wrapping himself in his cloak, left the house without another word. The next day the capitulation was signed, and the following day the army of James was seen approaching, and presently halted on a hill within cannon-shot of the town.

Londonderry stands in a bend of the river Foyle, and the position which the army took up at once isolated it from the surrounding country. The offer of capitulation had already been sent out to General Hamilton by Captain White, the bearer receiving instructions to stipulate that the army should not advance within four miles of the town until all was ready to hand over the city. In the meantime General Rosen, who was in chief command of the army, stationed it so as to extend from one corner of the bend of the river to the other, and so to cut off all communication between the city and the surrounding country; but in the course of the day a country gentleman named Murray made his way through their lines with a body of cavalry and rode up to the gate of the town.

The governor refused to open it, but in spite of his orders some of the townspeople opened the gate, and Murray rode into the town, and, going from point to point, exhorted the people not to surrender but to resist to the last, accusing the governor and council of foul treachery in thus handing over the city.

The confusion and excitement in the streets was now great, and while this was going on the governor sent a trumpeter to the king requiring one hour's time before the city should surrender.

Rosen took no notice of this, and, believing that all was arranged, rode forward with the king and a portion of the army. But Murray's exhortations and passionate harangues had their effect; a number of the townspeople ran to the walls, and, loading the cannon, opened, with these and their muskets, a heavy fire on the approaching troops. Several of the soldiers were killed, and among them was Captain Troy, who was riding close to the king.

Astonished at this unexpected resistance the troops drew back, as they were entirely without means of making an assault upon the city. The governor and council at once sent Archdeacon Hamilton to the royal camp to excuse themselves for what had happened, and to explain that the firing was the action of a turbulent body of men whom they were unable to restrain, and whom they represented as drunken rebels. The better class of citizens, they said, were all resolved to surrender dutifully, and were doing all they could to persuade the common people to do the same.

As the royal artillery had not yet arrived James drew off his troops to St. Johnston. Murray with a body of horse went out and skirmished with them, but returned into the town on hearing that the council still intended to surrender, and again harangued the people. Eight thousand men assembled on the parade, and after listening to a passionate harangue, declared that they would resist to the last. They at once chose a preacher named Walker and a Mr. Baker as joint governors, appointed Murray as general in the field, divided themselves into eight regiments, and took the entire control of the city into their hands. Archdeacon Hamilton, Lundy, and several of the principal citizens at once left the town in disguise, and were allowed to pass through the besieging army.

John Whitefoot had been present at all the events which had taken place that day, and although he had quite agreed with his cousin that resistance would do no good to the cause, and would entail fearful sufferings on the besieged, he was carried away by the general enthusiasm, and shouted as loudly as any in reply to the exhortations of Murray. The tanner was also present. John was by his side, and saw that he was deeply moved by the speech, but he did not join in the acclamations. When all was over he laid his hand on John's shoulder:

"The die is cast, my boy; I am glad that no act or voice of mine has had aught to do with bringing it about, and that the weight of what is to come will not rest upon my conscience; but now that it is decided I

shall not be one to draw back, but will do my share
with what strength the Lord has given me."

"May I join one of the regiments too?" John asked;
"I am young, but I am as strong as many men."

"It were better not at present, John; before the end
comes every arm that can bear weapon may be needed,
but at present there is no reason why you should do so;
doubtless plenty of work will be found for younger
hands besides absolute fighting, but I think not that
there will be much fighting save against famine.
Our walls are strong, and we have well-nigh forty
pieces of cannon, while they say that James has but
six pieces, and most of these are small. Methinks, then,
that they will not even attempt to take the city by
storm. Why should they waste men in doing so when
they can starve us out? It is famine we have to fight
in this sort of war. I do not think that James has
in all Ireland cannon sufficient to batter down our
walls; but ten days will bring our provisions to an end.
It will be with us as with Leyden; we have only to
suffer and wait. If it be God's will succour will come
in time, if not we must even perish."

With his spirits somewhat damped by his cousin's
view of the case, John returned with him to the house.
He would willingly enough have gone out to fight
against the besiegers, but the thought of the long
slow agony of starvation was naturally terrible to a
lad of good health and appetite.

The mob of Derry had shown good sense in the
choice which they made of their governors. Baker,
indeed, who was a military man, was a mere cipher in
the matter. Walker was in reality the sole governor.

He was a man of energy and judgment as well as enthusiastic and fanatical, and he at once gave evidence of his fitness for the post, and set himself diligently to work to establish order in the town.

He issued orders that all unable to bear arms who wished to leave the town could do so, while the able-bodied men, now formed into regiments, were assigned every man his place and every regiment its quarter on the walls. No less than thirty thousand fugitives, exclusive of the garrison, were shut up in the walls of Derry, and the army which was besieging the town numbered twenty thousand. The guns of the besiegers soon opened fire, and those on the walls replied briskly. The besiegers threw up works, but carried on the siege but languidly, feeling sure that famine must ere long force the town to surrender, and fearing, perhaps, to engage the fresh and ill-trained levies against a multitude animated by the desperate resolution and religious fanaticism of the defenders of the town.

Now that the die was once cast there was no longer any difference of opinion among the inhabitants, and all classes joined enthusiastically in the measures for defence. All provisions in the town were given into one common store to be doled out in regular rations, and so made to last as long as possible; and as these rations were from the first extremely small, the sufferings of the besieged really began from the first day. John Whitefoot found that there was but little for him to do, and spent much of his time on the walls watching the throwing up of works by the besiegers.

A regular cannonade was now kept up on both sides; but though the shot occasionally fell inside the town, the danger to the inhabitants from this source was but slight, for of the six guns possessed by the besiegers five were very small, and one only was large enough to carry shell. All day the various chapels were open, and here the preachers by their fiery discourses kept up the spirits and courage of the people who thronged these buildings. The women spent most of their time there, and the men when off duty from the walls, however fatigued they might be with their labour, flocked at once to the chapels to pray for strength to resist and for early succour. Never were the whole population of the town more deeply animated by religious excitement, never a whole population more thoroughly and unanimously determined to die rather than surrender.

When not upon the walls or in chapel John spent much of his time in amusing the children, of whom there were many in the tanner's house. The change from their country quarters, the crowded town, the privation of milk, and the scantiness and unfitness of their rations, soon began to tell upon the little ones, and John felt thankful indeed that his mind had been stored with stories from his varied reading of the last two or three years. With these he was able to interest and quiet the children who sat round him with wrapt attention, while the booming of the guns and the occasional rattling of musketry outside passed unheeded.

Scarce a day passed without active fighting, the initiative being always taken by the besieged, for in the royal army the policy of blockade rather than assault was steadily adhered to. The besieged, however, continually sallied out and attacked the parties engaged in throwing up works. There was no settled plan of operations; but the commander on each portion of the walls led out his men against the enemy whenever he thought he saw a favourable opportunity. The fights which ensued were stoutly contested, and many were killed, but no advantage was gained on either side. If it was the intention of the besieged to incite the Royalists to make an attack upon the city they failed altogether, and indeed would have served their purpose better had they remained quietly within the walls, for the energy and desperation with which they fought were well calculated to deter even the most energetic commander from attacking a town defended by eight or nine thousand men animated by such fiery energy.

So confident, indeed, were the besieged that the gates were often left open, and taunting invitations to come · on and take Derry were shouted to the besiegers. The supply of provisions found to be stored away was vastly greater than had been expected, for many of the fugitives had brought in large stores, and a great number of the inhabitants had been for weeks making preparation for the siege by buying up quantities of grain and storing it in their cellars. Thus, up to the end of the first month, although the allowance of food was short, no real suffering was undergone by the inhabitants; but as time went on the supplies doled out became smaller and smaller, and dysentery and fever broke out in the crowded town.

Fierce disputes arose between those belonging to the Established Church and the Nonconformists, and it was

with the greatest difficulty that Governor Walker prevented the two parties from engaging in open strife.
Day and night the besiegers' fire continued, and many
were killed by the shells which fell in the city. The
fighting men on the walls were far better off than those
who had nothing to do but to wait and suffer, and it
was among the women and children chiefly that disease
at first made its victims.

For a time the children of the families who had
taken refuge with the tanner remained healthy. The
visitors were lodged for the most part in the cellars, so
as to be in shelter from the fire of the enemy's mortar;
but John Whitefoot suggested to his cousin that the
children would soon pine and sicken unless they had
air. The tanner gave his consent to John's establish-
ing a shelter in the yard. A corner was chosen, and a
number of casks were placed along by either wall; on
these beams were laid, for it happened that the tanner
had intended shortly before the siege to build a large
shed, and had got the timber together for the purpose.

On the timber bark from the now disused pits was
heaped to a depth of some feet, which would effectually
break the fall of any shell which might light upon it,
and along the front of this low triangular building two
lines of sacks filled with tan were placed. These would
suffice to prevent any fragment of a shell which might
fall and burst in the courtyard from entering the
shelter, save by the opening about a foot deep between
the top of the sacks and the beams. When the whole
was completed John gathered the children there and
made it their headquarters, and established himself
as captain of the castle as he called it.

The elders entered warmly into his plans. It was a great relief to them to have the house cleared of the eighteen or twenty children. Their mothers had no longer any anxiety for their safety, and the children themselves looked upon it as great fun. There was plenty of air here, and in a short time John persuaded the parents to allow the children to sleep as well as to pass the day in the shelter. Here he told them stories, constructed toys for them, and kept them amused and quiet, appointing as his lieutenants three or four of the oldest of the girls, who had the little ones under their special charge.

John was rewarded for his pains by seeing that the children kept their health far better than did those of their neighbours, and up to the end of May not one of them had succumbed, although several of the parents had already fallen victims to dysentery and fever. Thus the month of May passed. With June the hardships rapidly increased; but on the 13th shouts of joy were heard in the streets. John ran out to ascertain the cause, and learned that a fleet of thirty ships had appeared in Lough Foyle, and was approaching the city.

The inhabitants, frantic with joy, ran to the walls, and both sides suspended their fire to watch the approaching fleet. Suddenly the ships were seen to turn and sail away. The people could not believe that they were deserted; but when they saw that the fleet was really making off, curses and cries of lamentation and grief rose from the crowd.

Why Major-general Kirk, who commanded the force on board the ships, which were laden with provisions, did not attempt to sail up to Londonderry, which, as was afterwards proved, they could have done without difficulty, was never satisfactorily explained. The besiegers had erected two or three small forts on the banks of the river, but these were quite incapable of arresting the passage of the fleet had it been commanded by a man of any resolution. Kirk anchored in Lough Swilly, and contented himself with sending messages to the town to hold out to the last.

A fresh search was now made for provisions, and parties of men entered houses which had been abandoned, or whose inmates had died, and dug up the floors of the cellars. Several considerable deposits of grain were discovered, and many inhabitants, moved by the intensity of the general suffering, voluntarily brought out hoards which they had hitherto kept secret. Early in the siege the water in the wells had become turbid and muddy, partly owing, it was thought, to the concussion of the ground by the constant firing, partly by the extra supplies which were drawn from them. As the time went on many of them dried altogether, and the water in the others became so muddy that it had to be filtered through cloth or sacking before it could be drunk.

During fishing expeditions previous to the commencement of the siege John had more than once had a drink of water from the well of a peasant living in a little hut near the river bank. This hut lay between the outposts of the two parties, and had at the commencement of the siege been deserted by its owner. After the water became bad John set out every evening with a bucket, leaving the town just before the

gates were shut, and making straight down to the
river. When it became dark he crawled along under
the shelter of the banks unperceived by the outposts of
either party until close to the hut. Then he filled his
bucket at the well and returned as he had come, lying
down to sleep on the bank well in the rear of the Protestant outposts until morning, when, as soon as the
gates were opened, he carried home the precious supply.

It was this as much as the light and air which
kept the children in comparative health; but on the
further diminution of rations, which took place after
Kirk's fleet retired, they began to fade rapidly. The
horses had now been killed for food. The sufferings of
the besieged inhabitants became greater daily, and
numbers died from sheer starvation. The little inhabitants of John Whitefoot's castle were mere skeletons. Most of their parents were dead, and a mourn-
ful silence pervaded the town, save when the bells
of the chapels called to prayer, or the yells of the mob
announced that the lower orders were breaking into
houses in search of food.

John could stand the sight of the faces of the suffering children no longer. He was himself faint and ill
from hunger, for he had each day given a portion of his
own scanty rations to the weakest of the children, and
he determined to try and get them some food or to die
in the attempt. He set out at his usual hour in the
evening. The tide was high, but just running out, and
entering the river he floated down with the stream.
Keeping close under the bank, he passed the batteries
which the besiegers had erected there without notice,
dived under the great boom which they had constructed

across the river directly Kirk's expedition had retired, and continued to float down to the mouth of the river, where he landed and boldly struck across the country, for he was now beyond the lines of the besiegers.

He knew that his friend Walter was in the Royalist army, for one of the last mails which entered the city had told him that he was to accompany his father, and that Captain Davenant's troop would most likely form part of any army that might march for the north. By the morning his clothes had dried upon him, and he then boldly entered the Royalist camp, mingling with the peasants who were bringing in provisions for sale. He soon learned where Captain Davenant's troop was stationed and made his way thither. He stood watching for some time until he saw Walter come out of a tent, and he then approached him. Walter looked up, but did not recognize in the thin and pallid lad before him his former companion.

"Do you want anything?" he asked.

"Don't you know me, Walter?" John said.

Walter started and gazed at him earnestly.

"Good heavens!" he exclaimed at last; "why, it can't be John!"

"It is what remains of me," John replied with a faint smile.

"Why, what on earth have you been doing to yourself, John?"

"I have been starving in there," John said, pointing to the city.

"Come into the tent, John," Walter said, grasping his friend's arm and then letting it fall again with an exclamation of horror at its thinness; "you needn't be afraid. My father is out—not that that would make any difference."

John entered the tent, and sat exhausted upon a box. Walter hastened to get some food, which he set before him, and poured out a large cup of wine and water, and then stood looking on in awed silence while John devoured his meal.

"I have wondered a thousand times," he said at last when John had finished, "what you were doing in there, or whether you left before the siege began. How did you get out?"

"I floated down the river to the mouth beyond your lines last night and then worked round here. I thought I might find you."

"Well, I am glad indeed that you are out," Walter said. "Every time the mortar sent a shell into the town I was thinking of you, and wishing that I could share meals with you, for of course we know that you are suffering horribly in the town."

"Horribly!" John repeated. "You can have no idea what it is, Walter, to see children suffer. As for men, if it is the will of God, they must bear it, but it is awful for children. I have had eighteen of them under my charge through the siege, and to see them getting thinner and weaker every day till the bones look as if they would come through the skin, and their eyes get bigger and bigger, and their voices weaker, is awful. At last I could stand it no longer, and I have come out to fetch some food for them."

"To fetch food!" Walter repeated. "Do you mean to say you are thinking of going back again?"

"That I am," John said. "I am going to take some

JOHN RELIEVED BY WALTER IN THE ROYALIST CAMP.

food in to them. You will help me, won't you, Walter? It isn't for the men that fight, but for little children, who know nothing about King James, or King William, or the Protestants, or the Catholics, but who are just God's creatures, and are dying of hunger. No one could grudge food to infants like these."

"I will help you, of course, John," Walter said, "if I can; but now tell me all about it."

John then gave an account of all he had been doing throughout the siege.

"And now what have you been doing, Walter? Fighting?"

"No. I have not been doing any fighting, except that once or twice I was out with the troop, when they had a skirmish with your horsemen, but I kept in the rear. I hope, ere long, my father will let me enter, but he is waiting to see what comes of it. No. I have been idle enough. Well, of course, I know all the officers in the cavalry now, and pretty nearly all the officers in the camp, and then with these constant skirmishes and attacks by your people and ours there is always plenty to interest one. General Hamilton has been conducting the siege lately, but General Rosen returned yesterday and took the command; but there's really not much to do. We know you cannot hold out much longer."

"I don't know," John said quietly. "I think that as long as a man has strength enough to hold his arms Derry will not surrender. When you march in it will be to a city of dead people. We had such hopes when the fleet came. If the people could have caught Kirk they would have torn him in pieces. He had five thousand soldiers on board, and if he had landed them we could have sallied out and fought instead of dying of hunger."

"Yes," Walter agreed, "we should have retired at once. We have only seven or eight thousand men here now, and if five thousand English soldiers had landed we must have raised the siege at once. I can tell you, that though he is on the other side, I was almost as angry at Kirk's cowardice as you must have been. I shall be glad when this awful business is over. I knew it was bad enough before, but after what you have told me about the women and children I shall never think of anything else, and I will gladly help you in any way I can. There can't be any treason in trying to prevent children from starving to death. What do you want me to do?"

"What would do the children more good than anything, the women say, would be milk. If I could get a keg that would hold two or three gallons, and a watertight box with about twenty pounds of bread, I could swim back with them just as I came. I would show you the exact spot where I landed, and would come out again in four days. If you could put a supply ready for me every fourth night among the bushes, at the mouth of the river, with a little lantern to show me the exact spot, I could come down with the tide, get the things, and float back again when the tide turns."

"I could do that easily enough," Walter said. "The mouth of the river is quite beyond our lines. But it is very risky for you, John. You might get shot if a sentry were to see you."

"I do not think that there is much fear of that,"

John said. "Just floating along as I do, without swimming at all, there is only just my face above water, and it would be hardly possible for a sentry to see me; but if I were shot I could not die in a better cause."

"I think, John, if you don't mind, I should like to tell my father. I am quite sure he would not object, and in case you should happen to get caught you could refer at once to him to prove that you were not a spy. They make very short work of spies. But if you were to demand to be brought to Captain Davenant, and say you were acting in accordance with his knowledge, no doubt they would bring you."

"Do as you think best, Walter, but don't tell him unless you feel almost sure that he will not object."

"There is no fear of that," Walter said. "He is constantly lamenting over the sufferings of the people of Derry, and has all along been in favour of attempting to storm the place by force, so as to put a stop to all this useless suffering. Now, John, you had better lie down on that straw bed of mine and get a sleep. After that you will be ready for another meal. I will tell Larry to go out among the market people and buy three gallons of milk and twenty pounds of bread. There are plenty of small spirit kegs about which will do capitally for the milk, and I don't think that we can have anything better than one of them for the bread. We can head it up and make it water-tight. How do you mean to get into the town? I should have thought that they were likely to be seized."

"So they would be," John said. "I shall hide them in some bushes at the foot of the walls, at the side of

the town facing the river. There are only a few sentries there. Then when it is light I shall go in and
tell my cousin and get him after dark to lower a rope
from the wall. I shall of course be below to tie on
the kegs. He can then walk with them boldly through
the street to our house, which is only a short distance
from that part of the walls. If anyone saw him they
would only suppose he was taking home water from
one of the wells."

John was soon fast asleep. Walter sat watching
him until, two hours later, his father returned with his
troop. John still slept on, while Walter told his father
the errand on which he had come.

"He is a brave lad," Captain Davenant said, "and I
honour him for his conduct. It is not many men who
at a time like this would risk their lives for a number
of children who are not any relation to them. Certainly I will gladly assist him. I am sick at heart at
all this. My only consolation is that it is brought on
solely by the acts of these men, who, though comparatively a handful, set themselves up against the voice of
all Ireland. If they had risen when an English army
arrived to their assistance I should say nothing against
it. As it is, without doing any good to their cause,
they are entailing this horrible suffering upon thousands
of women and children.

"By all means help the poor lad, and if he should
fall into the hands of our people let him mention my
name. Rosen would no doubt disapprove of it, but I
cannot help that. All the Irish gentlemen in the army
would agree that I had done rightly, and even if they
didn't, my own conscience would be quite sufficient for

me to act upon. I am fighting against the king's ene-mies, not warring against women and children. How soundly the poor lad sleeps, and how changed he is! He is a mere skeleton. I should not have known him in the least. If this is the condition into which a strong healthy lad has fallen, what must the women and children have suffered! I wish Kirk had not turned coward, but had landed his troops. We could then have brought up our scattered forces, and could have fought them in a fair field with something like equal forces. That would have been vastly more to my taste than starving them like rats in a hole."

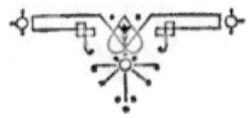

CHAPTER V.

THE RELIEF OF DERRY.

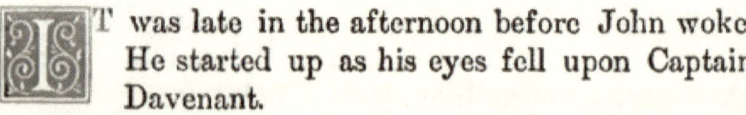

T was late in the afternoon before John woke. He started up as his eyes fell upon Captain Davenant.

"You have had a good sleep, and I hope you are all the better for it," Captain Davenant said kindly. "My son has been telling me all about your expedition, and I honour you very much for the courage you have shown in thus risking your life to get food for those starving children. I quite approve of the promise Walter has given to assist you, and if you should by any chance be taken prisoner I will stand your friend."

John expressed his gratitude warmly.

"It is a sad thing in these civil wars, when friends are arrayed against friends," Captain Davenant said. "Who would have thought three months ago that you and Walter would be arrayed on opposite sides? It is true you are neither of you combatants, but I have no doubt you would gladly have joined in some of the sallies, just as Walter is eager to be riding in my troop. If we must fight, I wish at anyrate that it could be so managed that all the suffering should fall upon the men who are willing to take up the sword, and not upon the women and children. My heart bleeds as I

ride across the country. At one time one comes upon
a ruined village burned by the midnight ruffians who
call themselves rapparees, and who are a disgrace to
our cause; at another upon a place sacked and ruined
by one of the bands of horsemen from Enniskillen,
who are as cruel and merciless as the rapparees. Let
the armies fight out their quarrels, I say, but let peaceful
people dwell in quiet and safety. But wholesale atrocities have ever been the rule on both sides in warfare
in Ireland, and will, I suppose, remain so to the end.
And now we are just going to have dinner, and another
hearty meal will do you good. Each night when my
son brings down the supplies for you he will bring a
substantial meal of cold meat and bread, and you must
give me your promise now that you will eat this at
once. You will need it after being so long in the
water, and having another swim before you besides.
Although I approve of sending in milk for the children,
I can be no party to the supply of food for the garrison.
Do you promise?"

"Yes, sir, I promise," John said, "though I would
rather save all but a mouthful or two for the people
who are starving at home. Still, of course, if you insist upon it, I will promise."

"I do insist upon it, John. The lives of these children
of yours depend on your life, and even one good meal
every four days will help you to keep enough strength together to carry out the kind work you have undertaken."

Larry now brought in the dinner. He had been
told by Walter of John's arrival, but he otherwise would
have failed to recognize in him the boy who had sometimes come down to the village with Walter.

"Are you quite well, Larry?" John asked him.

"I am," Larry replied; "but I need not ask the same question of yourself, for you are nothing but skin and bone entirely. Dear, dear, I wouldn't have known you at all, at all, and such a foine colour as ye used to have."

"I don't think starving would suit you, Larry," Captain Davenant said with a smile.

"Sure an' it wouldn't, yer honour. It's always ready to eat I am, though, as mother says, the victuals don't seem to do me much good anyway."

"You won't be able to come out and go back again the same night next week, John," Captain Davenant said presently; "the tide won't suit, so you must come up here as you have done to-day. You will always find a hearty welcome, and Walter shall go down and meet you early in the morning near the mouth of the river, so you can come up with him; and then, if you fall in with any of the other parties, no questions will be asked. I think everyone in camp knows him now. I wonder what your grandfather would say if he saw you sitting here at dinner with Walter and me?"

John laughed.

"I am afraid he would disown me then and there without listening to explanations."

"I have no doubt it's a sore grievance to him that he is not in Derry at present," Captain Davenant said.

"I am sure it is," John replied; "but the fasting would be a great trial to him. My grandfather is a capital trencherman; still, I am sure he would have borne his part."

"That he would," Captain Davenant agreed; "he

and the men of his class are thorough, fanatics as I consider them. Hard and pitiless as they proved themselves to those against whom they fought, one cannot but admire them, for they were heart and soul in their cause. There was no flinching, no half measures, no concessions for the sake of expediency. On the ground on which they took their stand they conquered or died. Would that a like spirit animated all my countrymen!"

After nightfall Larry brought round Walter's horse saddled and his own rough pony. Walter mounted the former, and John the latter. The two kegs were slung across Walter's horse.

" Will you meet me at the clump of trees half a mile out of camp, Larry?" Walter said; "in the dark no one will notice the difference between you and John."

Captain Davenant had furnished Walter with a pass-word, and now walked beside the two boys till they were well beyond the camp, and then returned to his tent. The lads made their way without meeting with anyone down to the mouth of the river; the kegs were then taken off the horse and placed in the water —they floated just above the surface.

"That is exactly right," John said; "they will not show any more than will my face. When I come down next time I shall fill them with water so as to keep them just at this level."

"I am afraid the moon will be up next time, John."

" Yes, it will. I shall lay some boughs of bush across my face and the kegs, so that there will be no fear of my face showing; and if a sentry should happen to catch sight of it he will suppose that it is merely a bush drifting in the stream."

"Well, good-bye, John, and may you get through without trouble."

"I have no fear, Walter. I am in God's hands, and He will take me safely through if He thinks fit."

The journey was achieved without detection, the only difficulty being the sinking of the kegs under the boom; this, however, was successfully accomplished, and by midnight the kegs were safely hidden in some bushes at the foot of the wall, and there John lay down and waited for morning.

As he entered the yard the children ran out to meet him. There were no loud rejoicings; they had no longer strength or spirit to shout and laugh; but the joy in the thin worn faces was more eloquent than any words could have been.

"We have missed you so, John. We have wanted you so much. Lucy and Kate, and Deby were so bad yesterday, and they did cry so for you. We were all so hungry. We don't mind so much when you are here to talk to us and tell us stories. Why did you stop away, John, when we wanted you so?"

"I went away to see if I could manage to get you something to eat."

"And did you?" was the anxious cry.

"I have got a little; but you must wait till evening, and then you will each have—" and he stopped.

"What, John? Oh, do tell us!"

"You will each have some milk and bread. Not much, dears," he went on, as there was a cry of gladness, which was pitiful from the intensity of joy it expressed,

" but there will be some for to-night, and a little curds
and whey and bread for you to-morrow and next day,
and I hope always as long as this lasts. Now, go,
dears, into your castle. I will come to you presently.
I have brought you some water as usual."

" I am heartily glad to see you back, John," his
cousin said as he entered the house. " The children
were in a sad state without you yesterday. I suppose you can tell me now what you have been doing.
You told me you would be away two nights, and
begged me not to ask any questions; but although I
know you to be discreet and prudent, I have been
worrying."

" I will tell you now," John said, and he recounted
the details of the expedition which he had accomplished.

" And you have swum the river twice, and been in
the camp of the Papists. Truly it is surprising, John,
and I know not what to do. Should your visit there be
discovered you will assuredly be accused of treachery."

" They may accuse me of what they like," John said
quietly. " I have done it, and I am going to do it
again every fourth night, and there is the milk and
bread at the foot of the wall ready for you to haul up
as soon as it gets dark."

" It ought to be fairly divided," the tanner said.

" It will be fairly divided between our children,"
John said; " but nobody else will get a drop or a crumb.
I have risked my life to get it for them. If other
people want to get it let them do the same. Besides, as
I told you, Captain Davenant and his son both pro-
cured it for me for the sake of the children, and them

only, and I should be breaking faith with them if any others touched it save those for whom it was given me. It is little enough among eighteen children for four days—a pound of bread and a little over a pint of milk each. They must each have a quarter of a pint when you bring it in to-night, and the rest had better be curdled. That way it will keep, and they can have a portion each day of curds and whey, and a fourth share of their bread. It is little enough; but I trust that it may keep life in them."

"Well, John, I will do as you say," the tanner said after a pause. "It goes somewhat against my conscience; but, as you say, it will make but a meagre portion for each of them, and would be nothing were it fairly divided; besides, you have brought it with the risk of your life, and I know not that any save you have a right to a voice in its partition."

Before the gates were closed John went out, and presently had the satisfaction of hearing a small stone drop from the wall above him, followed presently by the end of a rope. He sent up the kegs, and then lay down among the bushes and enjoyed the satisfaction of thinking of the joy of the little ones when the milk and bread were served out to them. As soon as the gates were open in the morning he went in.

"Thank you, oh, so much, for the milk and bread last night. We heard how you had swum so far and gone into danger to get it for us, and we're going to have some more for breakfast."

"It was not much, dears," John said.

"Oh, no, it was not much; but it was so nice, and we did all sleep so well last night—even little Lucy didn't waken and cry once—and Ruth Hardy said we ought to call you the Raven; but we don't like that name for you."

"The Raven, Ruth!" John said mystified. "Why did you want to call me the Raven?"

"I wouldn't do it if you didn't like it, dear John; but you know that chapter that Master Williams read us the other day about the ravens that fed somebody in a cave, and we have been wishing the ravens would feed us; and so you see when you sent us the milk last night I thought you ought to be called the Raven. I did not mean any harm."

"No, my dear, of course not, and you can all call me the Raven if you like."

"No, no, John. You are John, and that's much better than the Raven. They brought the man food, but they didn't nurse him and tell him stories as you do."

"Now, run inside the castle," John said, "and I will go in and get your breakfasts."

John soon returned with a great bowl of curds and whey, a platter piled up with slices of bread and a score of little mugs, and the feast began. Scarce a word was said while the children were eating, their hunger was too keen and their enjoyment too intense to admit of speech. When each had finished their portion there was a general exclamation.

"Oh, John, you haven't had any. Why didn't you have some too?"

"Because there is only enough for you," he said. "If I were to have some, and Cousin Josiah, and all the others, there would be a very little share for you;

besides, when I went out the day before yesterday I had as much as I could eat."

"Oh, dear, that must have been nice," one of the boys said. "Only think having as much as one can eat. Oh, how much I could eat if I had it!"

"And yet I daresay, Tom," John said, "that sometimes before you came here, when you had as much as you could eat, you used to grumble if it wasn't quite what you fancied."

"I shall never grumble again," the boy said positively. "I shall be quite, quite content with potatoes, if I can but get enough of them."

"The good times will come again," John said cheerily. "Now we will have a story. Which shall it be?"

As the children sat round him, John was delighted to see that even the two scanty meals they had had had done wonders for them. The listless hopeless look of the last few days had disappeared, and occasionally something like a hearty laugh broke out among them, and an hour later the tanner came to the entrance.

"Come to the walls with me, John."

"What is it?—what is the matter?" John said, as he saw the look of anger and indignation on the wasted features of his cousin.

"Come and see for yourself," the latter said.

When they reached the walls they found them crowded with the inhabitants. Outside were a multitude of women, children, and old men. These General Rosen, with a refinement of cruelty, had swept in from the country round and driven under the walls, where they were left to starve, unless the garrison would take them in and divide their scanty supply of food with them.

"It is monstrous," John cried, when he understood the meaning of the sight.

"What are we to do?"

"We can do nothing," the tanner replied; "the council have met, and have determined to keep the gates closed. We are dying for the cause; they must do so too; and they will not die in vain, for all Europe will cry out when they hear of this dastardly act of cruelty."

The people outside were animated by a spirit as stern as that of the besieged, and the women cried out to those on the walls to keep the gates shut and to resist to the last, and not to heed them.

The ministers went out through the gates and held services among the crowd, and the people on the walls joined in the hymns that were sung below. So for three days and nights the people within and without fasted and prayed. On the third day a messenger arrived from King James at Dublin ordering General Rosen at once to let the people depart.

The indignation among the Irish gentlemen in the camp at Rosen's brutal order had been unbounded, and messenger after messenger had been sent to Dublin, where the news excited a burst of indignation, and James at once countermanded the order of the general. The gates were opened now, and the people flocked out and exchanged greetings with their friends. A few able-bodied men in the crowd entered the town to share in its defence, while a considerable number of the women and children from within mingled with them and moved away through the lines of the besiegers.

John had the day before gone out when the gates
were opened for the preachers, and at night had again
safely made the passage to the mouth of the river and
back. He found the lantern burning among the bushes,
and two kegs placed beside it, with a bountiful meal
of bread and meat for himself.

So the days went on, each day lessening the number
of the inhabitants of the town. Fever and famine
were making terrible ravages, and the survivors
moved about the streets like living skeletons, so feeble
and weak now that they could scarce bear the weight
of their arms.

On the 30th of July three ships were seen approaching the mouth of the river. They were part of Kirk's
squadron, which had all this time been lying idle
almost within sight of the town. The news of his conduct had excited such anger and indignation in England, that at last, in obedience to peremptory orders
from London, he prepared to make the attempt;
although, by sending only two store-ships and one
frigate, it would almost seem as if he had determined
that it should be a failure. The besiegers as well as
the besieged saw the three ships advancing, and the
former moved down to the shore to repel the attempt;
the batteries on either side of the boom were manned,
and from them, and from the infantry gathered on
the banks, a heavy fire was opened as the ships
approached.

So innocuous was the fire of the artillery that it has
been supposed that Kirk had previously bribed the
officers commanding the forts. At anyrate the ships
suffered no material damage, and, returning the fire,

advanced against the boom. The leading store-ship dashed against it and broke it, but the ship swerved from her course with the shock and struck the ground. A shout of dismay burst from those on the walls, and one of exultation from the besiegers, who rushed down to board the vessel. Her captain, however, pointed all his guns forward, and discharged them all at the same moment, and the recoil shook the vessel from her hold on the ground, and she floated off, and pursued her way up the river followed by her consorts.

The delay of Kirk had cost the defenders of Londonderry more than half their number. The fighting men had, either by disease, famine, or in the field, lost some five thousand, while of the non-combatants seven thousand had died. The joy and exultation in the city as the two store-ships ranged up under its walls were unbounded. Provisions were speedily conveyed on shore, and abundance took the place of famine. Five days later General Rosen raised the siege and marched away with his army, which had in the various operations of the siege, and from the effect of disease, lost upwards of three thousand men.

"This has been a bad beginning, Walter," Captain Davenant said, as they rode away from the grounds on which they had been so long encamped. "If the whole force of Ireland does not suffice to take a single town, the prospect of our waging war successfully against England is not hopeful."

"It seems to me that it would have been much better to have left Derry alone, father," Walter said.

"It would have been better as it has turned out, Walter; but had the king taken the place, as he expected,

without difficulty, he would have crossed with a portion of the army to Scotland, where a considerable
part of the population would at once have joined him.
The defence of Derry has entirely thwarted that plan,
and I fear now that it will never be carried out.
However, it has had the advantage of making soldiers
out of an army of peasants. When we came here
officers and men were alike ignorant of everything
relating to war, now we have, at any rate, learned a
certain amount of drill and discipline, and I think we
shall give a much better account of ourselves in the
open field than we have done in front of a strong
town which we had no means whatever of storming.
Still it has been a frightful waste of life on both
sides, and with no result beyond horribly embittering
the feeling of hatred which unfortunately prevailed
before between the Catholic and Protestant popula-
tions."

The mortification and disgust caused by the failure
of Londonderry was increased by a severe defeat of a
force under General Justin M'Carthy, Lord Mount-
cashel, at Newtown-Butler, on the very day that
Derry was relieved. General M'Carthy had been
detached with a corps of six thousand men against the
Enniskilleners. He came up with them near Newtown-
Butler. Although but two thousand strong, the
Enniskilleners, who were commanded by Colonel
Wolseley, an English officer, at once attacked the
Irish, only a portion of whom had come upon the
ground.

M'Carthy, who was a brave and experienced officer,
sent orders to the cavalry to face to the right and

march to the support of the wing that was attacked. The officer gave the order "right-about face," and the cavalry turned and trotted towards the rear. The infantry, believing that they were deserted by the horse, at once lost heart and fell into confusion. M'Carthy, while endeavouring to remedy the disorder, was wounded and taken prisoner, and the flight became general. The Enniskilleners pursued with savage fury, and during the evening, the whole of the night, and the greater part of the next day, hunted the fugitives down in the bogs and woods, and slew them in cold blood. Five hundred of the Irish threw themselves into Lough Erne, rather than face death at the hands of their savage enemies, and only one of the number saved himself by swimming.

After leaving Derry the army returned to Dublin, where the parliament which James had summoned was then sitting. Most of the soldiers were quartered on the citizens; but, as the pressure was very great, Captain Davenant easily obtained leave for his troop to go out to Bray, where they were within a very short distance of his own house. The day after his return home Walter went over to give Jabez Whitefoot and his wife news of John, from whom they had heard nothing since a fortnight before the siege had begun.

"Your son is alive and well," were his first words. "He has been all through the siege of Derry, and has behaved like a hero."

"The Lord be praised!" Jabez said, while his wife burst into tears of relief, for she had gone through terrible anxiety during the long weeks that Derry had been suffering from starvation.

"But how do you know, Master Walter?" Jabez asked. "Seeing that you were on the side of the besiegers, how could you tell what was passing on the inside of the walls? How do you know John is alive?"

"Because I saw him first a month before the end of the siege, and because he came regularly afterwards to fetch away some provisions which I had placed for him." And Walter then gave a full account of John's visit to the camp in search of food for the children who were sheltered in the tanner's house.

"That is just like John," his mother said; "he was ever thoughtful for others. I am more pleased a hundred times that he should have so risked his life to obtain food for the little ones, than if he had taken part in the fighting and proved himself a very champion of Derry."

Parliament had met on the 7th of May. The session had been opened by a speech from the throne, in which the king commended the loyalty of his Irish subjects, declared his intention to make no difference between Catholics and Protestants, and that loyalty and good conduct should be the only passport to his favour. He stated his earnest wish that good and wholesome laws should be enacted for the encouragement of trade and of the manufactures of the country, and for the relief of such as had suffered injustice by the Act of Settlement; that is, the act by which the lands of the Catholics had been handed over wholesale to Cromwell's soldiers and other Protestants.

Bills were speedily passed abolishing the jurisdiction of English courts of law and of the English parliament in Ireland, and other bills were passed for the regulation of commerce and the promotion of ship-building. The bill for the repeal of the Act of Set-tlement was brought up on the 22d of May; it was opposed only by the Protestant bishops and peers, and became law on the 11th of June. Acts of attainder were speedily passed against some two thousand Pro-testant landed proprietors, all of whom had obtained their lands by the settlement of Cromwell.

A land-tax was voted to the king of twenty thou-sand pounds a month, and he proceeded to raise other levies by his private authority. The result was that the resources of Ireland were speedily exhausted, money almost disappeared, and James, being at his wits' end for funds, issued copper money stamped with the value of gold and silver; and a law was passed making this base money legal tender, promising that at the end of the war it should be exchanged for sterling money.

This was a measure which inflicted enormous loss and damage. At first the people raised the prices of goods in proportion to the decrease in the value of the money, but James stopped this by issuing a pro-clamation fixing the prices at which all articles were to be sold; and having done this, proceeded to buy up great quantities of hides, butter, corn, wood, and other goods, paying for them all with a few pounds of cop-per and tin, and then shipping them to France, where they were sold on his own account. It need hardly be said that conduct of this kind speedily excited great dissatisfaction, even among those who were most loyal in his cause.

Captain Davenant was shocked at the state of things he found prevailing in Dublin. "I regret bit-

terly," he said when alone with his wife and mother,
"that I have taken up the sword.   Success appears to
me to be hopeless.   The folly of the Stuarts is incredible; they would ruin the best cause in the world.
With a spark of wisdom and firmness James might
have united all Ireland in his cause, instead of which
he has absolutely forced the Protestants into hostility.
His folly is only equalled by his rapacity, and both are
stupendous."

This was said one evening when he had just returned from a visit to Dublin, depressed and disheartened by all he heard there.

"I am astonished, Fergus," his mother said sharply,
"to hear you speak in that way.   Who would have
thought that it was a Davenant who was speaking!
Doubtless there have been mistakes, as was only natural, but everything will come right in time.   I have
been longing for you to come home, looking forward
with such joy to welcome you as the possessor of the
broad lands of the Davenants.   Thank God I have
lived to see the restoration of my dear husband's lands,
and the discomfiture of those Cromwellian knaves
who have so long possessed them.   It was a grand day
when the act was passed repealing all Cromwell's
grants handing over the best part of Ireland to his
soldiers; and I saw in the *Gazette*, among the two
thousand grants specially mentioned as cancelled was
that of the Davenant estate to Zephaniah Whitefoot.
I am told that the old man and his son have taken no
notice of the act, but go about their work as if they
were still the owners of the land; but of course, now
that you are back, there will soon be an end of this."

Captain Davenant was silent.

"I shall be in no hurry, mother," he said after a pause. "It is true that an act of the Irish parliament has cancelled the iniquitous work of Cromwell, and restored the land to its rightful possessors. I do not say that this is not just, but I am quite sure that it is not politic. These men have been planted on the soil for two generations; they have built houses and tilled the fields, and made homes for themselves. It was essentially a case for arrangement, and not for setting right the first act of confiscation by another as sweeping. It has rendered the Protestants desperate; it has enlisted the sympathy of the Protestants of England in their behalf, and has done much to popularize the war there. It would have been vastly wiser had a commission been ordered to examine into the circumstances of each case.

"In the great proportion of cases the estates which the Cromwellites took possession of were vastly larger than they were able to till themselves; and, as in the case of Zephaniah Whitefoot, they let out the greater portion to tenants. All these lands I would have restored to their former owners, leaving to the Cromwellites the land they till themselves and the houses they have built upon it.

"As to turning the Whitefoots out, I shall certainly take no step that way at present: it will be time enough to do so when King James is firmly established on the throne. As things go at present I have but very faint hopes that will ever be. He has utterly failed to conquer the Protestants of the north of Ireland, and we have all the strength of England to cope with yet. It will be well, mother, if at the end of this strife we can keep Davenant Castle over our heads, with the few acres that still remain to us."

Two days afterwards Captain Davenant mounted his horse and rode over to the Whitefoots. Zephaniah and Jabez came to the door.

"I suppose you have come over to turn us out, Fergus Davenant," the old man said; "but I warn you that it will not be for long. The triumph of the ungodly is short, and the Lord will care for his own people."

"You are mistaken," Captain Davenant said quietly. "I have come over for no such purpose. I am of course aware that parliament has passed a law reinstating me in my father's lands; but I came over to tell you that at present I do not propose to take advantage of that law. I shall do nothing until this war is at an end. If King William's cause triumphs, the act will remain a dead letter; if King James's wins, and the act is upheld, I wish to tell you that I shall never disturb you in the land which you yourselves occupy. Your tenants, on the other hand, will be my tenants; but in the house which you have built, and in the fields which you have tilled, you will remain masters.

"I have thought the matter over, and this appears to me to be a just settlement, and one which I give you my word that I will hold to should King James triumph in the end. I think that the law turning out the Protestant settlers from the land which they have held for forty years is well nigh as unjust as that which gave it to them."

"I will take no gifts at the hands of the wicked," Zephaniah began, but Jabez interrupted him.

"Hush, father!" he said, "it is not thus that kindness should be met." Then he stepped forward, leaving his father too surprised at this sudden assumption of command on the part of his son to interrupt him.

"Captain Davenant," he said, "I thank you most sincerely on the part of myself, my wife and son, and, I may say, of my father too, although at present he may not realize the kindness of your offer. I do not think it likely that if James Stuart prevails, and Ireland is rent from England, we shall avail ourselves of your offer, for we have more than sufficient of this world's goods to remove to England, and there settle ourselves and our son, for assuredly Ireland would be no place where a Protestant could dwell in peace and quietness. Nevertheless, I thank you heartily, and shall ever gratefully bear in mind the promise you have made, and the fact that, although you have the power to turn us from our home, you have stayed from doing so. There has been much wrong done on both sides; and, from a boy, when I have seen you ride into or from your home, I have felt that I and mine wronged you by being the possessors of your father's lands."

"They were the spoil of battle," Zephaniah broke in fiercely.

"Yes, they were the spoil of battle," his son repeated; "but there are limits even to the rights of conquerors. I have read history, and I know that nowhere but in Ireland did conquerors ever dispossess whole peoples and take possession of their lands."

" The Israelites took the land of Canaan," Zephaniah interrupted.

" I am speaking of modern wars, father.   For centuries no such act of wholesale spoliation was ever perpetrated; and considering, as I do, that the act was an iniquitous one, although we have benefited by it, I consider the offer which Captain Davenant has made to us to be a noble one.   I have to thank you, sir, also, for your kindness to my son—a kindness which doubtless saved his life as well as that of many others in Londonderry; and believe me that, whatever comes of this horrible war, I and mine will never forget the kindnesses we have received at your hands."

" The affair was my son's rather than mine," Captain Davenant said; " but I was glad to be able to assist him in aiding your brave boy.   He is a noble fellow, and you have every reason to be proud of him."

" I must add my thanks to those of my husband," Hannah said, coming out from the house, having listened to the conversation through an open window. " We had suffered so until your son brought us news of John two days since.   It is strange, indeed, that your son should have been the means of saving one of a household whom he cannot but have learnt to regard as the usurpers of his father's rights.   It was but last night I was reading of Jonathan and David, and it seemed to me that assuredly the same spirit that they felt for each other was in our sons.

" The boys are very fond of each other, Mrs. Whitefoot, and I am glad of it; they are both manly fellows, and there is no reason why the feuds of the fathers should descend to the children."

With a cordial good-bye Captain Davenant rode off.

"Jabez," Zephaniah said, as they turned into the house, "I had not thought to hear a son of mine rise in rebellion against his father."

"Father," Jabez said, "for forty-five years I have been a good son to you; but it is time that I took my stand. It seems to me that the principles upon which the soldiers of Cromwell fought were the principles which animated the Israelites of old. Exodus, Judges, and Kings were the groundwork of their religion, not the Gospels. It has gradually been borne upon me that such is not the religion of the New Testament, and while I seek in no way to dispute your right to think as you choose, I say the time has come when I and my wife will act upon our principles."

"It is written, Honour thy father and thy mother," Zephaniah said sternly.

"Ay, father, I have honoured you, and I shall honour you to the end; but a man has no right to give up his conscience to his father; for it is written also that a man shall leave father and mother, and wife and home to follow the Lord. I have heard you, father, and the elders of our church, quote abundant texts from Scripture, but never one that I can recall from the New Testament. Hitherto I have been as an Israelite of Joshua's time, henceforward I hope to be a Christian. I grieve to anger you, father, and for years I have held my peace rather than do so; but the time has come when the spirit within me will no longer permit me to hold my peace. In all worldly matters I am still your obedient son, ready to labour to my utmost to gather up wealth which I do not enjoy, to live a life as hard as that of the poorest tenant on our lands; but, as touching higher matters, I and my wife go our own way."

Without a word Zephaniah took his hat and strode away from the house, and, after much angry communing with himself, went to the minister and deacons of his chapel, and laid the facts of the rebellion before them and asked their advice.

They were in favour of peace, for two of them were his tenants, and they knew that the time could not be very far off when Jabez would take the old man's place, and it would be a serious matter indeed to the chapel were he to be driven from its fold.

" We cannot expect that all shall see with our eyes, Zephaniah," the minister said, " and, indeed, the offer which thou sayest the man Davenant made was a generous one. It would be well indeed for our brethren throughout Ireland did all the original owners of their lands so treat them. Thousands who but a few months since were prosperous men are now without a shelter wherein to lay their heads. The storm is sweeping over us, the elect are everywhere smitten, and should James Stuart conquer, not a Protestant in Ireland but must leave its shores. Therefore, although I would counsel no giving up of principle, no abandonment of faith, yet I would say that this is no time for the enforcement of our views upon weak vessels. I mourn that your son should for the time have fallen away from your high standard, but I say it were best to be patient with him."

At home there were few words spoken after Zephaniah had gone out. Hannah had thrown her arms round her husband's neck, and had said:

"I thank God for your words, Jabez. Now I am proud of you as I have never been proud before, that you have boldly spoken out for liberty of conscience. I feel like one who has for many years been a slave, but who is at last free."

Jabez kissed her, but was silent. To him it had been a great trial to rebel; he knew that he was right, and would have done it again if necessary; but it was a terrible thing to him to have openly withstood the father to whom he had from childhood rendered almost implicit obedience. On his return Zephaniah did not renew the subject; but from that time there was a great change in the moral atmosphere of the house. Zephaniah was still master in all matters of daily work; but in other respects Jabez had completely emancipated himself.

CHAPTER VI.

DUNDALK.

AFTER the failure before Derry the utmost confusion prevailed in the military councils, arising chiefly from the jealousies and conflicting authorities of the French and Irish commanders. James was entirely under the control of the French ambassador, who, together with all his countrymen in Ireland, affected to despise the Irish as a rude and uncivilized people; while the Irish in turn hated the French for their arrogance and insolence. Many of the Irish gentlemen who had raised regiments at their private expense were superseded to make room for Frenchmen appointed by the influence of the French ambassador. These gentlemen returned home in disgust, and were soon followed by their men, who were equally discontented at being handed over to the command of foreigners instead of their native leaders.

Every day the breach widened between the French and Irish, and the discontent caused by the king's exactions was wide and general; and if William at this time had offered favourable terms to the Catholics it is probable that an arrangement could have been arrived at. But William was busily at work preparing an army for the conquest of the country. Had Ireland

stood alone it is probable that England would, at anyrate for a time, have suffered it to go its own way; but
its close alliance with France, and the fact that French
influence was all-powerful with James, rendered it
impossible for England to submit to the establish-
ment of what would be a foreign and hostile power
so close to her shores. Besides, if Ireland remained
under the dominion of James, the power of William
on the throne of England could never have been consolidated.

Although he had met with no resistance on his
assumption of the throne, he had the hearty support
of but a mere fraction of the English people, and his
accession was the work of a few great Whig families
only. His rule was by no means popular, and his
Dutch favourites were as much disliked in England as
were James' French adherents in Ireland.

In Scotland the Jacobite party were numerous and
powerful, and were in open rebellion to his authority.
Thus, then, if William's position on the throne of England was to be consolidated, it was necessary that a
blow should be struck in Ireland.

Torn by dissension, without plan or leading, the Irish
army remained for months inactive, most of the regiments having after the northern campaign returned to
the districts in which they were raised; and thus no preparation was made to meet the army which was preparing to invade the country. This, ten thousand strong,
under the command of General Schomberg, who, although eighty years of age, was still an able, active, and
spirited commander, embarked on the 8th of August
at Chester, and on the 13th landed near Bangor, in

Carrickfergus Bay. There was no force there of sufficient strength to oppose him.

Schomberg found Antrim and Belfast deserted; but the garrison at Carrickfergus, consisting of two regiments, prepared vigorously for a siege. Schomberg at once prepared to invest it, and in a short time attacked it by land and sea. The siege was pressed with vigour, but the garrison under M'Carty Moore defended themselves with the greatest skill and bravery. As fast as breaches were battered in their walls they repaired them, and repulsed every attempt of the besiegers to gain a footing in the town.

The garrison were badly supplied with ammunition, but they stripped the lead from the roofs of the castle and church to make bullets. But all this time no attempt whatever was made to relieve them. The French and Irish generals were disputing as to what was the best plan of campaign. The king was busy making money with his trade with France; and, after holding out until they had burned their last grain of powder, the gallant garrison were forced to capitulate. Schomberg was too glad to get the place to insist on hard terms, and the garrison marched out with all the honours of war—drums beating, and matches alight —and were conveyed with all their stores, arms, and public and private property to the nearest Irish post.

The effect of this determined resistance on the part of the little garrison at Carrickfergus was to impress Schomberg with the fact that the difficulty of the task he had undertaken was vastly greater than he had supposed. The success with which Londonderry had defended itself against the Irish army had impressed him with the idea that the levies of King James were simply contemptible; but the fighting qualities of the garrison of Carrickfergus had shown him that they were a foe by no means to be despised, and convinced him that the force at his command was altogether inadequate to his necessities.

He therefore moved south with extreme caution. He found the country altogether wasted and deserted. The Protestants had long since fled, and were gathered round Derry and Enniskillen. The Catholics had now deserted their homes at his approach, and the troops in their retreat had burned and wasted everything, so that he had no means of subsistence for his army, and was obliged to rely upon the fleet which he ordered to follow him down the coast. Schomberg was soon joined by three regiments of Enniskillen horse.

The appearance of these troops astonished the English. They resembled rather a horde of Italian banditti than a body of European cavalry. They observed little order in their military movements, and no uniformity of dress or accoutrement. Each man was armed and clad according to his own fancy, and accompanied by a mounted servant carrying his baggage. But, like the Cossacks, whom they closely resembled, they were distinguished by an extreme rapidity of movement, and a fierceness and contempt of all difficulty and danger. They calculated neither chances nor numbers, but rushed to the attack of any foe with a ferocity and fanaticism which almost ensured success, and they regarded the slaughter of a Papist as an acceptable service to the Lord. They

plundered wherever they went, and were a scourge to
the Irish Protestants as well as Catholics.

The troops furnished by Derry were similar in
character to those from Enniskillen. They could not
endure the restraints of discipline, and were little use
in acting with the regular army, and, like the Cossacks,
were formidable only when acting by themselves.
Schomberg and his successor, and, indeed, the whole of
the English officers, soon came to abhor these savage
and undisciplined allies.

Still the Irish army made no move. Report had
magnified Schomberg's strength to more than twice
its real numbers, and the military leaders could not
believe that, after so many months of preparation,
William had despatched so small an army for the conquest of Ireland.

Confusion and dismay reigned in Dublin. The French
Marshal De Rosen advised that Dublin and Drogheda
should be abandoned, and that the Irish army should
be concentrated at Athlone and Limerick; but Tyrconnell went to Drogheda, where the council of war
was sitting, and strenuously opposed this, promising
that by the next night twenty thousand men should
be assembled there. Expresses were sent out in all
directions; and by forced marches the Irish troops
stationed in Munster directed their course to Drogheda,
in high spirits and anxious to meet the enemy. Schomberg, although he had been reinforced by six thousand
men from England, fell back at the news of the gathering, and formed an intrenched camp in a strong position between Dundalk and the sea. His approaches
were covered by mountains, rivers, and morasses; his

communication was open to the sea, and here he resolved to wait for reinforcements.

Captain Davenant became more and more despondent as to the cause in which he had embarked.

"Without the king and without his French allies," he said bitterly to his wife, "we might hope for success; but these are enough to ruin any cause. Were the king's object to excite discontent and disgust among his subjects, he could not act otherwise than he is now doing. His whole thoughts are devoted to wringing money out of the people, and any time he has to spare is spent upon superintending the building of the nunneries in which he is so interested. As to the French, they paralyse all military operations. They regard us as an inferior race, and act as if, with their own five or six thousand troops, they could defeat all the power of England. It is heart-breaking seeing our chances so wasted.

"Had advantage been taken of the enthusiasm excited when King James landed; had he himself been wise and prudent, disinterested for himself, and desirous of obtaining the affections of all classes; and had he brought with him none of these French adventurers, he would long ere this have been undisputed King of Ireland from end to end, and we should have stood as one people in arms ready to oppose ourselves to any force that England could send against us. Never were chances so frittered away, never such a succession of blunders and folly. It is enough to break one's heart."

"I do hope, father, that when the troop marches again you will take me as cornet. I am six months older than I was, and have learned a lot in the last campaign. You have not filled up the place of Cornet O'Driscoll. I did think, when he was killed in that last fight you had before Derry, you would have appointed me."

"In some respects I am less inclined than ever, Walter," Captain Davenant said; "for I begin to regard success as hopeless."

"It will make no difference, father, in that way, for if we are beaten they are sure to hand all our land over to the Protestants. Besides, things may turn out better than you think; and whether or no, I should certainly like to do my best for Ireland."

"Well, we will think about it," Captain Davenant said; and Walter was satisfied, for he felt sure that his father would finally accede to his wishes.

It was late at night when the mounted messenger dashed up to the door of the castle and handed in an order. Captain Davenant opened it.

"We are to march in half an hour's time to Drogheda; the whole army is to assemble there."

"Hurray!" Walter shouted. "Something is going to be done at last."

A man was sent down to the village at once to order the twenty men quartered there to saddle and mount instantly and ride up to the castle, while another on horseback started for Bray to get the main body under arms. Mrs. Davenant busied herself in packing the wallets of her husband and son. She was very pale, but she said little.

"God bless you both," she said when all was finished, "and bring you back again safely. I won't ask you to take care of yourselves, because, of course, you must do your duty, and with all my love I should not wish you to draw back from that. When home and religion and country are at stake even we women could not wish to keep those we love beside us."

There was a last embrace, and then Captain Davenant and his son sprang on their horses, which were waiting at the door, took their place at the head of the party which had come up from the village, and rode away into the darkness, while the two Mrs. Davenants gave free vent to the tears which they had hitherto so bravely restrained. At Bray Captain Davenant found the rest of his troop drawn up in readiness, and after a brief inspection, to see that all were present with their proper arms and accoutrements, he started with them for Dublin, and after a few hours' rest there continued his way towards Drogheda.

The army then proceeded north to Dundalk, and bitter was the disappointment of the troops when, on arriving there, they found that Schomberg, instead of advancing to give battle, had shut himself up in the intrenchments he had formed, and could not be induced to sally out.

In vain King James, who accompanied his army, formed it up in order of battle within sight of the invaders' lines. Schomberg was not to be tempted out, and as the position appeared to be too strong to be attacked, the Irish were forced to endeavour to reduce it by the slow process of starvation. The English army was soon reduced to pitiable straits—not from hunger, for they were able to obtain food from the ships, but from disease. The situation of the camp was low and unhealthy. Fever broke out, and swept away vast numbers of the men.

The Dutch and Enniskilleners suffered comparatively little — both were accustomed to a damp climate, but of the English troops nearly eight thousand died in the two months that the blockade lasted. Had James maintained his position the whole of the army of Schomberg must have perished; but, most unfortunately for his cause, he insisted on personally conducting operations, and when complete success was in his grasp he marched his army away in the middle of November to winter quarters, thereby allowing Schomberg to move with the eight thousand men who remained to him from the pest-stricken camp to healthier quarters.

The disgust of those of James's officers who understood anything of war at this termination of the campaign was extreme. The men, indeed, were eager to return to their homes, but would gladly have attempted an assault on the English camp before doing so; and as the defenders were reduced to half their original strength, while most of the survivors were weakened by disease, the attack would probably have been successful. James himself was several times on the point of ordering an attack, but his own vacillation of character was heightened by the conflicting counsels of his generals, who seemed more bent on thwarting each other than on gaining the cause for which they fought.

The cavalry were not idle while the blockade of Schomberg's camp continued, frequently making excursions over the country to bring in cattle for the army, for the villagers had for the most part deserted their homes, and herds of cattle were grazing without masters. One day Captain Davenant's troop had ridden some thirty miles out of camp, and had halted for the night in a village. In the morning they broke up into small parties and scattered round the country. Walter with fifteen of the troopers, had collected some cattle and stopped for an hour to feed and rest the horses in a deserted village. He took the precaution to place two or three men on sentry round it.

The men were sitting on the door-steps eating the food they had brought with them, when one of the outposts dashed in at full gallop, shouting that the enemy were upon them; but his warning came too late, for close behind him came a body of wild-looking horsemen, shouting and yelling. There was a cry of "The Enniskilleners!" and the men ran to their horses. They had scarcely time to throw themselves in the saddle when the Enniskilleners charged down. For a minute or two there was a confused medley, and then three or four of the troopers rode off at full speed hotly pursued by the Enniskilleners.

Walter had discharged his pistols and drawn his sword, but before he had time to strike a blow his horse was rolled over by the rush of the enemy, and as he was falling he received a blow on the head from a sabre which stretched him insensible on the ground. He was roused by two men turning him over and searching his pockets. A slight groan burst from his lips.

"The fellow is not dead," one of the men said.

"We will soon settle that," the other replied.

"Don't kill him," the first speaker said. "Wait till

the captain has spoken to him. We may be able to get some information from him. We can finish him afterwards."

Walter lay with his eyes closed. He well knew that the Enniskilleners took no prisoners, but killed all who fell into their hands, and he determined to show no signs of returning consciousness. Presently he heard the sound of a party of horsemen returning, and by the exclamations of disappointment which greeted the news they gave, he learned that some, at least, of his men had made their escape. Some time later several men came up to him. One leaned over him and put his hand to his heart.

"He is alive."

"Very well," another voice said. "Then we will take him with us. He is an officer, and will be able to tell us all about their strength. Watkins, you have a strong beast, and do not weigh much. Do you mount, and then we will tie him to your back."

A minute later Walter was lifted up and felt that he was placed on a horse with his back to that of the rider. A rope was wound several times round his body. He remained perfectly passive, with his head hanging down on his breast. Then a word of command was given and the troop set off.

For a time there was no need for him to pretend insensibility, for the pain of his wound and the loss of blood overpowered him, and for some time he was unconscious. After two hours' riding the troop was halted. Walter felt the rope taken off him. Then he was lifted down, dragged a short distance, and thrown down on some straw. Then a door shut, and he heard a key turned. He felt sure that he was alone, but for some time lay perfectly quiet, as it was possible that one of the men might have remained to watch him.

After a quarter of an hour, hearing not the slightest sound, he opened his eyes and looked round. He was, as he supposed, alone. The place in which he was lying was a stable, lighted only by a small opening high up in the wall. Certain, therefore, that he was not overlooked, he made an effort to rise to his feet, but he was so weak and giddy that he was obliged for some time to remain leaning against the wall. Seeing a bucket in one corner, he made to it, and found to his delight that it was half full of water, for he was parched with a devouring thirst. After taking a deep draught he felt greatly revived, and then made a thorough survey of his prison. It evidently formed part of the house of a well-to-do man, for it was solidly built of stone, and the door was strong and well fitted.

The opening in the wall was out of his reach. He could at ordinary times, by standing on the upturned bucket, have reached it with a spring, and pulled himself up to it, but at present he was wholly incapable of such exertion. He thought, however, that after a night's rest he would be able to do it.

The door was so strong that he had no hope of escape in that direction. As he might at any moment be disturbed, he returned to the straw on which he had at first been thrown, laid himself down, and in a very short time dropped off to sleep. It was dark before he was awoke by the turning of the key in the lock, and two men entered, one of them bearing a horn lantern.

"Where am I?" Walter asked in a feeble tone as they approached him.

"Never mind where you are," one said roughly. "Get up."

Walter seemed to make an effort, and then fell back with a groan.

The man repeated his order, emphasizing it with a kick. Walter again made an effort, and as before sank back.

"Here, catch hold of him," the man said impatiently, "it's no use fooling here with him."

The men took Walter under the arms and lifted him up, and half dragged half carried him out of the stable and into the house adjoining. He was taken into a room where four or five men were sitting.

"Now, young fellow," one said sharply, "tell us what corps you belong to."

Walter looked stupidly at his questioner, but made no answer.

"Answer my question," the man said, levelling a pistol at him, "or I will blow out your brains at once."

Still Walter stared at him stupidly and made no reply, except to mutter "Water."

"It's no use," one of the other men said; "he hasn't got his right senses yet. It's no use shooting him now, after we have had the trouble of bringing him here. In the morning he will be able to answer you."

"He had better," the other said savagely, "or we will light a fire and roast him over it. There, take him back to the stable and give him a drink of water. I don't want him to slip through our fingers after the trouble we have had with him."

Walter was taken back as before to the stable, and one of the men brought him a mug of water and held it to his lips. He drank eagerly, and then the man placed the mug down beside him, the door was again closed and locked, and Walter was alone. He rose at once to his feet, and felt that his sleep had greatly refreshed and strengthened him.

" I will have another sleep before I try," he said to himself. " It will not be light till six, and it must be eight or nine o'clock now. I must make up my mind, before I dose off, to wake in about three or four hours; but first I must see what I can find here."

He felt round the walls, but failed to find anything like a rope.

" I must trust to luck," he said; " I don't suppose they will post many sentries. These fellows are not real soldiers, and no doubt they will all be sound asleep in a couple of hours."

So saying, he again lay down, and was speedily asleep. When he woke he felt sure that he had not exceeded the time he had given himself. He listened intently. He could hear a low confused sound, which he knew was made by horses feeding, but he could hear no human voices. He drank the rest of the water in the mug, then he turned up the bucket, placed it under the opening, and mounted on it.

His first spring failed to reach the sill, and he stood for a few minutes before making another attempt. He knew that it was a matter of life or death, for he had no doubt whatever that, even if he gave the required information, which he was determined not to do, however much he might suffer, he would be shot afterwards. He braced himself to the utmost, took a long breath, and then sprang. His fingers caught on the ledge of stone-work, and with a desperate effort he drew himself up, aided by his feet. He had before making the attempt removed his boots, partly to avoid the scraping noise which these would make, partly to enable him the better to avail himself of the inequalities in the stone-work.

It was a desperate struggle; and when he got his shoulders in the opening, which was just wide enough to admit them, he lay for three or four minutes panting heavily, with the perspiration streaming down his face. The aperture was too small to admit of his turning in any way, and there was nothing for it, as he knew, but to drop head-foremost.

Gradually he drew himself through the opening, lowering himself as much as he could by holding on to the upper edge by his feet. Then stretching out his arms to save himself, he let go. Fortunately the ground was soft, for a garden adjoined the stable; but the shock was a heavy one, and he lay for a minute or two without moving, having some doubt whether he had not broken his neck. Then he got up and listened.

Everything was still and quiet, and indeed his fall had been almost noiseless; he rose to his feet, felt along the wall until he encountered a low paling, climbed over it, and was in the road. He had, when he jumped for the window, tied his boots to his back, and now carried them in his hand. The night was very dark; but his eyes, accustomed to the greater darkness of the stable, had no difficulty in following the road. He walked slowly, for the exertion he had undergone and the shock of the fall had drawn greatly from his small stock of strength.

After going a quarter of a mile he put on his boots, and, climbing a wall of sods which bordered the road, struck across country. There were no stars to guide him, and a slight mist had begun to fall. There was but little wind, but this was sufficient to give a direction to the rain. Walter noticed this, and at once struck out in a direction which kept the rain falling upon the right side of his face; and he knew that, by so continuing, he was going in a tolerably straight line. As near as he could tell he walked for two hours, and then, utterly exhausted, lay down on the lee side of a turf wall.

There was as yet no gleam of light in the sky, and in a very few minutes he was again sound asleep. He woke up with a feeling of bitter cold, and on rising found that his limbs were completely stiffened by the wet. It was morning now, the wind had got up, and a driving rain shut out the view on all sides. Walter stamped his feet and swung his arms for some time to restore the circulation.

He had no idea in which direction he had been travelling, for he did not know whether the road from which he had started ran north, south, east, or west. He noticed that the wind had changed; for whereas he had lain down under the lee of the wall, it was now the weather side. He walked in the same direction as before for two hours, and could then go no farther. He had seen no signs of human habitation, and had not crossed a road or even a footpath. Since starting

(377)   I

in the morning he had passed no more walls or fences, and, as far as his eye could reach through the driving rain, nothing was to be seen save a desolate expanse of moor and bog. He was at anyrate free from pursuit for the time, and he thought more of obtaining food and shelter than of the Enniskilleners.

It was useless pushing further on, even had he been able to do so, while the rain lasted; for he might have passed within a quarter of a mile of a habitation without seeing it. He accordingly threw himself down beside some low bushes, which afforded him some slight protection from the rain.

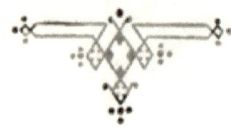

"CAN YOU GIVE ME SHELTER?" ASKED WALTER.

CHAPTER VII.

THE COMING BATTLE.

OME hours passed, and he was on the point of
dropping off to sleep again when he heard a
whistle repeated once or twice, followed by
the sharp bark of a dog. It was but a short distance
away, and leaping to his feet he saw a peasant standing at a distance of two or three hundred yards.

Walter hurried towards him at a speed of which
a few minutes before he would have thought himself
incapable. The man continued whistling at short intervals, and did not notice Walter till he was within
twenty yards distant; then he turned sharply round.

"Who are you?" he asked, clubbing a heavy stick
which he held in his hand and standing on the defensive.

The dress and appearance of the man assured Walter
that he was a Catholic, and therefore a friend, and he
replied at once:

"I belong to one of the Irish troops of horse. The
Enniskilleners surprised a party of us yesterday, and
wounded me, as you see. Fortunately I escaped in the
night or they would have finished me this morning.
I have been out all night in the rain, and am weak from
loss of blood and hunger. Can you give me shelter?"

"That I can," the man said, "and gladly. Those villains have been killing and destroying all over the country, and there's many a one of us who, like myself, have been driven to take refuge in the bogs."

'Is it far?" Walter asked; "for I don't think I could get more than a mile or two."

"It is not half a mile," the man said. "You do look nearly done for. Here, lean on me, I will help you along; and if you find your strength go I will make a shift to carry you."

"It is lucky I heard you whistle," Walter said.

"It is, indeed," the man replied, "for it is not likely anyone else would have come along to-day. My dog went off after a rabbit, and I was whistling to him to come to me again. Ah! here he is; he has got the rabbit too. Good dog! well done!"

He took the rabbit and dropped it into the pocket of his coat. Seeing that Walter was too exhausted to talk, he asked no questions and said nothing till he pointed to a low mound of earth and said: "Here we are."

He went round by the side; and Walter perceived that there was a sharp dip in the ground, and that the hut was dug out in the face of the slope; so that if it were approached either from behind or on either side it would not be noticed, the roof being covered with sods, and closely matching the surrounding ground.

The man went to the low door and opened it.

"Come in, sir," he said; "you are quite welcome."

The hut contained two other men, who looked up in surprise at the greeting.

"This is a young officer in one of our horse regiments," the man said. "He has been in the hands of the Enniskilleners, and has got out from them alive —which is more than most can say. He has had a bad wound, has been wet through for hours, and is half-starving. Look sharp, lads, and get something hot as soon as possible. Now, sir, if you will take off those wet things of yours and wrap yourself in that rug, you will find yourself the better for it. When a man is in health a few hours wet will not do him any harm; but when he is weak from loss of blood, as you are, the cold seems to get into his bones."

Fresh turfs were at once put on the smouldering fire, which one of the men, leaning down before it, proceeded to blow lustily; and although much of the smoke made its way out through a hole in the roof, enough lingered to render it difficult for Walter to breathe, while his eyes watered with the sharp fumes. A kettle had been placed on the fire, and in a very short time a jar was produced from the corner of the hut and a horn of strong spirits and water mixed.

"Here are some cold praties, sir. It's all we have got cooked by us now, but I can promise you a better meal later on."

Walter ate the potatoes and drank the warm mixture. The change from the cold damp air outside to the warm atmosphere of the hut aided the effects of the spirits; he was first conscious of a warm glow all over him, and then the voices of the men seemed to grow indistinct.

"You had better stretch yourself on that pile of rushes," the man said, as Walter gave a start, being on the point of rolling over. "Two or three hours' sleep will make a man of you, and by that time dinner will be ready and your clothes dry."

Walter fell almost instantaneously off to sleep, and it was late in the afternoon before he woke.

"I am afraid I must have slept a long time," he said, sitting up.

"You have had a fine sleep surely," one of the men replied; "and it's dinner and supper all in one that you will have."

Walter found his uniform and underclothes neatly folded up by his side, and speedily dressed himself.

"That sleep has done me a world of good," he said. "I feel quite myself again."

"That's right, yer honour. When you've had your food I will make a shift to dress that wound at the back of yer head. Be jabbers, it's a hard knock you have had, and a mighty lot of blood you must have lost!—yer clothes was just stiff with it; but I washed most of it out. And now, lads, off with the pot!"

A large pot was hanging over the fire, and when the lid was taken off a smell very pleasant to Walter's nostrils arose. Four flat pieces of wood served the purpose of plates; and with a large spoon of the same material the man who had brought Walter to the hut, and who appeared to be the leader of the party, ladled out portions of the contents. These consisted of rabbit and pieces of beef boiled up with potatoes and onions. A large jug filled with water and a bottle of spirits were placed in the centre, with the horn which Walter had before used beside it.

"We are short of crockery," the man said with a

laugh. "Here are some knives, but as for forks we just have to do without them."

Walter enjoyed his meal immensely. After it was finished the wooden platters were removed and the jug replenished.

"Now, your honour, will you tell us how you got away from the Protestant rebels, and how was it they didn't make short work of you when they caught you? It's a puzzle to us entirely, for the Enniskilleners spare neither man, woman, nor child."

Walter related the whole circumstances of his capture, imprisonment, and escape.

"You fooled them nicely," the man said admiringly. "Sure your honour's the one to get out of a scrape—and you little more than a boy."

"And what are you doing here?" Walter asked in return. "This seems a wild place to live in."

"It's just that," the man said. "We belonged to Kilbally. The Enniskilleners came that way and burned it to the ground. They murdered my wife and many another one. I was away cutting peat with my wife's brother here; when we came back everything was gone. A few had escaped to the bogs, where they could not be followed; the rest was, every mother's son of them, killed by those murdering villains. Your honour may guess what we felt when we got back. Thank God I had no children! We buried the wife in the garden behind the house, and then started away and joined a band of rapparees, and paid some of them back in their own coin. Then one day the Enniskilleners fell on us, and most of us were killed. Then we made our way back to the old village, and came up

here and built us this hut. It's a wonder to us how
you got here; for there are bogs stretching away in
all directions, and how you made your way through
them bates us entirely."

"Yours is a sad story, but unfortunately a common
one. And how have you managed to live here?"

"There are plenty of potatoes for the digging of
'em," the man said, "for there are a score of ruined
villages within a day's walk. As for meat, there are
cattle for the taking, wandering all over the country; some have lately strayed away; but among the
hills there are herds which have run wild since the
days when Cromwell made the country a desert. As
for spirits, I brew them myself. Barley as well as
potatoes may be had for the taking. Then sometimes
the dog picks up a rabbit; sometimes, when we go
down for potatoes, we light on a fowl or two; there's
many a one of them running wild among the ruins.
As far as eating and drinking goes, we never did
better; and if I could forget the old cottage, and the
sight that met my eyes when I went back to it, I
should do well enough, but night and day I am dream-
ing of it, and my heart is sore with longing for vengeance."

"Why don't you join the army?" Walter asked.
"There's plenty of room for good men, and yesterday's
affair has made some vacancies in my own troop. What
do you say, lads? You would have a chance of crossing swords with the Enniskilleners, and you could
always come back here when the war is over."

"What do you say, boys?" the man asked his companions. "I am just wearying for a fight, and I could

die contented if I could but send a few of those murdering villains to their place before I go."

The other two men at once agreed. They talked
well into the night, and Walter heard many tales of
the savage butchery of unoffending peasants by the
men who professed to be fighting for religious liberty,
which shocked and sickened him. It was arranged
that they should start on the following morning. The
men said that they could guide him across country to
Dundalk without difficulty, and assured him that he
would be little likely to meet with the enemy, for
that the whole country had been so wasted by fire
and sword as to offer but little temptation even to the
most insatiable of plunderers.

Accordingly, the next morning they set out and
arrived late that evening at the camp. Walter found
that his father and his followers were absent. They
had returned, much surprised at not having been rejoined by Walter's party, but on their arrival they
had found there the survivors of his command, who had
ridden straight for Dundalk.

After a few hours' stay to rest the horses, Captain
Davenant, with his own men and two of the troops of
cavalry, had ridden out in search of the Enniskilleners. Larry, who had been almost wild with grief
when the news of the surprise, and, as he believed, the
death of Walter, had been brought in, had accompanied the cavalry. It was late on the following
afternoon before they rode into camp. Larry was the
first to come in, having received permission from
Captain Davenant to gallop on ahead. They had met
the enemy and had inflicted a decisive defeat upon

them, but the greater part had escaped by taking to the hills on their wiry little horses, which were able to traverse bogs and quagmires impassable to the heavy troopers.

Captain Davenant had closely questioned two or three wounded men who fell into his hands. These all declared that a young officer had been captured in the previous fight, that he had been severely wounded, and carried away senseless, but that he had in some extraordinary manner managed to escape that night. This story had greatly raised Captain Davenant's hopes that Walter might yet be alive, a hope which he had not before allowed himself for a moment to indulge in; and as he neared Dundalk he had readily granted leave for the impatient Larry to gallop on ahead, and discover if any news had been received of Walter. Larry's delight at seeing his young master standing at the door of the tent was extreme. He gave a wild whoop, threw his cap high up into the air, and then, without a word of greeting, turned his horse's head and galloped away again, at the top of his speed, to carry the good news to Captain Davenant. Half an hour later the column rode into camp, and Walter was clasped in his father's arms.

That evening Walter's three companions were enrolled in the troop, and, hearing that there were vacancies for fifteen more, volunteered to return to the hills and to bring back that number of men from the peasants hiding there. This mission they carried out, and by the end of the week Captain Davenant's troop was again made up to its full strength.

The unsuccessful result of the siege of Schomberg's

camp greatly damped **Walter's** enthusiasm. He had been engaged in two long and tedious blockades, and, with the exception of some skirmishes round Derry, had seen nothing whatever of fighting. Neither operation had been attended by any decisive result; both had inflicted extreme misery and suffering upon the enemy, but in neither was the success aimed at attained. At the same time, the novelty of the life, the companionship of his father and the other officers of the regiment, and, not least, the good-humour and fun of his attendant, Larry, had made the time pass far more cheerfully to him than to the majority of those in the army.

As before, when the army arrived at Dublin, Captain Davenant's troop was posted in and around Bray, the greater portion of it being permitted to reside in their own homes until again wanted for active service. Walter on his return was glad to find that his friend John Whitefoot had made his way home from Derry, and their pleasant intercourse was at once renewed.

Schomberg's army, when moved to healthy quarters and bountifully supplied with all kinds of food and necessaries from England, speedily recovered their health and discipline, and in a very short time were again in condition to take the field.

Early in February, 1690, Brigadier Wolseley, with a detachment of Enniskilleners and English, marched against Cavan. James had no longer an army with which he could oppose Schomberg's enterprises. While the latter had been recovering from the effects of his heavy losses, nothing had been done to put the Irish

army in a condition to take the field again. They
lacked almost every necessary for a campaign. No
magazines had been formed to supply them when they
should again advance; and so short of forage were
they, that it was considered impossible to make any
move in force until the grass should grow sufficiently
to enable the horses to get into condition.

Nevertheless, the Duke of Berwick marched with
eight hundred men from Dublin, and Brigadier Nugent with a like force from West Meath and Long-
ford, and arrived at Cavan a few hours before the
English reached the town. The Irish force was composed entirely of infantry, with the exception of two
troops of cavalry. The English force consisted of
seven hundred foot and three hundred cavalry. As
Cavan did not offer any advantages in the way of
defence, the Duke of Berwick moved his army out
into the open field. The English lined the hedges and
stood on the defensive.

The Irish horse commenced the battle with a furious charge on the Enniskilleners and dragoons, and
drove them from the field, but the English infantry
maintained their position so stoutly, that after a pro-
longed fight the Irish retreated into a fort near the
town. The English and Enniskilleners entered Cavan,
and at once began to plunder the place. Hearing
what was going on, the Duke of Berwick sallied out
from his fort to attack them, and gained considerable
advantage. Brigadier Wolseley being unable to restore discipline among the Enniskilleners, who formed
the great majority of his force, ordered the town to
be set on fire in several places. The troops then

collected and repulsed the Irish with considerable loss.

The Duke of Berwick had two hundred killed, amongst whom were Brigadier Nugent and many officers. As the Irish remained in possession of the fort, and the town was almost entirely destroyed by fire, Brigadier Wolseley returned with his force to Dundalk. Shortly afterwards the Fort of Charlemont was invested by a strong detachment of Schomberg's army.

Teigue O'Regan, the veteran governor, defended the place with the greatest bravery, and did not capitulate until the 14th of May, when the last ounce of provisions was consumed. The garrison were allowed honourable terms, and the eight hundred men who defended the place, with their arms and baggage, and some two hundred women and children, were allowed to march away. The Enniskilleners treated the Irish soldiers and their families with great brutality as they passed along, but Schomberg humanely ordered that a loaf of bread should be given to each man at Armagh.

The Irish army were not in condition to render any assistance to the hard pressed garrison of Charlemont until after they had capitulated. In the meantime a great army, which was to be led by King William in person, was being collected in England. It consisted of a strange medley, collected from almost every European nation — English, Scotch, Irish Protestants, French Huguenots, Dutch, Swedes, Danes, Brandenburghers, Swiss, Norwegians, and Hessians. More than half, indeed, were foreigners. All were well disciplined, armed, and clothed. In all, including the force under Schomberg, the army amounted to forty-three thousand men and fifty cannon.

King William landed at Carrickfergus on the 14th of June, and the combined army at once began their southward march. Against this force King James collected but twenty thousand men. Of these six thousand were French; they had arrived under the command of the Count de Lauzun in March, but they had not increased the numbers of King James's troops, for he had been obliged to send in exchange an equal number of his best trained soldiers under Lord Mount-cashel for service in France. Of the fourteen thousand native troops, the Irish horse, which was raised and officered by Irish gentlemen, was excellent, but the infantry was composed for the most part of raw levies, but half armed, and the only artillery consisted of twelve guns, which had arrived with the infantry from France.

It was a sad parting when Captain Davenant and Walter left home for the front. The former was filled with gloomy forebodings. He could scarcely hope that the ill-trained levies of James could succeed against the vastly superior force of disciplined troops with whom they had now to cope; especially as the latter were led by an able and energetic general, while the former were hampered by the incompetence and vacillation of James. The day before they started Captain Davenant rode over to the Whitefoots and had a talk with Jabez.

"I know not how the campaign will go," he said. "If we are beaten we shall probably retire to the west

and maintain the war there. In that case, Dublin will
of course fall into the hands of William. Should this
be so I will ask you to reverse our late position, and to
extend what assistance you can to my wife and mother.
It may be that if I do not return here none will disturb them. I have not made myself obnoxious to my
Protestant neighbours, and no one may take the trouble
to bring it before the notice of the English that I am
absent fighting with the army of King James. If,
however, they should do so, and the castle and what
remains of the estates be confiscated, will you lend what
aid you can to the ladies and my younger boy until I
or Walter return from the war?"

"That will I do right gladly," Jabez said heartily.
"Should I hear any talk of what you speak of I will
go up to Dublin with some of our friends and ministers, and we will testify to the good relations which
have existed between you and your Protestant neighbours, and entreat that no measures be taken against
your estate. Should we not prevail, be assured that I
will look after the comfort of the ladies as if they were
of my own family. I can well understand that Mrs.
Davenant the elder would not accept the shelter of our
roof whatever her extremity. She belongs to the
generation of my father, and cannot forget the past;
but I will see that they are well lodged in Bray, and
have every protection from molestation and annoyance
there. Should I find, as, alas! may be the case, that
the spirit of religious persecution is fiercely abroad, I
will consult with them as to whether they may wish
to cross the sea until you can join them, and will make
arrangements as they may direct for their passage."

"I am truly obliged to you," Captain Davenant said. "It will make me comfortable to know that, whatsoever may befall me, they will have a friend in these stormy times."

"Say nought about it," Jabez replied. "Did not you and your son succour my boy in his extremity? If I do all and more than all that I can in this matter I shall not deem that we are quits."

The Irish army moved forward to the Boyne, which William was approaching from the north. James's officers endeavoured to dissuade him from setting everything on the hazard of the battle. They represented that his army, though now quite unequal to the contest, was rapidly improving in skill and confidence in itself; that reinforcements were every day expected from France, which would at least make them equal to the enemy in numbers; that they were in want of arms, artillery, and stores, all which might be expected also from France in a short period; and that their policy was clearly to protract the war, and wear out the enemy by a contest of posts and sieges.

Unskilled as his troops might be in the field, they had proved themselves steady and resolute in the defence of fortified places; they held all the great fortresses of the kingdom, and it would be easy to provide for the defence of these, and to occupy William's army in small affairs till the winter, when the climate would do execution upon the invaders, while the Irish would suffer little. Then would be the time to fight.

In the meantime, it was urged, the intrigues the French were actively carrying out in Britain, would have produced some effect: the French fleet was every day expected on the coast of England, and William would soon be compelled to return to that country, if not to recall the greater part of his army. In Scotland, too, the French were busy; and there were materials in that country for creating a powerful diversion. To fight now would be to forego every advantage, and to meet the views of William, whose obvious interest it was to bring the contest to an immediate decision now while every circumstance was in his favour.

But James, who had hitherto shown nothing but timidity and hesitation, was now seized with an impulse of valour. Having acted with unfortunate cowardice before Derry and Schomberg's camp at Dundalk, he was as unfortunately now seized with ardour to fight when prudence and discretion would have been his best policy. But while James was determining to fight in the teeth of the opinion and advice of his bravest officers, his true character was shown in his taking every precaution for his personal safety. He sent off his heavy baggage, and engaged a vessel at Waterford to convey him to France.

William, on the other hand, was naturally eager for an early engagement. He was still very insecurely seated upon the English throne. The people were either discontented or indifferent. They looked with impatience and indignation at the crowd of Dutch officers and civilians whom William had brought over with him; while the cold and ungracious manner of the king contrasted most unfavourably with the bearing to which they had been accustomed in English monarchs.

In Scotland the Jacobite spirit was gathering in strength, and William knew that unless he speedily

K

broke the strength of James's party in Ireland he would very shortly be confronted with difficulties and dangers on all sides.

The position which the Irish army occupied was a strong one. Its right rested upon Drogheda, a strong town in their possession. In front was the Boyne, with steep banks lined with thick hedges, with cottages scattered here and there, offering an excellent position for light troops. On the left the Boyne turned almost at a right angle, and formed a defence on this flank. To the rear the Irish position was covered by high hills and the village of Donore. Further back was the pass of Duleek.

The hedges and cottages by the river side were occupied by the Irish infantry, and upon some little hillocks which ran along the water's edge they erected some light batteries.

King William reconnoitred the position with great attention, and saw that it had been well chosen and its advantages turned to account. Notwithstanding the reports of deserters and others, he showed much anxiety to determine the exact strength of the Irish.

After examining the position for some time from a height he rode down towards the river accompanied by several of his officers. When within musket-shot of the bank, near the ford and village of Old Bridge, he perceived that a small island in the Boyne was occupied by a party of the Irish horse. Near the ford some field-works had been thrown up. It was at this point that the king determined to cross the river, and he spent some time conversing with his officers as to the arrangements for the passage.

KING WILLIAM RECONNOITRES THE IRISH POSITION.

He then rode slowly along the river bank until he arrived nearly opposite the left of the Irish line. Here he alighted from his horse, and sat down on rising ground watching his own battalions, which were marching with the greatest regularity and order into the positions assigned to them. While he was so engaged, some officers of James's army were observed riding quietly along the opposite bank of the river, and also engaged in watching the movements of the British troops.

These were General Sarsfield, the Duke of Berwick, the Marquis of Tyrconnell, the Count de Lauzun, and others. Some of the English dragoons approached the river and were fired upon by the Irish. They returned the fire, and while the attention of both sides was engaged by the skirmish a party of Irish cavalry moved slowly down towards the river and halted behind a low hedge, and then wheeling about again retired.

The movements of the king and the group of officers accompanying him had been observed in the Irish army, and two field-pieces were sent down concealed in the centre of the cavalry. The guns had been placed behind the hedge when the horsemen withdrew, and when William rose from the ground and mounted his horse fire was opened. The first cannon shot killed two horses and a man by his side. The next grazed the king's right shoulder, tearing away his coat and inflicting a slight flesh wound. Had the aim been slightly more accurate, or had the gunners fired with grape instead of round shot, it is probable that the whole course of history would have been changed.

The rumour spread through both armies that the

king was killed; but the wound was a slight one, and having had it hastily bound up the king rode quietly through the camps in order to show the men that the hurt was not serious. In the evening he called a council of war. The Duke of Schomberg was strongly opposed to an attack upon the enemy while posted in so strong a position, and urged that by making a turning movement and marching straight upon Dublin the enemy would be obliged to fall back and fight under less advantageous circumstances; but the king, relying upon his superior numbers and the discipline of his veteran troops, determined to attack at once, knowing that it was all-important to bring the matter to a decision as early as possible.

Schomberg then urged the necessity of occupying the pass of Slane upon the Boyne, considerably to the west of the Irish line, as he would thus cut off their retreat, and, in the event of victory, render their defeat a decided one; but the king saw that he should require his whole force to dislodge the Irish from their position, and that it was useless to occupy the pass of Slane with a small detachment, as these would be overwhelmed by the retiring Irish.

It was twelve o'clock at night before the council terminated, and then the king mounted his horse and rode through the camp. He examined into the state and preparation of each regiment, saw that the soldiers were abundantly supplied with food and refreshment for the morning, and that sufficient ammunition for the day's work had been served out. He directed the men to wear green branches in their caps, and gave "Westminster" as the word for the day.

The order of the battle finally determined upon was that the right wing of the army, under General Douglas and Count Schomberg, son of the duke, should pass the river at Slane and endeavour to turn the Irish left between Slane and Duleek. The left wing were to penetrate between the Irish right and Drogheda; the centre to force the passage of the river at the ford of Old Bridge.

A council was also held in James's camp, and here also there was difference of opinion. Some of the generals wished to hold the pass of Slane in force, but James decided against this. As the morning approached the king's new-born courage began to die out; he ordered some movements to the rear, and sent forward more of his baggage. He would probably have declined the combat altogether had it not been too late. Finally, just as day was breaking over the council, he determined that the army should retreat during the battle and not commit themselves in a decisive engagement. The French formed the left, and were to lead the retreat, while the Irish held the right and centre.

It is almost certain that if James had kept to his resolution to fight, imprudent as it appeared to be, and had brought the French battalion into action instead of leading them out of the field, the result of the battle of the Boyne would have been a very different one.

CHAPTER VIII.

BOYNE WATER.

THE morning of Tuesday, the 1st of July, 1690, broke calm and bright. At about six o'clock in the morning the English right wing, under General Douglas and Count Schomberg, marched towards Slane. It consisted of twenty-four squadrons of horse and six battalions of infantry. As they marched along at the back of the river they discovered several shallows, and crossed without proceeding as far as Slane. No serious resistance was offered to their passage of the Boyne, as the Irish had here only some parties of skirmishers, who fell back as they advanced.

After forming the troops in order Douglas and Schomberg advanced, but presently perceived the French battalions and a great part of the Irish cavalry, forming the left wing of James's army, drawn up in order at some distance. They consequently halted and sent for reinforcements. When these arrived they extended their lines to the right, so as to outflank the enemy, and, supporting their cavalry by alternate battalions of infantry, again moved forward. The Irish skirmishers fell back before their advance, taking advantage of the banks of the ditches, which divided the ground into small fields, and keeping up a galling fire upon the British as they advanced. With some difficulty the latter passed over this broken ground and formed in order of battle on the edge of what appeared to be a plain, but which was in fact a deep bog, which completely covered the Irish left. Here they came to a stand-still.

William had waited until he believed that his right would have had time to fall upon the Irish left, and then ordered his centre to advance and force the passage at Old Bridge. The Dutch guards, whom William relied upon as his best and most trustworthy troops, advanced in splendid order to the river side, with their drums beating the march.

When they reached the water's edge the drums ceased, and the soldiers entered the river. The stream rose as the dense column marched in and dammed it up, and the water reached the shoulders of the grenadiers, but they still moved on in regular order, keeping their arms and ammunition dry by holding them above their heads. On the opposite bank the hedges near the brink of the river were lined with skirmishers, while in the rear, in a hollow covered by some little hills, seven regiments of Irish infantry, supported by ten troops of horse and Tyrconnell's regiment of cavalry, were drawn up. The hills protected them from the fire of the British batteries, which passed over their heads.

The Dutch troops continued their way unmolested until they reached the middle of the river, when a hot fire was opened upon them from the Irish skirmishers; but the Dutch moved on unshaken and soon gained the opposite bank, where they rapidly formed up, the skirmishers retiring before them. Scarcely had the Dutch formed their squares when the Irish horse burst down upon them at full speed and charged them with impetuosity.

They stood the charge unbroken, but again and again the Irish horse charged down upon them with the greatest gallantry. William pushed two regiments of French Huguenots and one of British across the river to the assistance of the Dutch guards, and ordered Sir John Hanmars and the Count of Nassau's regiment to cross lower down the stream to support them.

As the supports were making a passage, General Hamilton advanced at the head of a body of Irish infantry to the water's edge, and dashing into the river encountered the French Huguenot regiments in the middle of the stream. A desperate fight ensued, but the French made their way across, and Hamilton, falling back with his infantry, opened to the right and left, permitting the Irish horse to charge through them.

These rushed with fury upon the French regiment of Colonel La Callimot, and cut their way right through them. Then wheeling they charged them in flank again, broke them and drove them into the river. La Callimot himself was killed, and but few of his regiment regained the opposite bank. In the meantime the Dutch guards, now reinforced, were advancing slowly, the Irish infantry holding fast to the hedges and brushwood, and contesting every inch of the ground, while, wherever the ground permitted it, the Irish horse burst down upon them, evincing a gallantry and determination which would have done honour to the finest cavalry in Europe.

The king continued to make repeated efforts to support his Dutch troops, and after the French were broken, he pushed forward the Danish horse; but no sooner had they crossed the bank than the Irish cavalry burst down upon them, broke them and drove them back into the river. They fled across the stream in disorder, and dispersed in all directions.

So far success had rested principally with the Irish; the Dutch guards alone remained unbroken in the centre; the French infantry and Danish horse were broken and destroyed. Old Duke Schomberg exerted himself to the utmost to restore the battle at this point, and having rallied the French infantry advanced with them, and a few French cavalry, towards the river, where he was met by some of the Irish horse returning from the pursuit of the Danes. The old duke was cut down and his party again routed, and at the same moment Walker, the clerical commander of Derry, received a mortal wound. After his successful defence of Derry, this man had gone to London, where he had been feted and made much of, and had then attached himself to King William's army, where he posed as a high military authority, although much discouraged by the king, whom his arrogance and airs of authority displeased.

While in the centre William's forces were getting worsted, and on his right Douglas and Count Schomberg were inactive and powerless, he himself was leading his left wing across the river. The passage was a difficult one, and the king himself was only extricated with much exertion from a quicksand into which his horse had plunged.

The Irish did not oppose the crossing, and as soon as his forces were across the stream William ranged them in order. They consisted of a large body of Danish, Dutch, and Enniskillen horse, and a considerable force of infantry. As soon as all were in order the king, though still suffering from the wound he had received the day before, drew his sword and put himself at the head of his troops. The Irish right wing, which consisted chiefly of infantry, moved forward to meet them, but perceiving the numerous cavalry, led by the king himself, preparing to take them in flank, they halted, faced about and marched slowly to the little hill of Donore. Having gained this point, they again faced round and charged down upon the British who had followed them closely.

At this moment the Irish cavalry, who had moved rapidly from the centre to the support of the right, charged down upon the Danish and Dutch horse led by the king, and no sooner had they come in contact than the Danes and Dutch turned and rode off with the Irish cavalry in pursuit. The king rode towards the Enniskilleners. Colonel Wolseley told his men that it was the king, and asked if they wished to follow him. They replied with a shout, and the king, placing himself at the head, rode towards the Irish infantry; but as they advanced they were met by a well-directed volley, and being much more fond of plundering and slaughtering than of close fighting, they turned horse and rode away.

Again and again the king rallied his infantry and

brought them back to the fight, but the Irish infantry
stood their ground with great steadiness until Hamilton, their general, was wounded and taken in a charge
of cavalry. After this they fell back from Donore
upon Duleek in good order, the enemy not wanting to
molest them, and the rest of the Irish infantry followed their example.

No more singular battle than that of the Boyne was
ever fought. In the morning, at break of day, part of
James's army, with most of his artillery, were in
march for the pass of Slane, and actually on their
retreat. The left wing, composed chiefly of French
infantry, supposed to be the best troops in the army,
never fired a shot. The centre and right, composed
entirely of Irish, most of whom had never before been
in battle, were alone engaged. With the exception of
his Dutch guards, all William's foreign troops had
been repeatedly broken; his cavalry had been driven
off the field by the Irish horse, while no division of
the Irish was broken or suffered a decided defeat,
until the infantry from the hill of Donore were compelled to retreat, which they did in perfect order.

Throughout the day the Irish cavalry showed a vast
superiority to those of the British, and even broke
and destroyed regiments of infantry; and when the
whole army fell back they closed up the rear, and
effectually prevented any attempt at pursuit. Thus
the battle of the Boyne was fought rather to cover a
retreat than defend a position. The loss on either side
was estimated at about five hundred, and General
Hamilton was the only prisoner taken by the British.

The honours of the fight certainly rested with the

Irish, who, against a vastly superior force, comprising some of the best troops in Europe, maintained themselves throughout the day, and gained, indeed, in most points, a decided advantage.

King James's valour had entirely evaporated before the first shot was fired. Instead of following William's example, and leading his troops in the conflict which was to decide the fate of his crown, and which he himself had precipitated, he took up his position at a safe distance from danger, on the hill of Donore, and as soon as the battle approached that point he rode off to Duleek, where he placed himself at the head of the French troops, and led their retreat.

He soon, however, rode on ahead, and arrived in Dublin in a state of consternation and despair, the first fugitive from the field of battle. In the meantime the army was whole and unbroken, marching in perfect order from the field of battle, while its king and commander was doing his best to ruin the cause by spreading dismay and alarm throughout the country. The next morning the king sent for the mayor and corporation of Dublin, and told them that he was under the necessity of taking care of himself, and recommended them to do the same, and to make the best terms they could with the enemy. He then at once mounted and made his flight to Waterford, ordering the bridges to be broken down behind him, although the British army had not yet moved from its position on the Boyne.

On reaching Waterford James at once embarked on board the ship he had ordered to be in readiness, and sailed for France. His conduct, and his conduct alone,

converted the battle of the Boyne, which was in effect
a kind of drawn battle, into a great victory for
William. It had, indeed, more than answered the
object which the Irish commanders proposed to themselves. Their plan was to accustom the new and
badly armed levies to stand firm against the steadiness
and experience of William's veteran troops, and then
to withdraw without committing themselves to a decisive combat, with a view of protracting the campaign
until William should be forced to leave Ireland, and
his foreign army should be worn out by winter service
in an uncongenial climate. Every day would, they
calculated, improve their own army and weaken and
reduce that of the enemy.

Their position at the Boyne enabled them to try
their plan of partial combat to what extent they chose
without danger of being forced into a more extensive
action than they deemed expedient. The Irish troops
had greatly surpassed the expectation of their own
officers, and had filled William's generals with amaze-
ment; and it is probable that, if a large part of the
infantry and artillery had not been sent off early in
the day, the experiment might have been turned into
a brilliant victory. As it was, William was so surprised and alarmed at the resistance he had encountered, that he remained some days at the Boyne without advancing.

He had been told by all except the Duke of Schomberg that the resistance of the Irish would be contemptible, and the most forward of those who had
scoffed at the courage of the Irish had been the Enniskilleners, who had themselves on the day of battle

shown so unmistakably the white feather. After this the king disliked and despised these troops, and hung them without ceremony when taken in those acts of plunder and slaughter to which they were so much addicted.

So far from the flight of King James discouraging the army, it caused universal joy. It was his constant vacillation, interference, and cowardly action which had paralysed his troops; and they felt that, now they were free to act without his interference, they would be able to cope with the invaders.

William at once offered favourable terms if Ireland would submit to his authority; but these were declined, partly owing to the powerful influence of France, partly to the fear that the terms would not be observed, partly to the apprehension of all the gentry that the lands which they had but just recovered from the hands of Cromwell's settlers would be again taken from them.

At the battle of the Boyne Walter Davenant with his father's troop had taken part in all the desperate charges upon the enemy. During the long hours the battle had lasted the cavalry had been incessantly engaged. Time after time they had charged down upon the Dutch squares, and no sooner had the ranks been reformed after recoiling from the line of fixed bayonets than they were called upon to charge in another direction.

Walter's heart beat high as they dashed into the midst of the French infantry, or shattered and drove before them the Danish horse; but there was little time to think, and looking back upon the day when all was over it seemed to him a chaos of excitement and confusion, of which he could hardly recall even the chief incidents. As the troops halted for the night they were in no way dispirited at the result of the battle, as the retreat had been begun before a blow was struck. They knew that it was neither intended nor hoped that the ground would be successfully held; and every man felt a pride in the thought that some eighteen thousand newly-raised Irish levies, of whom but a small portion of the infantry were armed with muskets, had sustained throughout a long summer's day the attacks of more than double their number of veteran troops, supported by fifty pieces of artillery.

The loss of the Irish horse had been comparatively small. Charging a square in the days when the bayonet was fixed in the muzzle of the gun was not the desperate undertaking that it now is, when from the hedge of steel issues a rolling and continuous fire. The French regiment, once broken, had been cut down with scarce any resistance, while the mercenary cavalry had been defeated with the greatest ease. Thus among the brigade of the Irish horse there were but few fallen friends to mourn, and nothing to mar the pride that every man felt in the behaviour of the Irish troops against such overwhelming odds. That the king had fled everyone knew, but the feeling was one of relief.

"His absence is more than a victory to us," Captain Davenant said as with a group of officers he sat by a fire made of a fence hastily pulled down. "His majesty has his virtues, and, with good counsellors, would make a worthy monarch; but among his virtues military genius is not conspicuous. I should be glad myself if Lauzun and the French would also take their departure, and let us have Mountcashel's division back again from France. If we are left to ourselves, with our own generals, Sarsfield and Mountcashel, we can tire out this continental riffraff that William has gathered together. The dissensions caused by French interference have been our ruin so far; leave us to ourselves and we shall do The Irish to-day have proved their fighting qualities; and, if proper use is made of the resources and difficulties of the country, I defy them to conquer us. I feel more hopeful now than I have done since the first day we took the field."

"Do you think we shall fight another battle before Dublin, father?" Walter asked.

"I have no idea what the generals will decide, Walter, but I should imagine that we shall march to the west. We had a strong position to-day, but in the open field at present we could not hope to cope with William's superior numbers and great artillery train. His guns were little use to him yesterday; but on level ground they would tear our ranks to pieces, without our being able to make any return. Among the rivers and bogs and mountains of the west we should find scores of places which we could hold against them. Besides, in my opinion we should not fight pitched battles, but should harass them with continuous marches and attacks, leaving them masters only of the ground they stand on, until at last we completely wear them out and exhaust them."

"Then you think we shall abandon Dublin altogether?"

"I think so, Walter."

"But will they not persecute the Catholics when they have them in their power?"

"There may be some disturbance in the city, Walter, before the English troops march in; but William will no doubt put an end to this as soon as he arrives. He cannot wish to drive the Catholics of Ireland to desperation. At anyrate I do not think we need feel at all uneasy about those at home; lying on the coast to the east of the town of Dublin, and altogether out of the track of the movements of troops, there is little fear of trouble there. In our district there is little preponderance in numbers of one religion over the other; and unless the presence of troops, or worse, of those savages from Enniskillen or Derry, excite them, there is little fear of the Protestants of that neighbourhood interfering with our people, especially as they have no grounds for complaint in the past. No, I do not think that you need disquiet yourself in the slightest about those at home."

As Captain Davenant had thought probable, the Irish army, after marching into Dublin in good order, with flags flying and music playing, left on the following day for the west. They were accompanied by most of the leading Catholic families; and on their departure the corporation at once wrote to William inviting him to enter the capital. Before his arrival, however, the Protestant mob destroyed a great quantity of property belonging to the Catholics, and carried their excesses to such a point that the town would probably have been destroyed by fire had not the better classes of Protestants armed themselves and taken energetic steps to repress the tumult.

(377)   L

As the troops marched into Dublin Walter said to
Captain Davenant:

"Can I ride over to see how they are at home?
They will have heard of the battle. Mother and
grandmother must be terribly anxious."

"I shall be glad for you to go, Walter, for it would
greatly ease their minds at home; but we are to start
again almost immediately, and probably the whole
army will have marched off before you get back in
the morning. There is no saying what may occur
after we have gone. There may be a general attack
upon the Catholics. At anyrate it will be dangerous
in the extreme for a single officer in our uniform to
be riding through the town after we have left. Even
in the country villages there must be intense excitement, and anyone in the king's uniform might be fired
at in passing through any of the Protestant settle-
ments."

"Well, father, suppose I do not start until it gets
dark, then I can get home without attracting notice;
there I can put on a suit of my old clothes, and bring
my uniform out in my valise."

"Well, perhaps you might manage in that way,
Walter; and I should be very glad to relieve their
minds at home, and to know how they are going on.
If you like you can stop there for a day or two. I
don't suppose that William will be here with his troops
for a few days. He has learned that our army is not
to be despised, and he may hesitate to advance upon
Dublin until he receives certain news that we have
moved away, and that he will not have to fight another battle for the possession of the city. Should you

hear that William's troops have arrived in the town, you will of course make a detour so as to avoid it on your way to rejoin us; and now I will write a letter at once for you to take to your mother."

As soon as it was dark Walter mounted and started for Bray, where he arrived without molestation on the way. His arrival was an immense relief to the ladies, who had been suffering an agony of suspense since the news of the battle had reached them. King James's hurried arrival and panic flight to Waterford had caused the most alarming reports as to the battle to circulate throughout the country, and by many it was supposed that his army had been utterly destroyed. Walter's arrival, then, with the news that his father as well as himself had passed through the day unhurt, was an immense relief; and they were grateful to learn that, so far from having been routed, the Irish army had accomplished its object of fighting the battle and then falling back in perfect order and without molestation.

"Father says, mother, that he believes next time, when we shall be no longer hampered by the interference of the king, we shall be able to make even a better fight of it, especially if, as we all hope, the French officers will follow the king's example and take themselves off."

"How long are you going to stay, Walter?"

"I shall stay over to-morrow, mother, and start next morning early. I ought to be able to come up to the army before night, but if not I shall overtake them on the march next day."

"I wish I was older," Godfrey, who had been listening to the account of the battle, said. "It is so hard to have to stay at home here while you and father are having such fun!"

"You would not think it was fun if you were with us, Godfrey," Walter said. "I used to think it would be fun, but I don't think so now. Just while the fighting is going on one is so excited that one doesn't think of the danger, but when it is over it is awful to see the gaps in the ranks, and to know that so many of those who were riding with you have fallen, and that it may be your turn next time."

"Ah, it's all very well for you to talk, Walter, because you are going through it all, but you would think just the same as I do if you were in my place."

"That is true enough, Godfrey. Anyhow, I am glad you are not old enough. I don't mean that I should not like to have you with us, but then there would be nobody at home with mother. Now if anything happens to father and me, she has got you, and as you grow up you will be able to look after her and take care of her. It is bad enough for her having two of us in the war; it would be worse still if there were three."

As the next evening Walter heard that there was news that William's troops had not yet moved from the Boyne, he thought that it was safe to take the direct road through Dublin. He had laid aside his uniform on reaching home, and in the morning started in his civilian clothes, with the uniform in the valise strapped behind the saddle. He carried his sword as usual, for almost all gentlemen at that time rode armed, and this would therefore excite neither comment nor attention. He carried also a brace of pistols

in a belt underneath his coat. On arriving in Dublin
he found the greatest uproar and excitement prevailing. Mobs of men were marching through the
streets smashing the windows of Catholics and sacking the houses. Fortunately, he was warned before he
got into the thick of the tumult by meeting some
women running and crying loudly. He asked what
was the matter, and learned that their houses had
been sacked, and that any Catholic found in the
street was being beaten and ill-treated. As Walter
was anxious to avoid anything which might arrest his
journey westward he made his way out of the town as
soon as possible, and was heartily glad when he reached
the outskirts and gave rein to his horse. He passed
many groups of people as he rode. Some were Protestants making their way to Dublin to join in the
greeting to William and his army on their arrival.
Others were Catholics afraid to remain in their abodes
now that the army had retired west, and journeying to
the capital, where they believed that William would
prevent disorder and pillage. It needed no inquiry as
to the religion of the respective groups. The Protestants were for the most part men, and these came along
shouting and waving their weapons, wild with exultation over the triumph of their cause. The Catholics
were of all ages and both sexes; many of them had
carts, and were carrying with them their most valued
possessions. All wore an expression of grief and
anxiety.

As Walter rode into one village a fray was going on.
A party of Protestants, riding boisterously along, had
knocked down a woman with a child in her arms, and

had answered the angry remonstrance of the peasants with jeers and laughter. Stones had begun to fly; the Protestants had drawn their swords; the villagers had caught up hoes, spades, and other weapons, and a fierce fight was going on. The women with shrill cries encouraged the peasants, and aided them by hurling stones at the rioters. Walter saw that his interference would be of no avail, and, with a heavy heart at the bitter hatred which the two parties in Ireland exhibited for each other, he turned from the road, made a circuit round the village, and continued his way. After that he avoided all towns and villages, and slept at night in the cabin of a peasant lying some little distance from the road. The following day he again pressed on, and before evening overtook the retiring army.

On the arrival of King William with his army in Dublin, a proclamation was issued assuring all save those who resisted his authority of his protection, and threatening severity against those who disturbed the peace or committed outrage on personal property. Letters of protection were granted to all who applied for them; and hearing this, Jabez Whitefoot at once went into Dublin to apply for protection for the family of Captain Davenant. On hearing, however, that no persecution of Catholics would be allowed, and that the army was likely to march west at once in pursuit of the Irish, he thought it better to leave the matter alone, as his application would only draw the attention of the authorities to the fact of Captain Davenant and his son being engaged in the hostile army. He felt sure that the ladies need fear no molestation save from the soldiers or Northerners, as his own influence

with the Protestants of his neighbourhood would suffice
to prevent these from interfering with the household
at the castle.

The Irish army marched towards the Shannon, and
were concentrated part in the neighbourhood of Athlone and part at Limerick. William shortly prepared to follow them. He, too, divided his army into
two columns. The main body, under his own command, took the road to Limerick, while the other
division, consisting of five regiments of cavalry and
twelve of infantry, was despatched under the command
of General Douglas for the purpose of investing the
fortress of Athlone.

As the armies marched west their path was marked
by wholesale outrage and destruction. Although pro-
tections were granted to the peasants and inhabitants
of the towns and villages through which the armies
marched, they were entirely disregarded by the soldiers, who plundered, ill-used, and sometimes murdered
the defenceless people, carrying away without payment all provisions on which they could lay their
hands.

The king sometimes hanged those who were caught
in these acts of plunder and slaughter, but this had
but little effect. The Dutch soldiers alone maintained
their order and discipline. The foreign mercenaries,
composed for the most part of the sweepings of the
great cities, behaved with a brutality and cruelty
almost without example, and which was acknowledged
by all the historians of the time, Protestant as well
as Catholic. Indeed, the Protestant inhabitants suffered even more than the Catholics, for many of the

latter fled at the approach of the army, while the
Protestants, regarding them as friends and deliverers,
remained quietly at home, and suffered every insult
and outrage at the hands of this horde of savages, who
were perfectly indifferent as to the religion of those
they plundered.

Captain Davenant's troop was with the force which
had retired to Athlone, and there awaited the approach
of the column of General Douglas. The reports of
the conduct of the enemy that were brought in by the
flying peasants filled the Irish troops with indignation
and rage, and when, on arriving before the town,
General Douglas sent a messenger to demand its surrender, Colonel Grace, who commanded, only replied
by firing a pistol towards him.

Athlone stood on either side of the Shannon. The
town on the eastern bank of the river was called " the
English town," that on the western "the Irish"—a distinction existing in many of the Irish towns, where
the early English settlers found it expedient to live
apart from the Irish for mutual protection against
attack. Colonel Grace had retired to the west bank
of the river, which was strongly fortified, destroying
the English town and breaking down part of the
bridge across the river.

The garrison consisted of three regiments of foot
and nine troops of horse; and when Douglas erected
his batteries and opened fire on the castle, they replied briskly, and their guns got the better of those
in the batteries. A strong detachment of horse and
mounted grenadiers was sent by Douglas to Lanes-
borough, some miles north of the town, with orders to

pass the river at that point, but the post was held by Irish troops, who easily repulsed the attempt.

It was next proposed to pass the river at a ford a short distance from the bridge; but the troops had little heart for the enterprise, as the ford was covered by field works erected by the Irish. The assailants were already reduced to considerable straits. They had consumed all provisions found in the town, plundering without mercy the Protestant inhabitants, who had been well treated by the Irish troops, while the conduct of the army effectually deterred the country people from bringing in provisions.

The circulation of the report that General Sarsfield, with fifteen thousand men, was on the march to cut off the besiegers of Athlone, determined General Douglas to make a speedy retreat. In his fear of being cut off he abandoned all his heavy baggage, and quitting the high-road, made his way by unfrequented routes, which added to the hardships of the march. In its retreat the column was accompanied by the unhappy Protestant inhabitants, who feared to remain behind lest the Irish should retaliate upon them the sufferings which had been inflicted upon their countrymen.

In the meantime the main English army had done but little. In Dublin a commission had been appointed to examine into and forfeit the lands of all Catholics and adherents of King James, and having set this machine at work, the king proceeded with his army southward through Carlow, Kilkenny, and Waterford, all of which places surrendered, the garrisons being allowed to march out with their arms and baggage to join their main army on the Shannon.

At Waterford the king received such serious news as to the state of things in England that he determined to return home. On arriving at Dublin he was overwhelmed with petitions from the inhabitants as to the shameful conduct of the troops left in garrison there, especially those of Trelawney's, Schomberg's, and some other regiments of horse, who, the people complained, treated them, although Protestants, far worse than James's Catholic soldiers had done. Inquiry showed these complaints to be well founded, and finding it impossible to restore order and discipline among them, the king at once sent these regiments back to England. Then, receiving better news from home, he again started to rejoin his army, and marched towards Limerick, being joined on his way by the division under Douglas, which had driven along with them all the cattle and horses of the country through which they had passed.

Limerick was at that time the second city in Ireland. The country, for a long distance along the mouth of the Shannon, was much wooded, but in the immediate vicinity of the town it was surrounded by thick inclosures, houses, orchards, gardens, and plantations. The cultivated land was everywhere divided into small fields inclosed by hedges, and intersected by lanes. To the east of the town the Shannon divides itself, forming an island on which part of the city is situated.

This was called the English town, and was connected by a bridge, called Thomond Bridge, with the Clare side of the river on the north, and on the south by another bridge with the Irish town on the county of Limerick side. The Thomond Bridge was defended by

a strong fort and some field-works on the Clare side, and
on the city side by a drawbridge flanked by towers and
the city walls. The bridge was very long and narrow.
The position of the English town was indeed almost
impregnable. It was built upon a rock of considerable
extent, and the land outside the walls was low and
marshy, and could at any time be flooded. The Shannon
was broad and rapid. The Irish town on the Limerick
shore was not strong, being defended only by ordinary
walls. If this were captured, however, the English
town could still hold out.

The king made his approaches to the city slowly,
being obliged to level the numerous inclosures as he
moved on. These were occupied by the Irish infantry,
who, lining every hedge, kept up a galling fire, falling
back gradually as heavy bodies of troops were brought
up against them, until they reached the cover of the
guns of the city and fort; upon these opening fire, William's army halted and encamped before the Irish
town.

Here, as at the Boyne, the king had a narrow escape,
a cannon-ball from the walls striking the ground at
his foot as he was passing through a gap in a hedge.

The king had learned that great dissensions existed
between the Irish and French, and relied upon this as
much as upon the strength of his arms to obtain possession of the city.

His information was indeed correct. King James in
his flight had left no orders as to who should assume
the supreme command. The Duke of Berwick had considerable claims. Lauzun and the French officers declined
altogether to receive orders from Tyrconnell, and the

Irish officers equally objected to act under the command of a Frenchman. Consequently, during the whole siege, the main Irish army, which, by acting upon William's rear, could speedily have made his position untenable, remained inactive. M. Boileau, a French officer, was governor of the town, but Lauzun, having examined the fortifications, pronounced the place wholly incapable of defence, declaring that the walls could be knocked down with roasted apples, and so ordered the entire French division to march to Galway, and there await an opportunity for embarking for France, leaving the Irish to defend the city if they chose.

Lauzun, in fact, was a courtier, not a soldier. He desired to get back to Versailles at any hazard, and had so inspired his officers and men with his own sentiments that there was a general cry among them to be recalled to France. They had indeed no interest in the cause in which they fought. They looked with contempt at their half-armed and half-trained allies, and they grumbled continually at the hardships which they had to undergo. It was indeed an evil day for King James's cause when he exchanged Mountcashel's fine division for these useless allies, who throughout the war not only did no service, but were the cause of endless dissension and disaster.

As soon as King William had taken up his position in front of Limerick he sent a summons to Boileau to surrender. The latter consulted with Tyrconnell, Sarsfield, and some other officers, for even to the last moment it was a question whether the place should be defended.

At last, however, a decision was made. The reply was addressed to William's secretary, Sir Robert Roultwell, as Boileau could not acknowledge the prince as king, and was too polite to hurt his feelings by a denial of the royal title. He expressed great surprise at the summons he had received, and said that he hoped to merit the good opinion of the Prince of Orange better by a vigorous defence than by a shameful surrender of the fortress which had been committed to his charge by his master King James the Second.

The king's camp was now formed in regular order; he himself taking his place on its right, having near him the Horse Guards, and the Blue Dutch Guards, who were always his main reliance. To the left of these were the English and Dutch regiments, further on the French and Danes, while the Brandenburghers and other German regiments formed the extreme left of the line. To their great satisfaction the post assigned to the Danes was one of the rude circular redoubts called in Ireland Danish forts, and probably constructed by their own far-off ancestors.

CHAPTER IX.

PLEASANT QUARTERS.

AFTER the termination of the short siege of Athlone the troop of Captain Davenant were despatched to join the army near Limerick, and on their arrival there were ordered to take up their quarters at the house of a Protestant gentleman named Conyers, four miles from the town on the Limerick side of the river.

It was a mansion of considerable size, standing in large grounds, for its proprietor was one of the largest land-owners in the county of Limerick, his grandfather having been a colonel in one of Cromwell's regiments. Mr. Conyers himself had gone to Dublin, upon the passing of the act sequestrating the property of all the Protestants by James's parliament, to endeavour to obtain a remission of the decree so far as it concerned his house and adjoining grounds. As he had influential friends there, he had remained urging his petition until the battle of the Boyne and the entry of King William into Dublin entirely changed the position. But he then, owing to the disturbance of the country, and the fact that the Irish army had retired to Limerick, found it impossible to return home. He had, however, travelled with William's army, to which he was able to give much useful information regarding the defences and details of the country round the town.

As Captain Davenant's troop rode up to the house a lady with a girl of some sixteen years old appeared at the door. Both looked very pale, for they feared that the brutal conduct of which they had heard of William's army would be followed by reprisals on the part of the Irish. They were somewhat reassured, however, by Captain Davenant's manner as that officer dismounted, raised his hat, and said:

" Madam, I have received orders to quarter my troop in the house, but I am anxious, I can assure you, to cause as little inconvenience and annoyance as possible under the circumstances."

" We are only women here, sir," Mrs. Conyers said. " The house is at your disposal. I myself and my daughter will move to the gardener's cottage, and I trust that you will give orders to your men that we shall be free from molestation there."

" I could not think of disturbing you in that manner," Captain Davenant said. " I myself have a wife and mother alone at home, and will gladly treat you with the same courtesy which I trust they will receive. Allow me in the first place to introduce to you my lieutenant, Mr. O'Moore, and my cornet, who is also my son, Walter. I see that you have extensive stables and out-buildings. I am sure that my men, who are all good fellows, and many of them the sons of farmers, will make themselves very comfortable in these. I myself and my two officers will quarter ourselves in the gardener's cottage you speak of."

" You are good indeed, sir," Mrs. Conyers said grate-

fully; "but I could not think of allowing you to do
that, and shall indeed be pleased if you and your officers will take up your residence here as my guests."

"I thank you kindly; but that I could not do. My
men will be well content with the out-houses if they
see that we are content with the cottage; but they
might not be so if they saw that we took up our quarters in the house. Therefore, if you will allow me, I
will carry out my own plan; but I need not say that
we shall be very pleased to visit you in the house at
such times as may be agreeable to you."

After expressing their grateful thanks Mrs. Conyers
and her daughter withdrew into the house. Captain
Davenant then addressed a few words to his men.

"The house will not hold you all, lads, and there are
only ladies here, and I am sure you would not wish to
disturb and annoy them by crowding their house;
therefore, I have arranged that you shall take up your
quarters in the out-houses, and that we shall occupy
a little cottage on the grounds. I hope, lads, that, for
the honour of the country and the cause, all will behave as peacefully and quietly as if in our own homes.
It would be a poor excuse that because William's
soldiers are behaving like wild beasts we should forget
the respect due to lonely women."

A fortnight was spent here pleasantly for all. The
first alarm past, Mrs. Conyers felt safer than she had
done for months. Ever since the troubles had began
she had felt the loneliness of her position as a Protestant, and she would have long before made her way
with her daughter to Dublin, had it not been that she
thought that so long as she continued in the house it

might be respected by the Catholic peasantry, while, were she to desert it, it would probably be plundered, perhaps burned to the ground.

Still, the position was a very trying one, especially since the Jacobite army began to gather in force round Limerick.

She now felt that her troubles were comparatively over. The troops caused no annoyance, and she heard but little of them, while she found in Captain Davenant and his officers pleasant guests. The troops on their part were well satisfied. Mrs. Conyers gave instructions that they were to be supplied with all they needed, and their rations of bread and meat were supplemented with many little comforts and luxuries from the house.

While Mrs. Conyers entertained the two elder officers Walter naturally fell to the share of her daughter, and the two soon became great friends, wandering in the grounds, and sometimes riding together when Walter was not engaged with the troop. The news came daily of the movements of William's army, and when it approached Captain Davenant's troop went far out to observe its movements and obtain an accurate idea of its strength.

It was late in the evening when they returned, and Captain Davenant said at supper:

"This is our last meal with you, Mrs. Conyers. We leave at daybreak, and a few hours afterwards William's army will arrive before Limerick. We shall be the losers, but you will be the gainer if, as you suppose, Mr. Conyers is with them."

"I shall be really sorry for your going, Captain

(377)   M

Davenant. It seemed a terrible thing having a troop of hostile horse quartered upon one; but in reality it has been a pleasant operation rather than not, and I have felt safer than I have done for months. I do hope that when these troubles are over we shall renew our acquaintance, and that you will give my husband an opportunity of thanking you for the kindness with which you have treated us."

"The thanks should be on my side," Captain Davenant said. "You have made what promised to be an unpleasant duty a most pleasant one. Our stay here has been like a visit at a friend's, and I regret deeply that it has to come to an end, a regret which I am sure Lieutenant O'Moore and my son share."

"We do indeed," the lieutenant said.

Walter and Claire Conyers said nothing. They had talked it over early that morning before the troop started, and Walter had expressed his deep regret that their pleasant time was at an end; and although the girl had said little she was far less bright and happy than might have been expected, considering that upon the following day she should probably see her father.

Captain Davenant's troop rode off at daybreak, kept down the Shannon to Limerick, and, crossing the bridge, entered the city and received orders there to take up their quarters in a village some four miles up the river. Thus they were less than a mile distant from Mrs. Conyers' house, although separated from it by the Shannon, and from an eminence near the village, the roof and chimneys of the mansion could be seen rising above the trees by which it was surrounded.

During the day the sound of the firing before Lim-

erick could be plainly heard; but little attention was
paid to it, for it was certain that no attack could be
made in earnest upon the town until the battering artillery came up, and there was but little hope that the
cavalry would be called up for any active service at
present. After dinner Walter strolled out to the eminence and looked across towards the house where he
had spent so happy a time, and wondered whether Mr.
Conyers had by this time arrived, and whether in the
pleasure of his coming all thought of the late visitors
had been forgotten. Presently Larry sauntered up and
took a seat on a wall a few paces away. Larry was a
general favourite in the troop. He did not ride in its
ranks, but accompanied it in the capacity of special
servant of Walter, and as general attendant to the
three officers.

"We had a good time of it, yer honour," he said presently.

Walter turned round sharply, for he had not heard
him approach.

"We had, Larry," he said with a smile. "We shall
find it rougher work now."

"We shall, yer honour. I was thinking to myself,"
he said confidentially, "that if you might be wanting
to send a bit of a letter it's meself could easily make
a boat with some osiers and the skin of that bullock
we had given us for the rations of the troops to-
day."

"Send a letter, Larry!—who should I be sending a
letter to?"

"Sure yer honour knows better than me. I thought
maybe you would be liking to let the young lady know

how we're getting on now, and to find out whether her
father has come home, and how things are going. Yer
honour will excuse me, but it just seemed natural that
you should be wishing to send a line; and a sweeter
young lady never trod the sod."

Walter could not help laughing at the gleam of
quiet humour in Larry's face.

"I don't know, lad. You have pretty well guessed
my thoughts; but it can't be. The opposite bank will
be swarming with William's men—it would be a most
dangerous business. No, it's not to be thought of."

"Very well, yer honour, it's just as you like; but
you have only got to hand me a bit of paper, and give
me a wink of your eye, and I will do it. As to
William's sodgers, it's little I fear them; and if all one
hears of their doings be true, and I had a pretty young
creature a mile away from me, with those blackguards
round about her, it's anxious I should be for a line
from her hand;" and Larry got down from his seat, and
began to walk away towards the village.

Walter stood silent for a moment.

"Wait, Larry," he said.

Larry turned with a look of surprise upon his face.

"Come here," Walter said impatiently. "Of course I
am anxious—though I don't know how you could have
guessed it."

"Sure yer honour," Larry said with an innocent
look, "when a gentleman like yourself is for ever
walking and riding with a purty colleen, it don't need
much guessing to suppose that you would be worrying after her with such creatures as the Northerners
and the furreners in her neighbourhood."

"And you seriously think you could take a letter across to her, Larry?"

"Sure and I could, yer honour; the nights are dark, and I could get across the river widout a sowl being the wiser, and make my way to the stables and give it to one of the boys, who will put it in the hands of Bridget, Miss Claire's own maid, and I could go back next night for the answer."

" But if you can do it I can," Walter said.

" What would be the good, yer honour? It's only the outside of the house you would see, and not the young lady. Besides, there's a lot more risk in your doing it than there is with me. You are an officer of the king's, and if you were caught on that side of the river it's mighty little trial they'd give you before they run you up to the bough of a tree or put a bullet into you. With me it's different. I am just a country boy going to see my cousin Pat Ryan, who works in the stables at the house. Pat would give me a character, no fear."

" Well, I will think of it," Walter said.

"And I will get the boat ready at once, your honour. A few sticks and a green hide will make a boat fit for Dublin Bay, to say nothing of crossing a smooth bit of water like this."

After Larry had left him, Walter walked up and down for some time. He had certainly thought vaguely that he should like Claire Conyers to know that he was still within sight of her house; but the possibility of sending her word had not occurred to him until his follower suggested it. Larry's suggestion of possible danger to her made him uneasy. Even if her father was with the king, and had already returned home,

he would frequently be absent in the camp, and who
could tell but some band of plunderers might visit
the house in his absence! The Protestants had been
plundered and ill-used by William's men round Athlone,
and might be here. It would certainly be well to
know what was going on across the water.

After the kindness they had received, surely it
would be only civil to let the Conyers know where
they were posted. At anyrate Claire could not be
offended at his writing; besides, he might arrange
some plan by which he might get news from Larry's
friend, Pat Ryan. As he went down to the village
he heard roars of laughter, and passing a cottage
saw Larry with five or six of the troopers round him.
Larry was seated on the ground, making a framework
in the shape of a saucer four feet in diameter.

"And what are you wanting a boat for, Larry?"

"Sure, I am mighty fond of fishing," Larry said.
"Didn't you know that?"

"I know you are a fisherman at home, Larry; but if
it's fishing you want, there are two large boats hauled
up on the bank."

"They are too big," Larry said. "I should want
half a dozen men to launch them, and then you would
want to go with me, and the bare sight of you would
be enough to frighten away all the fish in the Shannon.
But I will have a look at the boats; the captain might
want a party to cross the river, and it's as well to see
that they are in good order, and have got the oars and
thole-pins handy. I will see to them myself, for there
are not half a dozen of ye know one end of the boat
from the other."

When Walter reached his quarters he at once sat down to write. After many attempts he finished one as follows:

"Dear Miss Conyers,—After the kindness shown to us by Mrs. Conyers and yourself, I feel sure that you will like to know where we are posted. We are at Ballygan, just across the Shannon opposite to your house, and I can see your roof from a spot fifty yards from the village. It seems a pleasure to me to be so close, even though we are as much divided as if there were the sea between us. I hope that Mr. Conyers has returned, and that you will have no trouble with William's troops, whose reputation for good behaviour is not of the best. I hope that now that you are among your friends you have not quite forgotten us, and that you will let me have a line to say how you are and how things are going on with you. My boy Larry is going to take this across, and will call to-morrow night for an answer, if you are good enough to send one."

"When will your boat be finished, Larry?" he asked his follower as the latter came in, just as it was getting dusk.

"She will be finished to-morrow. The framework is done, and I could make a shift, if your honour wished, just to fasten the skin on so that it would take me to-night."

"If you could, I would rather, Larry."

"All right, your honour!" Larry said with a slight smile; "two hours' work will do it."

"I know where you are making it, Larry, and will come round when I go to inspect sentries, at eleven o'clock. We shall post ten men a quarter of a mile apart on the bank, and I will give orders for them to look out for you. The word will be 'Wicklow;' so when you come across they will shout to you, 'Who comes there?' You say, 'Wicklow;' and it will be all right."

At the hour he had named Walter went round for Larry, who was working by the light of a torch stuck in the ground.

"I have just finished it, yer honour; but I was obliged to stop till the boys got quiet; they were so mighty inquisitive as to what I was in such a hurry about that I had to leave it alone for a while."

"Look here, Larry, here is the letter, but that's not the principal reason why I am sending you across. You will give it to Pat Ryan, as you suggested, to pass on through Bridget to Miss Conyers; but I want you to arrange with him that he shall, to-morrow, get some dry sticks put together on the bank opposite, with some straw, so that he can make a blaze in a minute. Then do you arrange with him that if any parties of William's troops come to the house in the absence of Mr. Conyers, and there should seem likely to be trouble, he is to run as hard as he can down to the river; if it is day, he is to wave a white cloth on a stick; if it is night, he is to light the fire. Tell him to arrange with Bridget to run at once to him and tell him if there is trouble in the house, for as he is in the stables he may not know what is going on inside. I have been looking at those boats, they will carry fifteen men each at a pinch; and if the signal is made, we shall not be long in getting across. Pat would only have about half a mile to run. We will get the boats down close to the water's edge, and it won't take us many minutes to get across. Anyhow, in twenty minutes from the time he starts we might be there."

"That will be a moighty good plan, yer honour. Now, if you will go down to the water with me I will be off at once. I sha'n't be away half an hour; and I can slip up into the loft where Pat sleeps, and not a sowl be the wiser if there was a regiment of William's troops about the house."

"All right, Larry! I shall wait here for you till you get back."

Larry raised the light craft and put it on his head. He had made a couple of light paddles by nailing two pieces of wood on to mop-sticks.

Walter accompanied him to the water's edge, and told the sentry there that Larry was crossing the river on business, and would return in half an hour's time, and that he was not to challenge loudly when he saw him returning.

The night was dark, and Walter soon lost sight of the little boat. Then he waited anxiously; he had, however, but little fear that the enemy would have posted sentries so far down the river, especially as he would only just have pitched his camp opposite Limerick.

It was three-quarters of an hour before he heard a faint splash in the water. The sentry heard it too.

"Shall I challenge, sir?"

"No. Wait for a minute, we shall soon see whether it is Larry. Should there be anyone on the opposite bank he might hear the challenge, and they would keep a sharp look-out in future."

The sound came nearer and nearer.

"Who goes there?" Walter said in a quiet voice.

"'Wicklow!' and it's mighty glad I am to hear your voice, for it's so dark I began to think I had lost myself entirely."

"Is all well, Larry?" Walter asked as the light boat touched the bank.

"All is well, your honour," Larry said, stepping ashore and lifting the light boat on to his head.

"You had better stow it away close here, Larry, till the morning; it's so dark that you will be sure to pitch over something if you go further. Now, tell me all about it, he went on," as Larry stowed away the boat among some bushes.

"There is little enough to tell, yer honour. I just rowed across and landed, and made straight for the house. Everything was quiet and still. I went round to the stables and up into the loft where Pat sleeps. 'Are you there, Pat Ryan,' says I?

"'Who is it calls Pat Ryan?' says he.

"'It's myself, Larry, Mr. Davenant's boy.'

"'Why, I thought you had gone,' says he. 'Are you sure it's yourself?' says he.

"'And who else should it be, Pat Ryan? Don't yer know my voice?'"

"By this time I had got into the corner where he slept, and touched him."

"'I am glad to feel you, Larry,' says he, 'for I wasn't sure that you hadn't fallen in with the troopers, and it wasn't your ghost that come to visit me.'

"'Whist,' says I, 'I have no time to waste upon ye. The master and the troops are stationed just across the river at Ballygan. Mr. Davenant has given me a letter for Miss Conyers, telling her all about it. I don't exactly know what he said, and maybe she would like it given privately, so do you hand it to Bridget in the morning, and ask her to give it to her mistress, and to hand over to you any answer there may be. I will come across for it to-morrow night. But that's not all, Pat. You know the devil's work that William's men have been carrying on on the march.'

"'Av course, everyone has heard the tales of the villains' doings, Larry.'

"'Well, the young master is mighty anxious about it, as you may guess. Has Mr. Conyers come?'

"'Yes. He rode in at four this afternoon.'

"'Well, Mr. Davenant says you will all be safe as long as he's here, but maybe that at some time when he's away you may have a troop of these villains of the world ride in here, and little they care whether it's Protestants or Catholics that they plunder; so if they come here and begin their devilries, you run for your life down to the river, opposite Ballygan, with a white cloth or a shirt, if it's daytime, and wave it. You are to have a pile of sticks and straw ready, and, if it's night, ye will just set it in a blaze, and there will be help over before many minutes. You stop there till they come, to tell them how strong the enemy are.

"'The master says you are to tell Bridget about it, so that if they misbehave themselves inside the house she can slip out and let you know. You understand that?'

"'I do,' says he; 'and it's a comfort to me, for it's fretting I have been over what might happen, if a troop of those murderin' villains were to come here, and not a sowl save me and the other boys to take the part of the mistress and Miss Claire.'

"'Well, you know now, Pat, what's to be done, and see you do it; and now I must go, for the master is waiting for me. I will be with you to-morrow night for the answer.'

"And so I came back, and I lost ten minutes looking about for the boat, for it was so mighty dark that I could not see a fut. I kicked against it and very near fell over it. It's well I didn't, for I should have knocked it into smithereens entirely!"

"Capital, Larry! you couldn't have done better. Now I shall feel comfortable."

After breakfast Walter told his father of the mission on which he had sent Larry, and the arrangement he had made with Pat Ryan.

"You ought to have told me at first, Walter. I do not blame you, but you should not do things on your own responsibility."

"But so far, father, it has not been a regimental affair. I simply sent my own boy with a note to Miss Conyers just to say where we were; but as it may be an affair in which some of the troop may have to act, I have told you about it, so that you can make what arrangements you like."

"It's rather a fine distinction, Walter," his father said smiling. "It seems to me that you have engaged us to send a detachment across the river in case of trouble at Mrs. Conyers'. However, I heartily agree with you that our kind friends should be protected from injury and insult."

"How many will the boats hold?"

"Thirteen or fourteen men each."

"Very well, then. I authorize you at any time, if I am away with a portion of the troop, to take twenty-five men across if the signal is made. If I am here I shall, of course, go over myself. You can take any measures of preparation you may think necessary."

Walter availed himself of the permission, and at once gave orders to the sentry posted on the river in front of the village that if a white flag was waved by day or a fire lit by night on the opposite bank, he was to shout loudly and fire his pistol, and that these orders were to be passed on to the sentry who succeeded him at the post. Then he picked out twenty-five men and told them that at any time in the night or day, if they heard a shot fired by the sentry they were to seize their arms, rush down to the boats, launch them and take their places, and wait for orders. He told them to sleep without removing any of their clothes, so as to be ready for instant action.

The next night Larry again crossed and brought back a little note from Claire Conyers, thanking Walter for letting her know they were so close, telling him of her father's return, and saying that there was no fear of her mother or herself forgetting their late visitors. It was a prettily-written little note, and Walter was delighted at receiving it.

"Well, my boy," Captain Davenant said with a little smile when Walter told him next morning that he had heard from Miss Conyers, "as you seem specially in-

terested in this affair, I will let you have the honour
and glory of being the first to come to the rescue of
Miss Conyers and her mother if they should need it;
and therefore, whether I am here or not, I give you
permission to cross at once in the two boats if you get
the signal. But on reaching the other side you are to
send the two boats back at once, with two men in
each, and I will bring the rest of the troop across as
fast as possible. There is no saying what force you
may find there. I shall leave it to your discretion to
attack at once or to wait until I come up with reinforcements. You will, of course, be guided partly by
the strength of the enemy, partly by the urgency for
instant interference for the protection of the ladies."

Four days passed quietly; there was but little for the
cavalry to do. Small parties were posted at various
spots for some miles down the river to give notice
should the enemy appear on the opposite bank and show
any intention of making a crossing; and beyond furnishing these guards the troop had little to do. Walter
spent much of his time watching the opposite bank.
He hardly knew whether he wished the signal to be
displayed or not—he certainly desired no trouble to
befall the ladies; but, on the other hand, the thought
of rushing to their rescue was undoubtedly a pleasant
one. Larry spent much of his time at the water's-
edge fishing—a pursuit in which many of the troopers
joined; and they were able to augment the daily
rations by a good supply of salmon.

On the fifth day the officers had just finished supper
when the sound of a pistol-shot was heard. Walter
leaped from his seat, snatched up his sword and pistols,

and ran down to the river. The men were already clustering round the boats. A minute later these were in the water, and the men jumped on board. They too were eager for the work, for Larry had whispered among them that if the signal was made it would signify that a band of the enemy's marauders were at Mrs. Conyers'; and all had been so kindly treated there that they were eager to repay the treatment they had received. Besides, there was not a man in the Irish army whose heart had not been fired at the recitals of the brutality of the enemy, and filled with deep longings for vengeance upon the perpetrators of the deeds.

Walter counted the men as they rowed across, and was pleased to find that not one of them was missing. He ordered the two men who were at the oars in each boat to return, the instant the rest had landed, to fetch another detachment across. As they reached the land the men sprang out. Pat Ryan was standing at the landing-place.

" Well, Pat, what is it ?"

" A troop of Hessian horse, your honour. Half an hour ago they rode up to the doors. Mrs. Conyers came out to meet them, and told them that she was a loyal Protestant and wife of a gentleman high in the king's councils, who was in the camp. The blackguards only laughed. The officers, with some of the men, dismounted and pushed their way past her into the house, and the rest of the troop tied their horses up to the trees on the lawn, and shouted to me and some of the other boys who were looking on to bring forage. I suppose we weren't quick enough for them, for one of them drew his pistol and fired at me. Fortunately he only hit the truss of straw I was carrying. Then I went round to the back-door, where I had agreed that Bridget was to come to me if things were going wrong in the house. A few minutes afterwards she came out wid a white face and said: 'For the sake of the Holy Virgin run for your life, Pat, and warn the soldiers!' So I slipped away and ran my hardest."

All this was told as the party were running at full speed towards the house.

"How strong was the troop?" Walter asked.

"About eighty men, yer honour."

"We must trust to a surprise," Walter said. "We can get round to the back of the house without being seen. If we burst in there suddenly we can clear the house and hold it till my father comes up with the whole troop."

Five minutes after they had left the boat the party approached the house. Walter halted his men for a moment in the shrubbery behind it.

"Steady, lads, and take breath. You will follow me into the house and keep together. Give no quarter to the scoundrels."

Scarcely had he spoken than a piercing scream, accompanied by a pistol-shot, was heard within.

"Come on, lads!" Walter exclaimed as he rushed at full speed at the door, the men following close at his heels.

The door was open. In the passage lay one of the maid-servants shot through the head by one of the Hessian troopers, who still held the pistol in his hand. Walter's pistol cracked before the man had time to draw his sword, and he fell dead. Then he rushed on

THE HESSIAN TROOPERS DRIVEN FORTH.

into the hall, in which were a score of troopers gathered round a barrel of wine which had just been broached. In an instant the Irish were upon them. Many were cut down or shot before they had time to stand on the defensive. The rest were slain after a short and desperate fight.

"Bar the front door!" Walter shouted. "Sergeant Mullins, take six men and hold it against those outside. The rest follow me."

Short as the fight had been, it had given time to the rest of the Hessians scattered about the house in the act of plundering to gather on the stair, headed by their officers. Without a moment's hesitation Walter dashed at them; in point of numbers the party were well matched; but the fury of the Irishmen more than counterbalanced the advantage of position on the part of the Hessians.

For five minutes a desperate fight raged; those in front grappled each other and fought with clubbed pistols and shortened swords; those behind struck a blow as they could with sword or musket. But the Hessians, ignorant of the strength of the force which had thus suddenly attacked them, thought more of securing their safety than of defending the stairs, so several of those behind slipped away and jumped from the windows to the ground. Their desertion disheartened those in front, and with a shout Walter and his troopers bore back the Hessians on to the landing and the latter then broke and fled.

Most of them were overtaken and cut down at once; two or three only gained the windows and leaped out. The instant resistance had ceased Walter rushed into

N

the drawing-room, bidding the men run down and hold the lower windows. Mrs. Conyers lay in a dead faint on the sofa. Claire, with a face as pale as death, was standing beside her.

"Walter!" she gasped out; "then we are safe!"

She tottered and would have fallen had not Walter rushed forward in time to catch her, and place her in a chair:

"Don't faint, my dear Claire," he said urgently. "There is your mother to be looked after, and I must run down stairs, for they are attacking the house."

"I won't faint," Claire said, laughing and crying in a manner which frightened Walter more than her fainting would have done. "I shall be better directly, but it seems almost like a miracle. Oh, those dreadful men!"

"They have all gone now, Claire. We hold the house and have cleared them out. Pray, calm yourself and attend to your mother. I must go. Don't be frightened at the firing; my father will be here in a few minutes with aid."

"Oh! I am not frightened now," Claire said; "and oh! Walter, you are bleeding dreadfully."

"Never mind that now," Walter said; "I will see to it when it is all over."

Then, leaving her to look after Mrs. Conyers, he ran down stairs. His right arm was disabled, he having received a sweeping blow on the shoulder from one of the Hessians as he won his way on to the landing; but he had no time to think of this now, for his men were hardly pressed. For a moment a panic had reigned among the troopers outside at the outburst of firing, and at the sight of their comrades leaping panic-stricken from the windows; but inquiry soon showed them that they were still greatly superior in numbers to the party who had obtained possession of the hall; and, furious at the loss of all their officers and of many of their comrades, they attacked on all sides and tried to force their way in at the doors and lower windows in spite of the vigorous resistance from within. Walter hurried from point to point, cheering on his men by assurance that help was at hand, and seeing that no point had been left undefended.

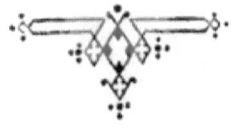

CHAPTER X.

A CAVALRY RAID.

STAUNCHLY as Walter's troopers maintained the defence they were sorely pressed, for the enemy still outnumbered them by three to one. Several times the Hessians almost forced their way in at one or other of the windows, but each time Walter, who kept four men with him as a reserve, rushed to the assistance of the defenders of the windows and drove them back; but this could not last. The defenders were hard pressed at several points, and Walter, feeling sure that his father would be up in a very few minutes, called the men off from their posts and stationed them on the staircase.

With shouts of triumph the Hessians burst in. The hall was filled with a crowd of furious soldiers, who hurled themselves like a wave at the defenders of the staircase. All the pistols had long since been emptied, and they fought sword to sword. Walter had detached five of his little party to hold the top of the other staircase should the assailants try to force a passage there; and he had but ten men now, and several of these severely wounded, to hold the staircase.

Great as the advantage that the position gave the defenders they were forced up step by step, and Walter

began to fear that he would be driven to the landing
before succour came, when a crowd of figures suddenly
burst in at the hall door, and above the cracking
of pistols, which at once arose, he heard his father's
voice:

"Down with the murdering dogs! No quarter!"

Taken wholly by surprise, ignorant of the force by
which they were attacked, and taken between two
bodies of enemies, the Hessians turned to fly. Walter
and his men at once pressed down upon them, while
the new-comers fell upon them with fury.

There was but little resistance, for the Hessians
thought only of flight. Some burst through their assailants and gained the door; more fled down the passages
and escaped by the windows through which they had
entered; but more than thirty of them fell in the hall.
The instant resistance was over Captain Davenant ran
out with his men to secure the horses. A few of the
Hessians who had escaped from the front door had
jumped on the backs of the nearest animals and ridden
off, the rest had fled on foot, and the exulting troopers
counted seventy-two horses remaining in their hands.
Captain Davenant at once returned to the house.

"Where are you, Walter?" he shouted; but there
was no answer. Getting more light Captain Davenant
searched hastily among the numerous bodies scattered
in the hall and soon came upon Walter, who was lying
insensible just at the foot of the stairs. The excitement had supported him so long as the defence had to
be continued; but as soon as succour appeared and the
assailants retreated he had stumbled forward with his
men and had fallen insensible from loss of blood at the

foot of the stairs. Captain Davenant hastily examined
him.

"Thank God," he said to Larry, who had smuggled
himself over with the second detachment, "he has no
other wound but this on the shoulder, and has only
fainted from loss of blood! Run up stairs and snatch
a sheet from one of the beds. We will soon make
some bandages."

Larry did as he was ordered. Slips were torn off
the sheets, and after cutting Walter's coat and shirt
from his shoulder Captain Davenant bound and ban-
daged up the wound. In the meantime Larry had got
some spirits from the buffet in the dining-room, and a
spoonful or two were poured down Walter's throat,
and in a few minutes he opened his eyes. For a
moment he looked confused, then he smiled at his
father.

"You were just in time," he said. "We couldn't
have held out much longer."

"Yes, we were just in time, thank God!" his father
said; "but where are the ladies?"

"In the drawing-room. Mrs. Conyers has fainted."

Captain Davenant ran up stairs. Claire had succeeded in restoring her mother, who had just sat up
when Captain Davenant entered.

"My daughter tells me that you have rescued us, you
and your son," she said faintly. "How can I thank
you enough?"

"Never mind that now, my dear lady," Captain
Davenant said hastily. "Just at present we have no
time to lose. The fellows who have escaped will carry
the news to William's camp, and in half an hour we

shall have a regiment of cavalry here. I must retreat
at once, and carry my wounded with me. What will
you do? Will you stay here, or will you and your
daughter come with us?"

"Oh I will go with you, please. If I was sure my
husband would come with them I would not fear; but
he may not hear of it, and there is no saying what they
might do."

"How is Walter, Captain Davenant?" Claire—who
had been waiting impatiently for her mother to finish
—burst in. "He was wounded, and there was such
terrible fighting afterwards, and he has not come back
with you."

"He fainted from loss of blood," Captain Davenant
said; "but I do not think his wounds are serious. Mrs.
Conyers, I can only give you five minutes. Take with
you any jewels or valuables you prize most. If they
should arrive without your husband they will be sure
to sack and burn the house."

Captain Davenant now hurried down stairs. The
wounded had already been collected. There were but
four so seriously wounded as to be unable to walk;
six had been killed. The wounded, including Walter,
lay on blankets. Men took each a corner and at once
started to the spot where the boats had been left.
Captain Davenant told four men to wait at the foot
of the stairs while he went up to the drawing-room.
Mrs. Conyers and her daughter were already prepared.
Each had thrown a shawl over her head and had in
their hands the dressing-cases, containing Mrs. Conyers's jewellery.

"Now, madam," Captain Davenant said, "if you will

point out your plate chest I have four men below in readiness to carry it to the boat. It is no use leaving that to be divided between the mauraders."

Mrs. Conyers pointed out two chests, in one of which deeds and other valuable documents were kept, and in the other the plate, of which Mrs. Conyers had a considerable quantity. Two men seized each of them.

"Now, Mrs. Conyers, please accompany them as quick as you can to the river. We will follow and cover the retreat. I think we have a few minutes yet before cavalry can arrive from the camp."

When Captain Davenant and the rear-guard reached the bank they found that the boats had already returned after taking over the wounded and a portion of the detachment. The rest, with the two ladies and the female servants, at once took their places, and were taken across before any sound betokened the arrival of the enemy at the Hall.

"I sincerely hope, Mrs. Conyers," Captain Davenant said as they landed, "that Mr. Conyers may accompany the first body of troops who arrive, for if not I fear they will set fire to the Hall. They must have lost considerably over fifty men, and in their rage at finding no one on whom to wreak their vengeance they will make no inquiry as to whom the house belongs; indeed, they will find no one there to ask. The servants of the house had already fled, and I sent my boy's servant Larry round to the stables to tell the men there to ride away with the horses. They will accompany fifteen of my men, who mounted as many of the horses we captured, and are driving the rest to a ford some miles away. They are a valuable capture, and altogether, as far as we are concerned, we have made a good night's work of it."

"But I do not understand now," Mrs. Conyers said, "how it was that you came across just in time. How did you know that we were in such trouble, because I am sure you would not have come across to attack the soldiers in our house without some special reason?"

"No, indeed, madam, I certainly should not have made your house a battle-field. The fact is, our fortunate arrival is due entirely to my son. He made all the arrangements without my knowing anything about it. He sent over his boy to one of your lads in the stable, and arranged that if there should be any trouble in the house in the absence of Mr. Conyers he should run down and signal across the river. Your daughter's maid was to let the boy know what was going on within. It was not till he had the whole business in train that Walter told me anything about it. As it was his plan and not mine, and I could see he was extremely anxious about it, I left the matter in his hands, and authorized him to lead the first party across whenever the signal was made, night or day. Our boats would only carry twenty-five men, and four of these had to return with them. As Walter would have but a quarter of our force with him I ordered him, in case the signal was made and he crossed, not to attack until I joined him unless the necessity seemed very urgent. I suppose he considered it was so, for he would hardly have fallen upon some eighty or ninety troopers unless he had deemed it most urgent."

"Thank God he did so!" Mrs. Conyers said, "for we owe him our lives and more. I cannot tell you all now.

It is too horrible to think of. But I shall never forget
the thankfulness and joy I felt when suddenly I heard
the noise of shouts and firing, and the men who were
trying to tear my child from my arms suddenly desist
and rushing out of the room left us alone. I fainted
then, and knew nothing more till I heard, in a confused way, the sound of shouting and conflict, and
Claire was bending over me, telling me that your son
was holding the stairs against the Germans, and that
he was expecting help to arrive every moment. Where
is he? I long to see him and give him my thanks
and blessing."

"He is in that cottage yonder, which is at present
our quarters," Captain Davenant said. "I told them
to send off a trooper to Limerick for a doctor as soon
as they got across."

"But you assured me his wound was not dangerous,"
Mrs. Conyers said anxiously.

"No, I am sure it is not. It is a severe wound, but
not likely to have serious consequences. But I fear
that some of the men are in a far worse condition."

"I shall install myself as head nurse," Mrs. Conyers
said decidedly. "We owe so much to you all, that that
is the least I can do."

"Very well, Mrs. Conyers. Then I appoint you head
of the hospital. I will have the four seriously wounded
men moved into the cottage next to mine. You will
be able to obtain plenty of assistance among the women
of the village. O'Moore and I will move into other
quarters and leave the cottage to you and your
daughter. Your servants can have the cottage on
the other side."

They had now reached the door.

"I will just go in and see him first," Captain Davenant said.

Larry was sitting by Walter's couch.

"Well, Walter, how are you feeling?"

"Oh, I am all right now," Walter said, "since Larry brought me word that the boats have brought every one across safely. I was anxious before, you know."

"How does your shoulder feel?"

"It throbs a bit, father; but that is no odds."

"Mrs. Conyers is coming in to see you. She is going to establish herself here, and O'Moore and I are moving out. She is going for the present to be head nurse."

"That will be nice," Walter said; "but I sha'n't want much nursing."

"I don't know, Walter. A downright cut with a heavy cavalry sword is not a light matter, even when it falls on the shoulder instead of the head. But you had better not talk much now, but when you have seen Mrs. Conyers try and get off to sleep. Larry, do you see to moving our things out at once."

So saying, Captain Davenant left the room, and a minute later Mrs. Conyers came in. She took the left hand that Walter held out to her.

"God bless you, my boy!" she said softly. "I shall never forget what Claire and I owe to you. All my life I shall be your grateful debtor, and some day I hope that my husband will be able to thank you for what you did for us. And now," she went on in a lighter tone, "I am going to be your nurse, and my first order is that you lie quite quiet and try to get to

sleep. I will make you some barley-water and put it
by your bedside. That is all I can do for you till the
surgeon comes to examine your wound. Claire wanted
to come in to thank you herself, but the child has gone
through enough for one night, so I have sent her straight
to bed. I do not want her on my hands too."

A few minutes later Larry, having established the
two officers in another cottage, returned and took his
place by Walter's bedside, while Mrs. Conyers went
out to see to the comfort of the other wounded. Half
an hour later a surgeon arrived from Limerick. Two
of the cases were pronounced at once to be hopeless,
the other two he thought might recover. Walter's
wound he said was a severe one, but in no way
dangerous. The sword had probably glanced off something as it descended, so that the edge had not fallen
straight on the shoulder-bone. It had, however, nearly
taken off the arm. Had it fallen truly it would probably have been fatal.

After he had attended to the more serious cases he
dressed the wounds of the other men, several of which
were quite as severe as that of Walter, although they
had not incapacitated the men from making their way
down to the boats.

Captain Davenant had kept a watch towards the
Hall. And as, in an hour after they had crossed, no
sheet of flame was seen arising thence, he was able to
tell Mrs. Conyers that he thought that it was safe, and
that either Mr. Conyers himself must have accompanied
the troops who would by this time have unquestionably
arrived there, or that some officer, aware that the
owner of the house was a friend, and with sufficient

authority over the men to prevent its destruction, must be in command.

In the morning he had a long talk with her. He suggested that she and her daughter should accompany him into Limerick, and be sent with a flag of truce across the bridge to join her husband in William's camp. This, however, she positively declined to accede to.

"In the first place," she said, "I consider that it is my duty to nurse the men who suffered for our sake. In the next place, after what we went through last night I refuse absolutely to place myself and my daughter in the hands of the ruffians who disgrace the cause of William. Hitherto as a Protestant I have been an adherent of that cause, as has my husband; henceforth I am an Irishwoman, and as such abhor a cause which can employ such instruments and inflict such atrocities upon Ireland. I will write a letter to my husband telling him exactly what has happened, and how we have been preserved, and say that nothing will induce me to trust myself and Claire among William's troops, but that I shall remain on this side of the Shannon. If, as I trust will not be the case, the English force their way across the river, I shall make for Galway, and thence take ship to England, where we can join him. I intend to remain here as long as I can be useful as a nurse, and I shall then retire with Claire to Galway, where I have some relations, with whom I can stay until matters are decided."

Mrs. Conyers at once wrote the letter, which Captain Davenant carried himself into Limerick, as he

was going in to report the occurrences of the preceding
night. The governor immediately sent the letter across
with a flag of truce. General Sarsfield, who was in
command of the cavalry, expressed himself highly
pleased with the result of the raid across the Shannon,
and appointed three officers to raise another troop of
horse with the captured animals, which had arrived
before morning at Ballygan, and to place themselves
under Captain Davenant's command.

"Your son must be a lad after your own heart," he
said to Captain Davenant. "It was indeed a most gallant action thus with twenty-five dismounted men
only to attack a strong troop of Hessians. I hope that
as soon as he is well enough to mount a horse again
you will introduce him to me. Keep your troop in
readiness for a move, for I mean to beat them up before long."

"Can't I see Walter to-day, mamma?" Claire asked,
after Captain Davenant had ridden off. "It seems so
unkind my being in the house with him and not going
in to tell him how sorry I am that he was wounded."

"Not to-day, Claire. He is very flushed and feverish
this morning, and I must not have him excited at all."

"But I would not excite him, mother. I would only
go in and speak to him quietly."

"Even that would excite him, my dear. I will tell
him that you want to come in and see him; but that I
think you had better not do so for a day or two."

But even without the excitement of Claire's presence
Walter became more feverish, and by evening was
talking wildly. The excitement and anxiety he had
gone through were as much responsible for this as the

wound, and by midnight he knew no one. The surgeon, who came over in the evening, ordered cloths constantly soaked with fresh water to be placed round his head, and that he should be given, whenever he desired it, barley-water sharpened by apples boiled in it.

Mrs. Conyers and Larry sat one on each side of his couch, and once or twice when he was lying quiet Claire was allowed to steal in and look at him; but at other times Mrs. Conyers kept her out of the room, for in his feverish talk Walter was constantly mentioning her name, and telling her he would come to her. Mrs. Conyers was troubled and perplexed in her mind. Regarding Claire as a child and Walter as a lad of eighteen, the thought that any serious consequence would arise from their intercourse at the Hall had not occurred to her; but now she could not doubt that on Walter's part at least a serious attachment for her daughter had sprung up, and Claire's face and manner told her a similar story. She was but sixteen, but having been her mother's companion and friend she was older than many girls of the same age. Mrs. Conyers would rather that it had not been so, for she foresaw much sorrow for Claire. She had thought that her daughter, as a wealthy heiress, would some day make a good match, and Walter, whose fortune in any case would be but a small one—for she knew that his father's estates had passed from the family—was a soldier on the side she believed would be the losing one. Still she felt that he had earned a right to Claire, and resolved that come what would, if it turned out that Claire's affections were really given to the lad, she

should have her support and championship with her
father.

For two days the fever continued, and then the care
of his watchers prevailed, and Walter sank into a quiet
sleep from which he awoke sensible and refreshed.   An
answer had been received from Mr. Conyers on the
same afternoon that his wife's letter was sent to
him.   He had been in council with the king, when an
officer came in with the news that some Hessians had
ridden in saying that the troop to which they belonged
had ridden out to a large house two miles beyond the
spot at which the regiment was quartered, and had there
been attacked by a body of Irish troops, who had killed
all their officers and three-quarters of the troop.

"Knowing where the regiment was quartered, it at
once struck me that the house might be our own, and
on the trooper being brought in I found that it was so,
and obtained permission from the king to accompany
the regiment of Danish horse who were at once sent
out.   The king gave stringent orders to the officer in
command that the house was to be respected, and a
guard was to be placed there to protect it from marauders.   You can imagine my anxiety as I rode out, and
how it was increased when I found the place absolutely
deserted.   From the trooper whom we took with us we
learned something of what had taken place.   He had
been in the garden, but the officers and nearly half the
troopers were in the house.   Suddenly the sounds of a
conflict were heard within.   Then many of his comrades jumped from the windows, and as they reported
the number of the assailants was not large, an attack
was made upon the house.   After considerable loss an

entrance was effected, and they were gradually over-coming the defenders when they were attacked in the rear by a fresh body of the enemy, and only a few of them managed to make their escape.

"The appearance of the house fully corroborated his story. The inside was piled with dead, who were found scattered all over the house. Among them were a few men in the uniform of one of the Irish cavalry regiments. This was some alleviation to my terrible anxiety. Had the assailants been a body of peasants I should have feared that they had wreaked on you and Claire the hatred which they feel, I own not unjustly, towards the king's foreign troops. As they were regular soldiers I had hopes that they had only carried you off as hostages.

"One of the female servants was found below killed. No pursuit was possible, as we could find no one of whom to inquire by which way the enemy retreated; but in the morning we found that the horses of the Hessians had been ridden to a spot some miles up the river, where they had swam or forded the stream. There was a strong party of the enemy on the opposite side. My anxiety was terrible till I received your letter, and you may imagine how great a shock it was to me to learn the frightful scene through which you had passed, and how my sentiments changed towards those whom I had regarded as your abductors, but whom I now learn were your saviours.

"I have read that portion of your letter to the king, who is furious at the evil conduct of his troops. He has all along done everything in his power to repress it; but when not under his immediate eye, it seems as

if all discipline was lost, and the troops behaved rather
as a horde of savages than as soldiers. After what had
happened I cannot blame you for the opinion you express in your letter, or for your determination not to
trust yourself and Claire in this camp, although I am
sure that the king would send a detachment of his own
Dutch guards with you to Dublin. I trust that you
will, as soon as the work you have undertaken is
over, go to our cousins at Galway and take ship without delay to England, where I will at once join you
when I hear of your arrival there.

"Please express to Captain Davenant and his son
the extreme obligation under which I feel towards
them, and assure them that I look forward to the time
when this unfortunate struggle shall be at an end,
and I can meet them and thank them personally. It
will be a satisfaction to you to be able to inform them
that I have this morning obtained from the king a
peremptory order on the commission in Dublin to stay
all proceedings in the matter of Captain Davenant's
estate near Bray, which was on the list of confiscated
properties. I am forwarding this by one of the royal
messengers, who leaves with despatches to-day, and when
I visit Dublin I shall do myself the pleasure of calling
on Mrs. Davenant, and of setting her mind at ease."

While Walter had been at his worst his father had
been away for only a few hours. After his interview
with Sarsfield in Limerick a messenger arrived from
that general ordering Captain Davenant to bring his
troop into the city at once. It was four in the afternoon when he arrived, and he at once went to General
Sarsfield's quarters.

"Let the men dismount, Captain Davenant, and let them and the horses feed. We have a long ride before us to-night. I have just heard that William's siege artillery is coming up under a weak escort, and I mean to get round in the Dutchman's rear and destroy it. He shall find that Limerick is not to be taken as easily as he expects. He has had a disagreeable sample of our quality to-day. A deserter brought in news of the exact position of his tent, and our artillery have been giving him such a peppering that from the church-tower we see that he has been obliged to move his camp."

As soon as it was night four hundred cavalry were in the saddle. Sarsfield placed himself at their head, and rode twelve miles up the Shannon to Killaloe. Crossing the river there he made a wide sweep with his cavalry until he was in the heart of the Tipperary mountains in rear of William's camp.

Quietly as the expedition had been carried out it was impossible that so large a body of horse should ride through the country unperceived, and a gentleman of county Clare, named O'Brian, thinking that he would gain honour and advantage by reporting their passage to William, set out for the British camp. Being unknown there, he was a long time before he could get access to the king. The officers to whom he spoke paid little attention to his story about a body of Irish horse passing through the country, and were much more interested in gaining information from him as to the state of the stock of cattle, sheep, and pigs in his part of the county; for owing to the terror excited by the conduct of William's soldiers the people for many miles round had driven off their stock and left the vil-

lages, and provisions were already becoming scarce in
the camp.

At length, however, one of those to whom he had
spoken mentioned his story to the king, who at once
sent for him and saw the importance of the news he
brought. O'Brian himself had no idea of the object
of Sarsfield's expedition, but the king instantly guessed
that it was the siege-train. He therefore ordered a
large body of cavalry to be immediately despatched to
meet the artillery on its way and protect it into camp.

All day Sarsfield remained in concealment among
the mountains, until towards evening the train came
in sight, moving slowly with its escort of two troops
of dragoons along the high-road. He watched it until
it halted and encamped for the night in a field beside the highway. He waited until the horses were
picketed and the men engaged in making their en-
campment for the night. Then the Irish cavalry
burst down from the glen in which they had been
hiding. The officer in command sounded to horse, but
it was too late; before the men were in the saddle
the Irish were upon them, and in a moment the two
troops of dragoons were dispersed or killed.

Sarsfield's men at once set to to collect the powder-
waggons, pontoons, and baggage of every description.
The great guns were filled with powder to the muzzle,
and then buried two-thirds of their length in the
earth, the whole mass of siege equipage was piled above
them, and a train of gunpowder was laid to the store
in the centre. The men then drew off to a distance.
A match was applied to the train, and the whole blew
up with a tremendous explosion.

The shock was heard in the far-away camp of William, and he knew that his cavalry had arrived too late to avert the catastrophe he feared. They had, indeed, just arrived within sight of the spot when the explosion took place. They rode on at full speed only to find the vast pile of ruined woodwork blazing furiously. The Irish cavalry was seen in the distance leisurely retiring; but although the English pursued for a short time, the Irish easily evaded them in the darkness among the hills. The whole of William's cavalry in camp were sent out, when the explosion was felt, to endeavour to cut off the Irish horse; but Sarsfield was well acquainted with the ground, and retired with his troops safely across the Shannon, having struck a terrible blow against the designs of William.

The king, however, found that in spite of the measures Sarsfield had taken, two of the guns remained uninjured by the explosion. These were brought to the camp, and another heavy gun was fetched from Waterford, together with a small quantity of ammunition. The regiments were at once set to manufacture fascines for the siege, and this work proceeded quickly, the orchards and plantations furnishing an abundance of wood. The fascines were used for filling up ditches, and the advances against the town were pushed forward with vigour. But the besiegers were not allowed to carry on their work unmolested, for a constant fire was kept up by the guns on the walls, and the besieged made several sorties, driving back the working parties, destroying their work, and retiring before any considerable bodies of troops could be brought up to attack them. The three heavy guns were, however, brought into position at a short distance from the wall, and began to play upon it.

The dissensions between the Irish commanders still continued, and beyond Sarsfield's raid against the battering train, nothing was done to annoy the enemy in the rear, although, had any vigour been shown, the Irish army lying idle west of the Shannon could have moved across, and speedily starved out William's army by cutting off all supplies. Even as it was, provisions could only be collected by sending out strong bodies of troops to plunder the country; for the peasantry had been goaded into fury by the evil conduct of the troops, and were now in a state of insurrection, cutting off and murdering all stragglers, and driving in small parties. William had good reason to regret that he had brought with him so small a contingent of British troops, owing to his doubts whether they could be depended upon, and his poor opinion of their bravery; for since the days of Agincourt English troops had been seldom seen on the Continent, and were consequently held but in small esteem there. He had with him now a regiment of English grenadiers and a few line regiments, but the bulk of the army was composed of his Dutch troops and foreign mercenaries; the latter had shown at the battle of the Boyne that their courage was not of a high order, while their excesses had not only produced a bitter feeling of hatred against them throughout the country, but had done immense harm to the cause by rendering it next to impossible to obtain provisions.

Walter's progress towards recovery from the day when he recovered consciousness was very rapid. The fever, though severe, had been short, and he gained strength almost as rapidly as he had lost it. The morning after he had come to himself, Mrs. Conyers brought Claire in to see him.

"Here is a young lady who is very anxious to see how you are getting on, Walter," she said cheerfully; "and now you are going on so well I shall hand you over a good deal to her care, as some of the others want my attention badly. You must not talk much, you know, else we shall be having you getting feverish again."

So saying she left the room.

Claire had stopped timidly near the door. The change which four days had made in Walter's appearance shocked her, and she scarcely recognized in the pale drawn face the youth who had burst in, sword in hand, to her rescue on that terrible evening. The tears were running fast down her cheeks as she approached the couch.

"Why, what is the matter, Claire?" he asked. "You must not cry. I am all right again now, and in a week shall be on horseback, I hope."

"Oh, Walter, what can I say!" she said. "To think that you should have suffered so for us!"

"There is nothing dreadful about it," he said smiling. "A soldier must expect to get wounded sometimes, and a slash from a German sword is not a serious matter. I am only too glad that I got it in your cause, Claire—only too glad that I was able to be of service to you—and your mother," he added as an afterthought. "It makes me very happy to think I have been useful to you, only I would rather that you didn't say anything more about it. I am quite content and happy as it is, and if it had been my life I would have gladly given it."

"I won't say any more if you don't wish it," Claire said quietly, "but I shall think of it always; and now," she said with an effort, "mamma said you were not to talk much, and you look quite flushed already, so you must lie quiet, and I will read to you, or work, if you like that better."

"I don't care which it is," Walter said, "so that I can look at you;" and this time Claire's cheeks were a good deal redder than Walter's.

Mrs. Conyers returned in half an hour and found Claire sitting working, while Walter lay looking at her.

"I think, Claire, you had better take your work in the next room again," she said. "Walter looks flushed, and I don't think your visit has done him any good. You have been talking too much."

"It has done me an immense deal of good, Mrs. Conyers," Walter protested; while Claire exclaimed that they had hardly spoken a word, which indeed was the truth, for Walter had been feeling too dreamily happy to want to talk, and Claire had felt so shy and embarrassed with Walter watching her that she had been unable to hit on a single subject for remark.

Another two days and Walter was well enough to get up and lie on a couch of heather, covered with the blanket, which Larry had prepared for him in the next room. His voice had recovered its natural ring, and Claire had got over her unaccustomed shyness; and Mrs. Conyers, as she moved in and out, heard them laughing and chatting together as they had done ten days before at the Hall.

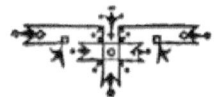

CHAPTER XI.

THE FIRST SIEGE OF LIMERICK.

THE three heavy guns thundered against the walls without intermission night and day until at length a breach was made. The garrison in vain attempted to repair it, and every hour it grew larger, until there was a yawning gap twelve yards wide. This William considered sufficient for the purpose, and made his preparations for the assault. The English regiment of grenadiers, six hundred strong, was ordered to take its place in the advanced trenches, and to lead the assault. It was supported on the right by the Dutch Guards, with some British and Brandenburg regiments in reserve.

On the left the grenadiers were supported by the Danish regiments, and a large body of cavalry were held in readiness to pour in behind the infantry. The storming parties were under command of Lieutenant-general Douglas. At three o'clock in the afternoon the signal for the assault was given by a discharge of three pieces of cannon. As the last gun was fired the grenadiers leaped from the trenches and dashed forward towards the breach.

As they approached the wall they discharged their muskets at the enemy upon the walls, and before as-

saulting the breach they hurled a shower of hand-
grenades at its defenders. The preparations for the
assault had been observed by the Irish, and they were
in readiness to receive it. The news had spread
through the town, and the excitement among the whole
population was intense. The guns on the walls ceased
firing in order that all might be ready to pour in their
shower of balls when the assault commenced. The
fire from the batteries of the besiegers had also died
away, and a silence which seemed strange after the
constant din of the preceding days hung over the camp
and city.

No sooner had the grenadiers leaped from the
trenches than the guns on the walls, and the musketry
of the defenders, poured their fire upon them, while all
the batteries of the besiegers opened at the same moment to cover the assault. Through the hail of fire the
grenadiers kept on without faltering, and as they
neared the breach the Irish rushed out through the
opening to meet them. There was a desperate struggle,
half hidden from the eyes of those on the walls by the
cloud of smoke and dust which arose from the combatants; but the grenadiers, fighting with the greatest
gallantry, won their way to the counterscarp, and half
the regiment forced its way through the breach and
entered the town; but the Irish troops, clustered behind
the wall, then closed in again, and barred the breach
to those following.

The Dutch and English regiments were marched up
to aid the rest of the grenadiers to cut their way in after
their comrades; but these troops were unable to imitate
the valour of the grenadiers. They got as far as the

counterscarp; but the fire from the walls was so deadly
that they could not be prevailed upon to advance. The
rain of fire mowed them down. Their officers urged
them on, and, unwilling to retreat and incapable of
advancing, they were shot down in scores.

Presently there was a sudden movement among the
Irish defenders on the breach, and a few of the grenadiers who had entered the city burst their way through
them, and rejoined their comrades. No sooner had
they entered the city than they found themselves assailed on all sides. The Irish troops and the citizens
attacked them with fury, and even the women, animated by the deadly hate which the deeds of William's
soldiers had excited, hurled missiles upon them from
the windows, and even joined in the attacks upon them
in the streets.

The grenadiers resisted obstinately, but they were
gradually overpowered by numbers, until at last a few
survivors gathering together, burst through their assailants, and succeeded in making their retreat. For
nearly three hours this furious conflict had raged
within the city; regiment after regiment had been
marched up to the assault, but none had proved brave
enough to fight their way up the counterscarp to the
aid of the hard-pressed grenadiers in the town.

When the little remnant of the grenadiers rejoined
them they continued for a time to keep up a constant
fire upon the defenders on the walls, but at last slowly
and sullenly fall back to their camp. In the meantime
a regiment of Brandenburgers had attacked the wall of
the battery known as the Black Battery, whose fire
was doing great execution upon the assailants. They

had brought scaling-ladders with them, and with these they succeeded, fighting with great bravery and determination, in gaining the walls.

The whole regiment poured in; but just as they did so the Irish fired the powder magazine that supplied the battery, and the whole battalion was destroyed.

William, from his position on a fort known as Cromwell's Fort, watched the struggle. Had he acted as Cromwell did at the siege of Drogheda, when, after his troops had been twice repulsed at the breach, he placed himself at their head and led them to the assault, the result might not have been the same, for the regiments which refused to follow their officers up the counterscarp might have followed the king; but William, although he had often proved the possession of no ordinary courage and coolness in danger, had not that species of courage which prompts a man to throw himself forward to lead a forlorn hope. Moreover, both as a general-in-chief and king, his place was not at the head of an assault.

The assailants lost more than two thousand men, and these the flower of William's army. The surprise of the troops at their defeat by an enemy they had been taught to despise was extreme, and so ashamed were they of their failure that the following day they were ready to renew the assault. The king, however, would not risk another such defeat. The bravest of his force had perished, his stores of ammunition were nearly exhausted, and the rains had set in with great violence.

On the day following the assault the king called a council of war, and it was resolved to raise the siege.

There was a great scarcity of waggons and horses in consequence of the loss sustained by Sarsfield's attack on the train. The few waggons which remained were not enough to convey the wounded men, many of whom were obliged to walk. The stores had therefore to be abandoned for want of transport. Some were thrown into the river, others blown up and destroyed, and on Saturday the 30th of August the army commenced its retreat.

It was accompanied by a great host of fugitives, for with the army went the whole of the Protestant inhabitants of the county of Limerick and the surrounding country, with their wives, children, servants, and such household goods as they could bring with them. In addition to these were the Protestant fugitives from the neighbourhood of Athlone, who had come down with the division of General Douglas after he had raised the siege of that city.

The Protestants round Limerick had not doubted the success of the besiegers, never questioning the ability of an army commanded by a king to capture a place like Limerick. The misery of this body of fugitives was terrible. They had abandoned their homes to pillage and destruction, and knew not whether they should ever be able to return to them again. They had, on the arrival of William, torn up the letters of protection which the Irish generals had given to all who applied to them, and having thrown in their fortunes with him, dared not remain among the country people who had suffered so terribly from the exactions and brutality of William's army. Not only had they to endure wet, hunger, and fatigue in the retreat, but they were robbed and plundered by the army which should have protected them, as if they had been enemies instead of friends.

William himself left his army as soon as he broke up the siege, and pushed straight on to Waterford, and the troops, relieved from the only authority they feared, and rendered furious by the ill success which had attended their operations, broke out into acts of plunder and insubordination which surpassed anything that they had before perpetrated. The siege of Limerick brought the campaign to a close, and so far the Irish had no reason to be disheartened. They had besieged and nearly annihilated the army of Schomberg at Dundalk; they had fought a sturdy battle on the Boyne, and had proved themselves a match for William's best troops; they had decisively repulsed the attacks upon Athlone and Limerick; half the troops William had sent to conquer the country had fallen, while their own losses had been comparatively small.

The sole fruit of all the efforts of William had been the occupation of the capital—a great advantage, as it gave him a point at which he could pour fresh troops into Ireland and recommence the war in the spring with new chances of success. When the British army reached Callan some of the arrears of pay were distributed among the troops, and the army was then broken up and the troops went into winter quarters.

William had returned at once to England, and sent over some new lords-justices to Dublin. These were received with delight by the townspeople, who had suffered terribly from the exactions and depredations of the foreign troops quartered there, and were, indeed, almost in a state of starvation, for the country people were afraid to bring in provisions for sale, as they were either plundered of the goods as they approached the city, or robbed of their money as they returned after disposing of them. As the only possible check to these disorders, the justices raised a body of militia in the town to cope with the soldiery, and the result was a series of frays which kept the city in a state of alarm.

By the time that Limerick beat off the assault upon its breach, Walter Davenant was quite convalescent. Rumours of the ill treatment of the Protestants who accompanied the retreating army circulated in Limerick, and Mrs. Conyers congratulated herself warmly that she and her daughter were safe under the protection of the Irish troops, instead of being in the sad column of fugitives.

As soon as the English army had left, Captain Davenant obtained for her an order of protection from General Sarsfield, and she returned for a while with her daughter to their house, to which the invalids were carried, Captain Davenant's troop being again quartered around it.

"I hardly know what is best to do," she said to Captain Davenant a few days after her return. "I am of course anxious to rejoin my husband, but at the same time I feel that my staying here is of benefit to him. With the order of protection I have received I am perfectly safe here, and I have no fear whatever of any trouble either with the troops or peasantry; but, on the other hand, if we abandon this place I fear that it will be pillaged, and perhaps burned, like the other houses belonging to Protestants which have been deserted by their owners. What do you say, Captain Davenant?"

"I should be sorry to give any advice, Mrs. Conyers. For the troops I can answer; the protection you have received from General Sarsfield will be sufficient to ensure you against any trouble whatever from them, but as to the peasantry I cannot say. Every village within reach of William's army, in its advance or retreat, has been destroyed, and the vilest atrocities have been committed upon the people. The greater part of the men have, in despair, taken up arms, and, when they get the chance, will avenge their wrongs upon inoffensive Protestants who have ventured to remain in their dwellings. Savagery has begot savagery, and even such a protection order as you have received would go for little with these half-maddened wretches. I should say, therefore, that so long as there are a considerable body of troops at Limerick, so long you may safely remain here, but no longer."

"At anyrate I will stay for a time," Mrs. Conyers said. "The winter may bring peace; and I am very loath to abandon the house, to which my husband is greatly attached, if it is possible to save it."

The party now fell back to the mode of life which had been interrupted by the advance of William's army. Captain Davenant drilled his men, and spent his evenings pleasantly in the house. Walter had so far recovered that he was able to stroll through the grounds or drive with Claire. The troopers enjoyed their rest and abundance of rations. Captain Davenant's mind had been set at ease by the receipt of a

letter which Mrs. Davenant had sent him by one of
the men of the village. It told him that she had seen
Mr. Conyers, who had obtained a stay of all proceedings against the property, and that she was well and
in as good spirits as she could be in his absence.

A month after they had moved across the river
their quiet life was interrupted by a trooper riding up
just as the party was sitting down to dinner, with an
order from General Sarsfield for the troops to be in
readiness to march at daybreak to form part of a force
which was about to undertake an enterprise against
the English stationed at Birr. There was silence at
the table after Captain Davenant had read the order.

"Then you must leave us?" Mrs. Conyers said at last.

"I am afraid so, Mrs. Conyers. Yes, sorry as I am
that our pleasant time here must come to an end.
There is no questioning the order; I have been, in fact,
expecting it for the last day or two."

"Then I shall move," Mrs. Conyers said decidedly.
"It will take us a day or two to pack up such valuables as I should like to take away and leave at
Limerick till the return of happier days. When that
is accomplished I shall carry out my intention of
making for Galway, and leave the house to take care
of itself."

"In the meantime, madam," Captain Davenant said,
"I will leave my son and four of the men, who are
now convalescent, as a protection. I fancy they are
all fit to take the saddle, but I can strain a point a
little and leave them still on the sick list."

"Thank you very much indeed," Mrs. Conyers
said, while a glance of satisfaction passed between

Walter and Claire. "That will be a satisfaction; indeed I shall feel quite safe so long as your son is here. I wish now I had moved the things before; but I had hoped that you would have been allowed to remain in quarters here all the winter. Had it not been for that I should never have decided as I did."

The next morning the troop started.

"The place seems strangely quiet," Walter said as he strolled out into the garden with Claire after breakfast. "It seems terrible to think that in three or four days it will be deserted altogether, and that you will have gone."

"It is horrid," the girl said, with tears gathering in her eyes. "I hate King William and King James both," she went on petulantly. "Why can't they fight their quarrel out alone, instead of troubling everyone else. I don't know which of them I hate the most."

"But there is a compensation," Walter said with a smile.

"I am sure I don't see any compensation," the girl said. "What do you mean, Walter?"

"I mean," Walter said, "that if they had not quarrelled we might never have met."

"There is something in that," Claire said softly. "No; I don't know that I ought quite to hate them after all."

By which it will be seen that Walter Davenant and Claire Conyers had already arrived at a thorough understanding as to their feelings towards each other. After this, as was natural between young persons so situated, their talk wandered away into the future, and the present was already forgotten.

In the house everyone was at work. Mrs. Conyers' servants had all returned when she came back to the house, and these were now busy, with the assistance of Larry and the four troopers left behind, in taking down and packing pictures, taking up carpets, and getting furniture ready for removal. In the afternoon Walter assisted in the work of packing. As he was dressing for dinner Larry, as usual, came into his room.

"I suppose, your honour," he said, after putting out Walter's clothes, "you will be setting a watch to-night?"

"Yes, Larry, I was intending to do so. You don't think there is any special occasion for it, do you?"

"I don't know, your honour. We hear tales of the Rapparees burning every Protestant house in the district. As long as the troop was here, av coorse the boys kept away; but there is a powerful lot of plunder in the house, and the news that the troop have gone will go through the country quick enough. The boys have had enough to turn them into devils with what they have gone through, and small blame to them if they take their chances when they find them. We know, yer honour, that Mrs. Conyers and Miss Claire are well-nigh angels, and there is small fear that the people around will lift a finger agin them, in spite of having had their own homes burnt over their heads; but folks from a distance don't know that, and the news that there is a rich Protestant house all ready for sacking will travel quick. I hope your honour will get the ladies to move out of the place to-morrow, whether the ould pictures and things are all ready or not."

" Do you think it is as serious as that, Larry?"

" Faith and I do, yer honour. You don't know how bitter the folks are!"

" But there cannot be any danger, Larry, as long as we are here. The Rapparees would never attack a house which has the general's protection, and with an officer and some troopers of the king to guard it."

" It's meself would not answer for them," Larry said, shaking his head. " The boys are just disperate, and would care nothing for the protection unless there were force to back it. They think that, as all the Catholics have been robbed by the Protestants, it's only fair that they should get their turn now; and if I were your honour I would lay all my plans out to-night, how to get away and the rest of it, just as if you were assured they would come before the morning."

" Why, you have heard nothing certain, Larry?"

" I have not, or I would tell your honour at once; but I know what the' people think and feel, and I know that the Rapparees have been plundering and destroying every Protestant house around, and they will guess that the ladies will be moving now that the troop is gone. Besides, won't they have heard that the news has gone round for waggons to come to take away the things!"

The earnestness with which Larry spoke convinced Walter that the danger was serious. Larry was not given to magnify danger, and usually treated all risks with carelessness and indifference. Walter knew that he would gather from the stablemen and the people who brought in provisions much more as to the state of popular feeling in the country than he was likely to

know, and he accordingly went down to dinner grave
and preoccupied.

Mrs. Conyers soon noticed the change in his manner,
and as soon as the servants had retired asked him if
he had received any bad news.

"No," he said, trying to speak lightly. "My boy
Larry has been trying to scare me about the Rapparees,
and although I do not think that there is any danger
to be apprehended from them, I do think that it would
be just as well to hurry on your preparations as much
as possible, and for you and Clare to go in to Limerick
to-morrow afternoon. We can finish the packing up
of the goods you wish to take, and any we cannot get
off to-morrow can be sent in the next day."

Mrs. Conyers looked grave.

"But we have heard of no Rapparees in this neighbourhood, Walter," she said. "We have heard of sad
excesses in some parts of the country, but nothing in
this neighbourhood."

"There has been small temptation for them about
here," Walter said, "for every house within miles was
stripped by the Williamites. Catholic or Protestant
was all the same to them. Besides, they knew well
that Sarsfield's horse would soon have put a stop to
that sort of thing. Now, I do not wish to alarm you
in the slightest, and I do not think that there is any
real cause for anxiety. Even if they are in the neighbourhood the Rapparees will hardly venture an attack
upon a house occupied by even a few of our troops.
Still it is always wisest to be prepared, and therefore
I should like for us to arrange exactly what had best
be done in the event of an attack. Of course I shall

see that all the doors and the lower windows are
securely fastened, and I shall have the men from the
stables into the house, so we shall be nine or ten men
in all, enough, I hope, for all circumstances. Still,
merely as a matter of discussion, let us suppose the
worst. Let us imagine the house surrounded, the
doors burst in, and the resistance on the point of
being overpowered. What would be our best plan
for making our escape? Do not be frightened, Claire,"
he went on, seeing how pale the girl had become.
"Every general, when he is going to fight a battle,
however sure he may be of success, decides upon the
route by which his army shall retreat in case of a
defeat, and I am only taking the same precaution."

"If there is to be a retreat made at all," Mrs. Conyers
said, "I prefer that it should be made now. Do you
really think that there is any real danger of attack?"

"I think that there is danger of attack, Mrs.
Conyers; but I have no reason for supposing that
there is any particular danger this night."

"Then Claire and I will at once start for the town
under the escort of two of your men. It would be
folly indeed to run the risk of another attack here.
If the house is to be burned it must be burned. For
if they were beaten off once they would come again
when the house was undefended. As for the things,
should all be quiet to-night they can be sent in to-
morrow as arranged. The things that are to go are
all got together."

"I do think that the best way," Walter said. "Of
course I shall ride in with you and hand you over to
the friends you are going to in the town, and shall

then come back here again with a light heart. But I own that I am nervous at the thought of you and Claire being here should the Rapparees attack the house."

"But mind, Walter, there is to be no fighting. If they come to-night I had rather that they took everything than that you should risk your life in its defence. The silver and valuables we took across before are all safe in Limerick. As for the other things, they can go. Now, mind, we shall not leave unless we have your promise, that if a band of these men come to-night to sack the place, you and your men will offer no resistance."

"If they come in numbers which render successful resistance out of the question, I promise you that we will not draw a trigger, Mrs. Conyers."

"In that case I am satisfied, Walter. Against you and your men these peasants have no quarrel."

Walter at once called Larry.

"Larry, get my horse saddled, and tell Browning to saddle his. Place two pillions behind the saddles. Mrs. Conyers and her daughter are going to ride into Limerick at once."

"The Lord be praised!" Larry said piously. "That's the best news I have heard this many a day."

"And, Larry," Mrs. Conyers said, "tell the three boys in the stable to saddle the three best horses and ride with us. If we lose everything else we may as well retain them, for it would not be easy to buy others now."

In ten minutes all was ready for a start. Walter and the trooper took their places in the saddles, chairs were brought out, and Mrs. Conyers and Claire mounted behind them. Walter had asked Mrs. Conyers to take her seat on the pillion on his horse, but she did not answer, and when Walter turned to see that she was comfortably placed behind him, he found that it was Claire who was seated there.

"Mamma told me to," the girl said. "I suppose she thought this was perhaps the last ride we should take together."

"For the present, Claire—you should say for the present. I hope it will not be long before we are together again. And for good," he added in a low voice.

Mrs. Conyers made no comment, when they dismounted and entered the house of a friend at Limerick, upon Claire's swollen eyes and flushed cheeks, but said "good-bye" lightly to Walter, thanked him for his escort, and said that she hoped to see him with her household goods on the following afternoon. On leaving them Walter went straight to the house where an officer of his acquaintance was quartered.

"Hullo, Davenant! I didn't expect to see you here at this time of the evening. I heard you were still laid up with your wound."

"That is an old affair now," Walter said. "I am not quite strong again, but there is little the matter now. I have come in to ask you if you will let me have five-and-twenty of your men. I have strong reason to believe that it is likely one of the bands of Rapparees will make an attack on Mrs. Conyers' house to-night. The tenants have been asked to send in their waggons to-morrow to remove some of the

furniture in here, and I think it probable they will
try to take what they fancy before it starts. I have
brought Mrs. Conyers and her daughter into the town,
but as I have only four men I cannot defend the house
if it is attacked in any force. I wish you would let
me have five-and-twenty men and a sergeant just for
to-night. I will march them in with the baggage in
the afternoon."

"Certainly I will," Captain Donovan said. "I need
not disturb the colonel at this time of the evening, but
will take it on myself. There are just that number
quartered in the storehouse close to the gate. I will
go down with you at once and turn them out and give
them orders. It will be a good thing for the Rapparees
to have a lesson. They bring disgrace upon our cause
by their doings."

In a few minutes the men, who had not retired to
bed, were turned out.

"You have got a four-mile march before you, boys,"
Walter said when they were drawn up; "but there
will be a pint of good wine and some supper for you
when you get there. So step out as briskly as you can."

After a cordial good-night to Captain Donovan
Walter placed himself at the head of the infantry,
and in little over an hour arrived at the house. He
knocked loudly at the door. A minute later Larry put
his head out of the window above.

"Who is there? What do you want knocking at a
peaceful house at this time of night? You had best
go away, boys, for the house is chock-full of soldiers. We are only waiting for orders to blow you to
smithereens."

Walter burst into a laugh.

"Very well done, Larry. It is I, with some soldiers. So you needn't give orders to the men to fire."

Larry gave a cry of satisfaction and ran down to open the door.

"It's glad I am to see you, Master Walter, entirely. I have been listening ever since you went, and when I heard the tramp of feet I made sure it was the boys."

"But I gave orders that there was to be no resistance, Larry."

"And I wasn't going to resist, your honour; but I thought I might just frighten them away."

"Now, Larry, get up a pint of wine for each of these good fellows, and what victuals you can find in the house. We need have no fear of an attack to-night."

When the soldiers had finished their supper they lay down in the hall.

Walter placed a sentry at a window at each side of the house, and he then lay down on a sofa, for the ride to Limerick and back had greatly fatigued him, much to his surprise, for he had no idea how far his strength had been pulled down. He was aroused just as day was breaking by a loud knocking at the door, and at the same moment a shot was fired from a window above. The soldiers had started to their feet and seized their arms as he ran out and bade them follow him up stairs. He threw up a window.

"Who are you? and what do you want?"

"Never mind who we are," a voice replied. "We want the door opened, and you had best do it quick."

"Look here, my man," Walter said in a loud steady

voice, "there are thirty soldiers in this house, and if I give the word you will get such a volley among you that half of you will never go home to tell about it, so I warn you to depart quietly."

"It's a lie," the man said. "If you are the officer you have got only four men, and you know it. We want to do you no harm, and we don't want to harm the ladies; but what's in the house is ours—that's the law of William's troops, and we mean to act up to it."

A chorus of approbation rose from a throng of peasants gathered round the door. A few of them carried muskets, but the greater part were armed with rude pikes.

"Show yourselves at the windows, boys," Walter said to his men. "Level your muskets, but don't fire until I give the word."

It was light enough for those without to make out the threatening figures which showed themselves at every window, and with a cry of alarm they ran back among the shrubs for shelter.

"Now you see," Walter said, "that I have spoken the truth. I have thirty soldiers here, and you know as well as I do what will come of it if you attempt to break into this house. For shame, men! Your deeds bring disgrace on the king's cause and on our religion. It is not because the scum who march with the Dutchman behave like brutal savages that we should do the same. There's plenty of work for you in fighting against the enemies of your country instead of frightening women and pillaging houses. Return to your homes, or better still, go and join the king's army and fight like men for your homes and your religion.

He listened, but there was no answer. The Rapparees knew they had no chance of breaking into the house so defended, and when Walter ceased each man slunk away in the darkness.

The next morning a number of waggons arrived, and Walter, with the aid of the soldiers, had the satisfaction of loading them with everything of any value in the house, and of escorting them without interruption to Limerick. Mrs. Conyers was filled with gratitude when she heard the events of the night and how narrowly she and her daughter had escaped another attack. One of the principal tenants had come in with his waggon and he agreed to move into the house with his wife and family until she should return. Seeing that now everything worth taking had been removed he thought there was little chance of any attempt to destroy the house.

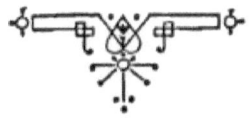

CHAPTER XII.

TWO or three days later Captain Davenant returned to Limerick with his troop. He had stopped at the house on his way and learned there of the move which had been made.

"Well, Walter, so you nearly had to defend Mrs. Conyers against odds again," he said, as Walter joined him in the market-place, where the troop was dismounting. "I have come here for a day only, for we are on our way south. It is thought likely that the enemy's next move may be against Cork, so some of us are detached in that direction. To my mind," he went on after he had seen the troop quartered in some houses which formerly belonged to the Protestants, but were now used as barracks,—"in my opinion we are wasting precious time. We ought not to allow the enemy to go into winter quarters. Our best season is just coming on. We can stand the wet far better than they can, and we ought not to give them a moment's rest, but should keep our army together and beat up one garrison after another; threaten the strongest places; compel them to keep constantly on the move; and, before the spring, completely wear out and exhaust those whom we cannot conquer. If England found that she had the whole work to begin over again she would think twice before she went further.

"These petty German princes would not find their men so ready to embark in a quarrel with which they have no concern when they learned that all who had done so had laid their bones in the swamps of Ireland, and without his mercenaries William would find it hard to gather an army, for the English themselves have no heart whatever in the war. If we remain inactive all the winter and enable them to retain their foothold everywhere, fresh reinforcements will arrive in the spring, and so bit by bit all Ireland will be won.

"It is disheartening in the extreme, after seeing the enemy retire repulsed and utterly disheartened from Athlone and Limerick, to allow them unmolested to rest and gather strength again. If we could but get rid of the French there would be some hope for us. They have scarce fired a shot since the war began, and yet they assume superiority over our generals. They thwart us at every turn; they not only refuse to combine in any action, but they prevent our doing so.

"Since the Boyne our army has lain inactive and has done nothing, although they might have done everything. All Ireland was open to them on the day when William, with all his forces, sat down here before Limerick. Why, they could have marched straight for Dublin and captured it, before William heard that they had crossed the Shannon. They might have cut off his supplies from Waterford; they might have starved him out in his camp here. They have had the game in their hands, and they have allowed it to slip altogether through their fingers. The only hope

I have now is that before the spring the French will go. It is but too clear that Louis has no intention whatever of helping us in earnest. Had he chosen he could any time during the last six months have landed an army here, which would have decided the struggle. Instead of that he has sent five thousand men, and had in return as many of our best soldiers; and the officers he sent seem to have been furnished with secret instructions not only to do nothing themselves, but to prevent us from doing anything."

"Whom would you like to see in command, father?"

"I should not care much, Walter, so that it was one man. I had rather have any soldier you might take at random from our army, so that he possessed a fair share of common sense, than the chaos which now prevails; but of course the man whom we would rather have is Sarsfield. Whether he is a great general or not we have no means of knowing, for he has never yet had the slightest opportunity of showing it; but I do not think myself that he has made the most of what chances he has had, save that one dash against the artillery convoy. He has done nothing; and as the cavalry are under his command, and he could if he chose, snap his fingers at the pretensions of the French and act independently, I think he might have done far more than he has done. Still he is our most prominent leader, and he possesses the confidence of the Irish of all classes. If he were in supreme command there would, I am sure, be a complete change in our tactics. Instead of waiting everywhere to be attacked we should take the offensive, and even if we were unable to meet William's forces in pitched battles, and I believe that

we are perfectly capable of doing so, we should be able
to harass and exhaust them to such a point that
William would be only too glad to grant us any terms
we might demand to bring the war to an end."

After having dined, Captain Davenant went with
Walter to call upon Mrs. Conyers. Hearing that he
was about to march with his troop to Cork, Mrs.
Conyers said:

"Oh, Captain Davenant, will you not take us under
your protection there? I am afraid of travelling with
Claire to Galway in the present disturbed state of the
country, and I should find it easier to take a passage
to England from Cork than from Galway."

"You certainly would, Mrs. Conyers. There is no
formal war between England and Ireland, and trading
vessels still ply between Cork and Bristol. I agree
with you that it would not be safe for two Protestant
ladies to travel without protection from here to Galway, and I shall be only too glad for you to journey
with us. Your daughter, I know, can ride any of the
country ponies; and for yourself—"

"I can ride too if there is an occasion. One of our
horses is perfectly quiet, and I have often ridden him
by the side of Mr. Conyers, so there will be no difficulty on that score."

"In that case," Captain Davenant said, "consider
the matter as arranged. Will you be ready to start
to-morrow early?"

"Certainly, Captain Davenant; I have no preparations to make. All our furniture—which, thanks to
Walter, was saved—has been stowed away in the cellars
of a warehouse here and is safe unless William returns

and batters the whole town to pieces. The silver and other valuables our friends here will take care of till better times, so we have only to pack two valises and mount. The servants will all find situations here. My daughter's maid, Bridget, and two or three others have offered to accompany us to England, but we have decided to take no one. Directly we get to Bristol I shall write to my husband, who has given me an address both in London and Dublin, so that he will doubtless join us in a very short time."

The party started the next morning and reached Cork without adventure, as there were no English troops in that part of the country. Three days after their arrival Mrs. Conyers took a passage for herself and Claire in a trader about to sail for Bristol. The evening before they sailed Mrs. Conyers had a long talk with Captain Davenant, while the two young people had slipped off for a last walk together.

"Of course, Captain Davenant," she began, "you have seen as well as I have how things stand between Claire and Walter. They are both very young, but the strange circumstances of the times and the manner in which they have been thrown together have combined to render their position peculiar, and I believe, nay, I am sure, that on both sides their affection is deep and will be lasting."

"I quite agree with you, Mrs. Conyers, at anyrate as far as my son is concerned. Walter has never spoken to me on the subject. I suppose fathers and sons are less given to confidences of this sort than mothers and daughters. But that Walter is deeply and earnestly attached to your daughter is unquestionable, and indeed it would be singular were it otherwise. I have stood passive in the matter, simply because I saw that you took no steps to keep them apart; and you could not but have seen at an early period of their acquaintance in what direction matters were tending."

"Frankly," Mrs. Conyers said, "I gave the matter no thought during your first stay with us. I had regarded Claire as a child, and it did not at first occur to me that there could be any danger of her falling seriously in love for years to come. When my eyes were opened to the true state of things, and I found my little girl had lost her heart, I could have wished it otherwise. I do not mean as to worldly matters," she went on hastily, seeing that Captain Davenant was about to speak. "That weighed absolutely nothing with me; indeed, they may be considered to be well matched in that respect. If the war is decided in favour of King William, Claire will be a rich heiress. If, on the other hand, your cause triumph, you will regain your confiscated estates while we shall lose ours. So that there is, I consider, no inequality whatever in their position. The difficulty, of course, to which I allude is their religion. This is naturally a grave obstacle, and I fear that my husband will regard it as such even more strongly than I do. He is, however, extremely attached to Claire, and will, I feel sure, when he sees that her happiness is at stake, come round to my views of the matter. There are," she said with a smile, " Catholics and Catholics just as there are Protestants and Protestants. I would rather see Claire in her grave than married to many Catholics I know; but neither you nor Walter are bigots."

"No, indeed," Captain Davenant said; "we came over to this country when Catholicism was the religion of all England, and we have maintained the religious belief of our fathers. I own that what I may call political Protestantism is hateful to me; but between such Catholicism as mine and such Protestantism as yours I see no such broad distinctions as should cause us to hate each other."

"That is just my view," Mrs. Conyers agreed. "The differences between the creeds are political rather than religious, and in any case I consider that when neither of the parties is bigoted, the chances of happiness are greater in the case where the man is a Catholic and the woman a Protestant than in the opposite case."

"I think so too," Captain Davenant said. "At any-rate I do not think that Walter and Claire would be likely to quarrel over their respective opinions."

"I think not," Mrs. Conyers agreed with a smile. "I do wish with all my heart that it had been otherwise; but as it is not so, I for my part am determined to make the best of the circumstances. They are both young, and it is possible that they may in time come to think alike one way or the other. I am not one of those who think that there is but one way to heaven; and should Walter some day win Claire over to his way of thinking, I shall not consider that she has forfeited her chances."

"It is quite as likely to be the other way," Captain Davenant said. "Walter is a good lad and a brave one; but with all Claire's pretty winning ways I question if the young lady has not more will of her own and more mind than Walter has. I hope they may agree each to go their own way, and I think that if they continue to live in this country they will probably do so, for here, unhappily, political differences build up a wall between the two branches of Christianity. But if it should come that they should some day leave this unhappy country and settle in England, where the same ill-feeling does not exist, there is no saying what may happen."

"Well, at anyrate, Captain Davenant, it is satisfactory that our views on the subject agree, and that we are both willing to make the best of what we cannot but consider to be a misfortune. But here come the young people. I have no doubt," she laughed, "that they have been swearing vows of eternal fidelity."

"Well, we were young ourselves once, and we are not too old yet, Mrs. Conyers, to feel enjoyment in the happiness of these young people."

The next morning Mrs. Conyers and Claire sailed for England, and the military events which shortly afterwards took place left Walter little time for thought on other subjects.

On the 21st of September, two days after the departure of Mrs. Conyers, a heavy cannonading was heard from the forts at the mouth of Cork harbour, and soon afterwards a horseman galloped into the town with the news that an English fleet had forced the entrance in spite of the fire from the forts. This fleet bore five thousand men under the command of the Earl of Marlborough.

The English party at court had long been mortified and disgusted at the manner in which the English had been ignored by William, and all the military commands bestowed upon foreigners. The discontent caused by the want of success which had attended the operations in Ireland had greatly strengthened this party, and they had now succeeded in getting an independent English expedition sent off under the command of an English general. William was much annoyed at this, for any brilliant success attained by Marlborough would have increased the feeling against his foreign favourites. He had therefore despatched the division of General Scravenmore to besiege the town on the land side, and had placed in command of it the Duke of Wirtemberg, whose rank as a prince and as a general of higher rank than Marlborough would enable him to claim the supreme command, and to carry off the honour of any success that might be gained.

This force arrived before the town within a day of the appearance of the fleet. Marlborough had already made good use of his time, for immediately the leading vessels had effected the passage, troops were landed in boats, and the batteries attacked in rear and carried. The rest of the fleet then entered, and on the 23d and 24th the troops were landed on the south bank of the river and commenced their march towards the city, the sailors dragging the guns. Wirtemberg immediately sent to Marlborough to claim the command of the whole force.

Marlborough replied that his commission was an independent one. He denied the authority of any of William's foreign officers in Ireland, and stated haughtily that his troops were British, and he a British officer. Wirtemberg was greatly offended that the

English general should affect to look down upon the Danes, Germans, French, and other foreign ragamuffins who composed his command, and he insisted strongly upon his claims. Marlborough maintained his position, and Wirtemberg was driven at last to propose that they should command on alternate days, and Marlborough agreed to the proposal.

The position of Cork was not a strong one, although in the days before the use of artillery it was considered well-nigh impregnable, being built upon the islands and marshes formed by the river Lea, and completely surrounded by two branches of the river. But upon three sides it was surrounded at a short distance only by high hills, which completely commanded it, and these hills were defended only by castles and forts of no great strength.

The garrison was but small, for the Irish were taken by surprise by the arrival of Marlborough's expedition, and had prepared only for a siege by Wirtemberg and his foreign division. They were therefore obliged to abandon Shandon Castle and two adjoining forts which defended the hills on the north of the city, and Wirtemberg's Danes at once took possession of these works, and planting their guns there, opened fire on the northern quarter of the city.

Marlborough constructed his batteries at a monastery called the Red Abbey on the south point of the river, where he was separated from the city only by the stream and narrow strip of marshy ground. These guns soon made a breach in the walls, and Marlborough prepared to storm the place, for at low tide it was possible to wade across the marsh and river.

The garrison, well aware that they could not long defend the place, now offered to capitulate on the same terms which William had granted to the garrisons of towns he had captured, namely, that they should be allowed to march out with the honours of war, with their arms and baggage, and to make their way unmolested to Limerick. The Prince of Wirtemberg was strongly in favour of these terms being granted, but Marlborough peremptorily refused. While a sharp dispute took place between the two officers, and before any conclusion could be arrived at, the tide rose, and the regiments drawn up ready to cross the river could no longer pass.

The firing then recommenced on both sides. Notwithstanding the efforts of the besieged to repair the injury to their wall, the breach daily increased in size. Wirtemberg moved his forces round from the north side to take their share in the assault, and at low tide the English and Danes advanced against the breach. Under a heavy fire from the walls they struggled through the marshes and entered the river, which even at low tide reached to their shoulders. Suffering heavily from the fire, they pushed forward until they nearly reached the breach. Here the Duke of Grafton, who commanded the British column, fell dead, with many officers and men; but the rest maintained their order and were about to make a dash at the breach when the governor, accompanied by Lord Tyrone, raised the white flag.

After a short parley it was agreed that the garrison should become prisoners of war, but were to be protected in their persons and private property; the city was to be preserved from any injury, and the citizens and their property were to be respected.

Captain Davenant's troop had remained idle during the siege, as there was no work for cavalry. They were quartered near an infantry regiment which had been raised by MacFinn O'Driscol from among his own tenantry, and was commanded by him. O'Driscol was a relation of Mrs. Davenant, and the two commanders were often together. Both felt that the city must speedily fall unless the Irish army moved down to its relief; but they agreed that if it surrendered they would make an effort to escape with their troops, for they had no faith in the observance of any terms of capitulation which might be made.

Accordingly, as soon as it was known that the governor had surrendered and that the gates of the town were to be handed over to the British, O'Driscol and Captain Davenant formed up their commands, and opening one of the gates marched boldly out. The exact terms on which the garrison had surrendered were not known, and Marlborough and Wirtemberg were near the breach arranging for the troops to take possession of the gates on that side; consequently the besieging forces opposite the gate from which the little column had marched out supposed that, in accordance with the arrangement, they were coming out to lay down their arms. They therefore stood aside as the column passed, being far more intent upon the plunder they expected to gather in Cork than on anything else. As, a few minutes later, the gates were opened and the troops poured into the city, no further thought was given to the little force which had marched out;

and the five hundred infantry and the troop of horse
were safe from pursuit before the news of the auda-
cious ruse they had practised reached the ears of the
generals.

Inside the town the articles of the treaty were at
once violated. The troops entered the town in crowds,
and, incited, as in Dublin, by a mob calling themselves Protestants, they proceeded to plunder the
houses and assault the Catholic inhabitants. The
governor, M'Carty, was wounded; the Earls of Tyrone
and Clancarty with difficulty made their escape from
the mob. Many were killed and a great destruction
of property took place before Marlborough and Wirtemberg entered the town and put a stop to the disorder, which inflicted great discredit upon them, as
they had made no arrangements whatever to ensure
the safety of the inhabitants, which they had solemnly
guaranteed.

It was now October, and Marlborough at once set
about the investment of Kinsale. On the very evening of the day he entered Cork he sent off five hundred horse towards that town, and the next day
marched thither himself at the head of his infantry.
The works of Kinsale consisted of two forts, both of
considerable strength, called the Old Fort and Charles's
Fort. They were well supplied with stores and provisions for a siege. On the approach of the besiegers
the governor set fire to the town and retired to the
forts, and, in answer to the summons to surrender,
replied that " it would be time enough to talk about
that a month hence."

Marlborough ordered General Tettau to cross the

river in boats with eight hundred picked men and to
carry Old Fort by storm. The assault was made with
great determination and bravery; but the works were
strong and stoutly defended, and the British were
about to fall back discomfited when fortune came to
their assistance. Some loose powder ignited and fired
the magazine, by which more than two hundred men
of the garrison were killed and the works seriously
injured. After this disaster the governor abandoned
the fort and withdrew with the survivors of its garrison to Charles's Fort. Marlborough at once commenced
the siege of this position, but for fifteen days the place
resisted all his efforts. The heavy loss, however, which
the garrison had suffered by the explosion in Old Fort
rendered them unable, by sallies, to interfere with the
works of the besiegers. These were carried on with
great vigour, for Marlborough feared that the approach
of the wet season would put a stop to his operations.
When, therefore, the governor offered to surrender on
the terms of his being permitted "to march away with
his garrison, their arms, baggage, and all the honours
of war, taking with them all persons who wished to
accompany them, together with their property, to
Limerick," Marlborough at once granted the terms
demanded.

The advent of winter now put a stop to regular
operations; but a war of skirmishes continued, and
the British in their quarters were greatly straitened for
forage and provisions. In Dublin the work of confiscation went on merrily; the greater part of the Catholic proprietors of the town were thrown into prison;
the various indictments against country gentlemen,

followed by the confiscation of their property, were hurried through the court with the merest shadow of legal form; for the defendants being absent and unacquainted with what was being done in Dublin, it was only necessary to recite the accusation to find the accused guilty and to pass sentence of confiscation—all this being the work of a few minutes only.

Nothing could be done, however, to carry the sentences into effect, for William's troops still possessed only the ground the troops stood upon and the towns they occupied. Outside those limits the whole country was against them. The Earl of Marlborough had returned to England immediately after the surrender of Kinsale; and General Ginckle, who had now succeeded to the command, determined to harass the enemy and to increase the resources at his disposal by an expedition into the south-west of Ireland, which, covered by Cork and Limerick, had hitherto been free from the presence of any English troops. He therefore pushed a strong body of cavalry and infantry westward from Cork and Kinsale; and these succeeded in making themselves masters of Castle Haven, Baltimore, Bantry, and several other castles on the line of coast. The district was wild and mountainous, and the passes might have been easily held against the advance; but the peasants had not been organized for resistance, and no serious opposition was encountered.

Colonel O'Driscol, a cousin of MacFinn O'Driscol, and Captain O'Donovan, two of the principal proprietors of the neighbourhood, soon arrived upon the spot and assembled a large irregular force, consisting chiefly

of mounted peasants, and with these they soon cooped
the invaders up in the castles they had taken. O'Driscol
next attempted the recovery of his own Castle Haven,
which was strongly defended and stood on a cliff over-
hanging the sea; but his wild peasants were ill adapted
for such work, and they were repulsed by the English
garrison and O'Driscol himself killed.   But another
force was advancing from the north; MacFinn O'Driscol
with his regiment pressed forward along the line of
Bandon river, besieged and captured Castle Haven, and
expelled the English garrisons from Baltimore and
Bantry.

General Tettau had also marched out from Cork with
several regiments of infantry and dragoons, with the
intention of penetrating into Kerry; but the enemy's
light troops harassed him night and day, wasted the
country, and defended every pass; and he was obliged
to return to Cork without having accomplished anything.   All this time Ginckle was urging upon the
lord-justices, who were now the real ruling party in
Ireland, to issue a proclamation offering pardon and
security for person and property to all who came in;
urging that it was impossible that he could ever sub-
due the country while the whole population had everything at stake in opposing him.

He was supported by King William, who was most
anxious to bring the struggle to an end; but the lord-
justices and the Protestant party at Dublin, who were
bent upon dividing among themselves the property
of the Catholics throughout Ireland, turned a deaf
ear to the arguments of Ginckle, and their friends
in London had sufficient power to prevent the king

from insisting upon his own wishes being carried into effect.

After taking part in the operations in Kerry, Captain Davenant's troop returned to Limerick, around which city the greater part of the Irish army were still encamped.

CHAPTER XIII.

A DANGEROUS MISSION.

WALTER," Captain Davenant said to his son one day when he returned from a council in which he had taken part at the quarters of General Sarsfield, " I have a mission for you in Dublin. It is necessary, in the first place, to communicate with some of our friends there, and in the second to ascertain, as far as we can, the plans of the enemy during the next campaign. There are few of us here who would not be readily recognized in Dublin; therefore, when there seemed a difficulty in selecting someone to undertake the duty, I said that I thought you would be likely to succeed better than most.

"You have not been any time in Dublin, and I question whether a single person there would be likely to recognize you. You will, of course, be in disguise, and your youth will be in your favour. I don't say there is no danger in such an undertaking, but I do not think the risk is greater than that which you have frequently run. I was sure you would readily undertake the mission, and I thought I could answer for your intelligence as well as your discretion."

"I will undertake it certainly, father, if you think

me capable of it," Walter said; "it is dull enough here now that the wet weather has thoroughly set in, and I shall really like the adventure. When am I to set out?"

"To-morrow. Your instructions and the letters you are to carry will be drawn up to-night, and you can set off after breakfast. I shall ride with you, with a part of the troop, until you are past the point where you are likely to fall in with any body of the enemy's cavalry; after that you will, of course, shift for yourself. We think you had best travel on foot, dressed as a peasant; in that way you will attract no attention and pass through towns occupied by the enemy without questioning."

"I think, father, I will take Larry with me, if you have no objection. He would be the real thing, and could do most of the talking; besides sometimes it is very useful to have someone to send with a message, or to put on guard when one went in anywhere."

"Take him, by all means, Walter, and, indeed, I agree with you that you may find him very useful."

Accordingly the following morning Walter and Larry, dressed as young peasants, mounted, and with the troop started from the camp. No signs of any parties of the enemy were seen during their ride, and after proceeding some five-and-twenty miles, they dismounted, and with a hearty farewell from Captain Davenant and a cheer from the men they started on foot.

The letters of which Walter was the bearer had been written on very small pieces of paper and had been sewn up inside the collar of his coat. His instructions as to the persons on whom he was to call had been learned by heart and the paper destroyed. Larry was in high glee at taking part in the adventure, and laughed and jested as they made their way along. They avoided the main roads running to Waterford and Dublin, as they would probably have fallen in with parties of troops journeying west, and might have been shot out of pure wantonness, besides being exposed to the risk of being asked awkward questions.

They slept at peasants' houses, where they were everywhere hospitably received as soon as their hosts assured themselves that they were Catholics. Larry was the principal spokesman, for although Walter, like all the Catholic gentry, spoke the native language, he was not so fluent as his follower, to whom it came naturally, as, although the peasantry in the neighbourhood of Dublin were all able to speak English, they always conversed in Irish among themselves. Larry gave out that he and his companion had been serving in the army and had obtained leave to pay a visit to their native village near Dublin for the winter.

" I doubt whether you will find much of it standing," one of their hosts said, " for I hear that county Wicklow and all round Dublin has been wasted by them foreign devils in Dublin. The curse of Cromwell be upon them! but we'll be aven wid them yet. They say next spring a big French army is coming, and they will set the Germans running so that they won't stop till the last man gets on board ship and ould Ireland is free from them, the murthering haythens. But you

must be careful, lads, and not let out to a sowl that ye
have been wid the boys in the west, or it's short work
they would make of you."

In every case they were asked questions about sons
or relations with the army, and were often able to
give news as to where the regiments to which they
belonged were stationed and of the part they had
taken during the last year's fighting. News travelled
slowly and was circulated principally by means of
travelling pedlars, who hawked their wares from village
to village and reported what was going on in the outside world. Thus, although the peasants were aware
of the general details of the fighting which had taken
place, they knew nothing of the part which the various
regiments had borne in it.

Reading and writing were rare accomplishments
and the post was altogether interrupted, so that many
remained in suspense, from the beginning to the end of
the war, as to the fate of those who had left them to take
part in it. The friends did not make long journeys, for
Walter was unaccustomed to walk barefooted, and his
feet at first were very sore and tender; but by the time
they reached Dublin they had hardened and he was
able to stride along by the side of Larry, who, until
he started with him for the war, had never had on a
pair of shoes in his life.

As soon as they reached Dublin they made their
way to the quarters inhabited by the working-classes.
There Walter purchased shoes and made such altera-
tion in their attire as to do away with their country
aspect and give them the appearance of two young

fellows belonging to the town. Having hired a room and made these changes they sallied out.

The streets were thronged with foreign troops, who behaved as if in a conquered country, swaggering along the streets, pushing the citizens out into the middle of the road, abusing the tradesmen who refused to part with their goods at nominal prices, making insolent remarks to any woman who hurried past them, and behaving with a freedom and license which showed how completely all bonds of discipline were relaxed.

"They look mighty bould," Larry whispered, "but it's mighty little of it they show when they see the Irish horse advancing agin them. No one would think, to see them now, as they were the men we saw spurring away for the bare life on Boyne Water."

"No, indeed, Larry," agreed Walter, who was furious at what he saw. "I wish we had a few squadrons of Sarsfield's horse here; we would clear the street of these vermin in no time. But you must be careful, Larry. Whatever happens we must not get into any brawl. We have a mission to perform, and must not think of ourselves."

"I will remember it, yer honour."

It was well that Larry had been warned, for the next moment a German soldier passing brushed against him, and then, with a savage oath, turned and struck him to the ground. Larry sprung up with his eyes blazing with passion, but he caught Walter's warning "Larry," and, hanging his head, moved away without a word.

"That's right, Larry," Walter said approvingly. "I

was afraid for a moment that you were going to spring at that fellow. If you had you would have been in a lock-up in five minutes, and as you could have given no good account of yourself, there you might have remained for weeks."

"If ever I meet that fellow outside Dublin," Larry muttered savagely, "I will pay him for the blow he gave me.'

Seeing the risk of another encounter of the same kind Walter led the way down to the bank of the river, and there they remained chatting until it became dusk.

"Now, Larry, I must begin my work. My first visit is to be to a merchant who lives in a street close to where the ships discharge. While I am in do you sit down on a door-step near and keep a sharp look-out to see whether the house is watched. It is not likely, but all the better class of Catholics who remain in the town are regarded with suspicion."

Walter had no trouble in finding the house he was in search of, and, knocking at the door, he told the servant who opened it that he wanted to see the master.

"You must come in business hours," the man said; "he can't see you now."

"I have a letter to him from his friend Mr. Fitzgerald of Waterford. If you tell him that I think he will see me now."

"That's all right," the man said. "He tould me if anyone came with a letter from that gentleman I was to show him up."

So saying he led him up stairs.

"Here's a young man, your honour, with the letter you tould me about from Mr. Fitzgerald.

"Show him in," a voice said; and Walter entered a sitting-room. The gentleman who was with him said nothing until the door was closed behind him: then he asked:

"Has the ship come in?"

To which Walter replied:

"She is sailing slowly, but she will come."

"That's right," the merchant said rising. "Where do you come from?"

"I am Walter Davenant, a cornet in my father's troop of horse, and I have come direct from Limerick. I have a letter for you in my collar."

He pulled off his coat, the merchant handed him a knife, he ripped open the collar, and taking out the papers concealed there picked out that intended for Mr. O'Brian, which was not directed, but had only a slight mark upon it to distinguish it from the others. The merchant read it in silence.

"I am disappointed, Mr. Davenant," he said as he finished it. "I had hoped that a dash would be made at Dublin this winter; but the general says that it has been decided to fight one more campaign on the defensive, and that in the autumn, when the French arrive, there will be a general advance. Now, I am ready to answer any question you are instructed to ask."

"In the first place, sir, how many men do you think would be ready to join in any rising in Dublin?"

"It would all depend upon whether an Irish army was advancing in this direction. In that case some seven or eight thousand men would rise. But unless there were a hope of early assistance I do not think that above a thousand could be relied on. I have about that number on my list. They, as you see, could do nothing unassisted. There are three or four thousand troops here, and the Protestant mob who would join them would number seven or eight thousand at the very least. Therefore any attempt to rise in the face of such odds, unless after a crushing defeat of William's troops, would be out of the question. But, as I said, if an army were marching on Dublin, the Protestants would be thinking more of taking to their ships than fighting, and all the Catholics in the city would then join the movement."

"I think the general hoped that you could have mustered a stronger force, sir."

"So I could a year ago," Mr. O'Brian said; "but the constant persecution and ill-treatment of the Catholics have caused large numbers of them to leave the town. Many of the younger and more determined men have made their way west and joined the army. I fear that the numbers I have given are quite as many as can be relied upon."

"The general was in hopes," Walter said, "that a diversion might have been caused in the spring by a rising in Dublin, which would, even if unsuccessful, compel the Dutch general to keep a large force here."

"It might have been done six or eight months ago,"

Mr. O'Brian said; "but the spirit of the people here has been very much broken as well as their numbers diminished. But you can rely upon it, that if anything like a general rising can be got up, we will do our share here. With but a thousand men I can rely on, I feel that any open insurrection would be hopeless; but we could fire the city at a score of points night after night, and so alarm the citizens that they would insist on a considerable force being kept here for their protection, and this would aid our friends outside. I know nothing as to what is being done there, I have only charge of the matter inside the city."

"I am well aware of that, sir, and have to call upon those who have the threads of the movement throughout the country in their hands. I only arrived to-day, and came to you first in order that I might know how matters stand here before I see the others. I shall, of course, call again upon you before I leave."

After leaving Mr. O'Brian Walter visited the houses of several others to whom he bore letters. The accounts of the feeling throughout the country were more encouraging than those which he had received from Mr. O'Brian. The hatred of the invaders was greater than ever, and the peasantry in all parts were in a state of sullen desperation: indeed the enemy could nowhere move in small parties without the certainty of being attacked. The pressing need was arms. A great part of the peasants who owned guns had already joined the army, and the rest possessed no weapons beyond roughly-made pikes and scythes fixed on long handles. These were formidable weapons in a sudden attack on

any small party, but they would not enable the peasants
to cope with any chance of success against considerable
bodies of troops, especially if provided with artillery.
The persons whom Walter saw were in communication
with the disaffected in all parts of the country, and
agreed in the opinion that a general rising should be
delayed until some striking success was obtained by the
Irish army, when the whole country would rise and fall
upon the enemy wherever met with. The plans for a
rising having been discussed and arranged after several
interviews, at some of which most of the leaders of the
movement were present, Walter prepared to start again
for the camp with the news that the first Irish victory
would be followed by a rising throughout the country,
aided by great conflagrations if not by a serious movement in Dublin.

The negotiations had occupied over a fortnight.
During the first ten days, Larry, who always kept
watch outside the house Walter was visiting, reported
that nothing whatever had occurred that was in the
slightest degree suspicious. Then he told Walter, on
his retiring to their lodgings, that he fancied their foot-
steps were followed.

"Do you think so, Larry?"

"I do, yer honour," Larry replied earnestly. "Three
times when you were in the house the same man came
along the street, and each time I saw him look up at
the windows, and somehow I felt that he was following us on our way back. I looked round several times,
and each time I fancied I saw a fellow slip into a doorway."

"That is serious, Larry. You don't think anyone in this house can have a suspicion of us?"

"Not they, yer honour. They all think it's just as you say; that the village was burned, and we have come to look for work in the city. Besides, if it was anyone here, he wouldn't have to take the trouble to track us back.".

"That's true enough, Larry. No; if there is a suspicion, it must be from some spy in the house of one of the gentlemen I have visited. We know that the leading Catholics are all suspected, and some of the servants may have been bribed to report everything which takes place in the house. We must be very careful; and let us arrange this, Larry, that if there is trouble and we get separated, we will neither of us come back to our lodging, but will meet at that burned-out village three miles along the western road. If anything happens to me, go to the first house I went to, and see Mr. O'Brian, and tell him that I have been taken. If there is anything to be done he will do it; if not, make your way straight back to Limerick. I have told you exactly what has been arranged with people I have seen, and you can tell my father, who will report to the general. But whatever you do, don't stop here with any idea of getting me out of their hands. The most important thing is that they should know at Limerick exactly what has been arranged. If you remain here you would almost certainly be caught also, for as the man who has followed us will be aware that we are together, a search will at once be made for you. So mind, my orders are that if you see I am in trouble you are at once to set out for Limerick. If you think that I may manage to get away, you are also to leave at once, but are to wait for me for twelve hours at the village three miles out. If I do not come by the end of that time, it will be that I have been taken, and you are to go straight on."

It was on the evening when all the arrangements were finally settled that a loud knocking was heard at the door of the house where eight of the principal persons in the affair were assembled. One of them looked out of the window and announced that the street was full of soldiers. All leaped to their feet and drew their swords.

"It is of no use to resist, gentlemen," Walter said. "Do you put bottles and glasses on the table and sit down quietly. I will try to escape. If they find you alone they can prove nothing against you, and if I get safe off you also are safe. Is there any way out on to the roof? No doubt the house is watched behind."

"There is a trap-door," the gentleman, in whose house they were, said, and led the way up stairs at full speed.

As he was unbolting the trap Walter ran into a bedroom and seized an armful of blankets, then ran up the ladder to the trap-door and stepped out on to the roof. The door was closed behind him, and he heard the bolts drawn, and then his host ran down stairs and told the frightened servants to open the doors, which had so far resisted the attack from without. Headed by an officer, the soldiers rushed in.

"What means this violence?" the gentleman asked. "Why is my house broken into in this way?"

"I arrest you and all who are in this house," the officer said, "on the charge of treason."

"Treason!" the gentleman said coolly; "you will find no treason here. I have a few friends up stairs who are cracking a bottle of port; but that is not, so far as I am aware, against the law."

The officer ran up stairs to the room where the others were standing, as if surprised at the tumult, round the table, on which were bottles and half-filled glasses.

"Take the names of all these persons," the officer said to the sergeant who followed him, "and then convey them in custody to the castle."

"There is no trouble about their names," the host said. "All are well known and peaceful citizens, as can be testified by any magistrate."

"Where is the man who was with you?" the officer said, looking round.

"There is, so far as I am aware, no one in the house, sir, beyond these gentlemen and my domestics."

"It is a lie!" the officer exclaimed furiously. "A man was seen to enter this house an hour and a half ago, and no one has left since."

"A young man! Oh, I suppose you mean the young fellow who brought me a message from my cousin at Waterford, and who called to ask if I had yet found him any employment. Oh yes, he has been here, but left some time ago, unless he is chatting with the maids in the kitchen."

The officer directed a rigorous search to be made of the house. The soldiers soon reported that every nook and corner had been examined, but that no one was to be found. At this moment a shot was fired in the street, and a sergeant ran in.

"Captain Peters bid me say, sir, that they have just caught sight of a man on the roof of a house some distance along the street."

"Take the prisoners to the castle under a strong guard, sergeant. You will be answerable for their safety," the officer exclaimed, as he ran down stairs.

Directly the trap closed behind him, Walter—sure that some minutes would pass before the method of his escape was known—tore the blankets he had brought with him into wide strips, tied the ends together, and twisted them up into the form of a rope; then, coiling this over his arm, he made his way along the roofs. The street below was now a mass of people. The report that a Popish plot had been discovered, and that a number of important arrests had been made, spread quickly as the soldiers were seen gathered round the house. The news was sufficient to stir up party feelings, and the mob which collected soon set up the shout which had of late been so often raised in the streets of Dublin—"Down with the Papists!"

Soon the crashing of glass was heard, as stones were hurled at the dwellings of known Catholics. Walter, anxious for the safety of Larry, who was, he knew, somewhere without, tried to look down into the street to see what was going on, believing that in the darkness he could not be seen. The flash of a musket, and

WALTER ESCAPES FROM THE ENGLISH SOLDIERS.

the whistle of a ball close to him showed him that his
figure had been seen against the sky-line. Drawing
back, he paused a moment in thought. The trap-door
would be discovered at once, and a search on the roof
commenced, and the soldiers would be placed behind
the houses. There was no time to be lost in continuing
his search for a house with a building projecting
behind on to which he could lower himself with his
rope, which was not nearly long enough to reach the
ground.

Looking over at the back between two of the sharp
ridges of the roofs, he hung his rope so that it would
fall across a window, fastened the end round a stack
of chimneys, and then taking hold of it, swung himself
over. He had been very careful in tying the knots,
and had tested them by pulling at them with all his
strength; but he did not feel at all certain that they
might not draw with his weight, in which case he
must have been dashed to pieces on the ground far
below him; but there was no time to hesitate, and as
fast as he could he began to slide down the rope, the
frequent knots affording good hold for his hands.

At last he reached the window. It was made of
the small diamond-shaped panes at that time in
general use. Holding the rope with one hand and his
legs, he dashed the other hand through a pane just where
he judged the fastening inside would be. Three panes
were beaten in before he felt the latch. This was
easily turned. The frame opened outward, and he
had some difficulty in pulling it past him; then, grasping the woodwork, he drew himself in, and with a

great effort succeeded in gaining a sufficient holding
to enable him to leave go of the rope and make good
his footing inside.

He had little fear of the inmates of the house taking
notice of the fall of glass; for had they noticed the
sound above the din in the street they would have
supposed that the breakage was caused by one of the
flying stones. He ran lightly down stairs and opened
a door at the back of the house and found himself in
the yard. The wall was not very high, and a spring
enabled him to get his fingers on the top. He was
soon sitting there, and then dropped into the road behind. The sound of his fall caught the ears of the
soldiers who were stationed at the back of the house
from whence he had started, some fifty yards away.

There was a sharp challenge, and then, as no answer
was given, four or five shots were fired, and there was
a rush of feet along the road.

As it was only in the principal thoroughfares that
a few lights were exhibited, the road would have been
in complete darkness had not the clouds just at that
moment blown away from the face of the moon, which
was half full.

The shots, however, had been fired hastily, and
Walter dashed off at full speed unhurt. He heard
shouts from the roofs of the houses, and one or two
shots were fired, but the chance of his being hit was
but small.

The sound, however, told the soldiers and crowd in
the front street that the fugitive was escaping at the
rear, and there was a general rush down the street to

the next turning. Walter was a hundred yards
ahead before the mob reached the turning, and was
rapidly distancing the soldiers who were pursuing
him. Unfortunately, however, there were many people
hurrying from all sides, attracted by the shouting and
firing. Several of these, in response to the shouts of
the soldiers, tried to stop him as he dashed past, and
failing to do so, at once joined in the pursuit.

Walter saw that he must be captured if he kept
straight on, for a group of men approaching, warned
by the shouts of his pursuers, prepared to seize him.
He therefore turned sharp down a narrow lane to his
left. Another fifty yards he was through this, and
found himself on the road running by the side of the
Liffey. Without a moment's hesitation he sprang
across it and plunged into the river.

Even in the moment of his spring, he perceived
that the tide was running up. Had it been ebbing
he would have made down and tried to gain the
shore under shelter of the shipping moored below.
But it was useless to think of swimming against the
tide. His pursuers were but a few yards behind him,
and the second time he rose to the surface for air two
or three shots were fired. He dived again, and when
he next came up took a deliberate look round in
order to judge of his chances. He was now about a
third of the way across. The shore he had left was
already lined with people, and several were gathering
on the opposite bank.

Two or three shots struck the water close to him,
and he knew that he was visible to his pursuers.

Taking a long breath he again went under water. He
was a first-rate swimmer and diver, having bathed
regularly summer and winter in the bay below the
castle.

He had this time turned his face towards the shore
he had quitted. The tide he knew was sweeping him
up. He kept under water as long as he possibly
could, swimming his hardest. When he could keep
under no longer, he turned on his back and permitted
himself to rise slowly to the surface.

The moment his mouth and nostrils were above
water he got rid of the pent-up air, took another
breath, and sank again. He swam on until he felt by
the ground rising rapidly in front of him that he was
close to the edge. He then cautiously came to the
surface and looked round. He was close under the
bank from which he had started, but two or three
hundred yards higher up. The bank rose straight up
some twelve feet above him, and he could hear persons
talking close to its edge.—"There he is."—"No, he
isn't."—"Pretty nearly over the other side."—"I don't
see him."—"They will catch him as he gets out."—"I
believe he has sunk."—"He never could keep under
all this time."—"One of the bullets must have hit
him."

Then a voice in the crowd shouted, "There's his head
just in the middle of the river," and a stone splashed
in the stream. It was followed by a volley of other
stones and several musket-shots in the same direction.

Walter having now got his breath, sank his head
quietly below the water, and swam on again, keeping

close under the bank. Whenever he came up for air he listened for a moment. Shots were still being fired below him, and he knew that the attention of all upon the shores was still directed towards the centre of the stream, and that there was but small chance of anyone leaning over to gaze down into the water close to their feet.

His hopes rose as every minute placed him further from his pursuers. He could no longer hear voices above him when he rose, but he swam on for upwards of a mile and struggled up the bank well beyond the walls of the town.

He lay down a few minutes to rest himself, walked half a mile along the bank, and then entering the river again, swam across, for the road he was to follow was on the south side of it.

He made his way across the country until he saw a small shed. He entered this, and finding some hay in the loft, stripped off his wet clothes, and crept deep into the hay to warm himself, for the water was cold, and he was shivering from head to foot. As soon as it was light he again put on his clothes and started at a run, which he maintained until he was in a thorough glow in spite of his wet clothing. He did not approach the village, at which he had arranged to meet Larry, until the sun was high and his clothes had dried so far that they would not attract the attention of anyone who might be passing. Then he went into the deserted village and took up his place in one of the ruined cottages, from which he could obtain a view of the road from Dublin.

(377) S

Half an hour later he saw Larry coming along it. Although there was no one else in sight, someone might be going the other way, and Walter therefore remained in his hiding-place till Larry was abreast of him, when he showed his head in the doorway and called him by name.

Larry gave a cry of joy, and rushing in, threw his arms round him and burst into tears.

"It's a terrible fright you have given me!" he exclaimed when he could find words. "I have been breaking my heart all night. Sure I thought you were at the bottom of the river."

"Not this time, Larry, though it was a pretty close thing. Did you see it all?"

"Sure and I did," Larry said. "I was sitting on a door-step watching the house when I saw the sodgers coming along. They turned up from a side street, and were so close that I saw I could not get across and get the door opened in time to give you the alarm. Then they began to knock at the door, and for a bit I felt so wake that I could not move. Then the crowd began to gather, and then I said to myself, The master will try to shlip out at the back of the house. So I went round, but I found the thieves of the world waiting for ye there. But I was sure ye weren't the one to let them take ye widout a struggle for it. So I moved a bit away, and jist waited.

"The time seemed long, when on a suddint I heard the sodgers sing out, and then fire and set out to run. I never doubted it was you, and so off I went behindt them as hard as I could tare. I wasn't long in coming

up to them, and at first I thought ye would get clean
away. Then my heart fell when I saw those villains
attempt to seize ye, but when I thought it was all over
ye turned sharp off and made for the river. I was
with the first of them to get there, and I ran accidental
against the first sodger who got his musket to his
shoulder, and there was no saying where the ball went
to. He cursed me for a clumsy baste, and would have
knocked me down, but he was in too great a hurry to
load again.

" I saw the bullets strike the water close to you when
you came up again. I saw you look round, and guessed
ye was thinking what was the best thing to do. Then
we saw no more of ye. I didn't think you had been
hit, for I saw you go down regular, as if you were
diving in the sea for pleasure, and not sharp as you
would have done if a bullet had hit you. I guessed as
you were meaning to swim up the stream, and I did
the only thing I could to stop them from following
up by shouting that I saw ye, and throwing a big
stone into the water close to where I had seen your
head before, knowing that by that time ye must be
nigh a hundred yards up.

" The fools didn't stop to think, but they took to
throwing stones and firing as hard as they could, and
by the time they had done I knew, if ye were alive,
ye must be nigh a quarter of a mile up the river. Some
of them did run up, and I kept with them, but sorrah
a glimpse of ye did we get. At last everyone made
sure that you were kilt entirely, and went their ways.
I went off to our lodgings, but took good care not to

go in. And it was well I didn't. For half an hour later a troop of sodgers came up, and some of them went in.

"They were led by that black villain who used to come wid messages from Mr. O'Brian, and I have no doubt it was he who set the sodgers upon you. Anyhow, they didn't find much there, but four of them waited till morning inside, the others all going away, so that if you had got out of the river they might catch ye in a trap. I waited till they had left this morning, thinking, I suppose, that it was no use to stay longer, and then started to see if your honour were here.

"Sometimes I thought I should find you, then again I towld myself that if you had been alive I must have seen you come up agin; for, knowing the strength of the stream and how fast you could swim, I could tell pretty nigh about where you would come up if you were keeping straight up the river. How did you manage it at all, Master Walter?"

"I turned and swam back again to the bank, Larry. I knew everyone would be watching the middle of the river, and would not be looking at the water in front of them. Of course the stream took me up a long way. I only came up once, on my back, took a breath, and went down again, and the second time I was right under the bank and well out of sight, though I could hear them talking above me. It was just when I looked round then that I saw them throwing stones and firing into the middle of the river two hundred yards lower down, and after that I had only to keep on swimming under water close to the bank."

"And that is how ye managed it! It was a grand thought entirely to swim back to us. I never thought of that. I was most afraid you would go for the opposite shore, and there were plenty had gathered there ready to seize you. I didn't think I could have missed you if you'd kept on in the middle, and I have been puzzled altogether as to what could have become of you if ye were really alive. I have got some bread in my bundle here, and a bottle of spirits, and you had better have a bite and a sup before we go on, for it's pretty nigh as white as a ghost ye are."

The meal seemed to put new life and strength into Walter, and after its conclusion he was ready to step out again with fresh energy. They thought it better at once to leave the road and tramp across the country. By so doing they avoided all parties of the English troops, and reached the Irish army without adventure. Walter at once reported himself to General Sarsfield, and related all that had taken place in Dublin.

"You have done excellently, Mr. Davenant, and your escape from capture was an extraordinary one. Unfortunately the betrayal of what was doing, and the arrest of our friends, is likely to upset all the plans you had arranged."

"I hope not, sir," Walter said. "I know that they were all careful to have no written documents, for it was always possible that the houses of the Catholics might be searched."

"That may be so," the general said; "but I fear that this traitor will have managed to overhear some of the conversation; and the fact of their meeting and of your escape will in itself tell against them sufficiently to ensure their being kept in prison at anyrate for a considerable time, and even if released they would be suspected persons, and would be unable to make the slightest move."

The general's previsions were justified. The whole of those arrested were retained in prison for some months, and no such general rising as had been planned was ever carried into effect.

During the winter stores and ordnance arrived from France for the supply of the Irish army, and from England for the use of the British, and a great number of officers from the Continent also joined both armies.

The discontent among the Irish at the apathy of France was extreme. They had embarked in the war on the strength of the promises of King Louis. None of these promises had been fulfilled. The supplies of arms and money had been most meagre, the few thousand troops sent had never taken part in any of the operations, and their coming had been much more than counterbalanced by the troops sent from Ireland in exchange for them. An additional cause of discontent was given by the fact that William exchanged all the prisoners taken in Ireland for Dutch prisoners in the hands of Louis, and the Irish so handed over were all incorporated in the French army.

So great was the discontent, that had a proclamation of pardon and protection been offered, the whole Irish army would have disbanded and all resistance ceased. But Louis, alarmed at finding that it was likely William would be freed from his troubles at home, and be at liberty to give his whole attention to the war on the Continent, sent fresh promises of large and speedy aid, and despatched General St. Ruth to take the command in Ireland in place of Lauzun, who had returned to France.

This appointment caused fresh discontent among the Irish. Their cause had already been well-nigh ruined by the interference and incapacity of the French generals, and on the retirement of Lauzun they had confidently expected that Sarsfield would be appointed commander-in-chief, and that henceforth there would be unity of design in their operations. St. Ruth was accompanied by a large number of young French officers, whose demeanour still further widened the breach between the French and Irish.

St. Ruth at once inspected the army, now concentrated between Limerick and Athlone. Except that there was a great deficiency in horses for the cavalry the army was greatly improved in discipline and appearance since the battle of the Boyne, for both officers, petty officers, and men had learned their duties. The army had passed the winter in comfortable quarters, and had been well supplied with food. The difficulty was to find horses. The Rapparees had carried off many of the chargers of the English cavalry by stratagem, and it was a common practice of the Danish and other foreign troops to sell their horses to the Irish at the outposts and pretend that they were stolen. Still the supply was altogether insufficient, and St. Ruth, finding that he could not get horses from the enemy, determined to take them from his friends.

A proclamation was accordingly issued inviting all the gentry throughout the country held by the Irish to meet him at Limerick, mounted and accoutred in the best manner. Reports were spread that an important communication was to be made to the gentlemen of the country from King James, and that many marks of honour and distinction were to be conferred.

Accordingly, there was a very numerous attendance of gentry on the day fixed. St. Ruth appeared on the ground with a large body of cavalry. He made a speech to the gentlemen — complimented them on their punctual attendance and gallant appearance; told them that it was necessary that every man should make sacrifices for the defence of his religion and his estates, and requested them to hand over their horses to the cavalry. He then at once rode off the ground, leaving the cavalry to take possession of the horses. Anger and expostulation were useless, and the gentlemen had to return on foot, sadder men; but the army obtained a large and valuable addition of horses, and St. Ruth was able to march out at the head of twenty thousand foot and five thousand well-appointed cavalry.

Their direction was Athlone, towards which point Ginckle was also directing his movements, having assembled his whole force at Mullingar, withdrawing the garrisons from almost all the towns, in order to raise his force in the field. The alarm in Dublin was, in consequence, extreme, and the council and lords-justices besought Ginckle not to leave them without protection; but he only replied, that they had it in their own power to put an end to the war by publishing such a declaration of pardon and security for person and property as would satisfy the Irish in James's army. But the council, even in this moment of alarm, refused to renounce their golden hopes of confiscation.

Ginckle's first attack was directed against the village of Ballymore, which lay between Mullingar and Athlone. It was defended by a thousand cavalry and infantry, and a sergeant and a few men were posted in a castle on an eminence some distance from the village. The first attack was made on the castle, but the sergeant and his little garrison made a long and gallant resistance, and the savage Dutchman was so infuriated at the opposition that when at last the post was taken he ordered the gallant sergeant to be at once hung.

He then sent word to the garrison of the village that if they did not surrender he would serve them as he had served the sergeant. They were unmoved by the threat, and made a long and gallant defence against the whole of Ginckle's army; and the Dutch general was unable to overcome their resistance till he at last offered fair terms of surrender. The position being a strong and important one, Ginckle spent some days in adding to the defensive works the Irish had erected before he moved forward and sat down in front of Athlone. His army was well provided with heavy artillery and everything necessary for a siege, and he was firmly resolved that there should be no repetition of the disastrous failure of the preceding autumn.

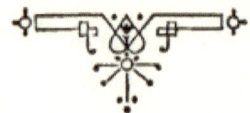

CHAPTER XIV.

ATHLONE.

THE Irish had this time determined to defend not only that portion of Athlone situated on the west of the river, but the English town on the east. The fortifications here were repaired and added to, and the town was abundantly supplied with stores and ammunition. It was, however, unable to resist the heavy artillery which Ginckle brought to play against it. Walls, buildings, and towers crumbled beneath the heavy cannonade; and although the Irish repelled, with great slaughter, several assaults upon it, the place became at last untenable, and they abandoned that part of the town and retired by the bridge across the river to the Irish town.

The British, on entering the eastern town, found it a mere mass of ruins, with the dead bodies of the soldiers lying everywhere, half covered with the wreck of the works they had died in defending. The taking of this portion of Athlone had cost Ginckle dearly, and he was but little nearer the object of his efforts, for he was separated from the Irish town by the Shannon, and the western arch of the bridge was broken down by the defenders.

Eleven large guns and three mortars now came up from Dublin, and he erected a succession of batteries upon the ruins of the English town, and opened fire upon the castle of Athlone, which, although a building of great strength, soon crumbled into ruins beneath the fire of the heavy artillery brought to bear upon it. A mill which stood in the river, and was connected with the bridge, was set on fire, and the sixty soldiers posted in it, being unable to escape, were all burned. Night and day seven great batteries played incessantly upon the town.

On the 26th of June thirty waggons loaded with powder and a hundred carts with cannon balls arrived from Dublin, and enabled the besiegers to keep up their fire without intermission. The interior of the town was reduced to ruins—nothing remained erect save the city walls, in which the breaches, as fast as they were made, were repaired by the Irish. The slaughter among those so employed was very heavy; but there was no lack of men, the places of those who fell being at once supplied by others willing to give their lives in the defence of the town.

At last there was nothing more that the besiegers could do. The town was reduced to ashes, but the river and the broken arch still separated them from the ruins. To remain much longer where they were was impossible, for the country on every side was exhausted, and no longer afforded food for man or horse. The country people had fled from the cruelty and spoliation of Ginckle's foreign soldiery, carrying with them all their effects; and the Irish light troops and armed peasantry hovered round the camp, laid the country waste, and intercepted their supplies and communications with Dublin.

Ginckle held a council of war to consider what was to be done. It was admitted that they must force the passage of the river without loss of time, or submit to the alternative of retreat and the utter failure of the campaign. It was finally resolved to attempt the passage of the bridge by throwing a wooden gallery over the broken arch, and forcing their way across at all cost. Additional batteries were now raised on the bank of the river, and a heavy fire was poured, without intermission, upon the Irish on their side of the broken arch.

Both parties had erected a breastwork on the bridge at their respective sides of the breach, and from behind this, day and night, a continued musketry fire was kept up, the grenadiers of the English army throwing grenades into the enemy's works. After some days the breastwork on the Irish side was set on fire by the continued assault of shot and grenades. The wattles of which it was composed, dried by the hot weather, were soon in a blaze, and under cover of the flames and smoke the English ran forward the great beams they had prepared in readiness, and threw them across the gap in the bridge.

The fire from all the batteries on the English side was directed against the burning breastwork, while the grenadiers hastened to lay planks across the beams to complete the bridge. The work was well-nigh done when an Irish sergeant and ten men all clad in armour, leaped through the flames of the breastwork, and began to hew with their axes at the beams and planks.

For a moment the British were paralysed at the daring action. Then the batteries and musketry fire again opened, a storm of shot and bullets swept across the bridge, and the whole of the gallant fellows fell dead, but in a moment another party, similarly armed, dashed through the flames and took their places.

Regardless of the fire they whirled their axes. Nine fell, but the last two gave the final stroke to the beams; the bridge fell with a crash into the river below, and the two survivors recrossed the breastwork and joined their friends within amid the wild enthusiasm of the defenders; an enthusiasm in which even the baffled assailants joined, for the British grenadiers gave a cheer in token of their admiration at the gallantry and devotion of the deed.

In all history there is no record of a more gallant action than this, performed by two sergeants and twenty men, who thus encountered almost certain death to maintain their post. The destruction of the temporary bridge filled Ginckle and his officers with consternation, and the manner in which their design had been baffled showed the spirit of the defenders and the magnitude of the task which they had undertaken; but it was resolved at another council which was called, to attempt one more effort before abandoning the enterprise. A finished platform was constructed. This was to be thrown over the arch, and a chosen body of the bravest troops in the army were to throw themselves across and try to force a passage. At the same time a division was to cross the river by a ford near the bridge, and another to attempt to cross by a bridge of pontoons prepared in readiness.

The Irish were informed, by French deserters, of what was going on in the English camp, and early on the morning of the assault several strong divisions of the Irish army were seen marching down from the camp two miles away into the town. Here they were drawn up in readiness to repulse the assault.

The British were some time before they were ready for the attack, but at ten o'clock the whole army stood in close order ready to advance. The first to move forward were those who were to carry the bridge. The Irish guns, which still remained intact, opened upon them, but they pressed forward along the bridge to the broken arch, and, with less trouble than had been anticipated, threw the platform across it. Instead of rushing forward at once the grenadiers stood behind their breastwork and hurled their grenades at the Irish grenadiers, who stood in close order on the opposite edge.

These, however, stood their ground and hurled their grenades with great effect into the column. One of these exploded against the English breastwork and set it on fire. It at once blazed up; a strong west wind was blowing and drove the smoke and flames into the faces of the English grenadiers, who for some time strove in vain to extinguish the flames, notwithstanding the heavy fire which the defenders poured into them. They had at last to fall back, and the Irish,

sallying from behind their breastwork, pulled down
the burning timbers on to the bridge, which was soon
in flames.

The other divisions of the English army, finding that
the grenadiers on the bridge made no progress, did not
attempt to perform their part of the work, and finally
the whole retreated to their camp. That evening
another council of war was held. Matters now looked
desperate, and the fact that the enterprise had this
time failed owing to the hesitation of the troops to
push forward to the attack of the enemy made the
prospect appear more hopeless. Nevertheless, in spite
of the opposition of Generals Ginckle and Mackey the
council determined that one more attempt should be
made, and that this should be carried out at daylight
next morning in the hopes of taking the Irish by surprise.

It was accordingly given out that the army would
retreat in the morning, and the heavy guns were with-
drawn from the batteries. St. Ruth, who was convinced that Athlone could not be taken, and who had
spent the greater portion of his time in entertaining
the ladies and gentry of the neighbourhood with balls
and fêtes, fell into the trap, and, contrary to the
opinion and advice of the Irish generals, recalled from
the town the regiments which had marched in that
morning and replaced them with only three battalions
of inferior troops.

The Irish officers remonstrated warmly, but St.
Ruth, to show his disdain for their opinions, invited a
large party of ladies and gentlemen to an entertain-

ment in the evening. In the night the British army prepared for the attack; the commanders of the respective divisions all led their troops in person. The garrison of the town were all asleep. In St. Ruth's camp the festivities were over, and the general and his officers had retired. The Irish sentinels, who noted the movement in the British camp, supposed that they were mustering to retreat, and thus the three British columns drew up inside the town wall in readiness to advance, without a notion of their purpose being entertained on the opposite side of the river.

One column, headed by sixty chosen men in complete armour, was to cross the bridge and throw a platform over the arch; another to cross by the ford; the third by a pontoon bridge. When the church bell tolled six the three columns advanced simultaneously, and before the Irish were thoroughly awake, the leading battalions had forded the river, the platform was in its place, and the troops pouring into the town.

A few guns were hastily discharged, and then the men of the three Irish regiments in the town fled in haste to avoid capture by the columns pouring across the river by the ford and pontoon bridge. Many indeed were captured whilst asleep. St. Ruth, roused from sleep by the sound of cannon, ordered the troops to arms, but it was too late. The town, or rather its ruins, were in the possession of the British, and the brilliant success which had been won by the valour and determination of the Irish troops was forfeited by the carelessness, folly, and self-confidence of the French general.

Had he listened to the advice of the Irish officers the attempt, like those which had preceded it, must have failed, and in that case there was nothing remained to Ginckle but a precipitous retreat to Dublin, with the loss of the whole of the advantages gained in the previous campaign and the necessity of bringing the war to an end by the concession of the rights and privileges of the Irish Catholics and landowners.

The whole course of history was changed by the folly of one man. Ginckle had taken Athlone, but it was at a vast cost of life, and he was more than ever impressed with the magnitude of the task of subduing Ireland so long as the people were driven to desperation by the threatened confiscation of all their lands and by the persecution of their religion. King William too was more anxious than ever for the termination of hostilities, and on the very day that the news of the fall of Athlone reached him he issued a proclamation offering protection, security of all possessions, and continuance in any offices which they held under James, to all who would lay down their arms in three weeks' time.

The issue of such a proclamation as this a year before would have satisfied the Irish and put a stop to the war; but it was now too late. The promises made had been broken over and over again, and the Irish had but too much reason to fear that when all opposition ceased the council and their train of greedy adherents would again obtain the ascendency, and would continue their work of spoliation and robbery. Moreover, the Irish army did not feel itself in any way

beaten. It was not its fault that the second siege of
Athlone had not terminated as the former siege and
that of Limerick had done, and that Ginckle's army
was not hurrying back defeated and disorganized to
Dublin. They felt that at the battle of the Boyne
they had suffered no defeat, although, in accordance
with the general plan, they had fallen back, and they
eagerly desired to fight one battle to prove that in the
open field they were more than a match for the mercenaries of King William. The council and lords-
justices, who were aghast at the proclamation which
threatened to destroy their hopes of dividing among
themselves and their friends all the lands of the
Catholics of Ireland, did their best to prevent its
acceptance by spreading rumours that it was a mere
bait, and that its promises would not be fulfilled, while
St. Ruth and his French officers did their best also to
set the Irish against it.

St. Ruth, who was really a good officer, was conscious
that, so far from having gained credit as he had expected from a command in Ireland, the misfortunes
which had happened were entirely attributed to him,
and he longed for an opportunity of wiping out the
slur on his military reputation. He therefore urged
upon the Irish generals that Ginckle had indeed gained
but little; that all the hopes of William rested upon
that army alone; and that with its defeat they could
demand and obtain any terms they liked to lay down;
besides which he was able to assure them by his
advices from France that Louis was making preparations for assisting them on a vastly larger scale than

he had previously done. Thus from a combination of circumstances the proclamation elicited no response.

While the siege of Athlone was being carried on the main body of Sarsfield's cavalry remained for the most part in the camp near the town, but commanders of small bodies of men like the corps of Captain Davenant, which were regarded as irregulars, had liberty of action. Some made long raids to the east and often spread confusion and dismay among the enemy by appearing suddenly when no Irish troops were believed to be within a hundred miles. Some went down and joined the peasants, who were keeping up desultory fighting in the neighbourhood of Cork, harassing the English whenever they moved from one point to another, or sent out parties to collect forage or provisions. Captain Davenant, who had more than once respectfully urged upon Sarsfield the immense benefit which would result were the whole of the Irish cavalry to place themselves upon the line of the enemy's communication, finding that the Irish general was unmoved by his arguments, several times endeavoured to carry out his ideas as far as could be done with his own small force.

The inactivity of the Irish horse throughout the long sieges of Athlone and Limerick, except only upon the occasion of the raid upon the siege-train, is almost inexplicable. They had nothing to fear from the enemy's cavalry, to whom they proved themselves immensely superior whenever they met during the war, and they had it in their power for months to cut the British communications and so oblige them either to detach so large a force to keep the roads open that they would have been unable to push on the siege, and would indeed have been in danger of being attacked and destroyed by the Irish infantry, or to raise the siege and fall back upon their bases, Dublin and Waterford.

The only possible explanations that can be offered are—first, that Sarsfield, although a dashing commander in action, was possessed of no military genius whatever; second, that he was prevented from moving by the jealousy of the French commanders-in-chief, who did not wish to see the credit of compelling the enemy to fall back monopolized by the Irish cavalry; or, third, that Sarsfield saw the advantages which could be obtained by throwing himself, with his cavalry, in the rear of the enemy, but deliberately remained inactive rather than leave the French generals to act unchecked by his presence at head-quarters. It can never be decided to which of these alternatives it was due that the Irish cavalry remained for so long a time inactive, and that William, and after him Ginckle, were permitted unmolested, save by a few detached bodies of horse, to maintain their long line of communications to their base unchecked

Upon one of his excursions in the rear of the English army Captain Davenant's troops dashed down upon a convoy of waggons. The dragoons who were escorting them were killed or driven off. The drivers were collected in a group, for Captain Davenant always ordered that these men should not be injured, as they were not combatants, and were in most cases obliged to accompany their teams, which had been requisitioned for the service. The men were collecting the waggons together preparatory to setting them on fire, when Walter, on riding near the group of drivers, heard himself called by name. Turning round he leapt from his horse and ran up to one of the prisoners.

"My dear John!" he exclaimed, "I am glad indeed to see you. Why, what brings you here?"

After exchanging hearty greetings Walter led him away from the group, and the two sat down together on a bank.

"What brings you here?" Walter repeated.

"All the waggons within miles round Dublin have been requisitioned," John said; "and as our three were called for, my father suggested that I should accompany them to see that the horses were fed and cared for."

"Which are your waggons?" Walter asked.

"The three last in the column."

Walter immediately ran to his father, told him what had happened, and begged that the three waggons should be exempted from the general destruction. Captain Davenant at once rode up to the men and ordered the waggons to be unloaded and their contents added to the pyre which was being prepared, but that the waggons themselves should be taken back a quarter of a mile along the road, and left there under the charge of their drivers, who were not to move until joined by their owner. He then rode back and shook hands with John.

"I am glad to see you," he said. "All are well, I hope, at both our homes?"

"Quite well, sir."

"Thank God for that! Now I must leave you to see that our work is thoroughly carried out. You will find your waggons safe a quarter of a mile along the road. I will leave you to tell all the home news to Walter, who will retell it to me afterwards."

"Now tell me all the news," Walter said when they were together again.

"The news is not altogether pleasant," John replied. "The whole of the country round Dublin is being harried by the cavalry in garrison there. They pay no attention whatever to papers of protection, and care but little whether those they plunder are Protestant or Catholic, friend or foe. They go about in small parties like bands of brigands through the country; and those who go to Dublin to obtain redress for their exactions are received with indifference, and sometimes with insult, by the authorities. Then, too, we have had trouble at home.

"My grandfather became more bigoted than ever, and would, if he had the power, have annihilated every Catholic in Ireland. My father and he had frequent quarrels, and I was in daily expectation of an open breach between them, and of my father giving up his share of the property and taking us to England. He was a backslider in my grandfather's eyes. The tales of battle, plunder, and murder seemed to have taken the latter back to his own fighting days; and he was rather inclined to consider the generals as lukewarm than to join in the general indignation at their atrocious conduct.

"Even the sufferings of the Protestants did not seem to affect him. The Lord's work, he said, cannot be carried on without victims. It horrified me to hear him talk. If this was the religion of our fathers, I was fast coming to the conclusion that it was little better than no religion at all.

"I think my father and mother saw it in the same light, and the breach between them and my grandfather daily widened. But I have not told you the worst yet. A party of cavalry rode up the other day, and were about, as usual, to seize upon some cattle. My father was out, and my grandfather stepped forward and asked them 'how they could lay it to their consciences to plunder Protestants when, a mile or two away, there were Catholics lording it over the soil— Catholics whose husbands and sons were fighting in the ranks of the army of James Stuart?'

"I was in the house with my mother, but we heard what was said; and she whispered to me to slip out behind and find my father and tell him what was being done. I made off; but before I had gone a quarter of a mile I saw the soldiers riding off towards the castle, with my grandfather riding at their head. I was not long in finding my father, who at once called the men off from their work and sent them off in all directions to raise the country; and in an hour two hundred men, armed with any weapon they could snatch up, were marching towards the castle, my father at their head. There were Catholics and Protestants among them — the latter had come at my father's bidding, the former of their own free-will.

"We hurried along, anxiously fearing every moment to see flames rise from the castle. Fortunately the soldiers were too busy in plundering to notice our approach, and we pounced down upon them and seized them unawares. They were stripping the place of everything worth carrying away before setting it on fire. We burst into the hall, and there was a sight which filled my father and myself with anger and shame. Your grandmother was standing erect looking with dignity mingled with disdain at my grandfather; while your mother, holding your brother's hands, stood beside her. My grandfather was standing upon a chair; in his hand he held a Bible, and was pouring out a string of denouncing texts at the ladies, and was at the moment we entered comparing them to the wicked who had fallen into a net.

"I don't think, Walter, his senses are quite right now. He is crazed with religion and hate, and I believe at the time he fancied himself in the meeting-house. Anyhow there he was, while two sergeants who were supposed to be in command of the troop were sitting on a table, with a flagon of wine between them, looking on with amusement. Their expression changed pretty quickly when we rushed in.

"It needed all my father's efforts to prevent the whole party being hung, so furious were all the rescuers at the outrage upon the good ladies of the castle. But my father pointed out to them that although such a punishment was well deserved, it would do harm rather than good to the ladies. They had orders of protection from the lords-justices; and he should proceed at once, with four or five witnesses, to lay the matter before the general at Dublin and demand the punishment of the offenders. But if the party took the law into their own hands and meted out the punishment the fellows deserved, the facts of the case would be lost sight of; there would be a cry of vengeance for the murder, as it would be called, of a party of soldiers, and it would serve as an excuse for harrying the whole district with fire and sword.

"Having at last persuaded the angry tenants and peasantry to lay aside their project of vengeance, my father went to the soldiers, who, tied hand and foot, were expecting nothing short of death. He ordered all their pistols and ammunition to be taken away and their bonds to be loosed; then told them that their escape had been a narrow one, and that with great difficulty he had persuaded those who had captured them while engaged in deeds of outrage and plunder to spare them; but that a complaint would at once be made before the military authorities, and the law would deal with them. Finally they were permitted to mount and ride off, after having been closely examined to see that they were taking with them none of the plunder of the house.

"Everything was then carefully replaced as they had found it; and my father at once rode off with six of the leading tenants—three Protestants and three Catholics—and laid a complaint before the general. The latter professed himself much shocked, and lamented the impossibility of keeping strict discipline among the various regiments stationed in the towns. How-

ever, he went down with them at once to the barracks
of the regiment, ordered them to be formed up, and
asked my father if he could identify the culprits.

"My father and those with him picked out fifteen,
including the two sergeants, as having formed part of
the body of plunderers; and the general had the whole
tied up and flogged severely then and there, and declared that the next time an outrage upon persons who
had received letters of protection came to his ears, he
would shoot every man who was proved to have been
concerned in it. He also gave orders that a well-
conducted non - commissioned officer and four men
should be sent at once to Davenant Castle, and should
there take up their quarters as a guard against any
party of marauders, with the strictest orders to cause
no annoyance or inconvenience to the inhabitants of
the castle.

"I learned afterwards that Mr. Conyers, who had
been interesting himself greatly on behalf of the ladies
of the castle, is a great friend of the lords-justices and
other members of the council, and is also acquainted
with the general, which will account for the prompt
measures taken to punish the marauders—a very rare
and exceptional matter, I can tell you."

"I am sure we are greatly indebted to your father
and you for so promptly taking measures to assist my
mother," Walter said. "I have no doubt the castle
would have been burned as well as plundered if it had
not been for your rescue of them."

"It is not worth thinking about, Walter. We are
heavily your debtors still for the kindness of your

father and yourself to me at Derry, and indeed on all other occasions; besides, it was the least we could do, seeing that it was my grandfather's hatred of your family which brought the matter about."

"What became of your grandfather," Walter asked, "when you interrupted his sermon?"

"He fell down in a fit," John replied; "and perhaps it was the best thing he could do, for I don't know what my father and he would have said to each other had it not been so. He was carried home, and he has not been the same man since. I don't think the subject was ever alluded to between my father and him; but I think that, being balked just at the moment when he thought he had obtained the object of his hopes and prayers for the last forty years, has almost broken his heart.

"He goes about the house scarce speaking a word, and seems to have lost almost all his energy. He has ceased to read the family prayers and to hold forth morning and night. I do think he considers that the Lord has cheated him out of his lawful vengeance. It is awfully sad, Walter, though it is strange, to see such a travesty of religion as the tenets of my grandfather and some of the old men who, like him, represent the views of Cromwell's soldiers.

"Their religion cannot be called true Christianity. It is the Judaism of the times when the Jews were among the most ignorant of peoples. To me it is most shocking, and I would infinitely rather be a Mohammedan than hold such a faith as theirs. I thank God that my father and mother have shaken off such a yoke, and brought me up according to the teaching of the New Testament rather than that of the Old."

By this time the waggons, with the exception of those under John Whitefoot's charge, had been collected in a mass, and fire had been applied to them. They were now a pile of flame. A few of the best and fastest-looking of the horses were set aside to be carried off by the troop. The rest were shot, as the great object of the raids was to deprive the English army of its means of transport. The troop then mounted. Captain Davenant and Walter took a hearty farewell of John, and intrusted him with hastily-written letters for home; and as the smoke of the burning train would soon bring down any parties of the enemy who happened to be in the neighbourhood, the troop then rode off at full speed, and arrived safely at Athlone without meeting with any further adventures.

After the fall of the city Ginckle remained inactive some time, but finding that his proclamation had no effect in inducing the Irish to lay down their arms he reluctantly prepared to advance against them. In the interval he occupied himself in repairing the western wall of the city, and as he had been joined by several regiments sent out to reinforce him, he resumed his advance with a force larger than that with which he had commenced the siege of Athlone. Before starting he issued the most peremptory orders against a repetition of the acts which had so disgraced his army, and had done so much harm to the cause by banding the whole peasantry against them.

St. Ruth chose his position with great skill. His camp extended more than two miles along a range of hills called the heights of Kilcomeden; his right was protected by a rivulet and by hills and marshes, on his left was a deep glen; beyond this, along his whole front, a vast bog extended, in most places impassable for horse or foot. On the borders of the bog on the left stood the ruins of the little castle of Aughrim, occupying the only spot of firm ground which led to the camp.

To pass the bog at this point it was necessary to go close by the castle wall, where there was a broken path only wide enough for two men to pass abreast. The passage on the right of the bog was more open, but it was marshy and unsafe. This position was much stronger than that which the Irish had held at the battle of the Boyne, and whereas on that occasion they had been very inferior in numbers to their assailants, they were now superior by some regiments in number. In the point of artillery the English had here, as at the Boyne, an overwhelming superiority.

Ginckle moved forward slowly and with caution, halting on the river Suck until he had been joined by every available soldier in Ireland.

On the morning of the 12th of July the British army halted on the edge of the bog, that like a great belt encircled the Irish within it. The morning was foggy, and the mist did not clear off until towards noon. The Irish prepared for battle by having divine service performed at the head of their regiments, and Dr. Stafford, chaplain to the royal regiment of foot, and some other priests, passed through the ranks, urging upon the men their duty and obligation as soldiers and Irishmen to make every effort they could to rescue their country from the oppression of the Prince of Orange and his army of foreigners.

Ginckle, on his part, as at Athlone, distributed money among the troops, and promised them the plunder of the enemy's camp. As the day cleared up the British army was put in motion, and a strong column advanced against the enemy's right, where stood the house and grounds of Urachree, occupied by some Irish horse A strong detachment of Danish cavalry headed the British column. They moved forward boldly, quickening their pace as they approached the Irish; but on the latter charging them at full gallop they wheeled about and rode off at once in disorder.

Ginckle immediately ordered two hundred of Cunningham's dragoons, who were considered the best cavalry in the army, to advance and drive back the Irish horse. The dragoons advanced at a trot, but seeing that the Irish quietly awaited their coming they halted behind a hedge and awaited the arrival of the infantry. When these came up the cavalry again moved forward. The Irish horse now fell back on a little hill in their rear, where a body of infantry were posted. They then faced to the front and charged and broke the English dragoons, who retreated as the Danes had done, in confusion.

Eppinger's dragoons were ordered up to support Cunningham's, but the Irish horse had also received reinforcements before they arrived, and after a fierce fight the two English regiments were routed and driven off the field. Ginckle rallied them, added Lord Portland's horse to their numbers, and again sent them against the Irish. These, however, had fallen back from Urachree, and had taken up a new position upon the rivulet behind it, in front of the solid ground by which alone the right wing of the Irish army could be approached. Here they remained waiting the onset of the British cavalry; but these, perceiving that the ground was becoming more and more difficult, soon came to a halt, and then wheeling about fell back upon the infantry.

Seeing the successful stand which was made by a small body of Irish horse to the advance of the left wing, and that the spirit with which his troops were behaving was greatly inferior to that of the Irish, Ginckle called a council of war. Opinions were greatly at variance. It was now nearly four o'clock, and it was at first decided to postpone the battle till the morning, and a messenger was sent to the baggage column in the rear to bring up the tents; but other counsels finally prevailed. The order for the tents was countermanded, and at half-past four the British infantry were ordered to advance.

They pressed forward in solid masses across the ground where the cavalry fight had taken place, and the Irish horse fell back behind their infantry, who were posted behind the substantial hedges which intersected the ground beyond the rivulet. A heavy musketry fire was opened upon the British infantry as they advanced, but they pressed forward in unbroken

order till they reached the hedges. These were long
and obstinately contested.

The Irish had cut openings through the hedges by
which they could retire, and as they fell back from
hedge to hedge the advancing British were received
by a fire from hedges on both flanks as well as from
the front. As the British poured regiment after regiment to the attack, St. Ruth moved some bodies of
horse and foot from his left to the support of his right
wing. This movement had been foreseen by Ginckle,
who now gave orders for several battalions of infantry
to cross the bog and attack the Irish centre.

At this point there was a path across the bog, or
rather a place where the mud and water were not so
deep as at other points, and where it was possible for
it to be forded. Ginckle had found a peasant, who,
for a large sum of money, disclosed the passage. It
traversed the bog at its narrowest point, the hill of
Kilcomeden here running out a shoulder far into it.
Four regiments entered the morass, with orders to
cross it and make their way to the nearest hedges
on the sloping ground, where they were to post themselves till the cavalry, who were to attempt the passage by Aughrim Castle, could come round to their
support.

The first part of the passage was unopposed, but
the difficulty of passing was great, for the men were
frequently up to their waists in mud, too soft to afford
any firm footing, but solid enough to render it extremely difficult for the feet to be disengaged from it.
At length, as they approached firmer ground, the Irish

infantry advanced towards the edge of the bog and received them with a steady fire.

The English, although suffering heavily, pressed forward without firing a shot, till the ground became solid under their feet, when the Irish withdrew, and, as upon the right, took post behind the hedges which everywhere intersected the slopes. The English, seeing the Irish retire, pressed forward, and another fierce contest raged in the inclosures; the Irish, according to their preconceived plan, falling gradually back. The British in their ardour forgot their orders to halt at the first hedge, and continued to press forward until the constantly increasing numbers of the enemy recalled to their leaders the danger of the position.

Before them were the heights of Kilcomeden with a strong force drawn up to receive them, while on both flanks the enemy were crowding down to intercept their retreat. Colonel Earl, who was the senior officer, looked anxiously towards the right, from which quarter he expected the British cavalry to arrive to his assistance; but no sound reached him from that quarter, while on the left the sound of the conflict, instead of advancing, appeared to recede, as if the British column was being forced back.

Advancing before his own regiment he called upon the soldiers to stand firm, for retreat would be destruction, and the only hope was to maintain their position till assistance arrived. When the Irish saw that the enemy had halted and could not be tempted to advance further they poured down to the attack through the passages in the hedges. The British might have defended these hedges as the Irish had done, but the soldiers saw that they would be taken in the flank and rear, and observing a large body of cavalry ascending the hill they were seized with a panic.

On the first shock of the Irish infantry the four regiments broke and fled. They were hotly pursued and slaughtered in great numbers, the Irish cavalry pouring through the openings in the hedges which had been prepared for them. At length the fugitives reached the edge of the bog, where they gathered in a confused mass, which the officers in vain attempted to form into order. The cavalry charged down upon them, broke and scattered them, and drove them into the morass, followed by the Irish infantry, who were better acquainted with the ground and more accustomed to traversing bogs. The soldiers were driven into the deepest and most difficult portion of the morass and a great slaughter took place.

The British artillery were planted on the edge of the morass, but so mingled were the two parties that they were unable to fire. Great numbers of the English were killed, Colonels Earl and Herbert with many officers and men were taken prisoners, and the remnant of the British were driven completely across the bog to the shelter of their own cannon.

While this was passing in the centre another division of Ginckle's army, consisting of English and French infantry, had crossed the bog by a passage more to the right. They also had met with no opposition in passing, and it was only when they reached the hedges on the firm ground that the Irish showed themselves, fired,

and retreated. This division, more cautious than that
of Earl, could not be tempted to pursue, but contented
themselves with maintaining their ground under a
heavy fire, awaiting anxiously the arrival of the British
horse.

They could see, however, no sign of them, but could
perceive the Irish cavalry descending in large masses
preparing to charge, while the infantry were forming
for an advance. So far the Irish had been successful
at every point; they had repulsed every attack made
by the British left, had crushed the brigade composed
of the flower of the British infantry which had as-
saulted the centre, and were now preparing to destroy
the division which stood unsupported on their side of
the bog. At this moment a tumult was heard on the
left wing of the Irish, the direction from which the
British division expected relief, and the Irish, aware
of the importance of the pass of Aughrim, suspended
their attack to await the events there.

St. Ruth had directed the operations of the battle
with as much skill as he had prepared for the assault.
He had taken up his position on a point of the hill
whence he had a complete view of the whole field of
battle, and had moved his troops with calmness and
judgment to meet each of the attacks made upon them,
and when he saw the destruction of the English regiment in the centre he exclaimed, in the full confidence
of victory, "Now I will drive the English to the walls
of Dublin!"

There was, indeed, but one hope, on the part of the
English, of retrieving the day, namely, the success of

the attempt to force the passage at Aughrim. But two horsemen abreast could pass under the castle walls. St. Ruth was aware of the passage, but thought it impassable for cavalry. It might easily have been made so by cutting a deep gap across it; but here, as at Athlone, his over-confidence proved his destruction. He had, however, taken the precaution to erect a battery commanding the passage, and had placed some battalions of infantry there.

General Talmash, who commanded the English cavalry, knew that the battle was lost unless he could succeed at this point, and at the head of his command he led the way along the pass, which was not only narrow, but broken and encumbered with the ruins of the castle wall. St. Ruth beheld the attempt of the cavalry with astonishment, and with the remark "They are brave fellows, it is a pity they should be sacrificed," sent orders for the Irish horse to move forward and prepare to charge them, and moved down the hill at the head of his officers to the battery.

There is no doubt as to what the result would have been had the Irish horse charged. They were greatly superior in number, and the English cavalry who had got across the passage were still in confusion and were suffering from the fire of the battery, and, indeed, even when in equal numbers, William's cavalry had never withstood the charge of the Irish.

It seemed that nothing could avert the defeat of the body on which Ginckle's last hope rested. But at this moment one of those events by which Providence overrules the calculations of man occurred. A cannon-ball struck St. Ruth as he stood in the middle of the battery and killed him instantly. The occurrence paralysed the Irish army. Sarsfield was away, there was no one to give orders, the news that some extraordinary calamity had happened spread rapidly, the men in the battery ceased firing, the cavalry, receiving no orders to charge, remained immovable.

Talmash took advantage of the pause to get the rest of his cavalry across the passage, and then with his whole force moved towards the centre. As he approached, the idea that the unknown calamity of which they had heard was that the British had defeated their own left spread among the Irish, and they began to fall back. The British column on the edge of the bog advanced, Ginckle pushed several fresh battalions across the morass in the centre, and the Irish infantry fell back, disputing every inch of the ground. The cavalry were still without orders, for strangely enough no one assumed the command on the death of St. Ruth.

As night came on the retreat of the Irish infantry became a rout, but the cavalry halted on the summit of Kilcomeden and covered the retreat.

The extraordinary circumstance of the Irish army being left without orders after the death of St. Ruth has never been explained. The command should have devolved upon Sarsfield, but none of the accounts of the battle speak of him as being present. He had certainly not been consulted by St. Ruth, and had not been present at the council of war before the battle, for the bad feeling which had existed between him and St. Ruth since that general arrived had broken out into open dispute since the fall of Athlone; but it is inexplicable that there should have been no second in command, that no one should have come forward to give orders after the death of the general, that a victorious army should have been left as a flock of sheep without a shepherd.

Up to the moment of the death of St. Ruth the loss of the British had been very severe, as they had more than two thousand men killed and wounded, while that of the Irish was trifling. But in the subsequent struggle the Irish, fighting each man for himself, without order or object, were slaughtered in vast numbers, their loss being estimated by the British writers at seven thousand men, a number which points to wholesale slaughter rather than to the loss which could have been inflicted upon a brave army during little over an hour of daylight.

But crushing as the defeat of the Irish had been the victory was far from inspiring William or his army with the confidence they had felt at the outset of the war. Here, as at Athlone, it was almost a miracle which had saved the English from a terrible disaster. The Irish had proved themselves fully a match for the best soldiers that William could send against them, and although their infantry had suffered terribly in the rout their ranks would be speedily filled up again; while the cavalry, the arm in which the Irish had uniformly proved their superiority, had moved away from the field of battle intact and unbroken. Athlone and Aughrim therefore rendered William and his general more anxious than ever to bring the struggle to an end, not by the force of arms, but by offering every concession to the Irish.

The imminence of the peril had cowed even the party of confiscation, and they offered no opposition to the issue by Ginckle of proclamations renewing the offers of William. Ginckle himself moved forward immediately after the battle and granted the most liberal terms to the garrisons of the various small posts which he came upon. On arriving before Galway he permitted that town and garrison to surrender on the terms of a pardon for all, security of property and estate, freedom of religious worship, and permission for the garrison to march away to Limerick with drums beating and colours flying, the British furnishing horses for the transport of their cannon and baggage.

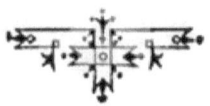

CHAPTER XV.

A FORTUNATE RECOGNITION.

AFTER the capitulation of Galway Ginckle moved towards Limerick. King William, who was absent on the Continent, was most anxious for the aid of the army warring in Ireland, and the queen and her advisers, considering that the war was now virtually over, ordered transports to Ireland to take on board ten thousand men; but Ginckle was allowed a month's delay. He himself was by no means sanguine as to his position. The Irish army was still as numerous as the British, and they were not discouraged by their defeat at Aughrim, where they considered, and rightly, that victory had only been snatched from their grasp by an accident. Ginckle relied rather upon concession than force.

The Irish were divided into two parties, one of which earnestly desired peace if they could obtain fair terms, while the other insisted that the British could not be trusted to keep any terms they might make. Sarsfield was at the head of the war party, and succeeded for the present in preventing any arrangement. Ginckle advanced slowly, for he had to march through a waste and desolate country. Sarsfield with his cavalry hovered round him, and intercepted his communications, and he was so short of draught-horses that it was only by forcing the gentry of Dublin to give up their carriage horses for the use of the army that he was enabled to move forward.

It was not until the end of August that he sat down with his siege-train in front of Limerick and prepared for the siege. For the moment the party in favour of peace among the Irish had been silenced by the news that twenty large ships-of-war, with a great number of transport and store ships, were being pushed forward at Brest and other French ports to come to their assistance.

Ginckle occupied the same ground which William's army had taken up in the first siege, but directed his attacks chiefly upon the English town.

As before, the Irish communication was open with the county of Clare, and the seventeen regiments of Irish horse were encamped on the Clare side of the river. Ginckle pushed on his works with great vigour, and the duty in the trenches was so severe that the cavalry were compelled to take their turn with the infantry; but notwithstanding that the siege artillery was much more powerful than that which William had at his disposal, but little progress was made. The town was set on fire several times; but the flames were speedily extinguished, and as the inhabitants had all left the city and erected tents on the Clare side under the protection of their cavalry, little harm was done to them.

While the siege was going on, a number of desultory

engagements took place in different parts of the country between the Protestant militia which had been lately raised, and the bands of Rapparees, with varying success.

The season was getting late; Ginckle was again becoming straitened for provisions, for the proclamations which he issued failed to inspire the peasantry with any confidence. He now erected a battery of thirty-five guns against King's Island, and after an incessant cannonade of some days a breach was effected in the wall between the abbey and Ballsbridge.

Preparations were made for crossing the arm of the Shannon and assaulting the breach; but the works constructed for crossing the river were repeatedly destroyed by the Irish, and the idea of assault upon the breach was at length abandoned. So desperate did Ginckle now think his position that he issued orders for the repair of the fortifications of Kilmallock, intending to raise the siege and establish his winter-quarters there; but he postponed taking this step for a few days, for to do so would be to bring almost certain disaster upon his army.

The French fleet was expected to arrive shortly, and the Irish, reinforced with men, arms, and supplies of every kind, would probably resume the offensive during the winter, and he would find himself cut off from all supplies and assistance. He determined therefore to make one more effort before retiring. He had throughout the siege been in communication with several Irish officers of high rank, and especially with

General Clifford, who commanded the cavalry posted on the river opposite to his camp.

These officers were as desirous as he was of bringing the war to an end, for they foresaw that if after the arrival of the French they succeeded in driving the English out of the country, Ireland would simply become a dependency of France, and they preferred the English connection to this. Ginckle determined to try again the same feint which had succeeded at Athlone. The workmen were kept busy repairing the works at Kilmallock, and preparing that place for the reception of the army. The greater portion of the baggage and a regiment of Danes were sent forward to that town. The batteries ceased firing, and the cannon were dismounted at several points, and the Irish were persuaded that the siege was about to be abandoned.

Meanwhile Ginckle was busy collecting boats and preparing a bridge across to a small island which lay not far from the Clare side of the river. On a dark night the boats were brought up and the bridge constructed, and, led by six hundred grenadiers, a strong force of infantry, cavalry, and artillery crossed to the island, and then waded through the shallow water beyond to the mainland. A few men posted on the island carried the news to Clifford, but he gave no orders to the four regiments of cavalry and two of infantry under his command, nor did he send any notice to the camp.

Some of the infantry and cavalry, however, ran without orders to the bank, and kept the grenadiers in check until the British cavalry had crossed and compelled them to fall back. The British cavalry then dashed forward to the Irish cavalry camp, which they took completely by surprise. Panic-stricken at this unexpected attack, the soldiers and the citizens in the town camp fled in all directions, and great numbers rushing to Thomond Bridge, entered the city by that narrow approach.

Had Ginckle at once pushed forward he would have captured almost the whole of the Irish officials and civilians on the Clare side of the river; but, fearing an ambuscade, he halted his troops before advancing to the Irish camp, and this gave time for most of them to escape.

Being afraid that the garrison would sally out from the town and attack his lines on the other side of the river, he recrossed the Shannon with his troops, carrying with them a crowd of civilians, among them a number of persons of rank, and officials with the records and public treasure.

The confusion and surprise in the town were so great that the Irish generals took no steps whatever either to hinder his passage back across the river or to attack either portion of his divided army. They knew that treachery must have been at work to have enabled the enemy to surprise the camp, and as they could not tell how far that treachery extended they abstained from all action.

Captain Davenant's troop had shared in the disaster inflicted by the night attack upon the cavalry camp. All were asleep when the English cavalry burst upon

them. Taken utterly by surprise, and ignorant as
to the strength of the force by which they were attacked, there was no thought of resistance; officers
and men leapt from the piles of rushes, which served
as beds, and rushed to their horses. The English
troopers were cutting and hewing in all directions, and
cutting the picket ropes, each man sprang on his horse
and rode for his life. Captain Davenant had at first
shouted to his men to keep steady; but his words were
lost in the din which prevailed, and seeing that nothing
was to done, he said to Walter:

"It is all over, Walter; we must ride for it like the
rest."

By morning the Irish cavalry was scattered all over
the country, and it was not for two or three days that
they again assembled in regiments, presenting a sorry
sight, the greater part having lost saddles and accoutrements of every kind. A few troops, composed of men
who had been fortunate enough to have left their
horses saddled when night came on, were sent back to
Limerick. The rest drew off towards Ennis and encamped there until they could procure saddles and accoutrements to take the field again.

In Captain Davenant's troop there were but six men
who had saved their saddles; and as it would have
been useless to send so small a detachment to Limerick,
these remained with the troop, and were at Walter's
request placed entirely at his disposal in order that
with them he might make scouting expeditions in
the enemy's rear. He had permission to consider
himself entirely on detached service, and to join any

body of Rapparees he might choose; but this Walter
did not care about doing, for he had a horror of the
savage acts which were perpetrated by the irregular forces on both sides, and determined to confine
himself to watching the roads, bringing in news of
any convoys which might be traversing the country,
and cutting off messengers going or returning with
despatches.

The service was one of no great danger, for parties
of peasants were on the watch night and day, and the
instant any movement was observed they started off
at full speed to warn all the inhabitants of the surrounding villages to drive away their cattle and carry
off their effects into the hills or into the heart of some
neighbouring bog where the cavalry would not venture
to penetrate.

One day when with his little band he was halting at
a village some ten miles in rear of the camp a peasant
ran in. "A party of their horse have just seized some
carts laden with potatoes at Kilcowan, and are driving
them off. The boys are mustering to attack them on
their way back."

"It is too bad," Walter exclaimed. "Only three days
ago Ginckle issued another proclamation guaranteeing
that no provisions or other goods should be taken by
his soldiers without payment. To horse, lads! We will
ride out and give the peasants a helping hand if they
really mean to attack the enemy."

Kilcowan was two miles away, and having learned
from the peasant that the people intended to attack
at a point where the road passed between two hills, a

mile and a half beyond the village, he galloped on at full speed. He arrived, however, too late to take any part in the fight. The peasants had rushed suddenly down the hillsides armed with scythes and pikes upon the convoy as it passed below them. Several of the cavalry had been killed, and the rest were riding off when Walter with his troopers dashed up. They continued the pursuit for a mile, cutting off a few stragglers less well mounted than the rest, and then returned to Kilcowan, where the peasants had just arrived in triumph with the rescued carts of potatoes.

"What are you going to do?" he asked when the excitement of the welcome accorded by the women to the captors had subsided a little. "You may expect a strong body to be sent out to-morrow to punish you for this."

"It's the general's own proclamation, your honour. Didn't he say himself that his soldiers were not to stale anything, and that they would be severely punished if they did, and didn't he guarantee that we should be paid for everything? He could not blame us for what we have done, and he ought to hang the rest of those thieving villains when they get back to him."

"I wouldn't be too sure about it," Walter said. "He issued a good many proclamations before, but he has never kept the terms of one of them. If I were you I would leave the village—man, woman, and child— for a few days at any rate, and see how the Dutchman takes it."

"KILCOWAN IS ON FIRE, SIR!"

But the villagers could not be persuaded that the Dutch general would disapprove of what they had done, and Walter finding his arguments of no avail rode off with his men to the village they had left an hour before, with the parting advice that if they would not follow his counsel they should at anyrate place watchers that night on the roads towards Ginckle's camp, to bring them news of the approach of any body of the enemy's cavalry.

But the villagers were too delighted with their day's work to pay much heed to Walter's warning, and after a general jollification in honour of their victory retired to rest thoughtless of danger. It was getting dark when Walter reached the village where he had determined to stay for the night. He ordered the men to keep the saddles on their horses and to hitch them to the doors of the cabins where they took up their quarters, in readiness for instant movement. He placed one mounted sentry at the entrance to the village, and another a quarter of a mile on the road towards Kilcowan. At nine o'clock he heard the sound of a horse galloping up to the door, and ran out. It was the sentry at the end of the village.

"Kilcowan is on fire, sir!"

Walter looked in that direction and saw a broad glare of light.

"Ride out and bring in the advanced sentry," he said, "as quick as possible."

He called the other men out and bade them mount; that done they sat ready to ride off on the return of their comrades.

(377)   X

"Here they come, sir," one of the men said, "and I fancy the enemy are after them."

Walter listened intently. He could hear a deep thundering noise, which was certainly made by the hoofs of more than two horses.

"Face about, men, trot! Keep your horses well in hand until the others come up, and then ride for it. Ah, what is that!"

As he spoke there was a shout from the other end of the village, followed instantly by the trampling of horses.

"They have surrounded us!" Walter exclaimed. "Shoulder to shoulder, lads, and cut your way through. It's our only chance. Charge!" And placing himself at the head he set spurs to his horse and dashed at the approaching enemy.

There was a fierce shock, a horse and rider rolled over from the impetus of his charge, then he cut right and left; pistol shots rang out, and his horse fell beneath him shot through the head, pinning his leg beneath it. The fall saved his life, for four or five troopers had surrounded him, and in another moment he would have been cut down. For a time he ran great risk of being trampled upon in the confusion which followed. Then some of the troopers dismounted, he was dragged from beneath his horse, and found himself a prisoner. He was placed in the centre of the troop, the only captive taken, for two of the six men had got safe away in the darkness and confusion, the other four had fallen.

The English, as he afterwards learned, had, immediately they arrived at Kilcowan, inquired where the Irish cavalry who had taken part in the afternoon's fight were quartered, and on hearing that they were but two miles away, the officer in command had forced one of the peasants to act as guide, and to take a party round by a detour so as to enter at the other end of the village, just as another party rode in by the direct road.

Walter was taken first to Kilcowan. There he found a party of twelve or fourteen peasants surrounded by cavalry. The whole village was in flames. Several of the inhabitants had been cut down as the cavalry entered; the rest, with the exception of those in the hands of the troops, had fled in the darkness. As soon as the detachment with Walter arrived the whole body got into motion, and reached Ginckle's camp shortly before midnight.

As the general had retired to sleep they were placed in a tent, and four sentries posted round it, with orders to shoot anyone who showed his head outside. In the morning they were ordered to come out and found outside the general with several of his officers.

"So," Ginckle said, "you are the fellows who attacked my soldiers. I will teach you a lesson which shall be remembered all over Ireland. You shall be broken on the wheel."

This sentence was heard unmoved by the peasants, who had not the least idea of what was meant by it; but Walter stepped forward:

"It is not these men who are to blame, but your soldiers, general," he said. "Your own proclamation

issued three days ago guaranteed that no private property should be interfered with, and that everything
the troops required should be paid for. Your soldiers
disobeyed your orders and plundered these poor people,
and they were just as much justified in defending
themselves against them as any householder is who
resists a burglar."

"You dare speak to me!" exclaimed Ginckle. "You
shall share their fate. Every man of you shall be
broken on the wheel."

"General Ginckle," Walter said warmly, "hitherto
the foul excesses of your troops have brought disgrace
upon them rather than you; but if this brutal order is
carried out your name will be held infamous, and you
will stand next only to Cromwell in the curses which
Irishmen will heap upon your memory."

The Dutch general was almost convulsed with
passion.

"Take the dogs away," he shouted, "and let the
sentence be carried out."

Several English officers were standing near, and
these looked at one another in astonishment and disgust. Two of them hurried away to fetch some of the
superior officers, and directly these heard of the orders
that had been given they proceeded to Ginckle's
tent.

"Can it be true," General Hamilton said, "that you
have ordered some prisoners to be broken on the
wheel?"

"I have given those orders," Ginckle said angrily,
"and I will not permit them to be questioned."

"Pardon me," General Hamilton said firmly; "but they must be questioned. There is no such punishment as breaking on the wheel known to the English law, and I and my English comrades protest against such a sentence being carried out."

"But I will have it so!" Ginckle exclaimed, his face purple with passion.

"Then, sir," General Hamilton said, "I tell you that in half an hour from the present time I will march out from your camp at the head of my division of British troops and will return to Dublin; and what is more, I will fight my way out of the camp if any opposition is offered, and will explain my conduct to the king and the British parliament. Enough disgrace has already been brought upon all connected with the army by the doings of the foreign troops; but when it comes to the death by torture of prisoners by the order of their general, it is time that every British officer should refuse to permit such foul disgrace to rest upon his name."

There was a chorus of assent from the other English officers, while Ginckle's foreign officers gathered round him, and it looked for a moment as if swords would be drawn.

Ginckle saw that he had gone too far, and felt that not only would this quarrel, if pushed further, compel him to raise the siege and fall back upon Dublin, but it would entail upon him the displeasure of the king, still more certainly that of the English parliament.

"There is no occasion for threats," he said, mastering his passion. "You tell me that such a punishment is

AN INDIGNANT OFFICER.

contrary to English law; that is enough, I abandon it at once. The prisoners shall be hung and quartered. I presume that you have no objection to offer to that."

"That, general, is a matter in your own competence, and for your own conscience," Hamilton said. "The men have simply, as I understand, defended their property against marauders, and they are, as I conceive, worthy of no punishment whatever. If you choose to sentence them to such a punishment it is your sentence not mine. I thought it was your policy to heal the breach between the two parties; it seems I was mistaken. Personally I protest against the execution of the sentence, beyond that I am not called upon to go. An act of injustice or cruelty performed by a general upon prisoners would not justify a soldier in imperilling the success of the campaign by resisting the orders of his superior, therefore my duty to the king renders me unable to act; but I solemnly protest in my own name and that of the English officers under your command, against the sentence, which I consider unjust in the extreme."

So saying, General Hamilton with the English officers left the general's tent. If they hoped that the protest would have the effect of preventing the barbarous sentence from being carried into execution they were mistaken. The fact that to carry out his first intention would have been absolutely unlawful had caused Ginckle to abandon it, but this made him only the more obstinate in carrying the second into execution.

The English officers stood talking not far from his tent in tones of indignation and disgust at the brutal sentence, and then walked towards their divisional camp. As they went they saw a number of men standing round a tree. Some Hessian soldiers with much brutal laughter were reeving ropes over the arm of the tree, and just as the officers came along six struggling forms were drawn up high above the heads of the crowd. The party paused for a moment and were about to pass on, their faces showing how deep was their horror at the scene, when one of them exclaimed:

"There is an Irish officer in uniform among the prisoners! This cannot be suffered, Hamilton. The Irish have several of ours prisoners in the town, and they would rightly retaliate by hanging them on the battlements."

General Hamilton and the others pressed forward.

"Colonel Hanau," the general said to a Hessian officer, "you surely cannot be going to hang this young officer? The general can never have included him with the others?"

"The general's orders were precise," the Hessian said coldly. "Twelve peasants and one officer were to be hung and afterwards quartered."

"It is monstrous!" General Hamilton exclaimed. "I will go back to the general and obtain his order for the arrest of the execution."

"You will be too late, sir," the Hessian said coldly. "I have my orders, and before you are half-way to the general's camp that prisoner will be swinging from that bough."

"I order you to desist, sir, till I return," General Hamilton said.

"As I do not happen to be in your division, General Hamilton, and as I have received my orders from the commander-in-chief, I decline altogether to take orders from you."

Walter, who had resigned himself to his fate, stood watching the altercation with a renewed feeling of hope. This died out when the colonel spoke and two of the troopers seized him, but at that moment his eye fell upon one of the English officers.

"Colonel L'Estrange!" he exclaimed.

The officer started at hearing his name called out by the prisoner, but he did not recognize him.

"I am Walter Davenant. You remember, sir, the wreck off Bray?"

"Good heavens!" Colonel L'Estrange exclaimed, pressing forward, "it is the lad who saved my life, General Hamilton! Gentlemen, this young officer saved my life at the risk of his own. I cannot and will not stand by and see him murdered."

The Hessian colonel signed to four of his men, who seized Walter and dragged him towards the tree. Colonel L'Estrange drew his sword.

"My men," he shouted to some English soldiers who were mingled with the crowd of onlookers, which had rapidly increased during the dispute, "stand by me and don't let this brave young officer be murdered."

A score of soldiers pushed through the crowd and

ranged themselves by Colonel L'Estrange. He dashed forward sword in hand, and in a moment Walter was torn from the grasp of the soldiers and placed in the centre of his rescuers, who were now joined by General Hamilton and the other officers.

Several men had ran off at full speed to the British camp to bring up aid. The Hessian colonel called upon his men to seize the prisoner and cut down all who interfered to prevent the general's orders being carried out. These hesitated before the resolute aspect of the English, but the crowd of foreign soldiers ranged themselves with them, and the attack was about to commence when a number of English soldiers were seen running, musket in hand, from their camp.

The Hessian colonel saw that to attempt to carry out his orders now would bring on something like a pitched battle, and he therefore waved his men back, saying to General Hamilton.

"I have nothing to do now, sir, but to report to General Ginckle that I have been prevented by force from carrying his orders into effect."

"That you will, of course, do," General Hamilton said coldly. "I shall be perfectly prepared to answer for my conduct."

There was no good-will between the English and foreign sections of Ginckle's army, and General Hamilton had some trouble in preventing the soldiers from attacking the Hessians and in inducing them to retire to their camp. As soon as he arrived there he ordered the drums to be beaten and the whole division to get under arms.

He then despatched an officer to General Ginckle, narrating the circumstances, and saying that the honour of the whole army was concerned in preventing an officer fairly taken prisoner in war, and not while acting as a spy, from being injured, and that indeed policy as well as honour forbade such a course being taken, as there were several officers of rank in the hands of the Irish, who would naturally retaliate on them the execution of prisoners of war.

He made a formal complaint against Colonel Hanau for refusing to delay the execution until he could lay the matter before the general. As for his own conduct in the matter, he said he was perfectly prepared to defend it before any military court, but that court must be held in England, where he purposed to return at once with the division his majesty had intrusted to his command.

The Dutch general had, long before he received the letter, been informed of what had taken place, and had also learned that the English division had struck their tents and were drawn up under arms. To allow them to depart would be to entail certain ruin upon the campaign, and he felt that it was more than probable that the course Hamilton and his officers had taken would be upheld by a military court in England, and that public opinion would condemn the execution of an officer taken in fair fight. He therefore wrote a letter to General Hamilton, saying that he regretted to find that he had been acting under a misapprehension, for he had understood that the person claiming to be an Irish officer was in fact a spy, and that he had severely reprimanded Colonel Hanau for his refusal to delay the execution until the fact had been explained to him. Far from feeling in any way aggrieved that General Hamilton had interfered to prevent such a mistake from taking place, he felt much obliged to him for what he had done, as the execution of an Irish officer taken in war would in every way have been a most unfortunate circumstance.

General Hamilton showed the letter to the colonels of the various regiments in the division, and these agreed that as General Ginckle was evidently desirous that the matter should go no further it would be as well to order the tents to be again pitched, and for the troops to resume their ordinary duties.

"My dear Walter," Colonel L'Estrange said, "I am happy indeed that we came up when we did. What should I have felt if I had afterwards learned that you, who had saved my life, had been murdered here, for your execution would have been neither more nor less than murder, as was that of the twelve poor fellows who were taken at Kilcowan—a brutal murder! They were perfectly justified in defending their property, and the idea of quartering them as well as hanging them, just as if they were traitors of the worst dye, is nothing short of monstrous.

"I only came out here with my regiment a month since, but I am heartily sick with what I see going on. It was terrible to see the ruined villages on the road from Dublin. I have seen fighting on the Continent, but nothing to equal the wholesale brutality with which the war is

conducted here. How God can continue to give success to an army which behaves, as this one has done is
altogether beyond me. Of one thing I am resolved,
whether we take Limerick or not—and I own I see
but small chance of it—I shall exchange, if possible,
into a regiment serving in Flanders; if not, I shall re-
sign my commission. And now how is your father? I
rode out from Dublin to see your mother, and was
very glad to find her and old Mrs. Davenant well. I
was glad too to find that owing to the influence of Mr.
Conyers they had not been troubled, and I was fortunately able myself to bring some influence to bear
upon the council, who seem to be bent upon squeez-
ing the last drop of blood from the Irish veins. But
the men are falling in, and I must put myself at the
head of the regiment. I will hand you over to the
care of an officer, and if we march out you will, of
course, go with us."

When the men were again dismissed Colonel
L'Estrange rejoined Walter.

"Ginckle has thought better of it," he said. "I
fancied he would not venture to push matters further,
for the loss of the one division he can really rely upon
would be fatal to all his hope of success to the campaign. Ginckle is a passionate man, but he is not a
fool, and he must have seen that if the matter had
been laid before the king his conduct would not have
been approved. I don't say that ours is right in a
military sense, but I am sure that public opinion would
have approved of it. The tales that have been circulated
of the doings of the army over here since the commence-

ment of the war have already roused a very strong feeling of irritation throughout the country."

Colonel L'Estrange now took Walter to General Hamilton's tent, and after formally introducing him he told the story of the wreck and of his rescue by Walter from certain death.

"What do you mean to do with him, L'Estrange?" General Hamilton asked.

"My intention is, unless you see any objection to it, to pass him through the lines this evening. I will provide him with a good horse and see him well away. After what has happened Ginckle will, I should say, feel obliged for our thus rendering him a service by getting rid of his prisoner. There are not likely to be any questions asked or remarks made afterwards. I am not without influence at court, and there is a very strong section who are bitterly opposed to Dutchmen being placed in every post in the king's gift, and there would be no difficulty in getting up such a hostile feeling against Ginckle in relation to this affair that it would cost him his command."

"Yes," the general agreed; "Marlborough would be only too glad to take the matter up, and as Ginckle must be pretty well aware that his want of success here must have already made his position precarious, I do not think he will trouble himself to ask any questions about the prisoner; and certainly William will not thank him for being the means by his unjust and arbitrary conduct of causing a split between the English and his foreign troops. I should like to put all their heads into one noose, and I should feel no

compunction in setting them swinging, for a greater set
of rascals were never collected under the sun. I must
say that the contrast between our army and the Irish
is very great, and that although many bloody deeds
are performed by the Rapparees there has never been
a single complaint brought against the Irish troops.
Anyhow, Mr. Davenant, I think you cannot do better
than fall in with Colonel L'Estrange's plan. There
will be no difficulty in getting out, and indeed I will
send a troop of cavalry to see you well beyond our
lines."

Walter spent the rest of the day with Colonel
L'Estrange, and told him all that had taken place
since they had last met.

"It is difficult to believe that it is but three years
ago," he said when he had finished.

"No, we judge the flight of time by the incidents
we crowd into it. The most uneventful days pass the
most unheeded. Now to me it seems but yesterday
that I stood on the deck of the ship and knew that
she was sure to go to pieces, and that the chance of
anyone reaching that rocky coast alive were small
indeed, when I saw what seemed little more than a
black speck approaching, and you and your fisher boy
made your way over the wave. By the way, how is
he? Doing well, I hope?"

"He might have done well if he liked. The present
that you left in my father's hands to buy him a boat
when he was old enough to start as a fisherman on his
own account would have made a man of him, but it is
hidden somewhere in the thatch of his father's cottage.

When my father first went to the war he handed it
over to Larry, as he could not say what might happen before his return. Larry was at first delighted
with the thought that some day he should have a boat
of his own, and a boat too larger than any on the
shore; but when I accompanied my father Larry insisted on going with me. 'It will be time enough to
buy a boat when the war is over,' he said; and as I
was very glad to have him with me, and my father did
not object, Larry had his way, and he has been with
me ever since. He is enrolled in the troop now, and
when he thinks there is any chance of fighting he takes
his place in the ranks, but at other times he acts as my
servant."

"Tell him I have not forgotten him," Colonel
L'Estrange said. "While you have been doing so
much I have had a quiet time of it. I could have got
a regiment at once had I cared for it, but I disliked
the thought of fighting over here, it was too much
like civil war. Six months ago, when things were
going badly with us on the Continent, I asked to be
employed, and was given a regiment they were just
raising. I had got them into fair order and was expecting to be ordered to embark for the Low Country
at any moment, when the news came of Ginckle's heavy
losses at Athlone and Aughrim, and the orders came for
us to proceed to Bristol and take ship there for Ireland.
I half thought of throwing up my commission, for the
news of the scandalous conduct of the foreign soldiers
had stirred every English heart with disgust and indignation, but I thought that the struggle was nearly

over. William was anxious for peace at any price, and would grant almost any terms to secure it; and on the other hand we knew that Louis was at last going to make a great effort. So that it was certain that either the Irish would make peace on fair terms before winter, or the French would land and there would be an end of any prospect of conquering Ireland until matters were settled on the Continent and William could devote his whole strength to this business."

"And which alternative do you think the most likely?" Walter asked.

"The latter," Colonel L'Estrange said gravely. "Frankly, Walter, the situation looks bad. There is, so far as I can see, no chance whatever of our taking Limerick, and in a fortnight ten thousand French troops will be landed. Of course it is probable that at the last moment the Irish may conclude that they prefer to be under England rather than France, for that is what it comes to. I hope they will have the sense to choose England, and if what we hear be true they can judge from the insolent arrogance of the French officers when they are but a fraction of your force, what they would be when they regarded themselves as your masters.

"William is ready to grant religious equality and the security of persons and estates. I think the Irish will be very unwise to refuse. At the same time they have suffered such villainous treatment at the hands of William's soldiers that I cannot blame them if they decide to throw in their lot with France."

"I think," Walter said, "that if they were but sure that all the promises would be kept the greater part would be in favour of making peace at once. Nine out of ten of us are of English descent, and have only been driven to take up arms by the cruel oppression which we have suffered. Why, at present five-sixths of the soil of Ireland is in the hands of Protestants, our religion is persecuted, and for years we have been trampled on and regarded as fair objects of robbery."

"All that you say is true, Walter, and no one can regret it more than I do. Still, I do think that you would be worse off under France than under England. Louis would drain the island of its men to fill his army. He uses you only as a cat's-paw in his struggle against England and Holland, and would not hesitate to turn you over to England again, did it at any time suit him to make peace on such terms or to offer Ireland as an exchange for some piece of territory he coveted beyond his frontier."

"I know my father is very much of your opinion," Walter said, "and that he has no confidence whatever in the King of France, and considers that French interference is responsible for the want of success which has attended us. At anyrate there is scarcely one of us who does not hate the French, and certainly if we had to choose between the two countries, we should choose England."

When it became dark a troop of cavalry mounted, and with Colonel L'Estrange and Walter in their midst rode out of camp. They went for several miles, and then Colonel L'Estrange said:

"We are now well outside the limit where you will be likely to meet any of our scouting parties. Two miles further along this road you will come to the village of Mulroon. It has, like all the others, suffered heavily, but there are two or three houses still standing, and when I rode through it a few days since I saw an old man standing at the door of one of them, so you will be likely to get information as to the best road to the town, and perhaps a guide."

"Thank you very heartily, Colonel L'Estrange. I know the village, for I rode through it only the day before I was captured, and if I can get no guide I can make my own way round as soon as it is daylight."

"You had better go on to-night if you can, Walter. Some party of rascally plunderers might arrive here, or Ginckle may, for aught I know, have sent out parties of dragoons. At anyrate I would not stop here, but make your way on among the hills even if you can only get a mile away and have to sleep by the side of your horse. No one can say he is safe under a roof within twenty miles of Ginckle's army."

There was a hearty leave-taking between Colonel L'Estrange and Walter, and the latter then rode straight forward, while the troop faced about and made their way back to camp.

On arriving at the village, Walter, as soon as he succeeded in convincing the inhabitants of a cottage in which he saw a light that he was an Irish officer, found no difficulty in obtaining a guide, a boy of fourteen volunteering at once to conduct him to the ford ten miles above Limerick. It was nearly twenty miles by the by-roads by which they travelled, and the morning was just breaking as they arrived there. Colonel L'Estrange had insisted on providing Walter with funds, and he was therefore able to reward his guide, who went his way rejoicing, while Walter crossed the river and rode for the cavalry camp, where he was received with delight by his father and friends, who had believed him to have been killed in the skirmish, for such was the report of the troopers who had managed to make their escape.

"I must not let you go on any more detached commands, Walter," his father said. "I do not say that you have been imprudent or to blame; but this is the second time that you have been surprised by the enemy, and as it is out of the question to expect that you can always have the good luck to get out of their hands when you are captured, as you have on the last two occasions, I shall keep you by me in future, for seriously, my boy, your absence has caused me terrible anxiety."

When Walter's account of the barbarous sentence passed upon the peasants, whose only crime was that they had defended their property against marauders acting in defiance of the general's order, was known in camp, the most intense indignation prevailed, and this was heightened by the fact that a cavalry officer taken in open fight should have been sentenced to a similar fate. So great, indeed, was the fury of both officers and men, that had they been in any condition to take the field, nothing could have restrained them from mounting and riding at once to strike a blow in revenge for the murder and mutilation of the peasants.

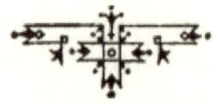

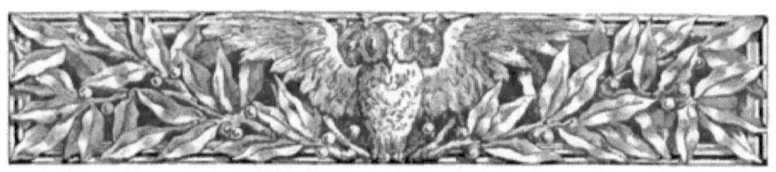

CHAPTER XVI.

PEACE.

GINCKLE'S expedition across the Shannon and his surprise of the Irish cavalry camp, successful as it had been, altered the position in no way. Several days passed, and then after a council of war it was determined to recross the bridge of boats, which remained undisturbed, to the Clare side, and try to force a way across Thomond Bridge. On the 22d of September all the cavalry of the army, ten regiments of infantry, and fourteen pieces of cannon made the passage without molestation and marched towards the bridge, which was defended upon the Clare side by two strong towers. As the British advanced guard of infantry approached the bridge it was charged by a body of Irish horse, broken, and driven back.

A strong body of cavalry rode up to support the infantry; the Irish horse were reinforced, and a hot fight continued until, at about four o'clock in the afternoon, the whole force of British infantry came up, and the Irish retired upon the infantry posted in the works which covered the bridge. Near the gate were high grounds cut up by gravel-pits. The Irish infantry were posted here as well as in the forts, and the English as they advanced were assailed with a very heavy fire from these positions, and also from the guns on the town walls.

In spite of the heavy loss they were suffering the English pressed on with the greatest gallantry. Success was now almost a necessity, for, if defeated, but few of them would ever have been able to recross the river. Foot by foot they fought their way, pressed on past the outworks, and pushed back the Irish infantry till the latter were gathered round the head of the bridge.

The Irish generals had thought that Ginckle's movement was but a repetition of the previous raid, and the force that had been sent over to guard the head of the bridge was altogether insufficient to withstand the determined attack by Ginckle's force. Reinforcements were now sent across the bridge, but this only added to the confusion. Pressed back by the weight and power of the English attack, the Irish were beginning to retire across the bridge when they met the reinforcements making their way over.

The bridge was of great length but extremely narrow, and a complete block took place. The English had pierced their way through the struggling mass at the head of the bridge and pressed on the rear of the mass of fugitives, literally hewing their way through them, and the pressure became so great that the regiments crossing were carried back. The head of the British column was pushed forward by those behind, and could only advance by slaying those in front of them and throwing their bodies over the bridge; for the mass were wedged so tightly that movement had now become impossible, while the Irish as they retreated formed ramparts of the slain and impeded the advance of the enemy.

While the struggle on the bridge was at its fiercest the French officer who commanded at the drawbridge across the arch nearest to the city, fearing that the British would press in at the rear of the Irish, and that he might not then be able to raise the drawbridge, ordered this to be done at once—thereby cutting off the retreat of the soldiers still on the bridge. These jumped over the parapet into the river and strove to reach the city wall by swimming. Some did so, but great numbers were drowned. This incident greatly increased the standing feud between the Irish and French, the former declaring that the latter not only never fought themselves, but were ready at the first alarm to sacrifice their allies in order to secure their own safety.

The success of Ginckle's second raid had been complete in so far that he had inflicted great slaughter upon the Irish infantry and had gained a moral victory; but he was no nearer capturing the town. An attack across the long narrow bridge was not even to be thought of; and he again retired across the river. The Irish were disheartened. Sarsfield, though a dashing cavalry commander, appeared wholly incapable of handling large bodies of men. Ginckle had twice given him a great opportunity, but on neither occasion had he made the slightest effort to utilize it.

On the first occasion surprise and uncertainty might excuse inaction on the part of the army in Limerick, but there was no such excuse the second time. Their force outside the town gate was but a small one; it was certain that the English could not push across the bridge; and as Ginckle had taken the best part of his army across, Sarsfield could have issued out with his whole force on the Limerick side, crushed the British force remaining there, and captured the camp and all its stores—in which case Ginckle's position would have been desperate. But not a movement was made to seize an opportunity which would have been patent to any military commander possessing genius and energy; nor until it was too late was any attempt made to reinforce the detachment which, on the other side of the bridge, was withstanding the attack of a vastly superior force.

Ginckle, relying upon the moral effect of the blow he had just struck, renewed his negotiations. Some of the Irish leaders had already received bribes; others were genuinely anxious that the war should cease now that William was ready to grant terms which would secure the ends for which they had been fighting; others, again, were animated by hostility to the French, and the fear that if the expected reinforcements arrived and the English were driven out, Ireland would become a mere appanage of France.

Sarsfield himself was no doubt swayed by his dislike to being again superseded in the command by the arrival of another French general. He was, too, influenced by the fear that the peace party might prevail, and that Clifford's act of treachery might be repeated, and the enemy be admitted into the city without any terms being arranged.

The French officers, eager to return home, made no attempt to stem the course of events; and on the evening of the day after the battle on the Clare side, the drums of the besieged beat a parley, and Generals Sarsfield and Waughup went out and had a conference with Ginckle. A cessation of arms was concluded for the night; and in the morning the truce was extended for three days to allow the cavalry, who were now encamped near Ennis, to be communicated with.

On the 25th the principal noblemen and officers from the cavalry camp arrived, prisoners were exchanged, and hostages on both sides were given, until the terms of a treaty of peace could be adjusted. On the 27th the Irish submitted their proposals to the English general, which were—that "all past offences should be pardoned; that the Catholics of the counties of Cork, Limerick, Kerry, Clare, Sligo, and Mayo be restored to the estates which they held previous to the war; freedom of worship to be allowed; Catholics to be capable of holding all employments, civil and military; the Irish army to be kept on foot, and those who were willing to serve to be received into the king's service; Catholics to be at liberty to reside in all cities and towns, and to have all rights of citizens; and that an act of parliament should be passed to confirm these conditions."

These terms were agreed to, and were held to be applicable not only to the garrison of Limerick but to

the whole of Ireland. Ginckle at once sent an express
to Cork to order the transports in that harbour to sail
round to the Shannon for the purpose of taking on
board such part of the Irish army as might wish to be
carried to France—this being one of the stipulations
of the treaty.

Sarsfield and most of his officers and the priests
used their utmost efforts to persuade the soldiers to
enter the French service in preference to the English.
Their exhortations were successful. Only about two
thousand Irish joined the British army, four thousand
laid down their arms and returned to their homes, and
a considerable number deserted on their march down
to Cork. The rest were shipped in transports to France,
where they entered the service of that country.

Two days after the treaty was signed the French
fleet, with ten thousand men and a great abundance
of stores, arrived at the mouth of the Shannon.

The Irish negotiators of the treaty have been greatly
and deservedly blamed, inasmuch as while they stipu-
lated that the proprietors of the neighbouring counties
should retain their estates, they abandoned those possessing property throughout the rest of Ireland to ruin
and beggary. There was no excuse for this. They
knew that the French fleet had sailed and must have
arrived in a few days, and that the English cause was
becoming so desperate that Ginckle would not have
resisted any terms they had laid down.

This cruel and wholly unnecessary desertion of their
friends has thrown a slur upon the memory of Sarsfield
and the other leaders who conducted the negotiations.

The officers and men who entered the service of France had bitter reason to repent their decision. Instead of being, as they expected, kept together in regiments, they were for the most part broken up and distributed throughout the French army. Louis was deeply enraged at the surrender just as the expedition he had made such efforts to send for the conquest of Ireland was within a few hours' sail of its shores, and he treated the whole of the Irish and French who returned from Ireland as men who had acted the part of traitors.

As soon as the terms of capitulation were arranged, Captain Davenant obtained papers of protection for all the men of his troop. He had formed them up on parade, and had put the question whether they wished to return home or to enter the service of France.

"I myself and your officers intend to return home," he said. "Of course each of you is free to do as he chooses; but it appears to me a most foolish thing to leave your country for ever, and exile yourself in the service of France, when you are free to return home. You know how little French promises have been kept during this war, and how little faith is to be placed on them in future."

The men were unanimous in their decision to return to their homes, and as soon as the protection papers were obtained the troop disbanded, and all returned to their homes and occupations in and around Bray.

It was a joyful meeting when Captain Davenant and Walter returned to the castle. Mrs. Davenant had always shared her husband's opinion that the chances of ultimate success were small, and of late even his mother had given up hope, and both were delighted that their anxieties were at last over, and husband and son restored to them in safety. There was an immense deal to tell on both sides, for it was months since any letter had passed between them.

"We have everything to be thankful for," Mrs. Davenant said when the stories on both sides had been told, "and it seems to me that it is to no slight extent due to Walter that we have passed so well through the last two troubled years. It was Jabez Whitefoot who first stood our friend, and who saved the castle from being burned, and his good-will was earned by Walter's friendship with his son. Then Mr. Conyers stood between us and the council, who would certainly have confiscated everything had it not been for him. And although he always expressed himself as greatly indebted to you also, he said that, so far as he understood from his wife, it was to Walter's foresight and arrangement that his wife and daughter owed their rescue. How was it that Walter was so forward in the matter, Fergus?"

"Walter was perhaps more particularly interested in the matter than I was," Captain Davenant said with a smile. "His thoughts were running in that direction."

Walter coloured up, and Mrs. Davenant, who was looking at him with some surprise at her husband's words, broke into a laugh.

"You don't mean to say, Walter, that you have been falling in love at your age?"

"You forget, dear," Captain Davenant said, coming to Walter's rescue, "that Walter is no longer a boy. Three years of campaigning have made a man of him, and I venture to think an earnest and thoughtful one. He is, it is true, only nineteen, but he has seen as much and gone through as much as men double his age. He has upon several occasions evinced an amount of coolness and judgment in danger which has earned him the approbation even of General Sarsfield, a man not easily satisfied."

"I don't mean to hurt your feelings, Walter," Mrs. Davenant said; "but of course it is difficult for me at first to realize that while you have been away you have changed from a boy into a man."

"I don't mind, mother dear," Walter said, "and you can laugh at me as much as you like."

"And is there anything in what your father says?" Mrs. Davenant asked, as she passed her hand fondly over Walter's head as he sat on a low stool beside her.

"Yes, mother," he answered manfully. "I am engaged to Claire Conyers. I have her mother's consent, but what Mr. Conyers will think about it I don't know. He must know long before this, for Mrs. Conyers said that she should tell him as soon as he joined them in England."

Mrs. Davenant leaned over and kissed her son.

"The Conyers are of good family," old Mrs. Davenant said, "although they did come over with Cromwell. I do not think that is any objection to a son of our house marrying into theirs."

Captain Davenant laughed.

"No objection at all on our side, mother. Any objection is likely to be on the other side, not on the ground of family, but on that of property. Claire Conyers is one of the richest heiresses in Ireland, while Walter's inheritance can scarcely be termed extensive."

Two months later Captain Davenant received a letter from Mr. Conyers saying that he had arrived with his wife and daughter at Dublin on the previous day, and should be glad to make his acquaintance and that of his son. "My wife," he said, "has informed me of certain love passages which have taken place between Claire and your son, and I shall be glad to talk to you concerning them."

Captain Davenant and Walter at once rode over to Dublin, the latter full of delight, and yet with a considerable amount of trepidation as to the interview between his father and Mr. Conyers. His mind was, however, speedily put at rest, for upon entering Mr. Conyers at once took him by the hand and said:

"I am glad, indeed, of the opportunity of thanking you in person for the inestimable service you rendered to my wife and daughter. I find from my wife that Claire has discovered a means of repaying you for your service, and as her happiness is, she tells me, dependent on my giving my consent to the plan, I tell you at once that I do so very heartily. I think you had better wait for a while, say two or three years, but we need not settle that at present. Come here, Claire." He placed the girl's hand in Walter's. "Take her," he said, "and make her happy."

The next day Mr. Conyers, with his wife and daugh-

ter, accompanied Captain Davenant and Walter back
to Davenant Castle, where they stayed for some days.

The Whitefoots did not long remain neighbours of
the Davenants. Old Zephaniah had passed away ere
the peace was signed, and soon after Captain Davenant
returned Jabez called at the castle.

"We are going away," he said. "John has made up
his mind to become a trader in London, and Hannah
and I would be lonely without him, and moreover we
are both weary of our life here, and have far more than
enough money laid by for our needs, and for giving
John the means of entering some well-established firm
when the time shall come. As to the lands here, they
are ours now; but the next turn of the wheel might
give them back to you. Besides we do not wish to be
troubled with their care. I therefore intend to revert
to the offer which you made me when the Parliament
restored the land to you. I have received a good offer
for our house and farm, and this I have accepted.
The rest of the estates I hand back to you, from whom
they were taken by the sword. My wife wishes this
as well as myself. John is eager that it should be so.
He will be glad that his friend should be heir to the
estates of his ancestors."

"But we could not accept such a generous offer," Captain Davenant exclaimed. "It is out of all reason."

"That I know not, friend Davenant; but I know
that I and my wife and John have so made up our
minds, and we are of a race not given to change. The
land would but be an incumbrance and a trouble to
us. John would far rather make his path in life as he

chooses it than live upon the rents of ill-gotten lands. You will receive your own again, and all parties will be satisfied."

Nothing could alter the resolution Jabez and his wife and son had taken, and so the Davenant estates came back to their former possessors.

Three years after the conclusion of peace Walter became Claire Conyers' husband, and in time succeeded to the wide estates of Mr. Conyers as well as those of the Davenants. Godfrey Davenant, on attaining the age of eighteen, obtained through Colonel L'Estrange's interest a commission in the English army, fought under Marlborough in the fierce campaign in Flanders, and fell at the battle of Oudenarde. Happily, during the lifetime of Walter and Claire Davenant there was never any renewal of trouble in Ireland, and they lived to see their children and grandchildren grow up around them in peace and happiness.

John Whitefoot became in time one of the leading merchants of the city of London, and spent the greater part of the fortune he gained in trade in works of charity and kindness. The friendship between him and Walter Davenant remained unchanged to the end of their lives. They occasionally paid each other visits, and when a son of John Whitefoot married a daughter of Walter Davenant, they felt that this was a fitting termination of the old feud between the families.

Blackie & Son's
CATALOGUE OF BOOKS
FOR YOUNG PEOPLE.

INCLUDING NEW WORKS BY

G. A. Henty.   G. Manville Fenn.   George Mac Donald, LL.D.

Prof. A. J. Church.   Harry Collingwood.

John C. Hutcheson.   Ascott R. Hope.   Henry Frith.

J. Percy-Groves.   Sarah Tytler.   Alice Corkran.

Rosa Mulholland.   Sarah Doudney.   Mary C. Rowsell.

and other popular Authors.

BY PROFESSOR POUCHET.

The Universe;

OR THE INFINITELY GREAT AND THE INFINITELY LITTLE. A Sketch of Contrasts in Creation, and Marvels revealed and explained by Natural Science. By F. A. POUCHET, M.D. With 273 Engravings on wood, of which 56 are full-page size. Ninth Edition, medium 8vo, cloth elegant, gilt edges, 7s. 6d.; also morocco antique, 16s.

"We can honestly commend Professor **Pouchet's** book, which is admirably, as it is copiously illustrated."—*The Times.*

"**As** interesting as the most exciting romance, and **a** great deal more likely to be remembered to good purpose."—*Standard.*

BY PROFESSOR CHURCH.

Two Thousand Years Ago:

Or, The Adventures of a Roman Boy. By Professor A. J. CHURCH. With 12 full-page Illustrations by ADRIEN MARIE. Crown 8vo, cloth elegant, olivine edges, 6s.

"Adventures well worth the telling. The book is extremely entertaining as well as useful, and there is a wonderful freshness in the Roman scenes and characters."—*The Times.*

"Entertaining in the highest degree from beginning to end, and full of adventure which is all the livelier for its close connection with history."—*Spectator.*

"We know of no book which will do more to make the Romans of that day live again for the English reader."—*Guardian.*

Robinson Crusoe.

By DANIEL DEFOE. Illustrated by above 100 Pictures by GORDON BROWNE. Crown 8vo, cloth elegant, olivine edges, 6s.

"One of the best issues, if not absolutely the best, of Defoe's work which has ever appeared."—*The Standard.*

"The best edition I have come across for years. If you know a boy who has not a 'Robinson Crusoe,' just glance at any one of these hundred illustrations, and you will go no further afield in search of a present for him."—*Truth.*

Gulliver's Travels.

A NEW EDITION. Illustrated by more than 100 Pictures by GORDON BROWNE. Crown 8vo, cloth elegant, olivine edges, 5s.

"By help of the admirable illustrations, and a little judicious skipping, it has enchanted a family party of ages varying from six to sixty. Which of the other Christmas books could stand this test?"—*Journal of Education.*

"Mr. Gordon Browne is, to my thinking, incomparably the most artistic, spirited, and brilliant of our illustrators of books for boys, and one of the most humorous also, as his illustrations of 'Gulliver' amply testify."—*Truth.*

BY G. A. HENTY.

"Mr. Henty is one of the best of story-tellers for young people."—*Spectator.*

Bonnie Prince Charlie:

A Tale of Fontenoy and Culloden. By G. A. HENTY. With 12 full-page Illustrations by GORDON BROWNE. Crown 8vo, cloth elegant, olivine edges, 6s.

The adventures of the son of a Scotch officer in French service who had secretly married the daughter of a noble. The boy, brought up by a Glasgow bailie, is arrested for aiding a Jacobite agent, escapes in a Dutch ship, is wrecked on the French coast, reaches Paris, and serves with the French army at Dettingen. Having discovered the convent in which his mother is confined, he establishes communication with her, and succeeds in obtaining through Marshal Saxe the release of both his parents. He kills his father's foe in a duel, and escaping to the coast, shares the adventures of Prince Charlie, but finally settles happily in Scotland. A book of the most stirring incident and of historic value.

For the Temple:

A Tale of the Fall of Jerusalem. By G. A. HENTY. With 10 full-page Illustrations by SOLOMON J. SOLOMON: and a coloured Map. Crown 8vo, cloth elegant, olivine edges, 6s.

Few boys have failed to find the story of the revolt of the Jews of thrilling interest when once brought to their notice; but there has hitherto been little choice between sending them to books of history and supplying them with insipid fictional transcripts of the story. Mr. Henty supplies a distinct want in this regard, weaving into the record of Josephus an admirable and attractive plot. The troubles in the district of Tiberias, the march of the legions, the sieges of Jotapata, of Gamala, and of Jerusalem, form the impressive and carefully-studied historic setting to the figure of the lad who passes from the vineyard to the service of Josephus, becomes the leader of a guerrilla band of patriots, fights bravely for the Temple, and after a brief term of slavery at Alexandria, returns to his Galilean home with the favour of Titus.

The Lion of the North:

A Tale of Gustavus Adolphus and the Wars of Religion. By G. A. HENTY. With 12 full-page Illustrations by JOHN SCHÖNBERG. Crown 8vo, cloth elegant, olivine edges, 6s.

"As we might expect from Mr. Henty the tale is a clever and instructive piece of history, and as boys may be trusted to read it conscientiously, they can hardly fail to be profited as well as pleased."—*The Times.*

"A praiseworthy attempt to interest British youth in the great deeds of the Scotch Brigade in the wars of Gustavus Adolphus. Mackay, Hepburn, and Munro live again in Mr. Henty's pages, as those deserve to live whose disciplined bands formed really the germ of the modern British army."—*Athenæum.*

BY G. A. HENTY.

"Surely Mr. Henty should understand boys' tastes better than any man living."
— *The Times.*

The Young Carthaginian:

A Story of the Times of Hannibal. By G. A. HENTY. With 12 full-page Illustrations by C. J. STANILAND, R.I. Crown 8vo, cloth elegant, olivine edges, **6s.**

"The effect of an interesting story, well constructed and vividly told, is enhanced by the picturesque quality of the scenic background. From first to last nothing stays the interest of the narrative. It bears us along as on a stream, whose current varies in direction, but never loses its force."—*Saturday Review.*

"Ought to be popular with boys who are not too ill instructed or too dandified to be affected by a graphic picture of the days and deeds of Hannibal."—*Athenæum.*

With Wolfe in Canada:

Or, The Winning of a Continent. By G. A. HENTY. With 12 full-page Illustrations by GORDON BROWNE. Crown 8vo, cloth elegant, olivine edges, **6s.**

"A model of what a boy's story-book should be. Mr. Henty has a great power of infusing into the dead facts of history new life, and as no pains are spared by him to ensure accuracy in historic details, his books supply useful aids to study as well as amusement."—*School Guardian.*

"It is not only a lesson in history as instructively as it is graphically told, but also a deeply interesting and often thrilling tale of adventure and peril by flood and field."—*Illustrated London News.*

With Clive in India:

Or, The Beginnings of an Empire. By G. A. HENTY. With 12 full-page Illustrations by GORDON BROWNE, in black and tint. Crown 8vo, cloth elegant, olivine edges, **6s.**

"In this book Mr. Henty has contrived to exceed himself in stirring adventures and thrilling situations. The pictures add greatly to the interest of the book."—*Saturday Review.*

"Among writers of stories of adventure for boys Mr. Henty stands in the very first rank. Those who know something about India will be the most ready to thank Mr. Henty for giving them this instructive volume to place in the hands of their children."—*Academy.*

True to the Old Flag:

A Tale of the American War of Independence. By G. A. HENTY. With 12 full-page Illustrations by GORDON BROWNE. Crown 8vo, cloth elegant, olivine edges, **6s.**

"Does justice to the pluck and determination of the British soldiers. The son of an American loyalist, who remains true to our flag, falls among the hostile redskins in that very Huron country which has been endeared to us by the exploits of Hawkeye and Chingachgook."—*The Times.*

"Mr. Henty's extensive personal experience of adventures and moving incidents by flood and field, combined with a gift of picturesque narrative, make his books always welcome visitors in the home circle."—*Daily News.*

BY G. A. HENTY.

"Among writers of stories of adventure for boys Mr. Henty stands in the very first rank."—*Academy*.

In Freedom's Cause:

A Story of Wallace and Bruce. By G. A. HENTY. With 12 full-page Illustrations by GORDON BROWNE, in black and tint. Crown 8vo, cloth elegant, olivine edges, 6s.

"Mr. Henty has broken new ground as an historical novelist. His tale of the days of Wallace and Bruce is full of stirring action, and will commend itself to boys."—*Athenæum*.

"Written in the author's best style. Full of the most remarkable achievements, it is a tale of great interest, which a boy, once he has begun it, will not willingly put on one side."—*Schoolmaster*.

Through the Fray:

A Story of the Luddite Riots. By G. A. HENTY. With 12 full-page Illustrations by H. M. PAGET, in black and tint. Crown 8vo, cloth elegant, olivine edges, 6s.

"Mr. Henty inspires a love and admiration for straightforwardness, truth, and courage. This is one of the best of the many good books Mr. Henty has produced, and deserves to be classed with his *Facing Death*."—*Standard*.

"The interest of the story never flags. Were we to propose a competition for the best list of novel writers for boys we have little doubt that Mr. Henty's name would stand first."—*Journal of Education*.

Under Drake's Flag:

A Tale of the Spanish Main. By G. A. HENTY. Illustrated by 12 full-page Pictures by GORDON BROWNE, in black and tint. Crown 8vo, cloth elegant, olivine edges, 6s.

"There is not a dull chapter, nor, indeed, a dull page in the book; but the author has so carefully worked up his subject that the exciting deeds of his heroes are never incongruous or absurd."—*Observer*.

"I can thoroughly recommend 'Under Drake's Flag.'"—*Truth*.

"Just such a book, indeed, as the youth of this maritime country are likely to prize highly."—*Daily Telegraph*.

A Final Reckoning:

A Tale of Bush Life in Australia. By G. A. HENTY. With 8 full-page Illustrations by W. B. WOLLEN. Crown 8vo, cloth elegant, 5s.

"Mr. Henty has never published a more readable, a more carefully constructed, or a better written story than this."—*Spectator*.

"Exhibits Mr. Henty's talent as a story-teller at his best. . . . The drawings possess the uncommon merit of really illustrating the text."—*Saturday Review*.

"All boys will read this story with eager and unflagging interest. The episodes are in Mr. Henty's very best vein—graphic, exciting, realistic; and, as in all Mr. Henty's books, the tendency is to the formation of an honourable, manly, and even heroic character."—*Birmingham Post*.

BY G. A. HENTY.

In the Reign of Terror:

The Adventures of a Westminster Boy. By G. A. HENTY. With 8 full-page Illustrations by J. SCHÖNBERG. Crown 8vo, cloth elegant, olivine edges, 5s.

Harry Sandwith, a Westminster boy, becomes a resident at the chateau of a French marquis, and after various adventures accompanies the family to Paris at the crisis of the Revolution. Imprisonment and death reduce their number, and the hero finds himself beset by perils with the three young daughters of the house in his charge. The stress of trial brings out in him all the best English qualities of pluck and endurance, and after hair-breadth escapes they reach Nantes. There the girls are condemned to death in the coffin-ships Les Noyades, but are saved by the unfailing courage of their boy-protector.

Orange and Green:

A Tale of the Boyne and Limerick. By G. A. HENTY. With 8 full-page Illustrations by GORDON BROWNE. Crown 8vo, cloth elegant, olivine edges, 5s.

The history of Ireland has assumed such immediate interest that Mr. Henty's fictional treatment of one of its important crises will be welcomed by all who desire that the young should realize vividly the sources of many of its troubles. The story is the record of two typical families. In the children the spirit of contention has given place to friendship, and though they take opposite sides in the struggle between James and William, their good-will and mutual service are never interrupted, and in the end the rightful owners come happily to their own again.

St. George for England:

A Tale of Cressy and Poitiers. By G. A. HENTY. With 8 full-page Illustrations by GORDON BROWNE, in black and tint. Crown 8vo, cloth elegant, 5s.

"Mr. Henty has done his work well, producing a strong story at once instructive and entertaining."—*Glasgow Herald.*

"Mr. Henty's historical novels for boys bid fair to supplement, on their behalf, the historical labours of Sir Walter Scott in the land of fiction."—*Standard.*

Facing Death:

Or the Hero of the Vaughan Pit. A Tale of the Coal Mines. By G. A. HENTY. With 8 full-page Illustrations by GORDON BROWNE. Crown 8vo, cloth elegant, 5s.

"If any father, godfather, clergyman, or schoolmaster is on the look-out for a good book to give as a present to a boy who is worth his salt, this is the book we would recommend."—*Standard.*

BY G. A. HENTY.

"Mr. Henty is the king of story-tellers for boys."—*Sword and Trowel.*

The Bravest of the Brave:

With Peterborough in Spain. By G. A. HENTY. With 8 full-page Pictures by H. M. PAGET. Crown 8vo, cloth elegant, 5s.

"Mr. Henty has done good service in endeavouring to redeem from oblivion the name of the great soldier, Charles Mordaunt, Earl of Peterborough."—*Athenæum.*

"Mr. Henty never loses sight of the moral purpose of his work—to enforce the doctrine of courage and truth, mercy and lovingkindness, as indispensable to the making of an English gentleman. British lads will read 'The Bravest of the Brave' with pleasure and profit; of that we are quite sure."—*Daily Telegraph.*

For Name and Fame:

Or, Through Afghan Passes. By G. A. HENTY. With 8 full-page Illustrations by GORDON BROWNE, in black and tint. Crown 8vo, cloth elegant, 5s.

"The best feature of the book, apart from its scenes of adventure, is its honest effort to do justice to the patriotism of the Afghan people."—*Daily News.*

"Not only a rousing story, replete with all the varied forms of excitement of a campaign, but, what is still more useful, an account of a territory and its inhabitants which must for a long time possess a supreme interest for Englishmen, as being the key to our Indian Empire."—*Glasgow Herald.*

The Dragon and the Raven:

Or, The Days of King Alfred. By G. A. HENTY. With 8 full-page Illustrations by C. J. STANILAND, R.I., in black and tint. Crown 8vo, cloth elegant, 5s.

"Perhaps the best story of the early days of England which has yet been told."—*Court Journal.*

"We know of no popular book in which the stirring incidents of Alfred's reign are made accessible to young readers as they are here."—*Scotsman.*

By Sheer Pluck:

A Tale of the Ashanti War. By G. A. HENTY. With 8 full-page Pictures by GORDON BROWNE. Crown 8vo, cloth elegant, 5s.

"'By Sheer Pluck' will be eagerly read. The author's personal knowledge of the west coast has been turned to good advantage."—*Athenæum.*

"Morally, the book is everything that could be desired, setting before the boys a bright and bracing ideal of the English gentleman."—*Christian Leader.*

Sturdy and Strong:

Or, How George Andrews made his Way. By G. A. HENTY. With 4 full-page Illustrations by ROBERT FOWLER. Crown 8vo, cloth extra, 2s. 6d.

The aim of the story is to show how steadfastness, truth, and watchfulness may aid a lad to win his way through the greatest difficulties and be of assistance to others in the endeavour.

BY GEORGE MANVILLE FENN.

"Mr. Fenn is in the front rank of writers of stories for boys."—*Liverpool Mercury.*

Dick o' the Fens:

A Romance of the Great East Swamp. By G. MANVILLE FENN. With 12 full-page Illustrations by FRANK DADD. Crown 8vo, cloth elegant, olivine edges, 6s.

A tale of boy life in the old Lincolnshire Fens. Dick o' the Fens and Tom o' Grimsey are the sons of a squire and a farmer living on the edge of one of the vast wastes, and their adventures are of unusual interest. Sketches of shooting and fishing experiences are introduced in a manner which should stimulate the faculty of observation and give a healthy love for country life; while the record of the fen-men's stealthy resistance to the great draining scheme is full of the keenest interest. The ambushes and shots in the mist and dark, the incendiary fires, the bursting of the sea-wall, and the long-baffled attempts to trace the lurking foe, are described with Mr. Manville Fenn's wonted skill in the management of mystery.

Devon Boys:

A Tale of the North Shore. By G. MANVILLE FENN. With 12 full-page Illustrations by GORDON BROWNE. Crown 8vo, cloth elegant, olivine edges, 6s.

"An admirable story, as remarkable for the individuality of its young heroes as for the excellent descriptions of coast scenery and life in North Devon. It is one of the best books we have seen this season."—*Athenæum.*

"We do not know that Mr. Fenn has ever reached a higher level than he has in *Devon Boys*. It must be put in the very front rank of Christmas books."—*Spectator.*

Brownsmith's Boy.

By G. MANVILLE FENN. With 12 full-page Illustrations by GORDON BROWNE. Crown 8vo, cloth elegant, olivine edges, 6s.

"Mr. Fenn's books are among the best, if not altogether the best, of the stories for boys. Mr. Fenn is at his best in 'Brownsmith's Boy.'"—*Pictorial World.*

"'Brownsmith's Boy' must rank among the few undeniably good boys' books. He will be a very dull boy indeed who lays it down without wishing that it had gone on for at least 100 pages more."—*North British Mail.*

Bunyip Land:

The Story of a Wild Journey in New Guinea. By G. MANVILLE FENN. With 12 full-page Illustrations by GORDON BROWNE. Crown 8vo, cloth elegant, olivine edges, 6s.

"Mr. Fenn deserves the thanks of everybody for 'Bunyip Land,' and we may venture to promise that a quiet week may be reckoned on whilst the youngsters have such fascinating literature provided for their evenings' amusement."—*Spectator*

"One of the best tales of adventure produced by any living writer, combining the inventiveness of Jules Verne, and the solidity of character and earnestness of spirit which have made the English victorious in so many fields."—*Daily Chronicle.*

BY GEORGE MANVILLE FENN.

"Our boys know Mr. Fenn well, his stories having won for him a foremost place in their estimation."—*Pall Mall Gazette.*

The Golden Magnet:

A Tale of the Land of the Incas. By G. MANVILLE FENN. Illustrated by 12 full-page Pictures by GORDON BROWNE, in black and tint. Crown 8vo, cloth elegant, olivine edges, 6s.

"This is, we think, the best boys' book Mr. Fenn has produced. . . . The illustrations are perfect in their way."—*Globe.*

"There could be no more welcome present for a boy. There is not a dull page in the book, and many will be read with breathless interest. 'The Golden Magnet' is, of course, the same one that attracted Raleigh and the heroes of 'Westward Ho!'"—*Journal of Education.*

In the King's Name:

Or the Cruise of the *Kestrel.* By G. MANVILLE FENN. Illustrated by 12 full-page Pictures by GORDON BROWNE, in black and tint. Crown 8vo, cloth elegant, olivine edges, 6s.

"A capital boy's story, full of incident and adventure, and told in the lively style in which Mr. Fenn is such an adept."—*Globe.*

"The best of all Mr. Fenn's productions in this field. It has the great quality of always 'moving on,' adventure following adventure in constant succession."—*Daily News.*

Yussuf the Guide:

Being the Strange Story of the Travels in Asia Minor of Burne the Lawyer, Preston the Professor, and Lawrence the Sick. By G. MANVILLE FENN. With 8 full-page Illustrations by JOHN SCHÖNBERG. Crown 8vo, cloth elegant, 5s.

"The narrative will take its readers into scenes that will have great novelty and attraction for them, and the experiences with the brigands will be especially delightful to boys."—*Scotsman.*

"This story is told with such real freshness and vigour that the reader feels he is actually one of the party, sharing in the fun and facing the dangers with them."—*Pall Mall Gazette.*

Menhardoc:

A Story of Cornish Nets and Mines. By G. MANVILLE FENN. With 8 full-page Illustrations by C. J. STANILAND, in black and tint. Crown 8vo, cloth elegant, 5s.

"They are real living boys, with their virtues and faults. The Cornish fishermen are drawn from life, they are racy of the soil, salt with the sea-water, and they stand out from the pages in their jerseys and sea-boots all sprinkled with silvery pilchard scales."—*Spectator.*

BY GEORGE MANVILLE FENN.

"There is a freshness, a buoyancy, a heartiness about Mr. Fenn's writings."—*Standard.*

Mother Carey's Chicken:

Her Voyage to the Unknown Isle. By G. MANVILLE FENN. With 8 full-page Illustrations. Crown 8vo, cloth elegant, olivine edges, 5s.

A stirring story of **adventure** in the Eastern seas, where a lad shares the perils of his father, **the captain** of the merchant ship *The Petrel.* After touching at Singapore, they are becalmed off one of the tropic isles, where the ship is attacked and, after a desperate fight, set on fire by Malay pirates. They escape in a boat and drift ashore upon a beautiful volcanic island. A volcanic eruption, while increasing their danger, relieves them of their enemies, and they finally escape and reach a civilized port.

Patience Wins:

Or, War in the Works. By G. MANVILLE FENN. With 8 full-page Illustrations by GORDON BROWNE, in black and tint. Crown 8vo, cloth elegant, 5s.

"**An excellent** story, the interest being sustained **from first** to last. One **of the best books of** its kind which has come before **us this** year."—*Saturday Review.*

"Mr. Fenn is at his **best** in 'Patience Wins.' It is sure to prove acceptable to youthful readers, and will give a good idea of that which was the real state of one of our largest manufacturing towns not many years ago."—*Guardian.*

Nat the Naturalist:

A Boy's Adventures in the Eastern Seas. By G. MANVILLE FENN. With 8 full-page Pictures. Cr. 8vo, cloth elegant, 5s.

"Among **the best of the many good books** for **boys that** have come out this season."—*Times.*

"**This sort** of book encourages independence of character, develops resource, and **teaches a boy** to keep his **eyes open.**"—*Saturday Review.*

BY DOUGLAS FRAZAR.

Perseverance Island:

Or the Robinson Crusoe of the 19th Century. By DOUGLAS FRAZAR. With 12 full-page Illustrations. Crown 8vo, cloth elegant, 5s.

"**A most** remarkable and fascinating book, and we are quite sure that **the thirty** chapters it contains will be read in less than thirty hours by hundreds of **bright** and adventure-loving English boys."—*Practical Teacher.*

"**This second** Robinson Crusoe is certainly a marvellous man. His determination to overcome all difficulties, and his subsequent success, should alone make this a capital book for boys. It is altogether a worthy successor to the ancient *Robinson Crusoe.*"—*Glasgow Herald.*

BY HARRY COLLINGWOOD.

"Mr. Collingwood stands far in advance of any other writer for boys as a teller of stories of the sea."—*Standard.*

The Log of the "Flying Fish;"

A Story of Aerial and Submarine Peril and Adventure. By HARRY COLLINGWOOD. With 12 full-page Illustrations by GORDON BROWNE. Crown 8vo, cloth elegant, olivine edges, 6s.

"The *Flying Fish* actually surpasses all Jules Verne's creations; with incredible speed she flies through the air, skims over the surface of the water, and darts along the ocean bed. We strongly recommend our schoolboy friends to possess themselves of her log."—*Athenæum.*

"Is full of even more vividly recounted adventures than those which charmed so many boy readers in *Pirate Island.* There is a thrilling adventure on the precipices of Mount Everest, when the ship floats off."—*Academy.*

The Rover's Secret:

A Tale of the Pirate Cays and Lagoons of Cuba. By HARRY COLLINGWOOD. With 8 full-page Illustrations by W. C. SYMONS. Crown 8vo, cloth elegant, olivine edges, 5s.

The hero of the *Rover's Secret*, a young officer of the British navy, narrates his peculiar experiences in childhood and his subsequent perils and achievements: the mutiny on board the *Hermione;* his escape with a companion to La Guayra, their seizure by the Spaniards, their romantic flight, and the strange blunder which commits them to a cruise to the headquarters of the notorious pirate Merlani, whose ultimate capture and confession come about in a way as exciting as unexpected. The narrative affords accurate descriptions of life afloat at the end of last century.

The Pirate Island:

A Story of the South Pacific. By HARRY COLLINGWOOD. Illustrated by 8 full-page Pictures by C. J. STANILAND and J. R. WELLS, in black and tint. Crown 8vo, cloth elegant, 5s.

"A capital story of the sea; indeed in our opinion the author is superior in some respects as a marine novelist to the better known Mr. Clarke Russell."—*The Times.*

"Told in the most vivid and graphic language. It would be difficult to find a more thoroughly delightful gift-book."—*Guardian.*

The Congo Rovers:

A Story of the Slave Squadron. By HARRY COLLINGWOOD. With 8 full-page Illustrations by J. SCHÖNBERG, in black and tint. Crown 8vo, cloth elegant, 5s.

"Mr. Collingwood carries us off for another cruise at sea, in 'The Congo Rovers,' and boys will need no pressing to join the daring crew, which seeks adventures and meets with any number of them."—*The Times.*

"No better sea story has lately been written than the *Congo Rovers.* It is as original as any boy could desire."—*Morning Post.*

BY GEORGE MAC DONALD.

"Mr. George Mac Donald is one of the few living authors who, while they enjoy a considerable reputation, are greater than their repute."—*Pall Mall Gazette.*

At the Back of the North Wind.

By GEORGE MAC DONALD, LL.D. With 75 Illustrations by ARTHUR HUGHES. New Edition. Cr. 8vo, cloth elegant, 5s.

"In 'At the Back of the North Wind' we stand with one foot in fairyland and one on common earth. The story is thoroughly original, full of fancy and pathos, and underlaid with earnest but not too obtrusive teaching."—*The Times.*

Ranald Bannerman's Boyhood.

By GEORGE MAC DONALD, LL.D. With 36 Illustrations by ARTHUR HUGHES. New Edition Cr. 8vo, cloth elegant, 5s.

"The sympathy with boy-nature in 'Ranald Bannerman's Boyhood' is perfect. It is a beautiful picture of childhood, teaching by its impressions and suggestions all noble things."—*British Quarterly Review.*

The Princess and the Goblin.

By GEORGE MAC DONALD, LL.D. With 30 Illustrations by ARTHUR HUGHES. New Edition. Cr. 8vo, cloth extra, 3s. 6d.

In the sphere of fantasy Dr. Mac Donald has very few equals, and his rare touch of many aspects of life invariably gives to his stories a deeper meaning of the highest value. His "Princess and Goblin" exemplifies both gifts, a fine thread of allegory running through the narrative of the adventures of the young miner, who, amongst other marvellous experiences, finds his way into the caverns of the gnomes and achieves a final victory over them.

The Princess and Curdie.

By GEORGE MAC DONALD, LL.D. With 8 Illustrations by JAMES ALLEN. New Edition. Crown 8vo, cloth extra, 3s. 6d.

A sequel to the *Princess and Goblin*, tracing the history of the young miner and the princess after the return of the latter to her father's court, where more terrible foes have to be encountered than the grotesque earth-dwellers. It is a book of unusually high literary merit and ranks among the most brilliant of Dr. Mac Donald's stories for the young.

Gutta-Percha Willie,

The Working Genius. By GEORGE MAC DONALD, LL.D. With 8 Illustrations by ARTHUR HUGHES. New Edition. Crown 8vo, cloth extra, 2s. 6d.

In *Gutta-percha Willie* Dr. Mac Donald has dealt rather with fact than with fantasy, the story showing how a country doctor's son, who was permitted to develop naturally in accordance with his own healthy instincts, educated himself in matters of practical utility. It is not given to all lads to have the wise curiosity and constructive genius of the hero; but the book is eminently calculated to bring out these qualities.

BY SARAH TYTLER.

Girl Neighbours:

Or, The Old Fashion and the New. By SARAH TYTLER, author of "Citoyenne Jacqueline," &c. With 8 full-page Illustrations by C. T. GARLAND. Crown 8vo, cloth extra, 5s.

A story specially adapted for girls, told in that quaint delightful fashion which has made Miss Tytler's former books so popular and attractive. The characters of the Girl Neighbours Sapientia (Pie) Stubbs, and Harriet (Harry) Cotton, who may be said respectively to illustrate the old and the new fashioned method of education, are admirably delineated; and the introduction of the two young ladies from London, who represent the modern institutions of professional nursing and schools of cookery, is very happily effected. The story possesses abundant humour, and piquant descriptions of character.

BY ALICE CORKRAN.

Margery Merton's Girlhood.

By ALICE CORKRAN. With 6 full-page Illustrations by GORDON BROWNE. Crown 8vo, cloth extra, 3s. 6d.

The experiences of an orphan girl who in infancy is left by her father—an officer in India—to the care of an elderly aunt residing near Paris. The accounts of the various persons who have an after influence on the story, the school companions of Margery, the sisters of the Conventual College of Art, the professor, and the peasantry of the neighbourhood of Fontainebleau—where some very weird adventures are experienced,—are singularly vivid. There is a subtle attraction about the book which will make it a great favourite with thoughtful girls.

Down the Snow Stairs:

Or, From Good-night to Good-morning. By ALICE CORKRAN. With 60 character Illustrations by GORDON BROWNE. Square crown 8vo, cloth elegant, gilt edges, 6s.

"A fascinating wonder-book for children."—*Athenæum.*

"The whole imagery is delicately managed, and the illusions of dreamland and their curious connection with the realities of life are cleverly described. The illustrations are excellent."—*Guardian.*

"A gem of the first water, bearing upon every page the signet mark of genius. All is told with such simplicity and perfect naturalness that the dream appears to be a solid reality. It is indeed a Little Pilgrim's Progress."—*Christian Leader.*

Adventures of Mrs. Wishing-to-be,

And other Stories. By ALICE CORKRAN. With 3 full-page Pictures in colours. Crown 8vo, cloth extra, 2s.

Simply a charming book for little girls."—*Saturday Review.*

Just in the style and spirit to win the hearts of children."—*Daily News.*

Sir Walter's Ward:

A Tale of Mediæval **Life.** By **WILLIAM** EVERARD. With 6 full-
   page Illustrations. Crown 8vo, cloth extra, 3s. 6d.

The chief scenes of this stirring **and** vivid story are in Thuringia, where
Sir Walter—a poet and minstrel knight, and his ward the youthful Dodo,
have to meet friends and foes. The youth, after remarkable vicissitudes,
joins the Crusade at the time that the Emperor is in danger from the
plots of the Knights Templars and Hospitallers, and is intrusted with
important duties, but afterwards incurs the displeasure of his imperial
master and returns to his own native place, where, by a series of strange
and interesting events, he recovers his inheritance. The story is interesting alike as a work of fiction or as a vivid historical picture of the mediæval **age.**

Dr. Jolliffe's Boys:

A Tale of Weston School. By LEWIS HOUGH. With 6 full-page
   Pictures in black and tint. Crown 8vo, cloth extra, 3s. 6d.

"Young people who appreciate 'Tom Brown's School-days' will find this story a
worthy companion to that fascinating book. There is the same manliness of tone
and healthy morality in this tale of school life as characterized the masterpiece of
Mr. Hughes."—*Newcastle Journal.*

Brother and Sister:

Or the Trials of the Moore Family. By ELIZABETH J. LYSAGHT.
   With 6 full-page Illustrations in black and tint. Crown 8vo,
   cloth elegant, 3s. 6d.

"A pretty story, and well told. The plot is cleverly **constructed, and** the moral
is excellent."—*Athenæum.*

The Lads of Little Clayton:

Stories of Village Boy Life. By R. STEAD. With 4 full-page
   Illustrations. Crown 8vo, cloth elegant, 2s. 6d.

"A capital book for boys. They will learn from its pages what true boy courage is. They will learn further to avoid all that is petty and mean if they read
the tales aright."—*Schoolmaster.*

Ten Boys

Who lived on the Road from Long Ago to Now. By JANE
   ANDREWS. With 20 Illustrations. Cr. 8vo, cloth extra, 2s. 6d.

"All are apt presentations in easy terms of the manners of their different ages,
and all lead well up to the moral, 'it is not what a boy *has*, but what he *is*, that
makes him valuable to the world and the world valuable to him."—*Athenæum.*

"The idea of this book is a very happy one, and is admirably carried out. **We**
have followed the whole course of the work with exquisite pleasure. Teachers
should find it particularly interesting and suggestive."—*Practical Teacher.*

The Wigwam and the War-path:

Stories of the Red Indians. By ASCOTT R. HOPE. With 8 full-page Pictures by GORDON BROWNE, in black and tint. Crown 8vo, cloth elegant, 5s.

"All the stories are told well, in simple spirited language and with a fulness of detail that makes them instructive as well as interesting."—*Journal of Education.*

Stories of Old Renown:

Tales of Knights and Heroes. By ASCOTT R. HOPE. With 100 Illustrations by GORDON BROWNE. New Edition. Crown 8vo, cloth elegant, 3s. 6d.

" A most beautifully produced volume. Mr. Ascott Hope has brought together nine famous stories, so prepared as to fit them to give real delight to all boys of healthy tastes. The designs are simply exquisite."—*Morning Advertiser.*

Reefer and Rifleman:

A Tale of the Two Services. By J. PERCY GROVES, late 27th Inniskillings. With 6 full-page Illustrations by JOHN SCHÖNBERG. Crown 8vo, cloth elegant, 3s. 6d.

" A good, old-fashioned, amphibious story of our fighting with the Frenchmen in the beginning of our century, with a fair sprinkling of fun and frolic."—*Times.*

" The author is quite at home in scenes of military and naval life, and writes with a picturesque dash which is fast bringing him to the front rank among the writers of boys' books."—*Daily News.*

The War of the Axe:

Or Adventures in South Africa. By J. PERCY GROVES. With 4 full-page Illustrations by J. SCHÖNBERG. Crown 8vo, cloth extra, 2s. 6d.

A story of the Caffre war, with an abundance of incident and the genuine local colouring. Tom Flinders, late of Rugby, sails to rejoin his parents in Cape Colony, goes up country, meets with many new experiences, gets mauled by a Cape lion, and finally joins the Cape Mounted Rifles. He falls into the hands of the Caffres, but after a strange escape succeeds in rejoining his friends. Many interesting campaigning memories are worked into the narrative.

Traitor or Patriot?

A Tale of the Rye-House Plot. By MARY C. ROWSELL. With 6 full-page Pictures by C. O. MURRAY and C. J. STANILAND, in black and tint. Crown 8vo, cloth elegant, 3s. 6d.

" A romantic love episode, whose true characters are lifelike beings, not dry sticks as in many historical tales."—*Graphic.*

" The character of the heroine, Ruth, is singularly pretty and attractive: we thank the author for so charming a creation."—*Bristol Mercury.*

BY JOHN C. HUTCHESON.

"Mr. Hutcheson is one of our best tellers of sea stories."—*Spectator.*

The White Squall:

A Story of the Sargasso Sea. By JOHN C. HUTCHESON. With 6 full-page Illustrations by JOHN SCHÖNBERG. Crown 8vo, cloth elegant, 3s. 6d.

"Few writers have made such rapid improvement in the course of a few years as has the author of this capital story.   Boys will find it difficult to lay down the book till they have got to the end."—*Standard.*

"The sketches of tropical life are so good as sometimes to remind us of 'Tom Cringle' and the 'Cruise of the Midge.'"—*Times.*

The Wreck of the Nancy Bell:

Or Cast Away on Kerguelen Land. By JOHN C. HUTCHESON. Illustrated by 6 full-page Pictures in black and tint. Crown 8vo, cloth extra, 3s. 6d.

"A full circumstantial narrative such as boys delight in.   The ship so sadly destined to wreck on Kerguelen Land is manned by a very lifelike party, passengers and crew. The life in the Antarctic Iceland is well treated."—*Athenæum.*

"Mr. Hutcheson is one who understands his subject and writes in that clear precise style which gives such a charm to the immortal pages of Robinson Crusoe."—*Bristol Mercury.*

Picked up at Sea:

Or the Gold Miners of Minturne Creek. By JOHN C. HUTCHESON. With 6 full-page Pictures. Cr. 8vo, cloth extra, 3s. 6d.

"The author's success with this book is so marked that it may well encourage him to further efforts. The description of mining life in the Far-west is true and accurate."—*Standard.*

"A capital book; full of startling incident, clever dialogue, admirable descriptions of sky and water in all their aspects, and plenty of fun."—*Sheffield Independent.*

The Penang Pirate

And THE LOST PINNACE. By JOHN C. HUTCHESON. With 3 full-page Illustrations. Crown 8vo, cloth extra, 2s.

"A book which boys will thoroughly enjoy. It is rattling, adventurous, and romantic, and the stories are thoroughly healthy in tone, and written by a skilful hand."—*Aberdeen Journal.*

Teddy:

The Story of a "Little Pickle." By JOHN C. HUTCHESON. With 3 full-page Illustrations. Crown 8vo, cloth extra, 2s.

"He is an amusing little fellow with a rich fund of animal spirits, and when at length he goes to sea with Uncle Jack he speedily sobers down under the discipline of life."—*Saturday Review.*

BY HENRY FRITH.

The Search for the Talisman:

A Story of Labrador. By HENRY FRITH. With 6 full-page
Illustrations by J. SCHÖNBERG. Cr. 8vo, cloth elegant, 3s. 6d.

"Is everything that a boy's book should be—healthy in teaching, instructive,
yet never dull. Mr. Frith is a thorough master of boy nature."—*Glasgow Herald.*

Jack o' Lanthorn:

A Tale of Adventure. By HENRY FRITH. With 4 full-page Illustrations in black and tint. Crown 8vo, cloth elegant, 2s. 6d.

"Will hold its own with the best works of Mr. Henty and Mr. Fenn."—*Morning
Advertiser.*

Aboard the "Atalanta:"

The Story of a Truant. By HENRY FRITH. With 3 full-page
Illustrations. Crown 8vo, cloth extra, 2s.

The hero, having received a flogging as the reward for saving a life, runs
away from school, and speedily finds that there are worse things in life
than floggings. He makes a perilous voyage in a barge laden with contra-
band ammunition, and ultimately finds himself on board the blockade-
runner *Atalanta*. He is compelled to share in the incidents of the siege
of Charleston, but eventually succeeds in escaping.

BY E. S. BROOKS.

Chivalric Days:

Stories of Courtesy and Courage in the Olden Times. By E. S.
BROOKS. With 20 Illustrations by GORDON BROWNE and
other Artists. Crown 8vo, cloth extra, 3s. 6d.

A collection of ten typical stories, turning upon some chivalrous action
either of courtesy or courage. They are taken from many nations and
ages, and amongst the leading figures are the Egyptian queen Nitocris,
Hannibal, Constantine and the Princess Valeria, Alfred the Great, Richard
II., Lazarus of Servia, Henry VIII., Jean Bart, &c. The work is the
worthy complement of the author's *Historic Boys.*

Historic Boys:

Their Endeavours, their Achievements, and their Times. By
E. S. BROOKS. With 12 full-page Illustrations by R. B. BIRCH
and JOHN SCHÖNBERG. Crown 8vo, cloth extra, 3s. 6d.

"This book will be voraciously read by every boy into whose hands it may
come; and no boy will read it without being thereby better fitted to fight the
battle of life."—*Literary World.*

"A wholesome book, manly in tone, its character sketches enlivened by brisk
dialogue. We advise schoolmasters to put it on their list of prizes."—*Knowledge.*

B

BY MRS. R. H. READ.

Silver Mill:

A Tale of the Don Valley. By Mrs. R. H. READ. With 6 full-page Illustrations by JOHN SCHÖNBERG. Crown 8vo, cloth elegant, 3s. 6d.

"A good girl's story-book. The plot is interesting, and the heroine, Ruth, a lady by birth, though brought up in a humble station, well deserves the more elevated position in which the end of the book leaves her. The pictures are very spirited."—*Saturday Review.*

Dora:

Or a Girl without a Home. By Mrs. R. H. READ. With 6 full-page Illustrations. Crown 8vo, cloth elegant, 3s. 6d.

"It is no slight thing, in an age of rubbish, to get a story so pure and healthy as this."—*The Academy.*

"One of the most pleasing stories for young people that we have met with of late years."—*Harper's Magazine.*

Our Dolly:

Her Words and Ways. By Mrs. R. H. READ. With many Woodcuts, and a Frontispiece in colours. Cr. 8vo, cloth extra, 2s.

"Prettily told and prettily illustrated."—*Guardian.*

"Sure to be a great favourite with young children."—*School Guardian.*

Fairy Fancy:

What she Heard and what she Saw. By Mrs. R. H. READ. With many Woodcut Illustrations and a Coloured Frontispiece. Crown 8vo, cloth extra, 2s.

"The authoress has very great insight into child nature, and a sound healthy tone pervades the book."—*Glasgow Herald.*

The Eversley Secrets.

By EVELYN EVERETT GREEN. With 4 full-page Illustrations by J. J. PROCTOR. Crown 8vo, cloth elegant, 2s. 6d.

"Is one of the best children's stories of the year."—*Academy.*

"A clever and well-told story. Roy Eversley is a very touching picture of high principle and unshrinking self-devotion in a good purpose, without any touch of priggishness or self-sufficiency."—*Guardian.*

The Family Failing.

By DARLEY DALE. With 4 full-page Illustrations. Crown 8vo, cloth elegant, 2s. 6d.

"'The Family Failing' is at once an amusing and an interesting story, and a capital lesson on the value of contentedness to young and old alike."—*Aberdeen Journal.*

BY MRS. E. R. PITMAN.

Florence Godfrey's Faith.

A Story of Australian Life. By Mrs. EMMA RAYMOND PITMAN. With 4 full-page Illustrations. Crown 8vo, cloth extra, 3s. 6d.

"This is a clever, and what is better still, a good book, written with a freshness and power which carry the story along unflaggingly to the close."—*Christian Globe.*

Garnered Sheaves.

A Tale for Boys. By Mrs. E. R. PITMAN. With 4 full-page Illustrations. Crown 8vo, cloth extra, 3s. 6d.

"This is a story of the best sort . . . a noble-looking book, illustrating faith in God, and commending to young minds all that is pure and true."—Rev. C. H. Spurgeon's *Sword and Trowel.*

Life's Daily Ministry:

A Story of Everyday Service for Others. By Mrs. E. R. PITMAN. With 4 full-page Illustrations. Crown 8vo, cloth extra, 3s. 6d.

"Shows exquisite touches of a master hand. She has not only made a close study of human nature in all its phases, but she has acquired the artist's skill in depicting in graphic outline the characteristics of the beautiful and the good in life."—*Christian Union.*

My Governess Life:

Or Earning my Living. By Mrs. E. R. PITMAN. With 4 full-page Illustrations. Crown 8vo, cloth extra, 3s. 6d.

"Full of sound teaching and bright examples of character."—*Sunday-school Chronicle.*

BY KATE WOOD.

Winnie's Secret:

A Story of Faith and Patience. By KATE WOOD. With 4 full-page Pictures in black and tint. Crown 8vo, cloth extra, 2s. 6d.

"A very pretty tale, with great variety of incident and subtle character study, written precisely in the style that is surest to win the hearts of young folks."—*Pictorial World.*

A Waif of the Sea:

Or the Lost Found. By KATE WOOD. With 4 full-page Illustrations in black and tint. Crown 8vo, cloth extra, 2s. 6d.

"A very touching and pretty tale of town and country, full of pathos and interest, told in a style which deserves the highest praise for its lucid and natural ease."—*Edinburgh Courant.*

The Bubbling Teapot.

A Wonder Story. By Mrs. LIZZIE W. CHAMPNEY. With 12 full-
page Illustrations by WALTER SATTERLEE. Crown 8vo, cloth
extra, 3s. 6d.

A book of delightful fantasy, appealing throughout to the interest and
comprehension of children. The metamorphoses of a teapot which, when
it bubbles, becomes a girl, and of the girl who, when she cries, becomes a
teapot, are novel in conception and excellently treated, and Flossy Tangle-
skein's search for the child's paradise carries her through experiences of
child-life all over the world. She is transformed into Hi-ski a little Chinese
maiden, then into the child of a Breton peasant, into a Spanish girl, a
Gypsy, a Moor, an Egyptian, a Lapp, a Hindu, and the like, hearing everywhere strange legends and seeing strange things. Finally, she decides that
there is no better child's paradise than an English home.

The Joyous Story of Toto.

By LAURA E. RICHARDS. With 30 humorous and fanciful Illustrations by E. H. GARRETT. Crown 8vo, cloth extra, 2s. 6d.

"An excellent book for children, which should take its place beside Lewis Car-
roll's unique works."—*Birmingham Gazette.*

"A comical book for children, capitally written. It is exactly the gift for a
bright merry child familiar with country life, and it will be no less welcome in
soothing hours of pain and *ennui* indoors."—*Dundee Advertiser.*

Brothers in Arms:

A Story of the Crusades. By F. BAYFORD HARRISON. With
4 full-page Illustrations by GORDON BROWNE in black and
tint. Crown 8vo, cloth extra, 2s. 6d.

"Full of striking incident, is very fairly illustrated, and may safely be chosen as
sure to prove interesting to young people of both sexes."—*Guardian.*

"One of the best accounts of the Crusades it has been our privilege to read. The
book cannot fail to interest boys."—*Schoolmistress.*

The Ball of Fortune:

Or Ned Somerset's Inheritance. By CHARLES PEARCE. With
4 full-page Illustrations. Crown 8vo, cloth extra, 2s. 6d.

"A capital story for boys. It is simply and brightly written. There is plenty
of incident, and the interest is sustained throughout."—*Journal of Education.*

Miss Fenwick's Failures:

Or "Peggy Pepper-Pot." By ESMÉ STUART. With 4 full-page
Illustrations. Crown 8vo, cloth extra, 2s. 6d.

"Instead of drawing a heroine of romance Esmé Stuart may be commended
for producing a girl far more true to real life, who will put no nonsense into
young heads."—*Graphic.*

Miss Willowburn's Offer.

By SARAH DOUDNEY. With 4 full-page Illustrations by ROBERT
FOWLER. Crown 8vo, cloth extra, 2s. 6d.

A young sailor on his deathbed writes to his mother and sisters asking
them to befriend and comfort the lady to whom he has become privately
engaged. They send for her readily; but while the mother and one sister
are enchanted with her, the other justly suspects that despite her curious
charm she is wanting alike in heart and uprightness. In the plot and
counterplot which follow the happiness of the family is on the verge of
destruction, till the reader, after a period of strained interest, finds that the
evil really works out good and defeats itself.

Hetty Gray:

Or Nobody's Bairn. By ROSA MULHOLLAND. With 4 full-page
Illustrations in black and tint. Crown 8vo, cloth extra, 2s. 6d.

"A pleasantly told story for girls, with a happy ending."—*Athenæum.*
"A charming story for young folks. Hetty is a delightful creature—piquant,
tender, and true—and her varying fortunes are perfectly realistic."—*World.*

Four Little Mischiefs.

By ROSA MULHOLLAND. With 3 full-page Pictures in colours.
Crown 8vo, cloth extra, 2s.

"Graphically written, and abounds in touches of genuine humour and innocent
fun."—*Freeman.*

Gytha's Message:

A Tale of Saxon England. By EMMA LESLIE. With 4 full-page
Pictures by C. J. STANILAND, R.I. Cr. 8vo, cloth extra, 2s. 6d.

"This is a charmingly told story. It is the sort of book that all girls and some
boys like, and can only get good from."—*Journal of Education.*
"The book is throughout most interesting, and shows in a very natural manner
the rough habits and usages in Saxon England."—*Schoolmistress.*

My Mistress the Queen:

A Tale of the Seventeenth Century. By M. A. PAULL. With
4 full-page Illustrations by C. T. GARLAND. Crown 8vo,
cloth extra, 2s. 6d.

"The style is pure and graceful, the presentation of manners and character
has been well studied, and the story is full of interest."—*Scotsman.*
"This is a charming book. The old-time sentiment which pervades the volume
renders it all the more alluring."—*Western Mercury.*

The Stories of Wasa and Menzikoff:

The Deliverer of Sweden, and the Favourite of Czar Peter. With 4 full-page Illustrations. Crown 8vo, cloth extra, 2s. 6d.

These stories form two of the most romantic narratives in history. Boys who delight in deeds of heroism will follow with enthusiasm the course of the Swedish patriot in his struggle for his country's freedom; and the account of how Menzikoff the pastry-cook's boy rose, through faithfulness to his master, to the topmost pinnacle of power in Russia, and how he again fell, through his own dishonesty, will interest and instruct them, while pointing to a high ideal of duty and honour.

Stories of the Sea in Former Days:

Narratives of Wreck and Rescue. With 4 full-page Illustrations by FRANK FELLER. Crown 8vo, cloth elegant, 2s. 6d.

"'Stories of the Sea' are a very good specimen of their kind, and some of the chapters, which are pleasantly written, are altogether fresh to us."—*The Times.*

Tales of Captivity and Exile.

With 4 full-page Illustrations by W. B. FORTESCUE. Crown 8vo, cloth elegant, 2s. 6d.

"It would be difficult to place in the hands of young people a book which combines interest and instruction in a higher degree."—*Manchester Courier.*

Famous Discoveries by Sea and Land.

With 4 full-page Illustrations. Crown 8vo, cloth elegant, 2s. 6d.

"Such a volume may providentially stir up some youths by the divine fire kindled by these 'great of old' to lay open other lands, and show their vast resources."—*Perthshire Advertiser.*

Stirring Events of History.

With 4 full-page Illustrations by JOHN SCHÖNBERG. Crown 8vo, cloth elegant, 2s. 6d.

"The volume will fairly hold its place among those which make the smaller ways of history pleasant and attractive. It is a gift-book in which the interest will not be exhausted with one reading."—*Guardian.*

Adventures in Field, Flood, and Forest.

Stories of Danger and Daring. With 4 full-page Illustrations. Crown 8vo, cloth elegant, 2s. 6d.

"One of the series of books for young people which Messrs. Blackie excel in producing. The editor has beyond all question succeeded admirably. The present book cannot fail to be read with interest and advantage."—*Academy.*

"A Pair of Clogs:"

And Other Stories for Children. By AMY WALTON. With 3 full-page Illustrations. Crown 8vo, cloth extra, 2s.

"Little Clogs," the child of a Yorkshire mill-worker, is stolen by gypsies during the mother's absence, but proving a dangerous encumbrance, is left by them at a rectory in the south of England, where she is brought up by the clergyman's wife. One of her small brass-tipped clogs is the only relic of her infancy retained by her; but it ultimately aids the mother in discovering her child. Her connection with the gypsies, her adventures, and her final recovery are all pleasantly described.

The Hawthorns.

By AMY WALTON. With 3 full-page Illustrations by J. J. PROCTOR. Crown 8vo, cloth extra, 2s.

"A remarkably vivid and clever study of child-life. At this species of work Amy Walton has no superior."—*Christian Leader.*

Dorothy's Dilemma:

A Tale of the Time of Charles I. By CAROLINE AUSTIN. With 3 full-page Illustrations. Crown 8vo, cloth extra, 2s.

"An exceptionally well-told story, and one that will be warmly welcomed by children. The little heroine, Dorothy Hardcastle, is a charming creation."—*Court Journal.*

Marie's Home:

Or A Glimpse of the Past. By CAROLINE AUSTIN. With 3 full-page Illustrations. Crown 8vo, cloth extra, 2s.

"An exquisitely told story. The heroine is as fine a type of girlhood as one could wish to set before our little British damsels of the present day."—*Christian Leader.*

Warner's Chase:

Or the Gentle Heart. By ANNIE S. SWAN. With 3 Illustrations printed in colours. Crown 8vo, cloth extra, 2s.

"In Milly Warren, the heroine, who softens the hard heart of her rich uncle and thus unwittingly restores the family fortunes, we have a fine ideal of real womanly goodness."—*Schoolmaster.*

New Light Through Old Windows.

A Series of Stories illustrating Fables of Æsop. By GREGSON GOW. With 3 Pictures in colours. Crown 8vo, cloth extra, 2s.

"The most delightfully-written little stories one can easily find in the literature of the season. Well constructed and brightly told."—*Glasgow Herald.*

The Squire's Grandson:

A Devonshire Story. By J. M. CALLWELL. With 3 full-page Illustrations. Crown 8vo, cloth extra, 2s.

An artist who had been disinherited for a supposed crime breaks down in health, and as the grim squire, his father, returns unopened all letters sent to him, the little grandson sets off, without consulting his parents, to endeavour to bring about a reconciliation. The squire adopts him and grows to love him; but the reconciliation is only effected after the heroism of the lad has led to the revelation of his father's innocence.

Magna Charta Stories:

Or Struggles for Freedom in the Olden Time. Edited by ARTHUR GILMAN, A.M. With 12 full-page Illustrations. Crown 8vo, cloth extra, 2s.

"A book of special excellence, which ought to be in the hands of all boys."— *Educational News.*

The Wings of Courage;

AND THE CLOUD-SPINNER. Translated from the French of GEORGE SAND, by MRS. CORKRAN. With 2 coloured Illustrations. Crown 8vo, cloth extra, 2s.

"Mrs. Corkran has earned our gratitude by translating into readable English these two charming little stories."—*Athenæum.*

Chirp and Chatter:

Or, LESSONS FROM FIELD AND TREE. By ALICE BANKS. With 54 Character Illustrations by GORDON BROWNE. Crown 8vo, cloth extra, 2s.

About a dozen highly dramatic sketches or little stories, the actors in which are birds, beasts, and insects. They are instructive, suited to the capacities of young people, and very amusing.

"The author has done her work extremely well, and has conveyed very many admirable lessons to young people. The illustrations are capital—full of fun and genuine humour."—*Scotsman.*

Little Tottie,

And Two Other Stories. By THOMAS ARCHER. With 3 full-page Illustrations. Crown 8vo, cloth extra, 2s.

"We can warmly commend all three stories; the book is a most alluring prize for the younger ones."—*Schoolmaster.*

Naughty Miss Bunny:

Her Tricks and Troubles. By CLARA MULHOLLAND. With 3 Illustrations in colours. Crown 8vo, cloth extra, 2s.

"This naughty child is positively delightful. Papas should not omit 'Naughty Miss Bunny' from their list of juvenile presents."—*Land and Water.*

BLACKIE'S EIGHTEENPENNY SERIES.

With Illustrations in Colour, and black and tint. In crown 8vo, cloth elegant.

NEW VOLUMES.

By Order of Queen Maude: A Story of Home Life. By LOUISA CROW.

An elder daughter, who has travelled for some time with an invalid friend, and has had high educational advantages, returns home with excellent notions as to how she will manage her father's household. She dispossesses the younger sister, introduces Kensington cookery and society graces, but fails for want of quick sympathy and wise tolerance. The story is told with much quiet satirical humour, and brings out the better points of the old as contrasted with the new training.

Our General: A Story for Girls. By ELIZABETH J. LYSAGHT.

A book for girls, the Story of a Motherless Household, and of the loving work of the elder sister. The little family in the "Crow's Nest," the kindly doctor and his sister, the trial that comes upon the young heroine, and the happiness that follows,—in all these things girls will take a real interest.

Aunt Hesba's Charge. By ELIZABETH J. LYSAGHT.

A story for children, relating the troubles of a maiden aunt, and various adventures of her niece and nephew. Young folk will take delight in reading about the wonderful king bird, and will sympathize with Aunt Hesba in her terror about the mad dog, and her grief when Jacqueline got mysteriously lost.

East and West: Or Scenes in Many Lands.

A selection of travel-experiences, adventures, &c., in illustration of the life, customs, and countries of various nations. Amongst special points of interest may be noted the history of the Seraglio—a trustworthy account of Roxalana, Roxana, and other heroines of romantic and historic fame.

The Late Miss Hollingford. By ROSA MULHOLLAND.

"No book for girls published this season approaches this in the charm of its telling, which will be equally appreciated by persons of all ages."—*Standard.*

The Pedlar and His Dog. By MARY C. ROWSELL.

"The opening chapter, with its description of Necton Fair, will forcibly remind many readers of George Eliot. Taken altogether it is a delightful story."—*Western Morning News.*

Yarns on the Beach. By G. A. HENTY.

"This little book should find special favour among boys. The yarns are full of romance and adventure, and are admirably calculated to foster a manly spirit."—*The Echo.*

BLACKIE'S EIGHTEENPENNY SERIES—Continued.

A Terrible Coward. By G. MANVILLE FENN.

"Just such a tale as boys will delight to read, and as they are certain to profit by."—*Aberdeen Journal.*

Tom Finch's Monkey: And other Yarns. By JOHN C. HUTCHESON.

"Short stories of an altogether unexceptionable character, with adventures sufficient for a dozen books of its size."—*United Service Gazette.*

Into the Haven. By ANNIE S. SWAN.

"No story more attractive, by reason of its breezy freshness and unforced pathos, as well as for the practical lessons it conveys."—*Christian Leader.*

Our Frank: And other Stories. By AMY WALTON.

"These stories are of the sort that children of the clever kind are sure to like."—*Academy.*

Miss Grantley's Girls, And the Stories She Told Them. By THOMAS ARCHER.

"For fireside reading more wholesome and, at the same time, highly entertaining reading for young people could not be found."—*Northern Chronicle.*

Down and Up Again: Being some Account of the Felton Family, and the Odd People they Met. By GREGSON GOW.

"The story is very neatly told, with some fairly dramatic incidents, and calculated altogether to please young people."—*Scotsman.*

Troubles and Triumphs of Little Tim. A City Story. By GREGSON GOW.

"An undercurrent of sympathy with the struggles of the poor, and an ability to describe their feelings, eminently characteristic of Dickens, are marked features in Mr. Gow's story."—*N. B. Mail.*

The Happy Lad: A Story of Peasant Life in Norway. From the Norwegian of Björnson.

"This pretty story has a freshness and natural eloquence about it. It seems to carry us back to some of the love stories of the Bible."—*Aberdeen Free Press.*

The Patriot Martyr: And other Narratives of Female Heroism in Peace and War.

"It should be read with interest by every girl who loves to learn what her sex can accomplish in times of difficulty and danger."—*Bristol Times.*

Madge's Mistake: A Recollection of Girlhood. By ANNIE E. ARMSTRONG.

"We cannot speak too highly of this delightful little tale. It is charmingly written, and abounds in interesting and laughable incidents."—*Bristol Times.*

Box of Stories. Packed for Young Folk by HORACE HAPPYMAN.

THE SHILLING SERIES OF BOOKS FOR YOUNG PEOPLE.

Square 16mo, neatly bound in cloth extra. Each book contains 128 pages and a Coloured Illustration.

"Quality is not sacrificed to quantity, the stories one and all being of the highest, and eminently suited for the purposes of gift books for either day or Sabbath schools."—*Schoolmaster.*

NEW VOLUMES.

The Children of Haycombe. By ANNIE S. FENN.

The story of a deformed child who was the sport of the other village children, whose love and companionship she craved, but who only learned to know her when she was dying. It is told with freshness and pathos, and should be one of the most popular as it is one of the most helpful of children's books.

The Cruise of the " Petrel:" And other Stories. By F. M. HOLMES.

An interesting story of adventure at sea, the hero being a lad from the training-ship *Mammoth*, who, by his pluck, alertness, and uprightness, saves the good ship *Petrel* from wreck and mutiny. The story of "The Miser's Million" combines with "The Cruise of the Petrel" to make a thoroughly attractive book for boys.

The Wise Princess: And other Stories. By M. HARRIET M. CAPES.

A charming collection of stories, several of which are narrated with exceptional skill and picturesqueness.

A Boy Musician: Or the Young Days of Mozart.

The early life of Mozart, who touched in many respects the ideal of clever childhood, abounded in interesting incident, and its setting in fictional form should give it a strong appeal to the minds of the young. Dealing with the life of a great musician the book should be welcome to all who care for the full culture of the young.

Hatto's Tower: And other Stories. By MARY C. ROWSELL.

The old legend of the cruel Hatto and his Tower on the Rhine is here re-told in a way to secure the eager interest of juvenile readers. The tyranny of the toll-taker, the famine in the village, the terrible invasion by the rats, and all the events of the tale are faithfully preserved. The story may indeed be called a miniature romance of history.

Fairy Lovebairn's Favourites. By J. DICKINSON.

A charming collection of fairy stories, recounting all that happened to the favourites—good little boys and girls—of the good fairy Queen Lovebairn, and the various marvellous chances that befell them in visiting and being visited by the fairy queen and her fairy husband King Fierce-eye.

THE SHILLING SERIES—Continued.

Alf Jetsam: or Found Afloat. By Mrs. GEORGE CUPPLES.

The Redfords: An Emigrant Story. By Mrs. GEO. CUPPLES.

Missy. By F. BAYFORD HARRISON.

Hidden Seed: or A Year in a Girl's Life. By EMMA LESLIE.

Ursula's Aunt. By ANNIE S. FENN.

Jack's Two Sovereigns. By ANNIE S. FENN.

A Little Adventurer: or How Tommy Trefit went to look for his Father. By GREGSON GOW.

Olive Mount. By ANNIE S. FENN.

Three Little Ones; Their Haps and Mishaps. By CORA LANGTON.

Tom Watkins' Mistake. By EMMA LESLIE.

Two Little Brothers. By HARRIET M. CAPES.

The New Boy at Merriton: A Story of School Life. By JULIA GODDARD.

The Blind Boy of Dresden and his Sister. A Story of great Pathos.

Jon of Iceland: A Story of the Far North.

Stories from Shakespeare. By A. J. MACFARLAND and ABBY SAGE.

Every Man in His Place: The Story of a City Boy and a Forest Boy.

Fireside Fairies and Flower Fancies: Stories for Girls.

To the Sea in Ships: Stories of Suffering and Saving at Sea.

Jack's Victory: and other Stories about Dogs.

The Story of a King, told by one of his soldiers.

Prince Alexis, or "BEAUTY AND THE BEAST." A Tale of Old Russia.

Little Daniel: A Story of a Flood on the Rhine.

Sasha the Serf: and other Stories of Russian Life.

True Stories of Foreign History. A Series of Interesting Tales.

SOMETHING FOR THE VERY LITTLE ONES.

By JENNETT HUMPHREYS.

Fully Illustrated with Woodcuts, and one Coloured Plate each. 64 pp. 32mo, cloth. Sixpence each.

Tales Easy and Small for the Youngest of All. In no word will you see more letters than three.

Old Dick Grey and Aunt Kate's Way. Stories in little words of not more than four letters.

Maud's Doll and Her Walk. In Picture and Talk. In little words of not more than four letters.

In Holiday Time. And other Stories. In little words of not more than five letters.

THE NINEPENNY SERIES OF BOOKS FOR CHILDREN.

Neatly bound in cloth extra. Each contains 96 pages and a Coloured Illustration.

NEW VOLUMES.

Jack and the Gypsies. By KATE WOOD.

Jack is a little boy who is being educated by a clergyman, but the governess takes a dislike to him, and the clergyman's little daughter and he set off together, lose their way in the wood, fall in with gypsies, and after many adventures, which are pleasantly narrated, reach home in safety.

Hans the Painter. By MARY C. ROWSELL.

Tells in an amusing and picturesque manner the tale of the early days and later honours of the famous Hans Holbein, painter to Henry the Eighth. The narrative is fresh and attractive, and will help to impart to young readers a taste for historical reading.

Little Troublesome. By ISABEL HORNIBROOK.

A brightly-told story. Life and energy are strong in Peter, and at times he is decidedly a *little troublesome;* but his aunt eventually discovers that he has many good qualities, despite his tricks and pranks.

My Lady May: And one other Story. By HARRIET BOULTWOOD.

This is the simple and pleasantly written autobiography of a doll who spends her infancy in a toyshop, her girlhood—not without its trials—in a pleasant home, and her maturer years in a children's hospital.

A Little Hero. By Mrs. MUSGRAVE.

The story of a little boy, born in India, who is sent home to reside with unsympathetic relatives, and who, in following his mother's counsels, grows up to be a brave man. It is told in part with very great pathos.

Prince Jon's Pilgrimage: Or Truth in Riddles for Little Thinkers. By JESSIE FLEMING.

A pleasantly conceived allegory, telling how Prince Jon is sent as a child from the land of Albricht to Stratherda, how he is helped and hindered, and how after many troubles he reaches the country from which he set out.

Harold's Ambition: Or A Dream of Fame. By JENNIE PERRETT.

A boy who thinks he has the genius of a great actor in him, runs away from home to fulfil his high destiny, but soon sickens of the new career. After some cleverly-told experiences he seeks a higher profession.

Sepperl the Drummer-Boy. By MARY C. ROWSELL

Aboard the Mersey. By Mrs. GEORGE CUPPLES.

A Blind Pupil. By ANNIE S. FENN.

Lost and Found. By Mrs. CARL ROTHER.

Fisherman Grim. By MARY C. ROWSELL.

THE SIXPENNY SERIES FOR CHILDREN.

Neatly bound in cloth extra.   Each book contains 64 pages and a Coloured Illustration.

NEW VOLUMES.

Little Neighbours. By ANNIE S. FENN.

Jim: a Story of Child Life. By CHRISTIAN BURKE.

Little Curiosity: the Story of a German Christmas. By J. M. CALLWELL.

Sara the Wool-gatherer. By W. L. ROOPER.

Fairy Stories: told by PENELOPE.

A New Year's Tale: and other Stories. From the German. By M. A. CURRIE.

———

The Tree Cake: and other Stories. By W. L. ROOPER.

Nurse Peggy, and Little Dog Trip.

Wild Marsh Marigolds. By DARLEY DALE.

Fanny's King. By DARLEY DALE.

Kitty's Cousin. By HANNAH B. MACKENZIE.

Cleared at Last. By JULIA GODDARD.

Little Dolly Forbes. By ANNIE S. FENN.

A Year with Nellie. By Do.

The Little Brown Bird.

The Maid of Domremy: and other Tales.

Little Eric: a Story of Honesty.

Uncle Ben the Whaler.

The Palace of Luxury.

The Charcoal Burner.

Willy Black: a Story of Doing Right.

The Horse and His Ways.

The Shoemaker's Present.

Lights to Walk by.

The Little Merchant.

Nicholina: a Story about an Iceberg.

"A very praiseworthy series of Prize Books. Most of the stories are designed to enforce some important moral lesson, such as honesty, industry, kindness, helpfulness, &c."—*School Guardian.*

A SERIES OF FOURPENNY REWARD BOOKS.

Each 64 pages, 18mo, Illustrated, in Picture Boards.

Della's Boots. By W. L. ROOPER.

Lost on the Rocks: a Story of a Storm. By R. SCOTTER.

A Kitten's Adventures. By CAROLINE STEWART.

Papa's Birthday. By W. L. ROOPER.

Little Tales for Little Children. By PENELOPE.

Holidays at Sunnycroft. By ANNIE S. SWAN.

Climbing the Hill. By Do.

A Year at Coverley. By Do.

Phil Foster. By J. LOCKHART.

Worthy of Trust. By H. B. MACKENZIE.

Brave and True. By GREGSON GOW.

Poor Tom Olliver. By JULIA GODDARD.

The Children and the Water-Lily. By JULIA GODDARD.

Johnnie Tupper's Temptation. By GREGSON GOW.

Maudie and Bertie. By Do.

Fritz's Experiment. By LETITIA M'LINTOCK.

Lucy's Christmas-Box.

*** These little books have been specially written with the aim of inculcating some sound moral, such as obedience to parents, love for brothers and sisters, kindness to animals, perseverance and diligence leading to success, &c. &c.

VERE FOSTER'S
WATER-COLOR DRAWING-BOOKS.

The Times says:—"We can strongly recommend the series to young students."

PAINTING FOR BEGINNERS.

FIRST STAGE. Teaching the use of ONE COLOR. Ten Facsimiles of Original Studies in Sepia by J. CALLOW, and numerous Illustrations in pencil. With full Instructions in easy language. 4to, cloth elegant, 2s. 6d.

"Sound little books, teaching the elements of 'washing' with much clearness by means of plain directions and well-executed plates."—*Academy.*

PAINTING FOR BEGINNERS.

SECOND STAGE. Teaching the use of SEVEN COLORS. Twenty Facsimiles of Original Drawings by J. CALLOW, and many Illustrations in pencil. With full Instructions in easy language. 4to, cloth elegant, 4s.

"The rules are so clear and simple that they cannot fail to be understood even by those who have no previous knowledge of drawing. The letterpress of the book is as good as the illustrations are beautiful."—*Birmingham Gazette.*

SIMPLE LESSONS IN FLOWER PAINTING.

Eight Facsimiles of Original Water-Color Drawings, and numerous Outline Drawings of Flowers, after various artists. With Instructions for Drawing and Painting. 4to, cloth elegant, 3s.

"Everything necessary for acquiring the art of flower painting is here: the *facsimiles* of water-color drawings are very beautiful."—*Graphic.*

"Such excellent books, so carefully written and studied, cannot fail to have great advantage in the creation and fostering of a taste for art."—*Scotsman.*

SIMPLE LESSONS IN LANDSCAPE PAINTING.

Eight Facsimiles of Original Water-Color Drawings, and Thirty Vignettes, after various artists. With full Instructions by an experienced Master. 4to, cloth elegant, 3s.

"As a work of art in the book line we have seldom seen its equal; and it could not fail to be a delightful present, affording a great amount of pleasurable amusement and instruction to young people."—*St. James's Gazette.*

SIMPLE LESSONS IN MARINE PAINTING.

Twelve Facsimiles of Original Water-Color Sketches. By EDWARD DUNCAN. With numerous Illustrations in pencil, and Practical Lessons by an experienced Master. 4to, cloth elegant, 3s.

"The book must prove of great value to students. Nothing could be prettier or more charming than the marine sketches here presented."—*Graphic.*

VERE FOSTER'S DRAWING-BOOKS—Continued.

STUDIES OF TREES.

In Pencil and in Water-Colors. By J. NEEDHAM. A Series of Eighteen Examples in Colors, and Thirty-three Drawings in pencil. With full Instructions for Drawing and Painting. Two Series, cloth elegant, 5s. each.

"We commend them most heartily to all persons of taste who may be wanting to cultivate the great accomplishment of Water-color Drawing, or who want a gift-book for a lad or girl taking up the study."—*Schoolmaster.*

ADVANCED STUDIES IN FLOWER PAINTING.

By ADA HANBURY. A Series of Twelve beautifully finished Examples in Colors, and numerous Outlines in pencil. With full Instructions for Painting. 4to, cloth elegant, 7s. 6d.

"Apart from its educational value in art training this is a lovely book: we have seen nothing to equal the coloured plates."—*Sheffield Independent.*
"The handsomest and most instruc- tive volume of the series yet produced."—*Daily Chronicle.*
"Coloured sketches of flowers which it is literally no exaggeration to term exquisite."—*Knowledge.*

EASY STUDIES IN WATER-COLOR PAINTING.

By R. P. LEITCH and J. CALLOW. Nine Pictures executed in Neutral Tints. With full Instructions for drawing each subject, and for sketching from Nature. 4to, cloth elegant, 6s.

SKETCHES IN WATER-COLORS.

By T. M. RICHARDSON, R. P. LEITCH, J. A. HOUSTON, T. L. ROW-BOTHAM, E. DUNCAN, and J. NEEDHAM. A Series of Nine Pictures executed in Colors. With full Instructions for drawing, by an experienced Teacher. 4to, cloth elegant, 5s.

"To those who wish to become proficient in the art of water-color painting no bet- ter instructor could be recommended than these two series."—*Newcastle Chronicle.*

ILLUMINATING.

Nine Examples in Colors and Gold of ancient Illuminating of the best periods, with numerous Illustrations in Outline, Historical Notes and full descriptions and instructions by Rev. W. J. LOFTIE, B.A., F.S.A. 4to, cloth elegant, 6s.

"The illuminations are admirably re- produced in colour. Mr. Loftie's prac- tical instructions enhance the value of an excellent handbook."—*Saturday Review.*

LONDON: BLACKIE & SON, 49 OLD BAILEY, E.C.
GLASGOW, EDINBURGH, AND DUBLIN.

www.ingramcontent.com/pod-product-compliance
Lightning Source LLC
Chambersburg PA
CBHW051520100726
47898CB00005B/1526